Dead Man's Switch
The Dominion Falls Series 10

Sarah Cass

Historical Romance
Romantic Suspense
Historical Western Romance

A Divine Roses Ink Book
Historical Romance
Romantic Suspense
Historical Western Romance

Copyright © 2023 Sarah Cass
First publication: February 2024

Cover design by Sarah Cass
Edited by Megan Koenen
Proofread by Mary Terrani
All cover art and logo copyright © 2023 by Sarah Cass

PUBLISHER
Divine Roses Ink
http://www.divinerosesink.com

Other Books in
The Dominion Falls Series

Independent Brake
Changing Tracks
Derailed
Dark Territory
Green Eye
Runaway Train
Home Signal
Red Zone
Chasing the Red
Blizzard Lights

Coming Soon in
The Dominion Falls Series

Bird Cage
A Highball Arrangement
Blood
Grave Digger
Bad Order

Books by Sarah Cass

The Tribe Series
The Tribe
The Wolf
The Chief
The Raven

The Lake Point Series
Santa, Maybe
Deep-Fried Sweethearts
Stalled Independence
Witch Way
A Thorough Thanksgiving
Eve's New Year
Heartstrings & Hockey Pucks
Luck of the Cowgirl
Stars, Stripes & Motorbikes
Free Falling
Love for Hire
Haunted Hearts

Stand Alone Novels
Masked Hearts
Leap

Dedication

To my family,
Who support me,
Even when they think it's weird.

Be proud. Be weird.
Be your unique selves.
Always

Table of Contents

*To travel hopefully is a better thing
than to arrive.
-Robert Louis Stevenson*

Jane stood before the mirror in her room. They'd arrived in Holle Creek early that morning. She'd longed to immediately go seek out Cole, but Charlie had convinced her she needed rest. It hadn't taken much to convince her, really, the journey had left her exhausted and weak. So she'd climbed into the terrible bed in the morose boarding house to attempt rest.

She'd obtained promises from both her brothers that they wouldn't go seek out Cole prematurely and give him warning of their arrival. She wanted to be there herself the first time he realized he'd been found.

After a nap in a bed only passably more comfortable than her hay pile in the wagon, her body still ached. Still, she felt more refreshed for the sleep.

She'd put on a subdued green dress. The cloak she'd brought nearly matched the color, so she'd wear that. She pinned her hat in place with minimal shaking to her hands. A strange mix of excitement and fear tangled her nerves taut as though she hadn't just slept.

Put back together into a semblance of human again, it was time to face whatever she might find. After she'd sent a telegram to Katherine assuring their family they'd arrived in Holle Creek safe and sound.

Seeing as she'd entrusted the carrying of the bulk of their funds and important paperwork to her brothers in the next room, her own room sat sparse. She'd packed only a few dresses, two cloaks, and a muffler for the coldest days.

Sunshine filtered weakly through the curtains. The day was drab, much like the town had seemed on first glance. There appeared to be no wind blowing, so she imagined she'd be fine without the muffler.

After a deep breath, she smoothed her hand over the swell of the baby. "Shall we send word home and see if we can find your pa?"

No response came from the child within. Not even a kick. When she'd been lying down the child had been quite active, so she didn't worry. "Well, let's go then."

Jane gathered her cloak and gloves from the bed on her way out. She locked the door behind her before knocking on the next room's door.

Charles pulled the door open. He offered her a warm smile and waved her in. Unlike her room, this room remained a disorganized mess. Nick had papers lying on the bed, more on the desk. His traveling case remained closed on a chair.

Charles' smile grew wan at her look. "Nick decided to get right to work instead of unpacking his things."

"This is a shock. I never imagined you to be such a messy sort, Nicholas." Jane surveyed the room. The half untouched by the mass of papers was neat as a pin, much as her own small room. Not that she had much in it to make it messy. "Is this why you've never allowed me in your home?"

"It isn't a matter of allowing such a thing. There's never been an occasion." Nick straightened a pile of papers, then set them aside. "I'm reviewing James' work on these divorce papers. He'd done as you asked, if that's what you still desire."

"I do. Especially after the inheritance I just received. I have no idea what we'll find here, and I need to protect myself." Jane kissed his cheek when he rose to greet her properly. "I'm going to head next door to the telegraph office to alert the family we've arrived safe. After that, I thought I might walk through the town."

"Give me a few minutes and I can join you." Charles stepped over Nick's carpet bag toward his side of the room.

"Nonsense." She'd managed to stop him with the simple word, thankfully. Expecting an argument, she pressed on. "I'll be thirty minutes at most. There won't be any trouble. This town is hardly the size of Dominion Falls."

"You said yourself you have no idea what we'll find here." Nick kept his sharp gaze on her. His eyes so similar to her own were heavy and dark with suspicion. "We don't know it's safe."

"We saw nary a soul when we arrived. Wagons in towns this small usually draw crowds and we only saw one or two people." She tried to smile reassuringly. "I don't think me taking a short walk will be an issue."

"Do you have your Remington, at least?"

"Do you see it?" Jane lifted her arms. She still hadn't donned the cape which would cover her holster. "It's one little walk. I will hardly shoot Cole on sight, even if the temptation exists."

Charlie frowned. "We don't know what's happening here."

"True." She pondered the necessity of returning to her room for her holster. The idea held merit. "I can't imagine I'd need it for a short walk. Do you?"

"At the very least, take this." Nick pulled a small weapon from the coat he'd hung over his chair. "It's only useful at close range but it could help you get away from a bad situation."

She wrinkled her nose at the sight of the Derringer. "Nicholas."

"Take it, or go get yours." Nick met her gaze meaningfully. "If it helps, it isn't the same one."

"It doesn't." She knew he referred to the weapon that had killed Alan Bingham. To that day only herself and Nick knew whom had truly pulled the trigger that night. Cole didn't even know. For that matter, it was one secret Tom wasn't privy to. With a sigh, she took the Derringer.

"Don't put it in your reticule," Charlie called from his side of the room. "You won't be able to get to it quickly enough if you need it."

With a frown, she slipped it into her left pocket. "Fine, fine."

"You know what to do if you run into trouble." Nick turned his attention back to the papers on his desk.

"Whistle." Jane nodded to Charlie seeing as he was the only one looking at her. She stepped from the room and swung her cape around her shoulders. On the way out, she noticed the gentleman manning the desk no longer stood at his post. Seemed odd at first. Then again, she didn't imagine this town got enough visitors to warrant standing sigil all of the time. There was likely plenty of warning before anyone came upon the mountain.

She stepped out into the chilly, dimly lit day. Sunlight struggled against the heavy swath of clouds offering nothing in the way of warmth. As she'd suspected there was no wind to add to the chill in the air.

The telegraph office sat two doors down. She made it there quickly through the empty street. Inside, she grabbed the pencil and paper. "I'd like to see this sent to Katherine Daughtery in Dominion Falls, Colorado please."

The weaselly young man behind the counter sneered at the telegram. "Thirty cents."

"Of course." Jane withdrew the funds from her reticule. She slid them across the counter toward him. He made no move to collect the funds or message. "Now, please. I'll wait here while you send it."

He huffed and snatched the paper away. Hunched over the key he sent a series of clicks and pauses. "There."

"No, sir. I asked you to send the telegraph, not put out a notice you were stepping away from the key." Jane stared him down. The dark look he cast her gave her plenty of suspicion as to where her own missives had disappeared, and Cole's if he'd sent any. "The woman you're sending that to is a dear friend and happens to help run the telegraph. She's taught me much about the code you use. Please, try again."

Once she'd heard the entire message send, she spun to leave the office without a word of appreciation. On the porch, she paused. The town boasted two saloons on the main road, each with a smattering of whores. It stood to reason Cole could be at either getting a drink.

The store straight down the road from her drew her gaze most, though. Cole had said his old father-in-law lived in and ran the store. The man had known where Cole had ended up and sent him an occasional missive. Perhaps she'd find Cole there instead of a saloon. Maybe the older man was ailing and Cole had been caring for him.

Maybe too hopeful for her current state, but she needed that shot of hope. After all, it was clear Cole wasn't in the small boarding house. Her and her brothers were the only guests there.

Right as she made up her mind to try the store, a figure emerged. Tall, muscular, every inch of the man drew her eye and called her heart. She gasped at the way her heart stuttered to a stop for a moment or two. Though he limped, everything about the way he moved was familiar. Her hand drifted to her heart when it sputtered to life only to race to fast she felt dizzy. She whispered, "Cole."

For a moment in time, he stood suspended. He had to have spotted her, for he was looking right at the office where she stood. Two steps toward her, features still shadowed by his Stetson so she couldn't read his expression.

A weak whistle carried through the air, and Cole turned toward his left. A heartbeat later his scream of *Ella* hit her like a physical blow. Ella? His wife? She backed against the window when a woman leaped into Cole's arms.

"Oh. Oh, no. No, no, no." Jane tore out from the porch toward the boarding house. Right as she'd made it to the cover of the saloon across from the boarding house, she skid to a stop. Out of sight of him and his—his wife—she leaned against the wall. The world spun around her, her vision growing blurry again. "No, no, no."

She tried to get a rein on the panic coursing through her veins. A headache bloomed across her skull despite her best efforts. Short breaths did little to ease her nerves. The first familiar stirrings of hysteria burrowed into her ears with a sharp buzzing. "Charles. Must get…Oh."

Her hand braced against the wall as she did her best to catch her breath. Somehow she managed to steady her breathing until the buzzing in her ears eased. Dizziness edged backward until she felt steady again. The headache clung stubbornly, though.

First, she had to see Charles. Then she would deal with the matter at hand. She straightened to return to the boarding house only to find a gun pointed right at her. Jane lifted her gaze further up the tall man's features, finding them unsettlingly familiar. Her brain raced to put the pieces together as she faced this man that looked so startlingly like her husband. "You must be the deceased Paul Spencer."

"I am." When her gaze drifted toward the windows of the boarding house he clicked his tongue. "Uh-uh. There'll be none of that. Come on, now. He clearly didn't care what happened to the other wife, maybe he'll care what happens to you."

Jane moved her hand toward her pocket, and the Derringer it held. A hand gripped her arm. She was spun around to find another stranger glaring at her. He also had a familiar visage, though mostly in the startling eyes that held more icy malice than she'd seen in Cole. She shook her head, now confused. "What? Who?"

He shoved aside her cape, his eyes widening. "Son of a bitch, she's gonna have his kid."

"Even better," said Paul. "Let's get her out of sight of the boarding house and check her for weapons. I'll take care of her, and you can get back to check on your dear ma."

"Like he'd believe that. I'll get back to the saloon, is what I'll do." The young man dragged her toward the woods. She didn't dare fight knowing there was a weapon trained on her. If he'd release her left arm for a simple two seconds she could get the Derringer. With two of them, that wouldn't increase her odds any. Damn her for not choosing to return to her room to get her holster with the two weapons it contained.

She was brought to a stop near a horse sheltered in the woods.

"Check for weapons." Paul leaned against a tree almost casually. His weapon didn't waver one second from her personage. He was clearly used to being listened to. How?

Jane turned her attention to the young man, thinking over how it was possible. Perhaps he was Paul's boy? Paul had referred to his ma, and the younger had scoffed derisively saying 'he' wouldn't believe he'd care to check on her.

Could they mean Ella? But how? Cole had been certain she'd died, and he'd seen her grave before he left town. Then again, Clara Young lay buried, too. Her cross still sat in the town cemetery.

The boy found her weapon quickly and pocketed it. Thankfully his check of her reticule was little more than perfunctory. He left her with all but a couple of small gold nuggets she could certainly live without. Everything else he left in place. Hopefully it would come in handy, seeing as she had no idea what this man was about to do with her.

She stared hard at the unknown young man. "And who are you? Or do I not get to know who's aiding in my kidnapping?"

He eyed her in suspicion. "Names Jimmy."

"Ah. Colton James Spencer. She named you after your pa, then." She imagined he wondered over her calm state. To be honest, she did as well. Her headache still beat against her skull, but her panic stayed at bay. Then again, even though the Derringer had been taken she still had another at her disposal. So long as she kept use of her hands, it was still going to help.

"That bitch did nothing."

Jane quirked a brow at his dark insistence. Funny how it was so similar to how Cole had always spoken of his pa. She turned her attention back to Paul. There was no telling quite how much the man knew. She went with what she did. The papers, when they had come, had been from Colton Spencer, not Cole. Could Paul not even know truly who his son had become? "This is pointless. My lawyer is better than whatever you used to send Colton's divorce decree. He doesn't have a dime to his name any longer. Or at least not by tomorrow."

Paul tossed a length of rope from the saddle to James. "Tie her hands behind her back, then it's on the horse with you."

She took a long step back from the approaching James. "No."

"Don't got much say, do ya?" James smiled coldly.

"I see that, however you cannot tie my hands behind my back."

Paul's eyes narrowed. "We will."

"If you expect me to get on that horse with this baby, you can't tie my hands behind my back. I'll never be able to maneuver." She raised her hands when James took a menacing step forward. "If you bully me on there I could lose the child. The pregnancy has not been easy. You lose the baby, you lose your only bargaining chip. Clearly by that letter of divorce I'm not worth much to Colton."

Paul seemed to consider her words. He gave one short nod. "In front then. I'll switch it when we get where we're going."

Jane folded her hands together, flexing the wrists and Tommy had taught her so she'd gain some flexibility of movement. When the rope pulled tight she flinched, but kept her wrists as flexed as possible.

On her way toward the horse, she had a passing thought to kick James on her way up. Only the fact that both of them now had one weapon each to her none kept her from following through. Instead, she grabbed the pommel with her right hand, hefting her foot into the stirrup.

With a bounce as though trying to get into the saddle she twisted her wrists so her left hand arched toward her. On the next bounce she pulled herself close enough to get her fingers in her mouth and blew a harsh whistle. It rang loud and clear through the trees, carrying far as it always had.

"Damn it," Paul cursed. Moments later a hard blow landed to the back of her head throwing her into darkness. Her body crashed to the ground with a pained groan and her grip on consciousness faded to black.

Many difficulties which nature throws our way may be smoothed away by the exercise of intelligence.
—Titus Livius

Sally settled back against the furs as the cutter flew over the snow. A soft sigh escaped her restraints. She ignored the look Patrick cutter as she watched the scenery fly by. They'd been on a ride out near to the Edward's ranch and were on their way back to town.

The day was lovely, though cold. Their ride had been spontaneous, a way to pass some time in the middle of the day. She was a little sad it was over, especially seeing as she had a very busy night ahead of her. With Ma now gone, too, she was covering the casino and brothel even more often than she had in recent weeks. She was due to cover the casino for a few hours that afternoon, in fact.

Coupled with the investigation, which she'd been working on whenever she could, it was lovely that Patrick had suggested the ride. Mams had insisted she go and have a little leisure.

"Don't tell me my imminent departure has sparked those feelings of deep adoration I know you've been suppressing." Patrick's tone and matching grin hinted at teasing.

"I'll not deny I'll miss the pleasure of your company." She allowed him a warm smile. "I have no idea where to begin to find another way to wile away some time within this town."

"That young man we just spotted seemed to enjoy the view when you passed."

"Matthew Coleman?" Sally glanced behind them to the ranch now barely visible. She shook her head, a low chuckle forming at the very idea. Yes, he was handsome and had caught her eye on the rare occasion she'd seen him. However, "I don't know that he has ever courted a soul. I don't believe he would know how to handle a relationship such as ours."

"And what of your friend Andrew?"

"Hopelessly enamored with miss Bonnie. Matthew's sister, actually." Sally wrinkled her nose. "Besides, I don't see him as anything other than a friend."

"I'm no more than a friend. Neither is Molly."

"Touché, Mr. Warner."

"I'm curious, then. If it isn't my leaving, though I know it wounds you more than you dare say to me."

She nudged his ribs, laughing outright. "Oh, stop. I've never known a more dramatic man than you can be sometimes."

He laughed with her. "Fine, fine. Tell me what brought on such a sigh. One that seemed to come from the very depths of your soul?"

She cut him a look at his continuing dramatics.

"In all seriousness."

"Nothing. Everything." Sally eyed the settlement as they passed by. She would need to see about making the supply run this week with Kat in Jane's stead. "I'm worried about Ma and Pa. Archie is still in danger. We lost Hammy, for heaven's sake. I don't know what this town will be without him."

"He is but one man. Now who is being dramatic?"

"You hadn't the pleasure of truly getting to know him as we all have over the years. A kinder man has never been seen in this life or the next." They drew close to the meadow. The skeletal remains of the church stuck out of the snow. She set her hand on Patrick's arm. "Swing by the old church, would you?"

"It's little more than ash and snow now." Despite his protest, Patrick pulled the rein to guide the cutter toward the rubble. He slowed near where the blackened wood marred the blanket of pure white. "I'm not quite certain where the edge of it is, actually."

"Right over there is where the steps were." Sally tossed aside the furs to hop out. What had been the church sat buried in the knee deep snow. The plans were to rebuild at the other end of the meadow. A similar, but larger, building. The last thing Hammy had done was to get the plans approved.

"What, pray tell, are we doing?" He'd also disembarked the cutter. Despite his finery, he trudged through the snow on a new path rather than follow Sally's.

"I'm not certain." She set her hand on a beam that stuck straight up out of the snow. By now all evidence had been trampled, melted, or buried in snow. Perhaps all three. She eyed the empty space where they'd gathered for service every week for years. In the past few years the church had overflowed with parishioners. Good people, led by a good Reverend. "Men of God."

"What?"

Sally's mind raced over her notes. She could picture the large swath of butcher paper much clearer than her notebook. Something clicked in her brain, and she emitted a squeal of surprise. "Oh my."

"Sally?"

She rushed back toward the cutter. "Let's get back, and hurry. I must speak with Tommy."

"Where is he? I haven't seen Thomas in nearly a week." He didn't hesitate at her rudely barked command. His composure in place, he even kindly tucked the furs back over her that she'd ignored in her haste.

"Oh. Ma got in a snit and kicked him out. He's been staying at the clinic. Come to think of it, though." Sally scooted forward in her seat. Anxiety clawed its way through her belly as she pondered when the last time she'd seen Tommy.

Patrick eyed her as the cutter slid along the homes on Main to circle around to the corral behind the hotel. "Come to think of what?"

"I haven't seen him in several days, either. I've only now realized, I've been so busy."

"Then be off." Patrick pulled the cutter to a stop behind the brothel without hesitation. "You sound worried."

"It isn't like him to not check on me," Sally admitted.

"I'll see to the cutter."

"Are we still on for tonight?" Half-distracted, Sally was already one leg out of the cutter. Tommy's recent threat to take a job and leave town reared in her memory.

"You, myself, and Molly at the brothel. Eight sharp."

Sally freed herself from the last of the furs. Quick as possible in the deep snow she cut down the alley toward Main Street. On her run to the clinic, she spotted Kat rushing toward the hotel. They both stopped simultaneously as they spotted each other. "Kat?"

"It's your ma. She's sent a telegram. They arrived safe in Holle Creek." Kat's grin grew brighter. "That means we know they can get telegrams through."

Sally wasn't sure whether to be happy or upset by that information. After all, if telegrams were coming through, why hadn't Cole sent more?

"Odd thing was," Kat continued seemingly oblivious to Sally's consternation. "The missive arrived almost immediately after the operator said he was stepping away."

"Really?" Sally pondered that tidbit. Seemed odd that the telegraph operator would say he was stepping away only to send Ma's message. She might have walked in right as he was heading out for an errand. It still rang as queer to her. "I'll pass the word onto Tommy."

"Thanks."

Sally continued her run toward the clinic as Kat rushed into the Inn. Without a word to Dr. Noe where she sat behind the desk, Sally raced up the stairs to room ten. She pounded on the door heartily. "Tommy! I've got news."

No answer came. Sally frowned at the silent door. Perhaps he'd gone to see Leanne for a few days. He was probably bored without the hotel to manage. Or maybe he was playing deputy today. She hadn't thought of either of those possibilities.

"Tommy?" She knocked again even though she knew he'd have answered by now if he was in.

Sally turned away, pondering where to try first. Then she stopped, another twinge in her gut making her turn back.

Trust your gut, Tommy had always told her. *If something seems off, it usually is.*

She reached toward the doorknob. Tommy kept his door locked more than even Cole had once upon a time.

The knob turned easily. Unlocked. Her stomach fluttered with worry, or nerves.

She pushed the door all the way open. While not as barren as his room at the Inn, she noticed his pack and a good number of his weapons were gone. "Damn it, Tommy. No. Tell me you didn't leave. Not without saying something."

Since he wasn't there to protest, she moved further into the room. He'd added no life to it, but then again the same could be said of his room at the Inn. Much like Molly's hotel room, it felt like they always had one foot out the door. Ready to leave at a moment's notice.

He must have taken a job. Done so without so much as a bye or leave. He'd told her she could handle the job, and she was doing fine with Molly's support. Then he and Ma had fought, or rather Ma had fought, Tommy had acquiesced without a peep. That was supposed to mean he'd stick around and help.

Now he was gone. Just gone.

She glared at the room as if it were its fault. "Ass."

When she turned to leave, she spotted a piece of paper on the pillow. With a glance around like he'd set a trap and was ready to jump out of the wardrobe, she swiped the note.

Sally,

I knew your nosy self would be up here soon enough. I'm off on a job. Can't tell you what it is or where, it's best certain people don't know. I'll leave you with this—I've never been good at listening to orders.

Take the notebook under my pillow. It's got all of my notes on your case.

Yes, YOUR case. Don't give me that look.

Trust your instincts and your memory. Use Molly. Lock up when you leave. It shouldn't have taken you this long to get in here. Hope none of my guns got taken.

Best,

Uncle Tommy

Sally slid her hand under the pillow to withdraw the notebook. After a reread of the note, she stared around the room again. "Where could you have gone?"

She exhaled long and slow on her way down to sit on the edge of the bed. Now what was she to do? Without Tommy or Ma around to tell her if she was being crazy, she'd never know if her ideas were too outlandish.

Trust your instincts. She scoffed as the words mirrored the recent memory of him telling her to trust her gut. "Easier said than done."

A knock on the door startled a shriek out of her. Andrew's mouth twitched in amusement. Oblivious to her flustered state, or completely aware, he let his grin form. "Hello to you, too."

"Andrew Cross, you scared the devil clean out of me."

"Good thing too. You've got too much devil in you for decency."

"You rotten friend." She laughed despite her attempt at a fit of temper.

"Dr. Noe said you came racing through the lobby without so much as a word. I was concerned and wanted to be assured you were in no distress. Am I to guess by that banshee shriek that you are, or you aren't?"

"Yes."

"What?" Andrew's grin flickered toward outright laughter. He remained respectfully at the door. "Where is your uncle? Why are you in here without him?"

"He's out." Sally tucked the note in the book on her way to the door. She tugged it shut behind her. Once she'd made sure it had locked, she laced her arm with his. "Tell me, dear Andrew. How much do you enjoy the detective work behind your autopsies?"

"I've always found it interesting. Why?"

"I need a fresh perspective. While we talk, you can show me how to test for other chemicals. A lesson and a chat rolled into one. Will that do?"

"I would enjoy it immensely."

"Wonderful."

*I like the dreams of the future better
than the history of the past.
-Thomas Jefferson*

Cole shoved his clothes into his pack haphazardly on top of the copy of *Leaves of Grass* Jane had sent with him. He had no idea why Paul had returned Ella, but he didn't have time to care. Now that she was back, he had to get them both out as as soon as possible. If he had to steal a horse and drag Ella kicking and screaming down the mountain. When he left the storeroom, Ella was once again digging through the drawers.

He pulled out his knife and knelt in front of the desk. Two weeks before he'd finally gained access to the desk, but had done so carefully. Inside he'd found that Richard had left the care of Ella, James, and the store to him. Paul wouldn't find any of that worth anything, so he'd left it aside. His pa had taken the financials of it. The savings box was thoroughly cleaned out. Whether by James or Paul, he didn't know.

No longer caring if Paul knew he'd managed to get into the desk, he stuck his knife into the lock and broke it clean off. With it free at last, he pulled out all the papers and shoved them into his bag. With a glance at Ella, he called to her. "Lydia's upstairs. Let's go."

He raced up the stairs ahead of her. She dug through the dresser he pointed to as a distraction. He pulled her bed away from the wall. The loose floorboard still meshed with the rest, which gave him hope Paul hadn't discovered his hiding place.

With the same knife he pried the floorboard up to reveal his money pouch. He pulled the funds free, giving them a quick count to ensure every dollar he had left was accounted for.

A sharp whistle cut through town. Cole knew that whistle all too well. His eyes widened. "Shit. They *are* here."

Cole shoved his money into his bag, replaced the floorboard, and shoved the bed back in place. He took a firm grasp of Ella's thin wrist. "We gotta go. Come on, Ella."

"Where, what?" She yelped as he tugged her down the stairs.

Each pounding step of his feet down the stairs aggravated the pain in his wound, but he didn't dare stop. The whistle had been the whistle of a Young, usually when there was danger. Maybe they'd spotted him and were alerting each other to end the search.

He yanked Ella out of the store and down the steps. In the distance he saw two familiar figures heading his way. Relief flooded through him. "Charlie! Nick!"

The pair made a beeline for him. Before Cole could say a word, Nick sprinted forward and dealt and uppercut to his chin. Cole's teeth rattled together. His grasp on Ella released as he stumbled. Another hit came to his jaw, nearly flattening him completely.

Cole bent over as the pain radiated through his jaw. After a shuddering breath he stood with no plans on retaliation. He likely deserved it. Hell, he knew he did. Before Ella could wander off, he grabbed her wrist again. He glanced between the brothers. "Which of you whistled?"

"We didn't." Charlie folded his arms across his chest. It was a relief that he didn't attack as Nick had. Cole didn't think his jaw could take another hit, deserved or not.

"You didn't—where's Jane?" Cole spun in a circle, but she was nowhere to be seen.

"That's what we'd like to know." Nick's gaze was fierce, but at least he didn't move to hit him again. Yet. The possibility lingered in the fierce darkness in his gaze.

"*Fuck.*" Cole stared at minute at Ella before looking into the woods. Paul had taken her from their old home before Cole could find her one night she'd wandered off. He'd had her for a week God-knew-where out in the woods. Cole's ability to search was limited by his injury and lack of horse. He'd returned Ella. Cole had wondered why. He couldn't believe Paul had found her so quickly. It wasn't possible.

"Colton," Ella whimpered.

"I told you to stop calling me that." Cole narrowed his eyes toward the saloon a short way down the street. For a second he could have sworn he'd seen Jimmy at the door.

"Colton?" Nick frowned toward Ella.

Cole ignored him. "Wasn't she armed?"

"She had one of Nick's Derringers." Charlie stared at the woman Cole fought to keep in place before she ran off in search of Lydia again. She kept muttering about their lost child, then talking of darkness. Charlie's gaze didn't soften, but took on the more clinical look he got when doctoring. "What's this?"

"No time." Cole turned his attention back to them. "You left your room empty. We'd best get back before they go nosing. I tried to tell Jane the inmates were running the asylum."

"What does that mean?" Charlie stepped forward, but not toward Cole. Toward Ella. He pried Cole's fingers from around her wrist. "Don't hurt her."

"I'd never hurt a woman, even if she was driving me batty. And we'll talk about it at your place. He ain't gonna hurt her. Not until he gets what he wants. I hope." Cole took Ella back from Charlie, ushering her down the street toward the boarding house. He rounded the corner when they got there, turning to meet them at the door. "Someone should go look for a trail. It oughta be you, Nick. I need Charlie to do something about her."

Charlie eyed him long and hard. Without a word, he turned to Nick. The pair stared at each other in silence in the annoying way Youngs had to speak without talking. They knew each other's ticks and tricks too well. They both nodded and Nick left to head off toward the woods. Charlie gestured. "Let's go upstairs."

Cole followed him willingly up to the room. At the door he pushed Ella inside behind Charlie. "You got a key to Jane's room? We should bring her stuff in here. Don't know if she left anything valuable, but it's best we keep to one room. We'll have to have someone keep an eye on the horses tonight if they're still there now."

Charlie held out a key. "Cole, what is going on?"

"Give her something." Cole avoided the question, he didn't want to have to repeat himself when Nick came back. He nudged his chin toward the woman half buried under the bed calling for Lydia. "Don't think she's slept in twenty years. I'll explain shortly."

Without waiting for Charlie to agree, Cole went to the next room and let himself in. The second he did the smell of her perfume hit his nose. His body went lax at the familiar scent. He leaned against the door, his eyes closed as he inhaled the scent that he'd linked with Jane from so early on.

As though that same day he could picture her leaning over the produce at Turners. The gentle breeze making the light tendrils of hair along her neck dance. The way she'd turned to face him, her breasts rounding over the edge of her bodice. "Jane."

He crossed to the dresser where her perfume bottle sat. He'd arranged to buy hundreds of bottles for her so she'd never have to stop wearing it, even if they stopped making it. He grasped the bottle and took a shaky breath. "Use your brain, Jane. Don't let him best ya like he did me."

It took a monumental effort to shake off the melancholy—no, terror—of what she might be going through. He set about gathering her things and shoving them in her case and carpet bag. She'd packed light and forgone the trunk, thankfully. When he pulled the muffler from the armoire, he paused. It was going to get real cold at night. He prayed to the God he still wasn't sure gave him a second thought that she was afforded some form of shelter.

Once he'd gotten her things together, he carried them to the next room where the door remained ajar. Inside he found Ella sleep on the bed, and released a huge sigh of relief. He dropped Jane's bags in the corner, then crossed to the window, staring off in the distance in hopes he'd get some flash of movement. He was facing the wrong way, down the mountain. Paul would never go that way.

"Your leg." Charlie looked up from his work of straightening a pile of papers on the desk. "You're limping. What's wrong with it?"

"Hoping I'm not gonna lose it." He dropped into a chair heavily. Lifting his trouser leg, he revealed the makeshift bandage he'd tied over it. "Got injured in the earthquake and haven't been able to get my hands on any medical supplies. I had it stitched up, but it kept ripping open."

Charlie dropped his bag on the table he'd just cleared. "What have you been using?"

"Only thing I could get my hands on. Alcohol. Ripped up one of her petticoats and cleaned it, but it's festering." Cole gritted his teeth when the cotton pulled away from the wound, sticking to the site. "Ain't been able to get a telegram outta here. He's got control of that, too."

"Who does?"

"It'll hold until Nick gets back." Cole hissed when Charlie poured water over the wound. Though it hurt like the devil, he held still. He didn't even complain a lick when Charlie dug at the wound.

"You're right. You'll be lucky if I can save the leg. If this has gone to the bone, you probably won't keep it." Charlie pulled several tools and medicines from his pack, along with muslin strips. "I can knock you out. It's going to hurt."

"No. I'll have some whiskey. I gotta be awake so's I can tell ya both all I can."

"Suit yourself." Charlie waited until Cole had grabbed one of the whiskey bottles from his bag before he took a scalpel to the edge of the woods. "It's too cold up here to get maggots to remove some of this dead tissue."

Cole froze in place, staring at his brother-in-law. There was no way he'd heard what he thought he had. "To what?"

"Maggots eat dead flesh, and you've got yourself quite a bit here." Sharp jolts of pain ran up his leg while Charlie worked. "Maybe in Fresno you'll get some help."

"What did I miss back home?" Cole stared at the window rather than the man digging into his flesh. "Is Mike free?"

"He was set free at Christmas, thanks to Sally and Thomas."

"Good. No way he did it. Are the kids all right?"

"They're getting by. Willow caught pneumonia, but she's much improved now."

"She what?" Cole hissed at a sharp stab of pain. "Damn it."

The door opened before Charlie could answer his question. They both turned their attention to Nick. He held up a pair of gloves. "Half a mile into the woods. There's a small spot of blood on the ground. Looks like several sets of footprints, including Janes and a horse. Who knows how far they could have gotten already."

Charlie's shoulders sagged. "It's not good for her to be in any sort of state of temper, or panic for that matter."

"I'm aware." Nick threw the gloves onto the desk.

"He won't kill her." Cole clenched his fists at the renewed pain when Charlie got right back to work on his wound. "He thinks he'll get more for her than that one."

"There are things much worse than death," Charlie said in an undertone. The brother's met each other's gazes in another silent conversation before Charlie turned back to the wound.

Fear ripped through Cole's gut, overriding the pain. "What is it? What don't I know?"

"A lot more than you could know." Nick perched on the edge of the bed. "Now tell us, who's this?"

Cole gaze settled on the bed. There'd be no way around revealing the truth now.

"She called you Colton." Charlie poured water over the wound again. His tone was less harsh than Nick's. "Like your son."

"We named Clara after who Jane used to be. Colton is for who I used to be." He turned his attention back to the wound as Charlie shoved wet bits of fabric in, then covered it with more muslin before he wrapped the leg up tight. "Before I left here."

Charlie cleaned his mess in silence. Once he'd settled in the chair beside Cole, he stared him down hard. "Then you haven't always been Cole Mitchell."

"No. Was born Colton James…" His lips twisted against the natural urge, and he couldn't fully fight the smile. "Spencer."

This time when the brothers looked at each other, he knew why. Jane had been going by Spencer since she'd survived her own hanging. With his permission she'd taken his birth surname rather than something else, and had kept it after their secret marriage.

"She took my name before…"

"Before you got married." Charlie smiled when Cole cut a sharp look his way. "She told all of us on Christmas. I don't believe she meant to, but she did."

Cole shook his head, pushing to his feet. "We were supposed to do that together."

"Hard to do when you up and disappear. Without another word, at that." Nick's tone hadn't warmed in the slightest. "She's been an absolute wreck dealing with the nightmare at home, along with the loss of you."

Cole rubbed his hand over his face, staring out the window. His secrets would be gone now. All of them. He couldn't bring himself to care, not with Jane missing. He got why she'd revealed theirs. Nothing mattered if she wasn't safe. "I wasn't born here. We moved here when my pa got it in his head to join the gold rush. Didn't know why he'd stayed here so long until I got here. There ain't nothing left here but empty mines and dry creeks."

"The woman, Cole." Charlie glanced toward the bed. "What's she got to do with it?"

"When we got here I started working at the general store. I wanted to earn the money to marry the store owner's daughter—Ella." Cole turned to face the unconscious woman on the bed. "She wasn't like this then. She was strong, capable. We had a baby within a year of getting married. Lydia."

Nick grunted but said nothing. He crossed to the desk to rifle through the papers there.

"We don't know why, never knew, but Lydia died before she was a year old. After she died, Ella changed. I tried to take care of her. She had some good moments, but only some. Her pa tried to get me to put her in asylum, but I thought I could take care of her. Then one night she was over me with a butcher knife." Cole's hand drifted toward the scar on his stomach. Every time he talked about it he could feel the pain like it was yesterday. "Drove it right in me. I tried to fight her off, get the knife away from her. Next thing I knew it was in her instead."

Charlie studied him long and hard as the silence lingered. Cole couldn't break it, the memory had him too choked up again. The woman lay alive on the bed across from him, but it didn't matter. She wasn't Ella, not anymore. The loss had been real.

Cole turned his gaze away, trying to get back to his story.

Charlie leaned forward. "And?"

"Her pa told me she was dead. I thought she was. Saw them bury her. Leastwise, that's what I thought I saw. Richard gave me the money to get out of town, to leave Holle Creek. I took it and ran. Ended up in Dominion Falls." Cole sat on the window sill with a heavy sigh. "Colton Spencer died that day she went in the grave. I never looked back 'til Jane. She knew all of this and so much more. Knew why I didn't want to come back. Knew why I didn't care if my pa lived or died. I put it all behind me. Heard from Richard once or twice, but he never told me she was alive. He never told me there was..."

Nick lifted his head as the sentence trailed off. He studied the woman on the bed. "What happened to her after you left, then?"

"Turns out she had another baby. Richard named him James after me, sent Ella to an asylum. I don't know where it all went wrong, but he brought her back here about five years ago. The kid can't stand her, and really hates me. Think it comes from hanging around my pa."

"Your pa. The one that died?" Charlie raised a brow. "Jane told us on the train ride here that's why you came."

"Only he ain't dead. He stuck around here because it still had something to offer, and he's got his thumb on it all. Telegraph is run by one of his wives' sons. Saloons by others. Owner of this place too, by marriage anyway. The well here is running dry, though. He got everything he could outta this dying town by selling it off and gambling the rest. He wants money to get out."

"Did you say—wives?" Nick's eyes narrowed. "As in, plural?"

"Pa liked to have more than one. Started when he took another wife while married to my ma. She had children with him."

"Alma," Charlie nearly yelped in surprise. He rose slow as molasses. "It makes sense now. Jane said she was a relation."

"That don't go nowhere beyond this room." Cole snorted at his own words. "Who the hell am I kidding? It's all over. Leanne is another one if you gotta know."

"Leanne, too?" Nick glanced at Charlie. "Does Tom know?"

"Of course he did. Where is he, by the way?" Cole hadn't expected Jane to bring these two brothers. Maybe Nick, since he was a lawyer, especially if Mike was free. But Charlie? He annoyed Jane half the time. It would have been Tom he expected. Even him in her stead because of the children.

Once again the brothers exchanged a significant look. Charlie chose to speak. "Jane and Thomas had a row. She kicked him out."

"What?" Cole stood at that news. "There's no way she'd do something so dumb."

"Jane is pretty fragile right now. Her trust is shaky and though what Tom did was out of the utmost in kindness, she wouldn't withstand the betrayal it included." Charlie focused on Nick, who nodded in some silent agreement.

"What are you two not telling me?"

Nick shook his head. "There's a lot you don't know, and we don't have time to go over it. You were concerned about our horses. Why?"

"They'll probably get stolen tonight, if they haven't been already."

"Why do you say that?"

"I've been trying to get out of here for weeks. I buy a horse only to have it stolen back and my ass in jail for a few days on a horse theft charge. I'm down hundreds of dollars at this point." Cole stared between the two of them. "Then there was the earthquake, and the snowstorm, and then Paul took her."

Charlie glanced at the bed when Cole jerked his thumb that way. "He must have gotten word Jane had arrived in town. How much does he know about the two of you?"

"Only that we got a hotel and some money. He didn't know we were married until I suggested the divorce in hopes he'd let me at least send that." Cole sank all the way to the floor at that. "I hated sending it."

Nick leaned on the desk, arms folded across his chest. "Didn't need to. If this is your wife."

"She ain't my wife. I told you, Colton is dead. And for all that matters, Ella did die that night. This woman ain't nothing but a vague memory. Nothing of Ella left in her."

Cole pressed his thumbs into his forehead to stem the growing headache. "Not that Jane's gonna want to still be married after all this."

"Jane is angry, hurt, and infinitely confused. She'll probably hold onto her anger for a while, but the Young's have an enormous capacity for forgiveness." Charlie let out a long breath. "Nick. You'll take care of the horses?"

"I will." Nick bent and dug through a bag, pulling free a holster with two weapons, then grabbed a shotgun from behind the door. "In the morning we'll go after her, then."

"I'll remain with this one." Charlie nodded to his departing brother. He frowned as the door closed. "You tried?"

"I'm not clever like you lot." Cole hauled himself to his feet, walking back toward the desk. He stared down at the papers on top, seeing the updated divorce decree staring back at him. A sick feeling settled in the stomach as he read down the page, taking in all Jane had ensured was part of her version of the divorce. The second he realized she'd made sure he had next to nothing as far as funds went, he lifted his head. "I should sign this."

"What?" Charlie straightened from his exam of Ella. "No, you shouldn't. Not until you talk to Jane."

"If I sign it, I've got nothing. Not a dime. He'll have no reason to keep her. She'll be free." He swallowed against the lump in his throat. "She'll be free of this mess, and me."

"We wouldn't be here if she truly wanted to be free. Those papers would have been delivered via one of Thomas's friends, not with her here." Charlie injected something into Ella's arm, then moved over to the desk. "Get some rest. You and Nick will be leaving early."

"Won't be early enough." He glared through the window at the setting sun. "It's gonna get damn cold on this mountain tonight."

Here shall he see no enemy
but winter and rough weather.
—William Shakespeare

Jane could feel the horse moving beneath her. Thin, cold air filled her nostrils. She didn't dare open her eyes or add any tension to her limbs yet. She wanted to groan at the aches and pains coursing through her from the blow to her head and subsequent drop to the ground.

Panic threatened to ruin her initial plan to remain lax against the pommel. The baby.

Slow and steady she measured her breaths, waiting for any sign from the child within it still fought for life as it had when its twin had left her. The moving hooves beneath her knocked stones loose that skittered downward. She counted each step, fighting the urge to move to apply pressure to her stomach to feel something, anything from within.

Then, finally, a kick to her ribs flooded her with such relief she nearly shouted in glee. Instead, she tried to get a firm grasp of her situation. The blow to her head had left her woozy enough for the ride that she had no idea how long they'd been traveling. The only reassurance being that at no time after the initial departure had Paul had the horse running. She only knew for sure because those first few minutes had jolted through her even in the haze of the head wound.

She allowed her eyes to open enough to figure out their surroundings. The sun hung low in the distant horizon. The chill air that had filled her lungs to awareness also whipped about her skirts. Sparse woods surrounded them on either side, those on the right climbing a steep hill, on the right they went down much the same way. Along the trail before them a familiar sight dotted the rocky face of the mountain. Deep holes lined with now-rotted wood.

Mines.

A cry of alarm crawled up her throat, nearly unchecked. Fear crawled across the back of her skull to deepen the headache still lingering after the blow.

Breathe. If you panic, it could hurt the baby. We are in a dire enough situation without you bringing harm to him as well. Her mind repeated the words over and over like a mantra. She'd faced worse terrors than Paul Spencer, even pregnant.

The horse drew to a stop in front of one of the narrow tunnels. She could no longer help herself, she lifted her head to stare into the darkness within. The idea of the cold that would intensify overnight threatened her loose grasp on calm. Another gentle kick to her ribs reminded her of the danger of such panics.

She schooled her breath back to the calm she'd felt within whistle distance of her brothers. Clearly the whistle had come far too late for them to find her, which meant she was on he own. Once again at the hands of a mad man. She grew tired of such things.

"You're awake." The hard pressure of a gun barrel pushed against her ribs. "Don't do anything else stupid. Next time I won't waste time knocking you out, I'll just shoot."

"I highly doubt that."

"Is that so?"

"The whole point of this exercise would be moot if you shot me. You'd not have me, my child, or whatever you were hoping to get out of us." Jane didn't move a muscle when he swung out of the saddle. The gun remained trained on her without wavering. She eyed him coolly. "Or out of Colton, for that matter. I've already explained to you that by tomorrow he won't have a dime. You're going about this all wrong."

"All he has to do is declare you an idiot and throw you in an asylum."

She didn't bother to wait for his prompting to leave the saddle. Hands grasping the pommel, she swung her leg over the horse to slide to the ground with ease. "What exactly *is* your plan here? Are you hoping he'll give you everything he asked for in the divorce? Are you hoping I'll go insane? Or perhaps just die so it's all his? I hate to disappoint you. I've shaken hands with death, I'm not scared by the likes of you."

"Get in here, come on."

She took a few steps toward the tunnel, careful to not take her eyes off him. Though his threats didn't scare her, she still didn't trust him. "I believe you've made a critical mistake."

"Shut up and move." He shoved her into the dim entrance. A match struck and flickered behind her. She used his distraction to slide her reticules around to her back. By the time he lifted the lamp she faced him dead on. His lip curled. "I said move."

"I was waiting for the light." She studied the walls and floors of the cave as the moved. Scraps of wood and rocks littered the floor of the narrow cave. Perhaps she would manage to survive this after all. A chair came into view only a dozen steps inside. The open entrance sat in full view of the seat. Jane eyed the chair as a blast of wind whipped into the tunnel with enough ferocity to make her cape and skirts stir around her. "I'll freeze to death."

"Entrance'll be boarded. You'll be fine. Now, sit."

She dropped into the chair a bit harder than necessary. The whisper of wood cracking under the sudden force echoed through the small space and down the black tunnel beyond. Good, breakable. She ignored the man tying her legs to a chair to scan the entire area as best she could while he worked. Something told her he'd not leave her the light as a kind gesture. The man hadn't a kind bone in his body. How had he charmed multiple women to marry him?

"I'm gonna untie your hands. Try anything and I'll shoot."

"That threat is truly getting old. Shoot or leave me be. I have no idea where we even are." She extended her arms to allow him to untie the ropes. The rough roped pulled from the raw spots on her wrist. She couldn't help the wince of pain when it did.

"Behind your back."

She wrapped her arms around the back of the chair so they stretched further than necessary. As before she clasped her fingers, but flexed her wrists to save her some slack on the rope when he'd tied it. "I told you already, my pregnancy hasn't been strong. At the very least leave me water and a bite of food. If I lose this baby you won't need to worry about money. I'll kill you myself."

A harsh tug on the rope against her raw wrists served as his only response.

She focused on her surroundings while she still had light. Several hefty chunks of wood across the way from her appeared to have come from a support beam. *Comforting*, she thought to herself before scanning onward around the furthest reaches of the lamp for more wood.

When he'd finished with the rope, she wiggled her fingers to see if the feeling remained. They were cold and stiff, but worked well enough. "Water? Food? I'm with child."

He dropped a canteen at her feet. "There's rodents in these tunnels. You can make do since you're so clever."

Jane leveled her gaze at him. "I never told you your critical mistake."

Paul crouched before her. The sneer he wore echoed with hints of Cole, enough to tug her heart strings. Not enough to keep her from hating the man in front of her. "Seems to me you're the one tied up in a mine. Not me. There's no mistake."

"But there is."

"Been playing the game a long time. I doubt it."

"You didn't look, *really* look into Colton's life beyond the fact he has money now, did you?"

"So?"

"You know nothing about me, or what he is like today. Nor any other pertinent information that could mean the difference between life and death for you." She curled her lip into a sneer to match his. "And that mistake will cost you your life."

He ignored her, as she'd expected. He carried the light toward the entrance where the last dregs of a weak sunset colored the winter sky. One by one large boards were set across the entrance to block even that pitiful bit of light. A squeal of ancient rusty wheels echoed into the tunnel until they stopped in a hard crash against the boards.

"Well, then." Jane turned from the entrance and closed her eyes against the increasing darkness of her surroundings. With deep breaths she still her internal panics one at a time. Until she'd counted to six hundred in slow, even breaths, she sat still in the chair. Six hundred seconds meant ten minutes. That gave Paul enough time to get a decent distance away.

On top of giving her space from her kidnapper, closing her eyes against the dark left her gaze in even deeper blackness. When she opened them slow and steady, the faint outline of jagged rocks met her careful gaze.

"That's better." A blast of wind hit the boards at the entrance. Enough slipped through the cracks to send a chill to her bones. "Not good, though. Breathe, Jane. Remain calm. Think of the baby. You can do this. Before you can deal with the cold or darkness, you must get free."

She collapsed her wrists against each other to ease the tight strain of the rope. With Paul long gone, she arched her back and straightened her elbows. Now she had room to move her arms and wrists. With care to those sensitive wrists, she twisted her hand against the rope.

The hemp burned her skin with every twist. She refused to give up until with one last twist of her hand, it burst free of the confine. Jane exhaled in relief. In short order she worked the knot to free her legs. Another blast of cold air had her turning her back on the door.

She shivered off that problem to face its resolution; to make a fire to keep warm. The wind being the way it was, her best bet would be to remain in the cave until daytime. Seeing as she couldn't see well in the dark and had no idea how they'd gotten where she was, she'd be in far more danger trying to get back to town in the dark.

She slid off the chair to gather the rope to her. The longer length she tucked in her belt. The shorter length she toyed with until it began to unravel. With several strands of hemp she made a birds nest of sorts by wrapping it around her shivering hands.

With that done, she set it on the ground and dug into her reticule to free her notebook and matches. After she'd set them near the nest she hefted her skirts to reach her petticoats. Two tugs at the hems later, she groaned in frustration. "I couldn't have brought a pair sewn by Bee so they'd tear easier."

After a deep breath she tugged again. Two more times, three, and on the fourth a rip finally broke the seam. Several more tugs later she managed to rip off a small length. It wasn't much, but it would have to do. With the fabric and several pieces of paper from the blank pages in the back of her notebook, she arranged them inside the little nest.

Jane grabbed the chair she'd been sitting in. Every bit of her shivered by now, but she didn't dare stop. With all the strength she could muster, she slammed the chair into the wall. It broke apart on impact.

She scrambled to grab every piece from small to large. By feel she arranged them by size. She took the matches in hand, then. Crouched low over the small rope nest to block the wind best as she could, she lit a match and slipped it between pieces of hemp.

A flicker of flame caught on some paper. Not wasting a bit of time, she lit another match and stuck it in the other side. Then a third, and a fourth. Small bits of flame flickered from the small nest of rope, fabric, and paper. She fed it a few more pieces of paper before placing several small pieces of wood on top. When they caught she began to truly ply the fire best she could.

Little by little, sometimes only by the aid of her own breath, the fire began to take on the larger pieces of wood. Warmth crackled against her freezing cold fingers sending tingling needles of fire through the stiff phalanges.

Once the fire was strong and holding she ripped at her petticoat again until another length freed itself. She wrapped it around the end of one of the chair legs and lit it. Now she had to find plenty of bits of wood to keep the fire burning all night. The chair would last, at best, a few hours.

Jane got to her feet, straightening out the kinks in her back. First wood, then she'd be able to rest by the fire. "Come morning I get out of here. Earliest opportunity, I kill that bastard."

To be a saint is the exception;
to be upright is the rule.
Err, falter, sin, but be upright.
—Victor Hugo

Tom remained tucked in the same crook of a branch he'd been in for over three hours. Another man darted away from the barn behind the boarding house like someone lit a fire under his ass. The third in as many hours. He wondered how long they'd been trying to get in there before he came along.

Soon as the coast was clear he climbed to the ground. He landed quiet enough to have the sound covered by the rustle of wind. He crept through the open area between trees and barn before pressing against the wall.

Horses could be heard moving inside. Huffs of breath, hooves on wood and straw. That was it. That meant the person inside was as capable of stillness as Tom. Could be either brother based on that. Charlie, as a spy and sniper would be perfect. Nick remained still when talking, although that had lessened and softened around their new sister.

No call of warning arose from the town at his movement, so Tom moved deeper into the shadows to circle the barn. He eased open the doors and slid inside. Before he'd pulled the doors shut the large barrel of what he assumed was a shotgun pressed into the nape of his neck.

He raised his arms in surrender, holding them there as the silence lingered. The man behind him made no threat, but he also didn't lower the weapon. If it had been Charlie, he would have said something for sure. Nick was more to hold a grudge. Then again, it was dark in here, maybe he didn't know who it was. Tom took a stab at which brother it was. "Is that any way to greet your brother, Nick?"

"Tom?" The gun didn't move.

"Last I checked."

"You were supposed to remain in Dominion Falls. With all that's going on, we don't need the only Young brother there to be Mike. He's of no use right now."

"True enough. James is there, though. As are Ma and Pa." Tom turned despite the long barrel pointing right at him. He nodded to the shadowy form of his brother. "Why are you guarding the horses?"

"There's been eight attempts to steal them tonight. Why do you think?"

"I've only been in the woods out back a few hours. Saw three of those attempts."

"Then don't ask ridiculous questions."

"What don't I know?"

Nick finally lowered the weapon. He turned up a lamp that barely had a whisper of a flame until it was light enough to see him. Nick met Tom's gaze with the same inscrutable apathy on his features. "Found Cole, lost Jane."

Tommy's heart dropped to his stomach. "You what?"

"You heard me just fine."

"I'm late by a day and you lost her?"

"She was right in the head. Had a weapon. Nobody expected her to disappear."

"Yeah, well, nobody ever expects it now, do they?" Tom's hand clenched into a fist to dispel some anger before he shouted at his brother. They didn't need to draw any further attention. "How long?"

"Hours now. That's how we found Cole so quickly. She whistled. When we came outside, we saw him and…"

Tom's already taut nerves jumped. His stomach curled into a knot. "And?"

"Ella."

"Son of a bitch." Tom could have punched his own damn self. Molly's point that he usually dug all the way to the bottom of the hole, but hadn't in these cases was proving true. He blamed Clara's hatred of him, and Jane's acceptance for making him soft. "I shoulda kept digging."

"Why didn't you?"

"I was worried Jane was making Clara's fool mistakes letting love blind her to facts. When I found out what sort of man Cole was, I didn't bother digging any further. I didn't bother digging around Holle Creek."

"How'd you figure out when to stop? What made you see?" Nick stared him down. "Did it have anything to do with Alma? Or maybe Leanne?"

"The man really spilled his guts, eh?" Tom ran his fingers over his beard. "He must be feeling as guilty as I am. What's kept him here so long?"

"Ella has a kid, it's his. An adult now. An adult that hates them both, but seems to love Cole's pa."

"The pa whose death brought him out here?"

"One and the same. Except he is not deceased."

Tom rolled his eyes to the rafters. "That'll teach me not to dig." It also made him more apt to dig where Molly had suggested when it came to Sally. That particular expedition would have to wait. For now there were more pressing matters.

"Room three. Expect another gun up there."

"I wouldn't expect any less."

"Cole doesn't know anything, by the way."

Tom halted to ponder the meaning. There were so very many things Cole had missed out on, things that would be pertinent information. "Elaborate."

"He doesn't know about Cora, Hammy, or Archie, and definitely not about the baby."

"For a man that hates my lies, you're keeping a lot from him."

Nick shrugged. "Over a month of silence. I don't much care. You didn't see her in that room after she kicked you out."

"Actually, I did. Who do you think got her to stop drinking all the laudanum?"

"Definitely not Ma. She was fine with it if it meant Jane was staying put to keep that baby safe."

"Which it isn't any longer."

"Something Ma doesn't know, and won't, until it's safe."

"Or otherwise."

Nick's tone was dark with anger. "Don't suggest such a thing."

Tom sighed. "It's probably best Cole doesn't know that detail until we get her back. It'll make him even more careless."

"Sure. Tell yourself what you want." The light dimmed again.

Tom slipped from the barn and back into the shadows. He pondered the boarding house in the darkness. A candle stood in a second floor window so he assumed they were there. If the owner of the place was at all alert and had a weapon, getting there would be tricky.

Well, then he'd just have to be quiet about it. He tested the door and found it unlocked. A good blessing to start. The door slid open with only one small creak. Another good sign. He closed the door quick and moved to the stairs.

No sound came from anywhere in the shadows of the first floor. He saw no sign of candle or fire light under any door. As if the building were empty save for the people upstairs. Since he wasn't sure it was as empty as it seemed, he crept up the stairs along the edge to avoid any creaking boards.

At room three he knocked once, paused, then twice more.

A muffled voice so quiet he couldn't be sure who it was spoke, "Who's there?"

"Tommy."

The door cracked open. The barrel of a Colt Walker leveled at his face as it swung wider. Cole relaxed his stance once the door was open. "It's him."

Charlie peered around the door. After a second he waved Tom in. The door had closed by the time he made it two steps inside. "Decided to ignore Jane, then."

"I'm terrible at following orders." Tommy extended a hand to Cole. "Glad to see you alive."

Cole eyed the hand, not extending his own. "Thought you'd hit me like your brother did."

When Tom glanced at him, Charlie held up his hands. "Not me. That was all Nick."

"Good man. Jane's been an absolute wreck." Tom kept his hand extended. "I'm not gonna hit you. Nick filled me in, briefly."

Cole shook his hand. His shoulders relaxed a little. "Paul's got his thumb on this town. It's about to break under the strain. No new folks coming in anymore, and gold's long gone. He's out for some cash to move on and find a new place to gather wives. He gambled everything away when they stopped letting him get fire insurance. Everything of Richard's has been wiped out. Only bare necessities in the store, and that's all that arrives. I ain't able to order anything myself because one of his wives' sons runs the telegraph."

"That explains that, then." Tom settled into the chair at the desk. He nodded to the lump under the covers. It hadn't moved an inch since he'd arrived. "That the wife?"

"It's Colton's wife, not mine. Then again, she ain't much like Colton's wife anymore, either." Cole sank heavily into a chair. "Spent years in an asylum. Not sure if it's what broke her, or if it was all Lydia."

Tome eyed the man he'd known for nearly five years. A man he considered not just a good friend, but a brother. Never had he seen him that defeated, broken down. What in blazes had happened in the past month? One thing he knew, despite all that had happened, what was really killing him now was his missing wife. "We'll get her."

"Of course." Cole stared at the candle sitting on the windowsill. Stress and sorrow lined his face in ways it hadn't even after the loss of one of the twins Jane had been carrying.

"It'll work out," Tom assured him. He knew Jane would be mad, but much of that would be resolved just seeing Cole. Hearing his story. Jane hated not knowing. Once she knew the facts she could deal with most anything.

Cole said nothing. A whiskey bottle sat beside him near full. He hadn't hardly touched it, and still didn't.

Charlie shrugged when Tom looked his way. After the silence lingered, he cleared his throat. "Cole's got a wound on his leg. I'll have to clean it again in the morning before you head out. He says he got it in an earthquake."

"Earthquake. Fun. What else happened?"

Cole's head dropped back, his gaze now on the ceiling. "Five times jailed for stealing horses I legitimately bought. Five different horses from five different men. The snowstorm. Ella driving me batty; constantly searching for Lydia, calling Jimmy Colton, calling me Colton, running off in the middle of the night to our old homestead or through the woods. Then Paul took her. Maybe James was right, I shoulda let her run. I'd be home and Jane would be safe."

"That's not who you are. You wouldn't let her suffer. You're not cruel." Charlie glanced toward the lump on the bed. "She's malnourished and delusional, which probably keeps her malnourished. Some sort of psychosis must have set in when the baby died."

Cole rubbed his side where a scar set. "She nearly killed me. I nearly killed her. Thought I had, Richard said…"

"Some people break," Charlie assured him. "Ella is one of them. Clara was one of them. Jane is not."

Tom eyed his brother-in-law with a hard gaze. "Jane'll get over it."

Cole's head popped up. "Should she?"

"It's not your fault you couldn't get word out. We'll get you both out of here and home, and it'll all blow over."

Cole turned his gaze on the bed, then back to the candle in the window. His brow furrowed as though he was willing it to be seen by Jane wherever she was.

"Trust me."

"Ella's still alive. She ain't gonna forgive that."

"It wasn't your doing."

"Does that even matter?"

"It does."

*Better to light a candle
than to curse the darkness.
-Chinese Proverb*

Cole sat in the saddle, his horse dancing as if his own impatience beat out of its hooves. Tom had gone to get his own horse from where he'd left it the night before. He was taking far too long. All too soon the sun would begin to rise, and they'd lose what little advantage they had.

Sure, the trail would be more difficult to follow in the dimmest of morning light they currently had. That didn't mean he didn't want to leave already. Hell, he'd rather have left the night before. The presence of Tom to help eased that desire only marginally.

Cole's mind raced over the places Paul could have taken Jane much as they had when he'd taken Ella. Difference was, this time he knew Ella was being watched and he could truly search with assistance. When it had been Ella gone, he couldn't go far for long.

The few places he knew truly remembered in the surrounding area he'd searched when looking for Ella. Would Paul use one of those thinking he'd dismiss them?

There were plenty of hiding places all around the town and up into the higher reaches of the mountains. Old shacks by the dried creek where miners had lived to pan for gold when it ran as fast as the water.

The actual mines that pockmarked the mountains. The deep tunnels within where men had dug along the veins of gold until tunnels collapsed on them.

He would search every single hovel and tunnel if it meant finding Jane. The ache in his heart that had stretched and burned when he couldn't reach her hadn't hurt near as bad as this. At least then he'd known she was safe, surrounded by people who would take care of her.

With her in danger now he swore his heart had split open. A mix of longing and pure fury poured out until his very fingers burned with the combined needs of finding her and killing his father. The man should have died long ago. He'd been no good then, and had grown more rotten as years passed.

Hooves stomped along the dirt. Tommy finally came over the ridge. At his nod, Nick urged his own horse forward to where he'd found her gloves the day before. A night of brutal wind meant any trail would be well scattered unless evidence remained in prints or damage to limbs higher up.

At the spot where Nick had found the gloves, Cole hopped out of his saddle along with Tommy. The urgent pressure of panic left Cole's mind spinning until he couldn't focus. All his brain could focus on and turn over and over until he was left dizzy, was what the men he considered brothers were keeping from him.

Even as recently as getting the horses and weapons ready that morning there'd been moments of hushed conversation and significant looks. Charlie's words, *There are things worse than death,* rang over and over in his head.

"Cole." Tom stared at him from atop his horse.

Cole adjusted his hat to cover his face better before climbing into the saddle. He couldn't let them know how off balance he was. "Lead the way."

"Get your head in the game. Won't do us much good if you're fretting." Nick clicked his tongue and his horse moved east up the mountain. Clearly, Cole hadn't been hiding it.

Tommy moved his horse next to Cole's. Both horses moved forward along the trail in synch behind Nick's. "She's been learning a lot from me along with Sally this past month. She's going to be fine. Focus on that, not whatever has you tied up in knots."

"Right." Cole spurred his horse to get ahead of Tommy. He didn't want understanding or reassurances. He wanted what he'd been looking for from the moment his train had crossed over the Wet Mountains. Jane.

For hours they searched on in relative silence. They'd pause to look for signs of a trail every fifteen minutes or so until the trail petered out at the creek.

Cole stared hard up along the near-dry creek bed, then along the trail to their left. The trail was old and worn, packed so hard no prints would make a dent. The rocky bed of the creek would prevent a surefire trail as well.

Tom studied both before he turned his attention to Cole. "What's your take?"

"There's shacks along the creek where the claims were packed tight for panners. Most of them are rotting and falling down, wouldn't make good cover or keep her pinned well. Mines up that way." Cole thumbed toward the left. "Same problem. Hard to contain someone if they're fit to escape."

"Nick?" Tom nodded to his brother. "What do you think?"

"Just tell us which way to go, you've already got an idea. No need for diplomacy when we're searching for our sister." Nick stared up the creek. When Tom didn't speak, he sighed. "Tree cover. The cabins afford minimal protection against the weather we had last night. Mines offer less unless the entrance is sealed in some way."

"Some of the mines were closed off after they collapsed." Cole turned his horse toward the trail. "I'm heading this way."

He didn't wait to see if they followed, he just raced up the trail quick as he could. The first mine he came to was almost fully collapsed at the entrance. Two hundred yards down the next mine entrance was fully covered.

He jumped from the saddle quickly. The boards were old and rotting, so he tugged hard until the first broke away. "Jane! You in here? Jane!"

Tom rode past him toward the next mine.

A couple of full boards cleared his way to step into the mine. He took a few steps inside. "Jane? You in here?"

All that echoed back to him was his own calls. He walked deeper in until the light wouldn't stretch any further. "*Jane.*"

Nothing. She wasn't there. He climbed back out of the mine to get back on his horse and ride further along the trails.

For another two hours he and Tom went mine by mine, breaking out their lamps to move deeper into the darkness in some of them. Cole didn't bother to ask where Nick was, he assumed he'd followed the creek to spread their search further.

Cole climbed back into the saddle, turning his horse on the spot to look back at the stretch of mines they'd just searched. "There's another group higher up, a little further north. Should we wait on Nick?"

"Nah. He'll alert us if he found anything. Let's ride." Tom spurred his horse and ran alongside Cole as they descended through a little valley before resuming the climb along the next stretch of trails.

The trail here was rockier so the horses had to slow their pace. Cole urged his horse on fast as he dared, pausing at the first mine entrance. When Tom dismounted to tug at the boards barring the entrance, Cole moved further along the path.

Around a slight bend he spotted something odd. Mining carts that littered the edge of their trail were a common sight, but this one was pushed against the entrance of a mine. Cole clicked his tongue at the horse to move closer.

The cart butted against boards blocking the entrance. Two boards near the edge were broken, smashed outward. "Jane. *Jane.*"

Cole clamored out of the saddle so fast he stumbled on the loose rock of the trail. He hauled himself over the cart toward the hole in the boards. "Jane? You in here?"

Silence echoed back. He paused there, glancing behind him. After he'd issued a sharp whistle to call Tommy, he climbed back out of the cart to grab his lantern. When Tom joined him just a minute later, they both shoved hard against the cart. The wheels squealed in loud rusted protest, but it moved away enough Cole could yank away several more planks.

He ducked into the tunnel, holding his lamp aloft. "Jane? Are you in here? Where are you?"

Once again only his own words echoed back to him. He crept deeper into the tunnel anyway. Those broken boards told him someone had been in here. An arc of light from his lamp flickered over the floor. "Tom, look."

Cole knelt next to the pile of ash on the floor. Bits of wood stacked against the wall, but there was nothing else there. He stood while Tom examined the site. "*Jane.*"

Heart pounding in his throat, he closed his eyes against the dark. They'd been searching for hours already. If she'd been here and gotten out, they'd have seen her on the trail, unless…no, he couldn't think of it.

"Fire's cold." Tommy brushed his hands together as he rose. Lamp in hand, he swung it around. "What about those planks at the entrance? Did you break them?"

"No. They were already broken. Outward like someone was coming out." Cole moved with him to the entrance. His heart sank as he searched either way on the trail, then lowered his gaze to the steep wooded mountainside below them. "You think she's out there?"

Tom's gaze also lingered in the woods beneath them. "She wouldn't have taken the trail, even if it's most sensible. She wouldn't want to run into your pa."

"On foot she'll never make it back to town today. It's going to get cold again tonight."

"She started one fire with few resources. She can do it out there"

"Damn it. *Jane.*" Cole cupped his hands around his mouth to bellow the last word. It echoed through the woods and off the mountain behind them. He stared deep into the woods in hopes of some sign of movement. A return call, anything. He put his fingers to his mouth and blew another harsh whistle.

Tommy did the same.

They both stood there in silence as the whistles died on the wind.

"Let's get Nick and head further down the mountain. We can break off the trail there."

Cole released a shaky breath. "We've gotta find her."

"We will. She hasn't learned to cover her trail yet."

"That doesn't help. She's unarmed. What If he finds her first?"

"God willing, Paul doesn't know she's gone yet."

"Like I tell Jane all the time, God ain't got much to do with me."

"Sure he does." Tom clapped his shoulder. "He brought you Jane."

Never let the future disturb you.
You will meet it, if you have to, but with
the same weapons of reason which
today arm you against the present.
-Marcus Aurelius Antonimus

Sally flipped through the pages of the catalog. She paused on every relevant page to write down numbers on the paper to her right. In her excitement, she worried she'd forgotten something from the surprisingly extensive suggestions Andrew had made. She bit her lip, flipping the pages back and forth.

"About done?" Andrew leaned on the counter beside her. He picked up her pad, running his finger along it. "Oh, you forgot something."

She handed off the pencil so he could jot down numbers. "I should have had you make the list in the first place."

"Then you wouldn't learn."

"You sound like Ma. And Tommy."

"Then you appreciate my words of wisdom and years of experience."

"You're barely two years older than me." Sally bumped his elbow, chuckling under her breath. Andrew had finished school at a very young age. No medical school would allow him in as young as fourteen, so he'd taken a position with the coroner. Soon as he'd been allowed in medical school, he'd breezed through that as well. "You're too smart for your own good."

"Only in school matters."

Sally studied the list. "Do you think this is good, then?"

"For a start." He handed it off to her.

She copied it into her notebook. "Good. I only want to get a good start on being able to run those tests myself. It isn't like I even have a place to set this all up, anyhow."

"Are you really looking for a place of your own?" He followed her to the counter. "I bet Dr. Young or even Sheriff Schaffer would give you space in the clinic or jail."

"I don't wish to be affiliated with either. I want this to be a proper business on its own when I'm ready for it." Sally smiled as Faith approached them. She handed off the list and catalog. "Could you get these ordered for me?"

"Of course." Faith ran over the list. A smile broke out. "Look at you, child. You even did the math for me."

"I know you're quite capable, but the store has been quite busy lately. I thought I'd help." Sally handed her twenty dollars. "That should cover it and some of Ma's credit. Pops and Mams will be by with the rest next week when they order."

"Thank you, Sally. Dr. Cross." Faith carried everything over to the back counter.

Sally turned her attention more fully on Andrew. "Now tell me, Dr. Cross."

"Dr. Cross?" He took a step back, eyes narrowed suspiciously. "You only call me that when you're up to no good."

"Are you going to ask the lovely nurse Bonnie to the Sweetheart Dance?"

"You are up to no good." He wagged his finger at her. A low chuckle carried under his scolding. "Why are you so insistent?"

"Because you are over the moon for that girl."

For a moment a bit of embarrassment brightened his pale features. A rosy hint to his cheeks lingered. "I doubt she'd even go with me."

"Nonsense. What young lady wouldn't want to dance on the arm of the elegant, well-bred Doctor Andrew Cross?" She curtsied low as she could, then lifted her eyes to gaze at him through her lashes. "Oh, my dearest Andrew, a girl would be a fool to say no."

"You stop that right now." He lifted her from the curtsy by her elbows. "I swear, you're as big of a brat as my darling sister ever was."

"It's why you like me so very much." She grinned through his hum of disapproval. "I do hope to meet her one day. She sounds simply charming."

A frown darkened away the light of embarrassment. "Unless you plan to go to Buffalo, such a thing is unlikely to happen. Since Father died…well, Mother has been rather protective of my sister. She rather despises that I am here. I doubt she'd ever allow Lisabeth to come."

"What a shame. From all you've told me about her, she'd rather enjoy it out here."

"I've no doubt she would." He held out his arm to her. "Now, if I were to invite Bonnie, whatever would you do for company? You say your friend Patrick is leaving in less than a week, after all."

"I wouldn't accompany Patrick to anything such as the Sweethearts dance. Our relationship isn't anything that would make such a thing appropriate." Sally turned to face him, her skirts swirling about as she did. "I imagine I would go alone. Perhaps I'd find some darling men that wish to dance with me."

"I'm certain there'd be no shortage of such men, but would they wish to dance with you for the right reasons?"

"Who cares? A dance is simply that, a dance." She dipped left, then spun right, twirling round and round until she hit a solid wall. "Oof."

Strong arms caught her before her stumble turned into a fall. "Easy there."

"My goodness." Sally held onto him as he righted her. Feet on the ground again, she lifted her gaze to find startling pale green eyes twinkling with laughter. The handsome face attached wasn't quite succeeding in hiding his amusement. "Mr. Coleman. I do apologize."

"No harm done, Miss." Matthew offered a crooked smile. His hands hadn't left her elbows, keeping her close to him.

"That's what I get for attempting to dance in the busy mercantile, I suppose. Though there are much worse things and people I could have bumped into than a handsome cowboy."

His tanned features ruddied. "I suppose so."

Warmth bloomed across her own face and neck as she lingered close to him. She couldn't deny her attraction to him, in a way that was different than those with Patrick and Molly. His warm gaze set her heart aflutter as much as her libido. "Hope I didn't step on your feet."

"No, my feet are safe. Much unlike any unfortunate soul that usually tries to dance with me, for I haven't one clue how to dance."

"No? Not a bit?"

"No. My Ma, Ma Edwards, and Bonnie all tried to teach me. It never stuck."

"What a shame."

"I'd best be getting to my shopping Miss Spencer—or is it Mitchell now that they say your ma and pa are married?"

"Oh, well I hadn't really thought about it." She leaned closer. "Why don't we make it easier for us both and say you can just call me Sally."

His ruddy cheeks darkened further, but he nodded. "That'll do, but only if you call me Matthew."

"Matthew it is. Thank you for rescuing me, even if you were the cause of my fall."

He chuckled low. "Any time, Sally."

"I'll remember that, Matthew." With a heaping pinch of regret, she took a step back. She let her fingers trail along his arm to his hands before she slipped free. At his nod, she offered a small curtsy before stepping on the porch where Andrew stood. The man was bright red with his concealed laughter. "You hush, Andrew."

"Oh no, no. That was *quite* a scene. I thought you weren't interested in the rancher."

"I honestly thought I wasn't." Sally glanced back not the store where Matthew stood in discussion with Abe. "Apparently I needed an up close introduction to learn the opposite. I'd be a fool to not be."

"Maybe you should ask him to the dance."

"Maybe I should." The suggestion wasn't without merit. Even though the man had just told her he couldn't dance, they could find other ways to occupy their time. She turned back to Andrew. "Only if you ask Bonnie."

"That's just cruel."

"Not even a little bit, and you know it." She laced her arm with his. "Now, where were we?"

"We were discussing you finding a place for your detective-type situation."

"Not situation, occupation." Sally surveyed the town from their perch, taking in the varied store fronts along First Street. "I'd hate to do something over on Second or Third, and definitely not on Fourth. I'd rather be right here in the middle of things. I don't need anything large. It isn't as though I plan to live there."

"Why not?"

"I'm perfectly content where I am. Ma gives me every freedom, but I remain close enough to help when it's needed. Now something similar in size to Lucky's barber shop would word. Or even right there where the church used to be, that would be perfect." She pointed to the one-story building on the corner of First Street and Miner's Row.

"Who's living there now? It clearly isn't a business front."

"Mr. Daughety's foreman has been using it as living quarters and office. Mrs. Daugherty was saying they are looking to build something larger near the old mines. They plan to bring on two more foremen. All of them are bachelors."

"Maybe you should make an offer."

Sally bit her lip as she pondered the idea. In order to purchase such a place, she'd need to borrow money from Jane, or get a mortgage. A mortgage would be near impossible for her to secure. She'd pay it, or her ma, back without question, but borrowing left a bad taste. "I can't, anyhow. Not without speaking with Ma or Tommy first."

"Them maybe mention it to Mrs. Daugherty. She seems to like you well enough, perhaps she'll ensure any sale is held for you."

"I'd hate to use Ma's connections for such a thing."

"It wouldn't be…" Andrew's voice trailed off. A wicked grin erupted as he nodded over her head. "Matthew."

"Dr. Cross." Matthew shook Andrew's extended hand.

"Bonnie is joining Sally and I for supper this evening. Would you care to join us?"

Sally cast Andrew a dark look before plastering on a smile and turning to Matthew. "It would be quite an evening. There's usually quite a crowd at supper at the Inn. My brother Jesse will probably be there. I think he and Stephen are friendly at school."

Matthew's gaze left Andrew to settle on her, warm and friendly. It didn't settle there, rather drifted along her form. Once again that warmth bloomed across her chest, all the way up to her cheeks. His smile lit his features as he nodded. "Stephen's mentioned him. I guess that'd be all right. If Bonnie ain't cookin', we're not eating fine at the ranch."

"Then we'll see you at six." Sally stepped closer until her skirts pressed into his legs. "If that suits you?"

Matthew never had a chance to reply. A large explosion across the street flashed bright enough to blind Sally briefly. A concussion pulsed right through the, knocking Sally to the ground. Matthew crawled toward her, shielding her body as another explosion went off.

Heat and shrapnel cut across Sally's arms as she ducked into a ball. She clutched Matthew's shoulder, calling out to Andrew, praying he was all right. Her eyes stung and flickered with dark spots as she coughed on dust.

Pure silence followed the blast at first, or perhaps it was the ringing in Sally's ears blocking any sound. Matthew shook her shoulders. "You all right? Sally? You good?"

"I…" her voice sounded strange to her own ears. She moved her limbs gingerly. Some bits of pain came, but nothing serious from what she could tell. "I think so."

His fingers brushed along her cheek. "Can you see? You were looking right at it."

"Sort of." Sally moved to rub her eyes, but he held her hands in place. "Don't rub 'em. Stay here, I'm gonna check Andrew."

Sally held her hands in the air when he'd left them, blinking against the spots still cluttering her vision. As her sight started to return, blurry and uneven, the site of the explosion came into view. Realization dawned when she realized where she was looking, what had been where the pile of rubble now sat.

The undertaker's office.

"My God, *Graham*."

*In peace, children inter their parents;
war violates the order of nature
and causes parents to inter their children.
-Herodotus*

Mike picked his way over the wreckage, following the same straight line as those on either side of him did. The blast had almost completely flattened the undertakers and the cooper's beside it. The barn in the back of each, as well as Graham's icehouse where several bodies waited for burial still stood.

No one had any idea if anyone was inside either building. Being as it was the middle of the day, it stood to reason there had been. Then again, he hoped that Graham's duties as mayor had kept him away. Mike lifted a board in his path, setting it aside. Then another.

Glass crunched under his feet. Burned wood and splinters scattered everywhere, even spread across the street. Mike moved another board, then a high-pitched scream paused all action. Every man picking through the wreckage turned as a small woman came tearing toward the building.

Linh was caught about the waist by Mr. Kilmurry. She screamed and shouted in Chinese, trying to pry herself away from the man holding her. Mike turned and met Abe's grim face.

Then one word came clear through Linh's foreign screams, "*Johua.*"

Mike froze in place, his heart stopped. A tremor ripped through his body as the impact hit him hard. His hands shook so hard he clenched them in fists. "She can't mean their son was in here, too."

Abe's features twisted in the same grimace of fear Mike himself felt. They both turned to look at the small, very pregnant woman still fighting to free herself from Kilmurry.

Dr. Noe pushed her way through the crowd to Linh's side. She administered a shot into Linh's arm, then urged Kilmurry to pick her up. With a dismal look their way, she followed the pair back to the clinic where casualties lined up for treatment. Someone must have told her about Linh to bring her out.

With a heavy sigh and a big dose of nerves, Mike continued his path through the destruction. Step by step he moved aside rubble. Ten minutes later loud calls went up, and men gathered in the area of the cooper shop. They dragged out an unconscious Bryan Kendrick.

All progress stalled as the man was tended to by Andrew. Mike crouched down and took a sip from his canteen. He offered it to Abe.

Abe accepted the offered canteen. After he took a sip, he returned it to Mike. "That's one. Kendrick got a woman?"

"Nah. He preferred whores." Even Mike heard the bitterness in his tone. Bryan had been one of Daisy's callers. He shook off the memory and took another swig of water. Once the group with Bryan had dissipated, David blew a whistle and everyone resumed combing through the rubble.

For near ten minutes there was silence. Another call went up and David's whistle blew. Just three men down from Mike a crowd gathered. Several boards later, Graham's prone form was revealed.

"Shit." Mike stared at the wreckage. If Graham was there, then it was a good bet Joshua was. Sometimes he'd send him with Sally to the library, but she hadn't been there that day. Mike's hands shook as he lifted his hat to run his hand through his hair.

Abe seemed to be feeling the same nerves as Mike. He bounced the balls of his feet waiting for the whistle to begin again. Due to Graham's large size, this time the removal took much longer. At least the calls being shouted about indicated he was alive as well. Perhaps barely, but alive none-the-less.

Mike waited anxiously the next twenty minutes while they cleared away Graham and got him to the clinic. His fingers twitched against the canteen, ready to start again, but moving would do no good without the men to help if they came upon anyone else.

They all knew a miner had been brought to the undertakers that morning after having a heart attack in the mines. There was also one of the ranch hands from the Keenan farm that had fallen from his horse. So far they hadn't found those bodies either. Thankfully, Hammy was in the icehouse so they wouldn't have to tell Jane his body had been in the building when it had blown.

The whistle finally sounded again. Mike tried to be careful in his movements through the rubble, but his nerves left his hands shaking. Five feet along his line, he stopped dead. Ice poured through his veins at what lay before him.

Peeking out from a shattered and burned board three feet ahead of him lay a small hand. The air disappeared from his lungs. Without regard to the three feet between them, Mike leaped forward. He threw aside the board and collapsed to his knees. Gingerly, he pulled the child from the surrounding rubble.

He reached for the boys' neck, praying against all hope he'd find a pulse. Joshua's eyes were closed, his lips nearly blue. The torn remains of his clothing clung to his similarly shredded back.

"Please," Mike whispered.

He held his hand against the artery as shouts went up around him. No beat from the boy's heart hit his fingers. Gasping for air, he pulled the boy close. He held onto him tight as tears burned down his cheeks. A horrified yell nearby pulled him from his focus on the boy.

When he lifted his gaze he realized the poor child was also missing a leg. Mike's head lowered, pressing to the silent child's forehead. "Get me a blanket."

A few minutes later a blanket settled on the ground in front of him. Mike laid Joshua in the middle, wrapping him with great care. He pulled the child back into his arms. Carefully he rose to stand.

With careful steps he walked back along the path he'd taken through the rubble. He ignored hands that reached for the child, blindly walking straight to the clinic.

The door stood wide open. He stepped through into the chaos inside. Dead silence fell over the room like a wave as he stood there.

Sally rose from her seat, her pale features cut from shrapnel. Slowly she approached him, her gaze falling to the blanketed child. "Joshua?"

Mike nodded once. He couldn't seem to make his mouth work. He feared if he tried it would only scream out his fury.

Sally wrapped an arm around his waist, guiding him through the waiting room to a room in the back. She pushed open the door for him, then put her hands on his arms to hold him still. "Wait just a moment. Let me make it comfortable for him."

He nodded numbly, staring at the simple wooden table in the room. Bottles of liquids and equipment lined the shelves, cluttering another table right next to where Sally now arranged several blankets.

When Mike spoke, he was surprised at the gravel in his tone. "What's this?"

"This is where Andrew does his autopsies. There isn't a room upstairs with a proper bed to lay him in. They're all full with patients getting treated." Sally rolled a blanket into a sort of pillow.

"He can't…" The words locked in his throat.

"That doesn't matter now, does it." Her tone was kind, with echoes of Jane's usual sort of understanding. She guided him over to the table. "Once the clinic clears out we'll get him into a proper bed and cleaned nicely so Linh can see him."

"Keep him covered. She doesn't need to see everything." Mike sent the boy on the table gently as he could. When Sally pulled the blanket aside to reveal the cherubic features of the young boy, a sob ripped its way through his gut.

Tears shimmered on Sally's cheeks as she smoothed Joshua's hair down. She wiped some soot from his cheek. "There. We'll see he's taken care of, Uncle Mike"

"Thank you." Mike took two steps backward and his legs gave out.

Sally knelt beside him, folding him into a hug. Thankfully, she offered no words of comfort, simply the reassurance of her presence. Mike held onto her in return, his head dropped to her shoulders. "It could've been the twins."

"I know."

"This has to stop."

"It will. I promise you that. I have an idea what's going on, but I need evidence."

"Find it fast, Sally. No one else should die."

"Too many have already."

Courage is resistance to fear,
mastery of fear –
not absence of fear.
–Mark Twain

Jane tucked herself against the trunk of a large tree. The wind had picked up again and swept across the hillside with ferocity on occasion. A headache had formed overnight, and she imagined her lack of water didn't help matters.

For hours she'd been carefully climbing down the steep grade. She had yet to find flat land or anything that could serve as a shelter for what promised to be another cold night. Her feet felt too big for her shoes, and her hands were stiff. The wind whipped at her nose, lips, and ears until she feared frost bite might set in. She kept pushing the collar of her cape up to stem this from happening.

While the wind moved about her, she leaned against the tree to rest and think. Her petticoats weren't offering much protection to her legs, thankfully her wool stockings saw to that task. Perhaps she could remove one layer of petticoat to serve as a hood and muffler. The cotton wouldn't serve her as well as a proper muffler, but it would be better than the nothing she currently wore.

She smoothed her hand along her waist to the back where the buttons lay for her skirts. Her clumsy fingers battled with the button for several minutes before she finally managed to get one petticoat free. With several hops and tugs, the skirt came free from her layers. She undid her cape during a break in the wind to secure the skirt about her head. With some gathers and tucks, she secured it in place with the cape. It wasn't warm, by any means, but the wind didn't strike quite as hard on the freezing features.

She had no idea how far from town she was but had a strong feeling she wouldn't make it by nightfall. Much earlier in the day she thought she'd heard several whistles. With the wind, she couldn't be certain. Plus, with the mountain rising at her back, it could have come from any direction.

The canteen remained hanging from her hip, though it now sat empty. She'd sipped careful as she could all day, there'd hardly been anything in there to begin with.

Her stomach rumbled now that she sat still. After she found a comfortable spot at the base of the trunk, she crossed her legs before her. Carefully she ran her hands along the swell of her stomach. "I know I've been moving a lot. Now would be a good time to let me know you're all right, little one. I'm going to rest here for a bit, then seek out some water and shelter. I doubt I'll find much edible in this landscape, but at least I should be able to build a fire."

She let her head drop back against the tree, closing her eyes. With every breath she willed her body to relax against the strain it was under. All day she'd been shaky, and the headache lingered interminably. She had a thought to see if she was bleeding, but the idea of finding any such thing terrified her too much to check.

"Please, baby. Please. Hold on." She exhaled long and slow, her hand continuing its circuit along her stomach. "As soon as I get back we'll head right home. No matter what. It was foolish to take this journey. Ma was right, but don't tell her I said that."

After three rounds of counting to six hundred, a light tickle of movement twitched near her ribs. Relief relaxed her shoulders a little more. "Thank you, little one. You are my hope. You keep going. I'll give you everything if you keep going."

Jane opened her eyes to scan the sky. Despite the brutal cold and wind, the bright blue of the sky shone down happily on her. As the baby moved again, Jane reveled in the moment of peace to her current situation.

The wind whipped about, changing direction to blow northward. Once again Jane thought she heard a whistle carry on the wind, but before she could be certain it changed direction.

She edged her way up the tree to standing, turning south. With her luck it was probably Paul, and she definitely didn't want that coming her way. Still, she searched in hopes it was Nick or Charlie searching for her.

For ten minutes she stood there searching the horizon for signs of life. She released her own harsh whistle though the wind seemed to carry away the sound before it fully left her lips.

Nothing. Not one sign of movement.

She exhaled slowly against the bitter disappointment. Another soft kick bumped against her hand, drawing her attention down. "Right. Let's try to find some water and shelter at the very least. Maybe there's something edible around here for us to get some form of sustenance, hm?"

With much regret, she abandoned the shelter of the tree to return to her descent. Foot by foot she slid along the rock face for what had to be another mile. Blessedly the ground began to level out as the sun lowered against the horizon.

Jane turned a circle, looking for somewhere to camp. A cluster of trees stood probably a quarter of a mile north. It wouldn't fully surround her, but it would offer some level of protection from the elements at least. If it began to snow she imagined she could use her cape as some form of shelter.

She made her way toward the trees, keeping her eyes peeled for any signs of wildlife. Now that she wasn't in a mine, her biggest worry was wild animals. Especially seeing as she didn't have any weapon but a fire if she could build one again.

Perhaps it was a good thing she didn't have food to cook. That would for certain attract animals to her. As if her mere presence in their territory wasn't enough.

Jane approached the copse slowly. She searched for any sign of an animal making its home there. Even a deer lay would mean that it could be a place that attracted animals like mountain lions. She circled the cluster of trees three times looking for prints, scat, or any nesting. Short of a squirrel chattering at her from above, she found nothing.

"Thank heavens. Still no signs of water, though. I almost wish it would snow to give us some melt to use for water."

She set about gathering sticks, twigs, and larger branches scattered on the rocky ground.

In absence of anyone to talk to, she continued to talk to the baby. "I have no idea how close to the town we are. I don't want to attract attention. We should keep the fire smaller. Only as large as we need to keep the frostbite away."

Once she'd gathered enough to create and maintain a fire for the night, she encountered another problem. Where to build the fire.

The best way would be inside the arc of trees where it would be protected on most sides from the wind. However, that would leave her back open to the woods climbing the hills behind her. The fire would be protected, she would not. Plus, then the fire-no matter how small-would be at the trees where it could catch.

The fading light left her little time to decide. She blew out a long breath and began to dig at the ground with a large branch to create a depression near the opening of the trees. She lined rocks around the circle, then checked her surroundings once more.

Before the sun hit the horizon she rushed out through the woods to find several longer, thicker branches. She'd ignored them for the fire, fearing making it too large or being unable to break them. Now she carried them back to her spot.

She pulled the length of rope out of her belt and unraveled it as she had the smaller rope the night before. Once she had four separate strands of hemp, she dropped three by where she'd build the fire. The fourth she clamped in her teeth while she lined the large branches up.

The bottom ends of each spread out in a rough triangle while she angled the tops together. The whole thing barely came to her chest, but she didn't need a lot of room. Once the tops were crossed together, she pulled the strand from her teeth and wrapped it around, under, over, and through the branches to brace the pieces together.

When it was tied as tight as possible, she pushed on it a couple of times. Though it wobbled, it was secure enough to do the job. Before she could add the final touch, she needed to build the fire. She dropped to her knees and began as she had the night before with her nest of hemp.

The fire built slow and steady. By the time the sun sank below the horizon it held strong enough to satisfy Jane. She dragged the tripod of branches close enough that they stood at the edge of the fire, but not over it.

Satisfied with its position, she dug down at each end to secure the poles in the ground. She set rocks over them so the wind wouldn't carry her measly protection, and her only cape, away. This time when she pushed on it, it hardly moved.

She undid her cloak and draped it over the branches to form a sort of shelter. She'd not have the warmth of the cloak on her, but it would block any snow and help keep the heat and light of the fire contained.

She sat on the edge of the fire, soaking in the warmth. "Now I almost wish it would snow, just not a blizzard. Light and fluffy like we'd get back home. When everything is clean and crisp, the air smells so clear."

A soft sigh slipped free from the momentary homesickness. She ran her hands along her stomach again. "Although right now I'd prefer it so we might be able to get some water. Tomorrow we'll get back to town, I'm sure of it. Then we can eat something that'll tide us over until Fresno where we will dine on something absolutely sinful to make up for this grievance. What do you think?"

A soft bump hit her hand. Jane brushed aside some dead leaves to curl on her side. "And a feather bed so soft we'll almost sink right through it. Nothing but the best."

The fire crackled, dancing along her lids even as they closed.

Fear secretes acids;
but love and trust are sweet juices.
-Henry Ward Beecher

Cole stared into the woods, searching for any sign of movement. The lump in his throat wouldn't budge. The night had gotten brutally cold. Despite their exhaustive search before nightfall they'd found no sign of Jane. He knew in his heart that she was resourceful and capable, but fear tugged at his gut.

In the darkest part of the night, Tom had climbed a nearby tree in hopes of spotting any fire Jane might have started. He'd seen nothing. Their whistles the day before had given them no response. Outside of the remains of a fire in the cave, they'd seen no sign of her.

"Cole." Tom clapped a hand on his shoulder. He even threw in a shake as though it might stir Cole out of his fear. It didn't. "We'll head back toward town. That's where she's heading. We'll keep searching along the way."

"She doesn't know the way. Resourceful as she is, she doesn't know these mountains like those back home."

"She knows to head down the mountain west. The rest will work itself out."

Cole couldn't turn away from the woods. She was out there, somewhere. Alone, cold. "She should have never come out here. At least in Dominion Falls I knew she was safe."

"I wouldn't count on that. Things have gotten bad at home."

"She was surrounded by you all, and her friends. She was safer than out there all alone." Cole kept his eyes on the horizon as if she'd magically appear to ease the panic in his soul. "When she got taken by Bingham I knew she was safe because you were there. That was better than this."

"Let's move." Tom urged him back toward the horses. "Standing around here isn't going to do a damn thing."

"Why didn't she stay in Dominion Falls?"

"Because despite everything she still held onto the belief that you loved her as much as she loved you." Nick glared down from his horse. "Only to find you with your first wife."

Cole thought back to the moments before Ella had been returned by Paul. The flash of bright green he'd seen, how he'd thought for sure it was Jane. Now it seemed likely it had been her. He swallowed down the lump of guilt in his throat. Avoiding Nick's glare, he climbed into his saddle. "Let's just keep looking. We've got to find her. Who knows if he left her with any food or water."

"There was some snowfall last night, I'm sure she got some water from that." Tom hefted himself into the saddle. Before they moved, he turned back toward the woods. Fingers to his lips, he blew a long harsh whistle.

Cole held his breath as the sound died away, praying the wind hadn't kept it from carrying far enough to reach Jane. Several minutes of silence passed with no return. Resigned, Cole turned his horse to follow the pair of brothers.

The remaining two hours of slow descent it took them to get back town went much the same. They'd ride for ten minutes, whistle loud and long as possible, then wait for a reply. When none came they'd move on. Cole prayed with all of his might that she'd be at the boarding house waiting for them. Weakened by her ordeal, but no less ready to fight.

He'd take a fight, even the worst fight they'd ever had, if it meant she was alive. That was all that mattered to him now.

As they came in sight of town, Cole slowed further. He popped open his holster so he would be able to grab it at the first sign of trouble. He noticed the Young brothers did the same. The quiet town sat much as it had before they'd left the morning before. Yet, somehow it seemed even more silent.

No whores lingered outside of the saloons. There was a small measure of sound from within, but nowhere near the usual boisterous drunkenness. The general store remained still and silent as he'd left it.

Cole narrowed his eyes toward the telegraph office. The place appeared dark. The line going to it from down the mountain was gone, likely cut. "Either Paul cleared out or he's planning to attack us."

"My thoughts exactly." Tom urged his horse on toward the boarding house.

Cole pulled his weapon free as they passed the saloon, keeping an eye peeled for any hint of trouble. When Tom dismounted Cole stayed where he was, weapon at the ready.

He nodded to his brother-in-law, taking up position next to Nick with their backs to the building.

For five long minutes everything sat silent. Tom offered no signal of reassurance, but there was also no signal of warning. Finally Tom emerged from the front door. "Owner is gone. Took everything. Clothes, and some furniture. The place is pretty well cleaned out. At least there's food in the kitchen. No, still no sign of Jane. Charlie's concerned for the long-term effects of her disappearance if she's had no food or water."

Once again the brothers stared hard at each other. For a second Cole was dead certain he'd heard a sniffle from Nick. His anger rumbled from his chest. "What in blazes are you lot not telling me about my wife?"

Nick didn't bother to look at him again, his gaze on the hill rising up behind the general store. "Which wife would that be?"

"Jane. Jane Mitchell. My wife, not Colton's." Cole met Nick's gaze when he turned to look at him. "You accept Jane ain't Clara."

"Jane doesn't remember. You do."

Cole drew his horse closer to Nick. He didn't waver at the man's cold gaze. "I ain't a liar, neither."

"Enough. Nick, drop it. You're only goading him, and you know it." Tom hauled his rifle from the saddle holster.

"He needs to be angry. It makes him sharper." Nick turned his attention back to the hills. "She can't be far so long as she's heading west."

"Let's get moving. On foot this time." Tom hesitated at Cole's look. "We're not going overnight. Nick'll get the horses in the barn and lock it up our way. We'll hear anyone trying to get in."

Despite the assurance, Cole hesitated to get out of the saddle. After a few minutes, he conceded and hopped to the ground. His hand twitched over his second weapon, but he returned his Walker to its holster without locking it in. If he needed it, he'd need it quick.

Nick was gone so long Cole began to wonder what Tom meant by locking up the horses their way. Then again, he figured it wasn't something he wanted to know.

Once Nick rejoined them, they moved down the street together. Each man on his guard for any movement from the buildings around them. This caution made their progress past the saloons exceptionally slow. For all they knew Paul was hiding out in one of them.

Then a movement down the street caught Cole's eye. A figure came around the corner. Filthy from toe to wild curls.

Cole's heart caught in his throat as she crept into view. Her green dress ratted at the edges, her cloak askew. Though her gait was stiff, it was unmistakably, *"Jane."*

*We shall find no fiend in hell can match
the fury of a disappointed woman—
scorned, slighted, dismissed
without a parting pang.
—Colley Cibber*

Jane leaned against a tree, staring at the town. She'd come down a little too far north, but she'd found it in the end. The smart thing to do would be to go around the town center and straight to the boarding house from behind.

She didn't have the energy to fight the woods any longer.

It had snowed lightly the night before. She'd managed to gather some snow in the canteen, but the gritty water that had resulted from her efforts hadn't been nearly enough to sufficiently hydrate her.

Her whole body hurt from the journey, lack of sleep, and nourishment. Her lips were chapped, mouth parched like a desert. The pains in her stomach had begun that morning by the fire. Panic had been all that had gotten her moving with any hint of speed.

The headache that had been her constant companion had increased until she thought her brain might leak from her ears. The sight of the town, while a happy one, was blurry.

Another pain stretched across her stomach. She whimpered, closing her eyes and taking a deep breath. "Charles will help us. He has to. First, I have to get there."

She clutched her cloak around her. With a push off the tree, she headed down the path into town slow and steady. Thankfully she saw no one on her path, though she feared being seen by the wrong person. She didn't think she had the strength to fight off a flea.

After several minutes of slow movement, a wave of dizziness overtook her. She leaned against a building, taking a few deep breaths. Her eyes closed against the headache and double vision that left her dizzy.

"A few more yards and we can rest. We can see you're taken care of. Stay with me, little one. We've fought hard enough to get here, we can't lose everything now." She took a few deep breaths to still the panic for the tenth time that morning.

When she felt settled she moved again. A mix of panic over being seen, and relief of being right there coursed through her as she rounded the corner. Then Cole's yell hit her. *Jane.*

For a moment her heart leapt. He was there and sounded panicked. He'd worried. With every step he took toward her the disappointment, loss, fear, and anger shoved aside any bit of joy over seeing him.

His arms wrapped around her to pull her close. She braced her arms out to keep him far enough he couldn't truly hold her. He didn't seem to notice. "Thank God you're alive. Did he hurt you?"

She pushed him back hard. Before he could speak or protest, she hauled off and slapped him. In the moments of his stunned silence, she grabbed his weapon from its holster and held it on him. Adrenaline spiked through the fear and pain until only fury remained as she glared at him down the barrel of his own weapon.

"Jane." Cole raised his hands in the air. He made no move to draw closer. "You don't—"

"Shut up." Anger and relief welled so fast, her own words choked off. She used her free hand to hold her cloak closed over the evidence of their child. "Weeks I waited. Cora was shot, I heard nothing"

"Jane." This from Tommy, whom she hadn't even realized was standing there. Which meant he'd ignored her request to stay away. "You should know what's been going on."

"I don't care." Jane forced the words out through gritted teeth. She fought to keep her breath and tone steady. "Willow got desperately ill and still I heard nothing. Not one word. I fought worry and gossip until I couldn't stand it any longer and told them all the truth.

Cole still didn't move. His usually bright ice blue eyes dull. A tear sat on his cheek. He didn't waver his gaze one bit as she spoke.

"Then Hammy."

Cole's eyes widened when she said his name. "What—what about him?"

"You didn't even care that he *died*."

His features went slack, hands dropped to his side. Cole shook his head. "What? *No.*"

Jane's hold on the weapon shook when a pain stretched across her stomach. Her arm began to drop. "Then divorce papers? A *divorce*? You left me devastated, alone. Meanwhile you were here with your real wife."

"No, Jane. It ain't like that." Cole took a step toward her, pausing when the gun returned its aim on his face. "You gotta listen."

"And a son. You have a son that was all too happy to help kidnap me right along with your dear Pa."

"He *what*?"

This time the pain that arced across her stomach couldn't be ignored. Jane gasped, doubling over. She clutched her abdomen. "No. No, *Tom.*"

"I've got you." Tom scooped her into his arms.

"What's going on?" Cole's voice grew quieter as the jarring steps of Tommy carried her away from him.

She whimpered, clutching her stomach protectively. Tom's bellow echoed through the boarding house and she curled into him as they moved up the stairs. She was set on a bed, her cape removed within minutes.

"Jane. Jane, look at me." Charles got right in her face. "Try to relax."

She snorted at the absurdity, but it only made her double in pain again. "Charles, please. Help me. Help him. Please, please."

"Shhh." A needle jabbed into her arm. "When's the last time you had food or water?"

"Food...never." Jane blinked as the sedative rolled over the worst of her nerves. The room spun as the effects took hold. Even with the sedative another pain stretched across her. "Oh God."

"Jane. Water. When?"

"A day. I think. Some today. Very little."

"Thomas. Get the bag under the desk. It has a new treatment I've been researching. It's probably her best bet. I don't care, do it."

Jane tried to focus on the brother in front of her. She'd heard nothing Tommy had said. Her hand rested on Charlie's arm. "Water."

"Here." He pressed a glass in her hand.

She slurped at the water desperately until the glass was pulled from her lips.

"Easy. You drink too fast, and you'll feel even worse. Sips. I'm going to try to hydrate you another way that'll be faster. If we don't, there may be nothing I can—"

"What the hell?" Cole's cry cut through Charlie's explanation. "Jane!"

Charlie set the glass back in her hand. "Sip only. Cole, Jane is pregnant."

Cole circled into her line of sight. "I can see that. How the hell can I see that? If she—what is—how?"

"Get *out*." Jane shrieked. Or at least she thought she did. The sedative made her brain a little fuzzy. "Get the *hell away from me*."

Cole backed into the wall, staring at her wide-eyed.

Another round of pain hit. She cried out, doubling over.

"Lie down." Charles pushed her back onto the bed.

Jane closed her eyes. The glass slipped from her fingers to shatter on the floor. She vaguely heard Charlie say something about bleeding. No, no. It couldn't be. She whimpered. Against her upset, one word slipped free, "Cole."

Her head lifted and within moments she rested back against his familiar chest. A soft kiss dropped to the top of her head. "I'm here, Jane. I love you."

She was certain if she had the water to produce tears, she'd be crying. "Don't lie."

"I'm not a liar."

"I know."

Men acquire a particular quality by constantly acting a particular way...you become just by performing just actions, temperate by performing temperate actions, brave by performing brave actions.
-Aristotle

Sally leaned on the autopsy table, chin in hand. Glass clinked nearby as Andrew attempted to clean the clutter on his desk. She stared at her notebook, more specifically at the most recent notes she'd jotted down.

"Go over it again," prompted Andrew. He replaced some bottles on the shelves where they actually belonged.

"All the men that have died were good men, well-loved men, men of God. Not a Sunday went by when we didn't see them in church. Even after their wives died, if they had them. They were always kind to everyone in town. Very little bad could be said of any of them. Even Ellis, and it was widely known he liked his moonshine."

"What about Horace?"

"Chauncey?" She straightened, stretching against a kink in her back. "He worked in the saloon forever, but he was a good man. To answer your next question, yes. He also attended church every Sunday with Opal. Pa is the only one from the original saloon that still doesn't attend church on the regular."

"Right. Now onto the women."

"Whores—or at least thought of as such. Even Ma, though she's told me she was only ever loyal to Pa. She pretended otherwise sometimes to stoke his jealousy, but many thought her loose and spread rumors of her with Major Webb, the Sheriff, and half the army camp."

"You're including your mother?" He dusted off his hands as he approached the table.

"I know that one seems specific to her seeing as Ma and Mac had a long rivalry, but it still fits the pattern. All of the women with the exception of Miss Bee were whores either in the present or the past. We also all attended church regularly. Daisy missed alternate Sundays to attend to the clinic, but she went often until near the end of her life."

Andrew's brow furrowed. "Then how would Miss Bee fit in? Why attack her?"

"I don't know. It's a discrepancy from every other attack. She didn't attend our church. She went out to Pastor Eckles' Glorious Valley church from the time she arrived in town." Sally stared at her notebook. Bee being such a discrepancy rankled her. Something was off there.

"What about the man that attacked your mother? He died."

"He killed himself." Sally flipped back in her notebook. "No one knows why. It's not like it was the first time he'd been in jail."

Andrew waited until she'd added a note about Mac's suicide. "Outside of Miss Bee, do you have any idea what it all means?"

"No. That's the best connection I've come up with so far." Sally closed the notebook. "I'll be sitting down with Molly tonight to go over it as well. I feel like it's right there at the edge of my thoughts and if I pluck the thread enough it will fall loose."

"Plucking at threads can unravel things, you know."

"That's what I'm hoping. I'd like it to unravel. It's all a tangle." She sighed, tucking the notebook in her reticule. "How is Linh doing?"

"Poorly. The baby is ready to come, but she's taken to melancholy and does nothing but stare out of the window. If she waits too long there could be consequences."

"Graham still being in bad shape likely doesn't help. When he wakes, I don't know what he'll do. You didn't know him before Joshua. He could be one mean son of a bitch."

"He still has his wife and soon another child."

"I hope that's enough. I don't know how Ma would handle the loss of one of us, she took the loss of the baby's twin so hard. Graham—he's going to be devastated, just as Linh is."

"His friends will have to be here for him."

"That would be easier if his friends were here. We haven't heard from Ma since she first said she'd arrived. It's like Pa all over again."

"Sally, it's been three days."

She stared out the window rather than meet his gaze. If the internal panic she was feeling over Jane's silence was anything at all compared to what Jane had felt at Cole's silence—well, she had renewed sympathy over what her Ma had gone through. "I suppose."

A light knock sounded on the door, interrupting whatever hopeful line Andrew was bound to issue. "Excuse me. Sorry for interrupting."

Sally turned toward the familiar voice. A smile broke free despite her temperament when she found Matthew's gaze on her. "Matthew. What brings you by?"

"I was in town sending a telegram. Had some time before I need to get Stephen from school." Matthew leaned on the frame, one ankle crossed before the other. With his Stetson off, one lock of rich brown hair draped over his eye. "Thought I might see if you wanted lunch since we never did to have supper the other night."

"Supper was a family affair. This would be just the two of us." A flutter of excitement stirred inside when a crooked smile lifted a corner of his lips.

His tone was warm, "I'm aware."

Andrew scoffed behind her. "I guess I'm not invited."

"Close your hole, Andrew." Sally stepped closer to Matthew. "I would be delighted."

He brushed the lock of hair from his face and returned his Stetson to his head to keep it in place. Much was her disappointment, she rather liked the unruly lock. He offered his arm. "Shall we?"

She laced her arm through his without another word to Andrew, even as the infuriating man laughed outright behind him. It took all her effort not to scowl back at him. Then again, not so much as it was easy looking at her escort. "Ignore him. He has much too high an opinion of himself."

"Bonnie seems to like him well enough." He grabbed her coat before she could. She obliged him by sliding her arms into the sleeves.

"I can't believe those two aren't officially courting. Ma swore they'd be courting by Christmas." She ducked her head against the brutal wind. The sheer force of the wind prohibited any conversation on the trek across the street.

Matthew helped her out of her coat one inside the Inn. He draped her coat and his own on the rack by the door. His hat dropped to a chair, that adorable lock of hair dropping forward soon as it was off. "Bonnie's worried about them working together and courting. Plus…"

Sally sat in the chair he held for her. "Plus, Andrew is too yellow to dare ask properly. I keep telling him to ask her to the dance. That's actually how I stumbled into you the other day."

"You didn't stumble, you spun."

"I spun and then stumbled."

"Fair enough."

She leaned closer, pleased to see his eyes light up at her approach. "What if we came up with a way to get them to the dance together without either of them having to ask? I'd rather not watch Andrew continue to get all embarrassed and fumbling around her. It's becoming rather pathetic to see."

He opened his mouth to reply, but they were interrupted by the waitress. Soon as their orders were placed, he stared her down. "Bonnie seems to think he might like you, too."

An uncouth, loud bark of laughter rushed out of her before she could school it. Heat flooded her cheeks. "That was ruder than I meant. No. Andrew is a dear friend, for certain. We get along famously but I'm not attracted to him in the least."

"That so?"

She gave a slow nod before leaning closer to him. Her hand settled on his knee. "When I have an attraction, a man knows it."

Her actions brought the reward of his cheeks growing red again. The pale green of his eyes seemed to darken as he took a breath. Their food arrived, giving him a distraction that eased the embarrassment. Much was the shame, she thought he was cute when his eyes darkened like that.

She settled into her meal easily. After a few bites, she glanced at him out of the corner of her eye. "Tell me, Matthew. Did you run many trails?"

"Not as many as most of those that come through town." His whole energy brightened at the mention of his time as a cowboy. "Pa Edwards preferred me on the ranch learning how to run it, but I liked running trails, too. I got to go twice a year for five years, and once a year since."

"And you're twenty-one now, so if you started at fifteen…"

"Twelve."

"Twelve? That's awful young to be running trails."

"Edwards had a nephew that ran the trails to keep an eye on me. The first ride was a fluke. I wasn't supposed to go, but there was an emergency."

Sally got distracted from his story at a movement near the door to the casino. Mams led Alma in precisely at one, but Sally could tell immediately that Alma was in a right state.

She'd been bad since Cole had left, and once Jane did as well, there were far more bad days than good. "Oh dear. Mams."

"What?" Matthew followed her gaze as the pair approached the table. He wiped his mouth and rose. He offered a gentlemanly nod as he moved his hat. "Mrs. Young. Miss Alma."

Alma's hands clenched and unfurled at her sides. Then one arm jerked and she hit her own thigh. She shook her head, eyes closed.

"Mams. It's not a good time for her." Sally flew to her feet, around Matthew to Alma's side. "Alma, do you want a song?"

"Sorry. I thought she was settled enough." Mam's looked the most frustrated Sally had ever seen her. She wondered at what sort of morning Mams had been having with Alma.

Alma let out a squawk, her arms flexing until her hands hovered near her head. Another squawk and she hit herself in the head.

"Let's go to the office." Sally's attempt to move closer got her an accidental elbow to the eye. "Ow. Damn."

Matthew touched her shoulder. "What can I do?"

"Bear hug. Get her arms down and carry her to the office. She'll fight you until we can get her calm. Mams, a blanket." Sally tried to distract Alma while Mathew circled behind her. When he got Alma's arms pinned, Alma let out a bold screech that stilled all action.

Without hesitation, Matthew lifted her off the ground. He followed Sally's rushed steps to the office. Somewhere along the line Mams showed up with a blanket. Sally clutched it to her. "Take a break, Mams. We'll take care of Alma."

"I don't mind."

"Really." Sally squeezed her hand before she closed the door in Eunice's face.

"Let her go." Son as he did, she threw the blanket around Alma's shoulders. "And again."

Matthew wrapped his arms around Alma again. His brow pursed at Alma's insensible protest. "This really gonna help?"

"Hold her tight as you can, even if you think it's too tight. Trust me, it works."

"I trust ya."

"Alma, do you want a song? A song?"

Alma grunted, but her fight lessened.

"Um, oh dear. What should I sing? Oh, right." Sally immediately thought of the one song that always seemed to help calm Alma. The tempo and tone were right within her favorite comfort zone. "Beautiful dreamer, wake unto me. Starlight and dewdrops are waiting for thee."

To her surprise, Matthew joined in on the next line. "Sounds of the rude world, heard in the day."

She met his gaze. His brow relaxed as she offered an encouraging nod. When he began the next phrase, she dropped her tone to harmonize with him. While they sang she withdrew her pencil from her reticule. In time with their pace she tapped on the desk in measured, rhythmic pulses.

Finally, Alma's fingers began to tap the same steady pace against her thigh. Sally pushed on until the final words of the song faded. She stepped closer to Alma, taking the edges of the blanket. At a nod to Matthew, he released his tight hold.

Sally kept her tone level and even. With every syllable she tried to follow the same beat and tone as she'd just used to sing. "Is that better for you now?"

Alma nodded, her head low.

"Did you want to go home or stay here?"

"Home."

Sally smiled softly. "Then we will. We have to go through the noise to go home, all right?"

Alma nodded again.

"Might Matthew join us until he must leave to pick up his brother?"

Alma's eyes slid to the edge of their sockets to peek at Matthew. She turned back to Sally, reaching out to play with the pin at her collar. After some hesitation, she nodded.

"Fair enough. Thank you, Alma. Let's go home." Sally wrapped an arm around her fellow ward. Matthew stepped ahead of them to open the door. The whole way back to the apartment she let Matthew lead the way and sort of clear their path so there'd be little resistance.

The moment they hit the apartment, Alma drifted to the piano. Ada glanced up from the book she was reading to the twins. She cast a curious glance at Sally. "Everything all right?"

"It will be now. I think. Mams is staying in the restaurant for a little break. I'm sure she'll be back shortly with some food for Alma." Sally took Matthew's hand and tugged him over to the table in the corner of the room. With a heavy sigh, she sat. "You didn't get to finish your lunch, or your story. I do apologize."

"It's no matter. She gonna be all right?" The gaze he directed toward Alma held no pity or disdain for what had just happened. If anything, he looked concerned. It was touching.

Sally relaxed with that realization. "With time she will be. Having Ma and Pa so far away has led her to be much worse off than normal. Alma likes things ordered and predictable. With Ma and Pa gone, they no longer are."

"Nothing wrong with that."

"Thank you." The words rushed out of Sally without censor.

"For what?" Matthew turned back to her.

"For being so understanding. Not everyone can tolerate her, they call her all sorts of names. They say she's not normal."

"Normal ain't nothing but your way of thinking."

Sally sat straighter. The words held familiarity, something she'd once read that had struck her much as it had impacted Jane. "What did you just say?"

"Normal ain't nothing but your way of thinking. Why?"

"It's funny. Pa once said the same thing to Ma a while ago. I read it in her journal."

A warm smile brightened his features. "Is that so?"

"It is. Guess that means you aren't half bad."

"But does it mean I'm all good?"

"I sincerely doubt it."

Love truth, pardon error.
—Voltaire

Cole bit his tongue as long as he could.

Nick came in and muttered something to Charlie before disappearing. Tom arrived with the case Charlie had asked for. Charlie hung a bottle of what looked like water to the end of some tubing. When he attached it to Jane with a large needle, panic jolted through him again.

"What's that?" He held Jane's hand near as tight as she held his, worried at what was happening to her.

"It's a treatment for her dehydration." Charlie checked the tubing before lifting his head. "They started using something similar to treat cholera patients years ago. I've tried it myself with moderate success."

"Moderate?"

"In the past. Andrew and I have been working on a ratio of additives that make it safer. His assistance has been immensely helpful. It should bring her no harm."

Tom leaned on the end of the bed, staring Cole down. "I'm heading out. You all leave soon as you can. Get off this damned mountain. Let her recover a few days in Fresno. I'll do my best to meet you there."

Cole nodded. He knew better than to ask Tom what he was up to. He'd tell soon enough. Jane's near-panicked grip on his hand grew lax. Cole did his best to remain calm.

He knew that though she'd called for him, and held onto him until she'd lost consciousness, once she was back in control of her faculties and no longer terrified he'd likely find himself back on the business end of his own gun. Or hers. Either way, he wasn't forgiven. If he even should be.

To that end, he would be damned if he left her side until then. He rested his cheek on her head, holding her close as he could from their position. Once he was certain she slept, he ran his hand over the swell of the baby inside. He didn't know how it was possible she still carried his child, but he couldn't have been happier. It gave him a sliver of hope that he might be forgiven with time.

Then again, that would only happen if she didn't lose the child after what his damn fool pa had done to her. Fear tightened his arms around her to hold her close to him like it would save her by sheer force of will. A soft whimper whispered from her lips, but she remained relaxed.

When Charlie's flutter of movement finally settled and the room sat still and silent, Cole released a long breath. It was time to question his brother-in-law and find out what he could. First things first, Jane. He ran his hand over the swell of the baby again. "She gonna be all right? The baby?"

"I can't say for sure. If she loses the baby, she won't be." Charlie rubbed his hand over his face, a heavy sigh escaping.

"Tom's right, we need to get her down to Fresno, away from this place. I need her more stable to move her, but I'll feel better if she's not here."

"She gonna be all right?"

"The bleeding has eased. The pains she was having as well. Those are good signs. If we can keep her calm after she wakes, all the better."

Cole glared toward the next room where he'd seen Ella still lying unconscious on the bed. "She won't be if I'm around, or if that one is."

"I've been around that woman for the past couple of days while you've been out looking for Jane. She is not sane, nor is she well."

"I know." Cole turned his attention back to Jane and the baby. "How? I mean, how is this possible? I buried a baby. We mourned the loss."

Charlie's features softened. He rubbed a hand along Jane's arm. "With the birth of Colton and Clara at near term we thought Jane had broken the curse. Our ma lost four twin pregnancies. Two complete losses, and two much like Jane did with this one."

"Twins?"

"Yes. One was passed, but the other lingers. That's why her corset wouldn't fit right even after she lost the child."

Cole closed his eyes against the rush of emotion. The grief they'd been going through when he'd left home. What relief and joy she must have had knowing they still had a child growing. How much he would have loved to have known. "Thank God."

"The baby gave her a lot of hope when your absence lingered."

That put the lump of fear and guilt right square back in his throat. It wouldn't do to release his emotions right there with a witness. Cole pulled it all back as best he could, clinging to Jane like a lifeline. He cleared his throat against that blasted lump that would give him away. He had to change the subject. "What was that about Cora being shot?"

"She was walking home from the Inn one night, she'd left early. Sally has a notion the bullet was meant for her because she was supposed to be going to visit Arthur at that time."

"Why would she visit Arthur?"

"Because she accidentally beat on him when he startled her."

Cole's attempt to cover his own laughter resulted in a loud snort that startled Jane. He took her hand again, waiting until she settled to glance back at Charlie.

"What else have I missed?"

"The new dressmaker was killed. She was left in a mine to be found."

Cole's brow furrowed. That was odd. Why in a mine? "What?"

"They're still trying to figure out that one."

"In a mine?"

"Yes. Sally and her little friend Molly did something that resulted in Reuben Miller—"

"That manager at the Sage Brush?"

"That's the one. He confessed to Daisy's murder. Mike was set free at Christmas." Charlie sighed heavily. He glanced at Jane as though to check if she was awake. "Then there was Hammy."

"Tell me it ain't true. Hammy ain't dead." Cole hadn't even had a chance to give the man a proper good-bye. He'd never thought he wouldn't see him again.

"Shortly after Christmas he was at the casino when he had a massive stroke right in front of Jane. Over the next week his condition worsened. He continued to have strokes and seizures. It was right after midnight on the new year when he passed away."

Cole clenched his jaw against the wave of grief that swept over him. He'd always had a soft spot for the old coot. He'd found the man's adoration of Jane amusing, and his generosity when Cole had first arrived had never been forgotten.

That was nothing to how Jane cared for the man. She'd always treated him like family, worried over him like one of her own constantly. He clung to her unconscious hand. "She must have been a wreck."

"She was with him when he passed. His stroke actually delayed her trip out here so she could stay with him." Charlie turned his attention back to his sister. His eyes widened. "Welcome back, Jane. Can you remain calm, or do you need more medicine?"

"Fuzzy," she whispered.

"That's fine. I won't give you any more. Is it safe to leave you here with him while I check on my other patient? I'll send Nick to prepare the wagon. I want to take you down the mountain immediately, and now that you've had some fluids I think it's safe to. We don't want to linger where there could be more danger."

"Go." Jane waved at her brother, then paused. Her arm lifted and turned so the needle and tubing were more in front of her. "What?"

"I'm getting you fluid faster than you can drink it. I imagine you'll be feeling much better in another thirty minutes. We'll leave right after." Charlie leaned down to kiss her forehead. "Be nice."

"Go." Through it all, Jane never released her hold on Cole's hand. It wasn't until Charlie left before she bothered to acknowledge his presence, though. "I'm…I don't even know."

"Can I talk, or are ya still fuzzy?"

"Talk—like my Cole. My Cole, not her Colton."

"Huh?"

"Vernacular."

"I've been talking rough." He sighed at her nod. Much like at home when Sally had pointed it out, he hadn't even realized he'd slipped back. Being around Jane had changed him, but when he was around the right sort it was easy to go back. When he spoke again he did his best to think before the words emerged. "I've been stuck here for a month with the mining sort. It was easy to fall back. You said I did it at the saloon, too."

"Didn't mind then. Hate it now." Her hand left his to run along her belly.

"I'm so sorry. I tried, I really did. I sent telegram asking you to come, asking Tom. I never heard anything."

"The telegraph operator tried to fool me. Instead of sending my telegraph to Katherine, he said he was stepping away."

"He's the boy of one of Paul's wives. I'm sure that's why none of my messages went out, or my letters. I tried to leave, to get a horse. They kept throwing me in jail for stealing horses I'd bought and paid for."

She didn't respond, didn't look at him. Worse, she didn't take his hand back.

"I hurt my leg in an earthquake. Then there was the blizzard. He took Ella like he did you. The whole last week she was gone." In his arms, she tensed. After a moment she even tried to sit. He set his hands on her shoulders. "I don't love her, Jane. That doesn't mean I'd want him to kill her."

"Go away."

"No."

"Leave me alone, Cole. I don't want...I don't." She managed to sit, but her whole body swayed. "Please go. Send Charles back."

"Jane."

"I said *go*."

*I am tired.
My heart is sick and sad.
—Chief Joseph*

Jane did her best to ignore the man staring at her with pitiable sadness from across the room. Instead, she focused on her brother as he removed the needle from her arm.

When it came out, blood bloomed from the wound. He pressed cotton to it and bent her arm up. "Hold it there, that will stop the bleeding."

She didn't argue. Whatever he'd done had left her feeling better. No more pains, and even her headache was diminished. However, her body still ached from head to toe. The idea of traversing down the mountain was not pleasing. "Must we really get back in that blasted wagon again? For days?"

Charlie's lip quirked. "Do you want to leave this place?"

"I do. Forever."

"Then yes."

She sighed. "Fine. I want the softest bed there ever was when we get to Fresno."

"I'm certain we'll have no problem attaining the best for you, Jane." The wry tone spoke of her newly vast wealth, without saying it aloud before the man that had no idea. Charlie rose with a kiss to her forehead. "Cole. Before we leave, I need to clean your wound."

Wound? Jane pondered what wound Charlie could mean. Then she remembered Cole mentioned getting injured in an earthquake. The limp he still had, as well. It couldn't be all that serious, could it?

Cole didn't broach a word of argument. He didn't speak at all, as though waiting her permission. Instead, he sat in a chair. His right leg propped on the table as he lifted his pant leg.

Jane kept equal silence while Charlie removed the bandage from the leg. The ugly wound revealed itself as the cotton wound away. It looked horrible, deadly even. She whimpered at the thought he could be lost again after she just found him. Her stewing anger wavered despite her best intentions. "Oh, no."

Cole's gaze flickered her way before returning to her brother. Charlie poured water over the wound without care to the floor. He leaned in close, pulling some tools from his bag. When he began to scrape at the edges, Cole winced. His eyes closed and his head dropped back.

Jane fought against the building worry. They weren't on a battle field where proper treatment didn't exist, but how long had Cole gone without proper treatment? When was the earthquake? Her heart twisted. "Will he lose the limb?"

Charlie didn't turn from his work. "I don't believe it's made it to the bone, so we should be able to save the limb. I need better supplies than what I brought. We'll get that in Fresno."

Three more days, maybe two as they were descending rather than climbing. She did her best to ignore Cole when he turned his gaze on her. It would do her no good to have him see her concern. Still, she found his earnest and pained expression. Her resolve crumbled. She wanted to run to him and comfort him. Her hands shook as she buried her head in them. "I can't handle this."

"You can handle anything," Cole said in an undertone. "Always could. Better than me."

She tore from the room before she gave in to the flood of emotions. On her way out she paused by the room where Ella still lay unconscious. She stared at the woman Cole had described as strong and capable. The frail figure on the bed didn't match what he'd said about her.

Jane backed away from the room and made her way down the stairs. By the time she reached the wagon Nick guarded, her legs were wobbly.

Nick immediately set down the gun to wrap his arm around her waist. "Jane?"

"I'm fine. I needed air."

"Where are the others?"

"Charles is cleaning Cole's wound. I had to—I need to—I don't..."

"It's going to take time." Nick's voice was soft and soothing in its kindness. None of the sharp edges so familiar to his tone. He was worried about her. That, at least, was comforting. He lifted her into the wagon bed where there now sat two beds of hay instead of one. Hers by the wagon seat, and a second by the tail.

She wrinkled her nose against the idea of sharing the wagon bed with Cole's former wife. "I can't do this."

"You have to." Nick guided her toward her bed by the wagon seat. "When we get to Fresno, Charlie will find a place to put Ella. She's too far gone for anything now but a hospital."

"You mean asylum." The idea of putting Alma in one had disgusted her. Even with her bitter feelings against the woman through no fault of her own, Jane shuddered at the idea.

"Unfortunately, yes." Nick helped her get settled, then took a seat so he sat hip to hip with her. His gaze wandered to search the environment before facing her dead on. "Clara died. That's what you say."

Her heart lodged in her throat. It was such a bitter topic with him, so much so that the harsh edges had returned to his voice. She nodded a weak agreement.

"When Clara died, you became you." His tone softened again, but he'd looked away to search the area again.

"Yes," she admitted. The bitterness in her own tone couldn't be helped.

"Cole says the same about Colton. He says Colton died when Ella died."

"But she didn't."

"He thought she did. If it's true for you, how can it not be true for him?"

"I don't remember. He does."

A sad smile crossed his usually stoic features. His intense blue eyes so much like her own shimmered. He leaned in to kiss her forehead. "Sometimes that makes it easier to become someone else."

"What about when the past comes back to you?"

"Yours came back. We are all here, part of your life. Yet, you're still Jane. Not Clara."

She turned her gaze away, staring unseeing into the woods where she'd been taken. Tears flooded her eyes until everything warped and shifted with each blink.

Nick took the hint, climbing over the seat to settle in. Rifle in one hand, reins in the other, his sharp gaze never stopped moving. She wondered where Tom had gone, why he wasn't helping secure their departure.

It probably didn't matter. The town seemed almost deserted now. She closed her eyes against the new flood of tears. Colton was dead, or so he said. She'd seen the way he'd called for her, the way she'd rushed into his arms, though.

That's what it should have been for her. She supposed he'd tried, but she'd aimed his gun at his face. He'd deserved it. He said he tried, but it wasn't hard enough.

I don't love her, Jane. That doesn't mean I'd want him to kill her.

Cole always took care of his family, even when he didn't want to name them as such. Look at what he'd done for Leanne and Alma all of those years. The man he'd once been had loved Ella. He'd shoved away so much to protect himself after her supposed death.

Jane's heart twinged. She hadn't loved David when he'd returned to her life, but she didn't remember him. It was so different, even in its similarity. She didn't know what to think or do.

Ten minutes went by before Cole emerged from the boarding house, laden with the bags Nick hadn't already brought down. He loaded them in the wagon in silence, then disappeared back inside. Charlie came out next, carrying Ella. He set her into the hay bed near the back of the wagon, then lifted the gate closed.

Cole appeared again with Charlie's two medical cases. He handed them to Charlie, who tucked them under the wagon seat. After Charlie squeezed Jane's leg, he climbed into the seat beside his brother.

Using a wheel for leverage, Cole hauled himself into the bed near Jane's feet. He settled in, then clapped his hand on the wagon bed. "Let's get out of Hell."

"Happily." Nick slapped the reins, guiding the wagon toward the road down the mountain.

Jane gripped the edge of the wagon, trying to not react to every jolt that made her exhausted body ache even more. One hand on her stomach, she breathed out slow and steady to try to keep her nerves at a minimum. She definitely didn't feel back to full strength. She needed a hot meal and a long night's sleep to even get marginally close.

Nick and Charlie apparently decided to ignore them, bantering back and forth in annoyingly jovial tones. They were either trying to cover the tension behind them, or truly excited to be heading home. More likely it was a combination of both.

When they'd been traveling for barely ten minutes, Cole shifted.

Jane glared his way, though she doubted it was effective with the tears still blurring her vision. It must not have been because he drew closer until his back was against her side of the wagon. He set a canteen down by her side, then inched closer.

"Please don't," she whispered.

"Is this one of the times I'm supposed to listen to you, or one of the times I should ignore you? I'm out of practice."

"I told you to go away." She closed her eyes so she couldn't see whatever look he gave her. She'd longed for the comfort of his arms for so long, but now she couldn't bear him so near. Not with *her* right there. Everything was wrong and mixed up.

Cole's warmth faded from her side, but there was no shuffling to indicate he'd gone back to the other side of the wagon again. His heavy sigh carried over the jovial conversation and rattle of the wagon.

His hand rested on hers, gentle and warm. All of her resolve nearly crumbled. Her wounded heart beat hard against her chest. She took a shaky breath.

"Please, Jane. Look at me."

If she did, her pain would soften under the sanctuary she'd so often found in him. The sanctuary he'd always provided her. "You're married still. Everything we built—"

"Ella died years ago. Before she was buried. Just like Clara. So did Colton."

She opened her eyes, but kept them downcast rather than look directly at him. There was no way she'd be able to bear whatever she found in his gaze. Whether earnest intensity or lies. "Please unhand me."

He did as she asked. The warmth of his hand drifted away. "I know you're hurting. You may never forgive me. I love you, though. I am yours. I have been since I first laid eyes on you."

Though she knew he wasn't a liar, the words felt inconsequential. Nothing in the chasm that had formed in the past weeks. She turned on her side, willing her tears to not fall. Much as he wanted forgiveness, she wanted to grant it to him.

She had no idea how to begin to do so. None of it was his fault, her brain knew. Her heart wouldn't listen to such logic.

"I'll spend every day for the rest of my life proving it. You can count on that."

The wagon lurched over a bump, giving her the opportunity to release her sob without notice. She nestled in deeper to the hay, pulling her arms close to keep from the instinct to reach for him.

She'd once been told that her heart often made a fool of her, ignoring all logic when it came to matters such as love.

Was she being a fool?

*From the lightest words
sometimes the direst quarrel springs.
—Cato the Elder*

Sally and Matthew tore down the street at a dead run, heads ducked as snowballs landed on and around them. She yanked him to the right as soon as they hit First Street. Across Kat's porch and into the alley they ran, pausing halfway down.

Her breath strained against her corset, but she laughed with every breathless exhale. "Why on earth did you start such a thing?"

"Stephen was being a brat." Matthew turned to cover her as a group of laughing kids ran by the end of the alley.

She grabbed the lapels of his coat. Her brow furrowed in her attempt to appear stern through her continuing laughter. "Well, your attack on your brother got me caught in the crossfire."

"I'll have to apologize right-proper, then."

"I expect you to, sir." She flattened her hands to push him away, but paused before she made any effort. Her ears strained for any further signs of laughter. "I think they're gone. Perhaps we can make it to the Inn in relative safety. It's just across the street."

"It is." In her distraction he managed to surprise her by tucking a finger under her chin.

Her breath caught as he turned her face up to his. His gaze locked on hers, he leaned in close. She managed another shaky breath. "Oh."

His lips brushed across hers gently, a soft touch that sent a spark of warmth through her. After the brief moment, he withdrew just enough to meet her gaze.

She slipped her hands under his coat to circle his waist. Her heart seemed to hold its breath as she hovered close to him. No heat of passion spurred her on as it had in the past. No rush to get to business. This was a slow burn she wanted to linger in forever.

His fingers brushed along her jaw in a whisper-light touch before he closed his lips over hers, pulling her in with gentle insistence. The lightest brush of his tongue across the seam of her lips sent shivers of heat through her. She opened to him easily.

The warmth that built between them came along slow and steady. She could revel in the soft touch of his lips all day and into the night. Fingers buried in her hair, his other hand slipped around her waist to edge her closer. She obliged without hesitation, pressing her body flush against his.

Flumpff. Flumpff.

Ice cold hit her cheek, dribbling down the neck of her cape. The shock ripped them apart. Sally spotted the remains of a snowball on Matthew's cheek and shoulder. Laughter echoed down the alley before disappearing.

She sucked in her lips to hold back her laughter. The wet mass of snow on his shoulder and melting drips on his face brought a giggle anyway. "I think Stephen got you."

"You got it, too." His fingers brushed some moisture from her cheek. "Jesse got one of us, Stephen the other, I think."

"It would appear they came at us from both sides," she said with a measure of annoyance.

He brushed the snow from her shoulder. When he touched her cheek again, he took his time there. His thumb trailed along the cold, wet trails of melting snow. Even through his amusement there was a tenderness there. The way his fingers lingered near her neck made her think he was disappointed at their interruption as well. "Remind me to give that kid what-for later."

"I'll do the same with Jesse. I think the pair of them are dangerous together. Add in Isaac and we'll have real trouble on her hands." She knocked the remnants of the snowball off his coat. "Well, then."

"I suppose I oughtta get you back home and wrangle my kid brother before he terrorizes anyone else."

"I suppose you should. Such a shame, though. I was rather enjoying myself."

"Perhaps I'll take ya for a ride in that cutter your Inn's got on Sunday."

"What if it's already rented for the day?" She hesitated to part from him, but she was due back to work on the casino floor soon. "Whatever should we do then?"

"Then we'll have to ride separate."

"That is fun, but not as much fun as snuggling under furs."

"Definitely not."

She chuckled low, meeting his gaze. "We should go. I'll check the schedule and add our names so you might see about our brother. This evening I'll deal with mine."

He set a hand at the small of her back as they approached the end of the alley. While he held her back, he peeked around the corner of Kat's. Then his head turned the other way. "They must think they've won. No sign of 'em."

"Then let's make haste." Sally darted across the street. She rushed up the steps fast, pausing at the door.

Matthew stopped short behind her, that same warm smile he'd had in the alley before he'd kissed her on his features. "Thank you for the walk. I'm deeply sorry it ended in such a way."

"Sorry for which part?" She couldn't help but tease him. "The kiss, or the snowballs?"

"Definitely not the kiss." He winked before brushing his lips across hers. "If I don't see ya before then, I'll see you Sunday."

"Sunday." She leaned against the door as he hopped down the steps to his horse. At his parting nod, she offered one of her own before slipping into the Inn. Though she tried to calm herself, the smile wouldn't leave her lips. What an effect that man had on her.

"My, my Miss Sally," Patrick called from a nearby table. Molly sat beside him, her lips pursed, gaze fixed on her tea. Patrick raised his brows. "What's this we saw?"

Sally sighed as she sank into the chair he pointed toward. "What's what?"

"That kiss?" Patrick chuckled low. He leaned in, wearing a conspiratorial grin. "Young Mr. Coleman seems to have charmed you rather well. You are quite smitten with the cowboy."

"You exaggerate." Sally took the teapot he offered. Warmth flooded her cheeks at his continual chuckling. She poured herself a cup of tea. "I'm not smitten."

"Sally, I have spent many hours around young women infatuated with me. I know the look. You have it when you look at him."

"Excuse me." Molly stood up so fast the table bumped, knocking Sally's tea right over.

Sally and Patrick scrambled to grab the teacups before they rolled off the table where they'd surely shatter. By the time they got everything straight, Molly was gone. Sally stared at her seat in confusion. "That was odd."

"Was it?" Patrick poured another cup of tea. He continued to wear the annoyingly knowing smirk he'd had since she entered.

"What on earth was that about? I thought she'd join you in teasing me."

He added some sugar to his cup, seemingly oblivious to her frustration. "Perhaps you not knowing what it's about *is* the problem."

"Can you not just tell me if you know so much?"

He shook his head. After a sip of tea under her continual glare, he sighed. "No. I believe that's a matter best left to Molly. Off you go. I'll see you at supper. Please, do me a favor."

"What's that?"

"Remember I leave in four days and would hate to not see you for any of them because you are busy basking in your newfound affections."

"Oh you." Sally slapped his arm at his teasing. His laughter followed her as she headed to the stairs.

What had made Molly leave so abruptly without a word? She'd truly thought Molly would tease her as much, if not worse, than Patrick. They'd always joked about the young women being courted staring at the men much in the most embarrassing way she imagined she was looking at Matthew minutes before.

By the time she got to Molly's door, the answer was no clearer. She knocked gently on the door. "Molly?"

"Not right now, Sally." Though she couldn't be sure, Sally thought she heard a wobble in her friend's voice. Something she'd certainly never heard before.

"Please, Molly. What's wrong?"

"Nothing."

"Did I do something wrong?"

The door flew open. No evidence of tears lingered on Molly's cheeks, but her eyes were rimmed red. "Of course not. Why would you think such a thing?"

"Because you ran off when I sat down. Then when I arrived here, you wouldn't let me in. You always let me in." Sally stepped close as she could without crossing the threshold. "Have you been crying?"

"I don't have time for this." Molly turned her back on Sally. She crossed to the window, staring out onto the street. "I'm fine, Sally. Go on about your business."

"This is my business. You're clearly not fine. Something's upset you. You're my friend." Sally's words cut off at a snort from Molly. "What?"

"Friend. I thought we were more."

"More?" Sally stepped into the room. Her mind raced to make sense of what Molly meant. They'd always gotten along famously, but Molly had always been—well, Molly. A ruse, a character in her long stream of characters as a Pink. What could she mean, more? "I don't understand. You mean a great deal to me."

"Do I?"

"As much as Patrick does, probably more. You've taught me so much these last months. I very much enjoy your company."

"Patrick was a mere dalliance."

"Yes, he was. For both of us. You certainly enjoyed him as much as I did." Sally thought over the past several months. Together she and Molly had flirted with half the men in town, often. Always a game, always fun. How Molly acted now didn't make sense. "Perhaps I'm not clever enough to understand what you mean, but I truly don't."

"Now there's Matthew."

Unbidden, a smile crossed Sally's lips at the name. She managed to school it in time for Molly to turn around. This time there were tears on her friends' cheeks. Sally studied Molly quietly. "Yes. Matthew and I have been getting to know each other. I told you I'd flirted with him at the mercantile, and several times after."

"Flirted is not what you were doing."

"What was I doing, then?"

"Patrick seems to think you're smitten."

Once again the smile rose before she could stop it. Molly's lip curled in response. Sally's brow furrowed. It seemed too much like an emotion that didn't match their relationship. "Are you jealous? Of Matthew? Why?"

"If you have to ask why, it doesn't matter now does it?"

Sally walked over to stand before Molly. She took her friends' hands in her own. "Patrick was a dalliance. We've been a dalliance, too. I care for you a great deal as a friend."

"I care for you. I thought…" Molly's words trailed off. For the first time since Sally had known her, the young woman looked lost.

Realization struck Sally finally, like a lightning bolt. She released Molly's hands. "Love?"

"Maybe."

"Molly, be fair." Sally didn't know where this was coming from. Perhaps she wasn't as wise to certain ways as she'd thought. She'd told Molly she didn't know what love was. Plus, there was the one thing that wouldn't allow it between them. "How could we possibly fall in love?"

Molly's eyes narrowed. "Just because we're women—"

"Because we're not equal."

"What?" Molly's upset faltered, her face growing blank.

"I know nothing about you. Nothing but the fact you are a Pinkerton that can put on any face she desires. You—you are the queen of the ruse, the master of voices. You even managed to become Daisy, a woman you've never met."

"What does that have to do with anything?"

"You know nearly all about me, both from my own lips and Tommy's, or word about town. Yet you haven't extended me the same courtesy. I never know if your tales are true or tall. I don't even have the courtesy of your real name."

"That's neither here nor there. A name is nothing. You know who I am."

"I know the sort of person you are for me, certainly."

Molly's eyes flashed in anger, her hand clenching at her side. "Are you saying I'm pretending when I'm around you?"

"No, not exactly. I know Molly Malone. My mentor, my friend, and yes, my lover. I know we get along very well, but I don't know *you* underneath Molly. You've been a Pinkerton so long I never expected you to turn it off."

"I did."

"Did you? I still don't know who you are. Where you came from, how you became a Pinkerton, your life before you came to be one, if you've ever been in love, if you've broken hearts, or if you are even capable of showing the real you. We've spent hours together and I've only had lessons or tales."

Molly's features paled. From wide eyed surprise, her face fell into a stoic mask that hid all. "You never asked."

"If you thought it could be love, should I have had to?"

"I think you should go."

"Molly." Sally reached for her hand again, but it slipped from her grasp. "I still want to remain friends. I enjoy your company, and I still have so much to learn. Perhaps if I got to know the real you—"

"I said I think you should go."

"I'm sorry, Molly."

"So am I."

*Get the facts, or the facts will get you.
And when you get them, get them right,
or they will get you wrong.
—Dr. Thomas Fuller*

Sally leaned on the porch railing of the Inn. The biting winds of the previous week had dissipated so that the sunshine almost seemed warm. The hint of warmth and the prospect of a cutter ride with Matthew the following day did little to disperse the lingering melancholy since her spat with Molly.

To be honest, she felt terrible. Perhaps she should have seen that Molly was coming to care for her in such a way. The continued dalliance with Patrick and the frequent flirtations elsewhere had left her with no idea of any such thing. Perhaps she was still too naïve to carry on as she had been.

Then again, she didn't plan to. Though still new, things with Matthew were different somehow. They talked about so many things, including her past and hopes for the future. He'd proven funny and kind and had a few tales of his own from his days riding the trails.

It was hopeful, and warm, and so unlike the brash excitement of her liaisons with Patrick and Molly. She didn't know what to call it, but she liked it a lot.

She sighed, resting her chin on her hand. Had she been cruel in her honesty? Had her words hurt more than the lack of deep affection? Ma had taught her to be honest and to see things with logic, but she'd also said logic had little place in matters of the heart.

"Sally." Patrick's voiced doused her thoughts for a moment. He climbed the steps toward her, a bright smile splitting his features. At least he held no grudge toward her. "I have something for you. My darling Kat insisted I bring it straight away."

"What?" Sally gasped at the paper he held toward her. Hope sprung through her melancholy to warmth. "A telegram. Is it from Ma?"

"Read it yourself, you silly thing."

She unfurled the paper, holding her breath as she read the note from Charlie. "It's from Uncle Charlie. He says they're in Fresno and able to send and receive communications again, whatever that means. Pa is with them, too! Oh, how wonderful. Oh dear."

"What oh dear?"

"He says they'll be staying on in Fresno at least three days before they head home. Drat. I really need to talk to Ma, or to Tommy. I guess I'm on my own."

"Oh." His voice cracked with his dramatic sorrow. He clutched a hand to his chest.

"What is wrong with you?"

"The lady doth wound me."

"That isn't what I meant, you beast." She smacked his arm with the telegram.

"If you're certain. I'd hate to be thought of as a ghost before I actually leave this place."

"You most certainly are not." She studied him a moment. "I could talk to you about what I wanted to talk to Ma about. You certainly have experience and I'm feeling rather out of sorts again all of a sudden."

He clasped her hands in his. "Sally, darling. Slow down."

"Sorry."

"Would this have anything to do with our mutual friend, Molly?"

"It does." Her shoulders sagged, but she clutched his hands tighter. "I fear I was cruel."

"You haven't a cruel bone in your body." When she lifted her gaze, he smirked. "Fair. You haven't a cruel bone toward your friends."

"I worry it's much like it was with Arthur. I was trying to be logical, reasonable, and speak my truth as Ma taught me. It only seems to hurt those I do care about when I do."

"Sometimes the actions we take, and the words we use, can be seen as cruel when you and the other soul are looking through different lenses. I've often had to use reason and logic with the women I have wooed. It rarely goes well."

"I thought we both knew it was a dalliance. Much as you and I did."

"Ah, yes." His thumbs stroked the back of her hands in a soothing manner. "It was a matter we discussed directly before we began our little adventure. Did you do the same with—"

"Molly!" Sally squeezed Patrick's hands so hard, he withdrew them. She stared at the woman who'd just exited the Inn.

Molly's features registered surprise before transforming into a bright, friendly smile by the time Patrick turned her way. "Good afternoon, you two. I was heading over to the brothel."

Patrick bowed his head toward her. "You didn't think to ask for company?"

"I believe I'll be going by myself today." Molly's eyes flickered toward Sally before returning to Patrick. Her smile softened as she drew closer to him. "If you'll be free around three I wouldn't mind some company."

Sally turned away as the pair chatted. It had been like that since their argument. Molly didn't completely ignore her existence, but kept a cool distance. Sally truly missed her friend. She had no idea how to make things right.

In her distraction she almost missed Andrew waving frantically from the clinic porch. His call echoed across the street. "Sally. Archie is awake."

"Oh goodness. He's awake!" Sally scooted around behind Patrick. "We'll talk later, Patrick. I have to go talk to Archie about his accident."

"Of course." Patrick offered a warm smile and touched a finger to his hat.

Sally froze at the bottom step, turning to face Molly. She mustered the politest tone she could. "You're welcome to come if you still have any desire to work the case with me."

She ignored Molly's harumphed reply to rush across the street. Soon as she skidded onto the porch, Andrew held the door open for her. "He's been awake for a couple of hours, but relatively out of sorts. He's started talking lucid now."

"Good." She followed him up the steps, pausing partway when she heard footsteps behind them. A quick glance told her Molly followed. With a sigh, Sally rushed the rest of the way up the stairs to Andrew's side. "How is his leg looking?"

"Better. I believe Dr. Young's treatment helped a great deal. He'll keep the leg."

"Thank heavens."

"I don't know how well he'll move any longer, but at least he'll have all of his limbs." Andrew paused outside the door while Molly caught up. "He's still in a lot of pain. Please keep your questioning brief."

"Of course." Sally bustled in soon as the door opened. Archie sat on the bed, looking the worse for wear, but sitting up and awake. She moved closer. "Archie. It's so good to see you awake again. You had me so worried."

"Sally." Archie grunted when he shifted his weight. He squeezed her hand as she leaned in to kiss his cheek. "How's your ma?"

"I'm sure she's fine. I just got word that they're all safe. She's got Pa with her now."

"Wait, she isn't here?"

"No. I'm afraid you've been out of it for a while. Ma left to go find Pa. Good news is she did, bad news is it'll be a few days. There's some other things—"

"We're here to ask questions, Sally." Molly took a seat on the opposite side of the bed. She dug her notebook out of a pocket. "You can gossip and catch up another time."

Sally frowned at Molly, but managed to smile when Archie looked at her curiously. "Well, I suppose she has a point. We'd best make quick work of it. I imagine you'll get tired quite quickly."

"Based on what you said, I'd wager I've been sleeping a lot. If I were a betting man, that is." Archie rubbed his hand over his face. "I remember bits and pieces. I think I woke up some."

"You did. You've been in far too much pain for much more than moments at a time." Sally scooted her chair closer. "Before you lost consciousness you told me someone kicked out the supports on that wagon."

He nodded slowly. "Yes. It's fuzzy, but there was someone there."

"Obviously you were under the wagon where you couldn't see them," Sally supplied.

"Don't lead, Sally," Molly spoke sharp like a schoolmarm scolding a child. She kept her head bowed, scribbling in her notebook. "Let him speak."

Archie frowned at the woman opposite Sally. "Don't know what ya mean by that. She's right. I couldn't see who it was."

Molly jotted something down. "Did they speak?"

"Yes." Archie rubbed his injured arm, wincing. "Sounded familiar, too."

Sally abandoned her chair to sit on the edge of the bed. "That's good, Archie. You knew who it was. Don't try to think too hard on it."

"Sally. I told you—"

"I know what I'm doing. Leave me be. Sorry, Archie." She set her hand on Archie's wrist. "You've been mayor for several years here in Dominion Falls. I don't think there's a person in town you haven't talked to one way or another. That's a lot of familiar names and voices to go through. Don't think so hard. What did they say?"

"He called out my name. I told him I'd be with him in a minute." Archie's gaze wandered away from Sally. It became unfocused, fixed on a point beyond the wall he stared at. "He said he had a question."

Sally glared at Molly when she interrupted with a hum. The woman wasn't even looking at her. She remained scribbling in her notebook.

Thankfully, Archie was still focused on the memory. "A question about his carriage. I thought it was odd because he didn't have a carriage. He had a wagon."

"Good," Sally said in an undertone. She didn't want to pull too much focus from what he was remembering. "You know he had a wagon. What about horses?"

"Two. Old girls, not much good for a decent carriage—Jake."

Sally straightened at the name. "Jake? As in…" She hesitated rather than lead him toward the answer on the verge of her lips. Last thing she needed right then was for Molly to snap at her again.

"Jake Bosen. Two work horses because he's a farmer. Bach's north of town."

"Great, Archie. You're doing wonderful. What happened after he asked about the carriage?"

"I began to slide out because I thought it was odd. Next thing I knew, he kicked out the supports. I don't remember much after that."

"That's fine. You did really well." Sally patted his hand. "I'm going to see that you get some of Cora's stew sent your way. Ma says it fixes most any ailment. I'll be back in a few hours to catch you up on all that's happened since the incident."

"A bowl of Cora's stew sounds like it'd hit the spot. Thank you, Sally." Archie released a shaky breath, his hand keeping hers tight. "Why would Jake do that?"

"I honestly have no idea. We'll go talk to him and see what he has to say."

"Take Tommy." Archie squeezed her hand. "You shouldn't go alone."

"We'll take someone," she reassured him. She didn't want to worry him more to tell him that Tommy wasn't here either. "Andrew told us not to keep you too long. I'll be back later. I'll bring you supper. How about that? We'll catch up on all the news."

"That would be nice. Thank you."

Sally kissed his forehead, then backed toward the door. She held it open for Molly, following her down the stairs. She tossed a wave Andrew's way before darting out on Molly's heels. "What on earth was that about?"

"You weren't focused. You wanted to learn. I'm teaching."

"That wasn't teaching, that was berating. You had no problem with how I asked my questions before." Sally grabbed Molly's arm when she kept walking fast. "Hold on, now. We need to talk about this."

"We already talked." Molly turned to face her. "You wanted a teacher, you got her."

"No. I wanted my mentor, my friend. Not this, whatever it is."

Molly sighed, diverting her attention away. She went so far as to change the subject, slightly. "We need to figure out how Jake fits into all of this."

"I'm aware of that. We also need to pay him a visit. Will you sit and talk with me? We can go over all of this and then head out to Jake's farm."

"Why don't you ponder a while, and we'll meet in an hour."

"Molly." Sally caught her hand before she could slip away. "I'm really sorry. Please. I know I was…I mean…we need to talk about this."

Molly stared at their hands. A weak laugh trickled from her. "It's funny."

"What is?"

When she lifted her head, Molly's eyes shimmered with tears. "Tommy was so busy telling me to not break *your* heart, he didn't think to tell me to protect my own."

Sally let her go this time. "I'm so sorry."

He who spares the wicked injures the good.
—Seneca

"Jane." Cole brushed his fingers along her forehead. He hated to disturb her sleep for anything. After the rough journey in the wagon she'd collapsed into the soft feather bed at the nicest hotel Fresno had to offer. Outside of occasionally waking to nibble on some food, she'd been asleep ever since. Almost a full day.

He'd crawled into the bed beside her during the night. Though he'd followed her instructions to not touch her, he wanted to be close. At some point during the middle of the night she'd actually turned to curl against him.

For a few hours he'd been able to relax for the first time in over a month. He'd dozed for a while before reluctantly leaving, knowing she wouldn't tolerate finding herself wrapped in his arms, even if she'd put herself there.

He kissed her forehead. At that moment he'd give anything to climb into bed with her and hold her again. If he did there'd be ugly pounding at the door soon. Tom hadn't given him any leeway in getting Jane up and out the door for something. "Jane. Wake up."

Jane's eyes fluttered open. A warm smile brightened her features. Her hand rested on his cheek, the thumb tracing his cheek. "Good morning, you…oh." Darkness and pain hardened her expression until every bit of affection disappeared.

His heart sank, but he pushed on. "Tom wants to see us. Now, apparently."

"Tom?" she sat up fast. Immediately she swayed and groaned. "Oh. Dizzy."

"You've pretty much been asleep a whole day." He crossed to the armoire and flung it open. She'd packed light, leaving few options. "Blue or purple?"

"Purple. Oh dear, I need a bath."

"I brushed your hair. Would have cleaned you some, but you told me not to touch you." He kept his gaze averted while she got dressed. After so long away from her, it killed him to keep his distance. He wanted nothing more than to reconnect with her and prove he'd not once been tempted by Ella or his past.

"That's right, I did." Her voice wavered again. She still seemed so weak after her ordeal and the horrible journey in the wagon. Weak in everything but her resolve to be angry and hurt.

"I figured once you slept you'd like a real bath. The tub is back there, and the water too. You only need to heat it on the stove a bit."

"Thank you." She moved into his line of vision. With her dress in place, she fiddled with her hair in the mirror. She caught him staring, and lowered her gaze. "Why?"

"I told you I'd spend every day proving it. I told you I'm not a liar."

"I know." Her lip trembled, as did her hands. She lowered them from her attempt at crafting a knot of her curls.

He stepped closer. "I ain't—"

Jane shuddered, turning a glare on him. Even though he could only see her reflection, the spark of anger was clear. "Go away now."

"Sorry. I've got to get back in the habit. I didn't mean—"

Thud. The door rattled under the heavy knock. Tommy's voice boomed through the door loud enough for the whole city to hear. "Let's go."

"Damn him." Cole groaned. The timing couldn't be worse. He needed some time with Jane in the worst way. The well-rested, not fresh off her death-bed Jane. The one that might see reason, and the truth of his last weeks. "Get your hair finished. I'll meet you outside to help you downstairs."

"Right. I—Cole."

"Yeah?"

She set her hand on his forearm. Her gaze locked with his. After a step closer, she seemed to hold her breath. "Colton is dead?"

"As a doornail." Another pound startled them both. In that second, her hand left his arm. No longer did she look at him.

Her brow furrowed toward the floor. "You should get that."

He wanted nothing more than to pull her into his arms and make it all right again. To make her see he'd never wanted Ella for a minute. She was wounded, he knew it. He didn't blame her. If he'd been cleverer he would have left, forced Ella down the mountain with him to get the hell out of there. He hadn't, though. He blamed himself as much as Jane did.

Another knock banged through their silence.

Cole stalked to the door. He yanked it open to find Tom grinning like a fool. "Waking the whole damn hotel wasn't necessary."

"You weren't answering." Tom shrugged. "You coming? It'll cheer you both up, I swear it."

"I'll be down in a minute." Jane glared at her brother from where she stood. "If I feel like it. You aren't forgiven."

"This'll help. I promise, you'll like it."

"Your promises mean nothing." Jane turned her back on them to focus on her own reflection.

Soon as the door closed, Tom's joviality dissipated like smoke in the wind. "How is she?"

"Seems better since she slept. Still a wounded mountain lion. More likely to kill than cuddle." Cole stared at the door helplessly. "Can't say that I blame her."

"You didn't mean to be gone so long. She'll see it after a time."

"Rather than get down the mountain for help, I stayed to help Ella. I coulda done it, I shoulda done it. I didn't know what Paul would do." Cole closed his eyes. "I thought she was safe and sound. It took a couple weeks to realize they weren't sending my telegrams."

"She's got a brain. The logic will win eventually. I hope." Tom blew out a noisy breath. "For me, too."

"What *did* you do to piss her off so bad?" Cole eyed his brother-in-law. "She's been mad at me often enough. Don't know I've ever seen her so mad at you."

The door opened, revealing Jane. As though to prove his point, she eyed her brother cold as she'd been eying Cole. "Thomas. What are you doing here? I thought you left because I've told you on multiple occasions to leave me alone."

"Yeah, I'm not that good at listening. Besides, I have a present for you and Cole. You're going to want to see this." Tom gestured down the hall. "Let's go."

Jane hesitated a moment on the threshold. Clearly her curiosity won out for she slipped from the room. Her arm reached out as if to wrap around Cole's waist. She realized too quick what she was doing and pulled it back in front of her.

Cole's heart dropped even further into his stomach. He had no clue how to repair things. All the way down the stairs he fought his own urge for a gesture of familiarity. In the end, he couldn't help himself. His hand drifted to the small of her back. They followed Tom down the stairs to the front doors. Outside they found Nick talking with a strange man who wore a Sheriff's badge. Behind them both on a horse with his hands tied behind his back sat Cole's pa.

Jane froze in place. With one step, she pressed back into Cole. He set his hands on her shoulders to offer comfort. The plummet his heart had taken upstairs got buoyed by her instinct to lean into him for support.

Paul looked a bit the worse for wear. Bruises bloomed on both eyes, his nose sat crooked. Blood soaked the front of his shirt and dried in his beard. A deep cut ran along his cheek. Cole had to admit he wasn't upset by the sight, only disappointed he hadn't been able to help Tom make the damage worse.

"Gary, you made it." Tom shook hands heartily with the Sheriff. "It's good to see you again."

"Tommy. Last I heard from you was four years ago. Where've you been hiding at?" The Sheriff wore a warm smile. "Did you finally get out?"

"Mostly. Been living in Colorado. I see you've met my brother Nick. This is my sister Jane and her husband, Cole Mitchell." Tommy gestured toward them. "Jane is here to identify him."

"I'm what?" Jane cleared her throat when her voice cracked. "Thomas, would you care to explain what's going on?"

"Jane, this is Sheriff Davis. Old colleague of mine at the agency. He's here to arrest the man that kidnapped you, if you can identify him."

"Cole glared up at his pa. "Did you mention all of his wives?"

"Polygamy?" Davis glanced at Paul before turning to Tommy. "Always a surprise when it comes to your cases."

"Not sure if it matters," Cole added. "I also found the papers he kept from me with my inheritance. It wasn't much, but he destroyed what little it was worth and stole all the product to use for his families."

Nick made some notes on a paper. "I'll need to see the documents, Cole. Sheriff, I can write up a formal complaint for that as well."

Davis grinned, rubbing his hands together. "This should be fun."

"I was hoping you'd say that." Tom folded his arms across his chest. "Is our old buddy Ben Kern still the judge 'round these parts?"

"He is." Davis turned his attention to Jane. "Are you sure this is the man that kidnapped you?"

"I am. He left me with a half-full canteen, no food, no light, and no heat." Jane lifted her chin, as if to look Paul dead in the eye. "I told you. You made a critical mistake."

"She's right." Tom chuckled low. "You should have never messed with my family. I got more connections than you could ever know. Gary, will you see he gets taken care of? I don't want Jane to have to suffer through a trial or anything."

"We've got it handled. Send me her statement, and any other necessary papers, I'll get it to Ben." Gary shook Tom's hand. "If you're around for a couple of days, let's meet for drinks to catch up."

"I am. You can find us here." Tom stepped back closer to them as Gary led Paul away. Once he was out of hearing distance, Tom turned to Cole. "Didn't figure they needed to know the family connection. If you got the names of those wives, I'll need them to pass on. Don't worry, Jane. Ben and Gary will see he's well taken care of."

"You should have just killed him." Jane turned on her heel and walked back into the hotel.

Tom sighed, his head falling back. "That woman can hold a grudge."

"I'll ask again. What in hell did you do?" Cole glanced his way. "She seems to like Nick better than you these days. Hell, she likes Charlie more than you, and he always annoys her with his doctor fussing."

Nick chuckled. When Tom glared at him, it grew into a full-on laugh. "He's got a point. That'll teach you to do a kindness wrapped in betrayal."

"What are you talking about?" Cole looked between them.

"You should probably talk to your wife. She has a great many stories to tell you." Nick's head tilted upward as though looking for her through the windows. "Life has been interesting the past few weeks, to say the least."

"Don't think she's much in a talking mood." Cole grimaced. "Not that I blame her."

"Only thing you can do is tell her what happened." Nick's sharp gaze returned to him. The anger he'd shown on the search for Jane no longer darkened his eyes. He actually seemed worried. "She doesn't have the facts, and Jane loves facts. They help her head—"

"And her heart," Tom added.

"Yes, I was getting there you impatient brute." Nick shook his head. "It helps her make sense of things."

"I suppose. Don't think she wants to hear about Ella, though." Cole rubbed the back of his neck. "Even though she isn't Ella, not anymore. Not for a long time."

"Has she eaten?" Nick turned to his attaché to put his papers away.

"Nothing more than scraps when she's woken." Cole frowned. "I should get her something."

"Yes. While you do that, I'll go talk to her." Nick glanced at his brother with a wicked smirk crossing his usually stoic features. "You know, since she actually likes me these days."

"You're hilarious," Tommy snarked. He glared at Nick's departing back. "He's feeling his oats now, but wait until she starts meddling. He'll be running for the hills."

Cole frowned at Tommy. "You can't just tell me what you did?"

"Would that I could, but its wrapped in a much bigger story that's only Jane's to tell. That's if she chooses to tell you all things considered."

"That sounds…ominous."

Reason has always existed,
but not always in reasonable form.
-Karl Marx

Jane paced back and forth across her room. Any minute now Cole would return and wish to talk. She didn't feel ready to talk. Her mind raced, her heart panged, and her stomach ached.

Three days in the wagon followed by a full days sleep had done little to ease the chaos of confusion still settled in her soul. Not even being in the presence of Ella had helped. No matter that she'd witnessed what the woman had become, her damnable memory kept replaying Cole calling for Ella when she'd first arrived in Holle Creek.

Jane poured herself a glass of water. Her hands shook too much and water spilled onto the table. She cleaned the water quickly. "Damn it. I need to get myself together."

She'd send Cole away and go downstairs to eat something. There was no way she was read to talk, certainly not on an empty stomach. He'd do as she asked, the man was acting as though he'd do anything she asked, except perhaps leave forever.

She closed her eyes against a sudden rush of tears. He'd complied with her request to not touch her. For three whole days in that wagon he'd not complained once. Every time she'd needed to move he'd asked permission before assisting her. He'd barely given Ella any attention at all. Charlie had handled her every time she'd woken from her drug-induced slumber.

"Colton is dead," she whispered to herself, willing her heart to remember.

No matter, she wasn't ready to reveal all that had happened in his absence. Would enough time ever pass? Would enough of his acts of attrition soften the shard of ice his absence had shoved into her heart?

A knock sounded on the door. Not demanding or impatient, but soft. Jane turned to stare at the door in confusion. Would Cole have bothered to knock?

Another soft knock echoed into the room. "Jane?"

"Nicholas?" Jane scurried to the door to open it. She searched his face for any sign of panic or anger. Only warm concern shone from his deep blue eyes. "Is there something wrong? Did something else happen?"

"Relax. I'm here to check on you is all. I sent your husband to get you a meal."

"Husband." The word fairly spat from her mouth. She walked back toward her bed. A new panic climbed through her veins like spiders rushing from the dark. She balled her hand into a fist at her side so hard the nails dug into her palm.

"Yes. As you blurted to half the town at Christmas, if you remember. Wait, you remember everything so I'm certain you do."

"Is he really?" She turned to face her brother.

"Really what?"

"My husband." She focused over his shoulder to the door. Though it sat closed, she knew across the hall Ella lay in a nearly similar room with Charles as her doctor and watcher. "The dead wife is not so much any longer."

Nick's features softened from their normal stoicism. "You are still married. There was no Colton at your wedding. Cole Mitchell and Jane Spencer—"

She shuddered. "Don't."

"Fine, Jane Doe Mitchell are married. For that matter, Ella Spencer is dead as well. I saw the grave. By all accounts that woman is Ella Decker, and thoroughly insane."

"I know that." She turned away at the hint of a shriek in her tone. "In my head I know she's insane. I know she's not— I know…but I can't get my heart to hear it. I'm so hurt, so angry."

"Anger hurts you more than anything. Whether at a country, a legion, a person, or yourself." Nick's voice dropped at his last words. "Don't linger there too long. It changes you in ways you cannot change back."

All of her anger flew away at the pain in his tone. She turned back to her brother. He no longer looked right at her, rather more out of the window. She swept him into a hug. "Oh, Nicholas."

He embraced her right back, tight. "Learn from my mistakes, Jane—and Clara's. You always said you learned from her weaknesses. Don't let them become yours."

"You're right." She let him hold on until he was ready to let go. When he did, she let out a shuddering breath. "I don't know where to begin. I missed him so much and long to have him take it all away. I worry over the injury he suffered. The moment he opens his mouth to explain, I want to scream at him to shut his trap and go far away."

One corner of Nick's mouth twitched in a hint of a grin. "A silent Cole isn't entirely a terrible option. I'm sure many would appreciate it."

She laughed despite herself, the strain of anger and worry rushing away at the sound. "Perhaps fewer now than there were when I first met him."

"A handful, maybe."

"Maybe." She clasped his hands in hers. "That's twice on this trip you've come to his defense. Could you actually be growing to like him?"

"Don't let him know. I think he's a little scared of me. I don't mind that one bit."

"I'll take your secret to my grave." Now that the initial burst of emotion had blown away, her headache crept up out of nowhere. She rubbed her hands together, hoping he wouldn't notice her new discomfort.

"What is one thing you thrive on?"

"Hm?" Distracted by the change of subject and her headache, she tried to focus on him.

"Knowledge. You don't like not knowing. When Hammy got ill, you wanted to know every detail of what would happen and what to expect. When Cole left you were worried, you missed him, but you carried on all right until the silence grew too long. When you had no way of knowing where he was or what was happening, that is when you became unsettled."

"I remember quite clearly."

"Knowledge, Jane." He clasped her hand in his. "Much as you might wish to scream at him to not say a damned thing, you need to know what he went through."

"I know. I don't feel ready."

"The longer you wait, the less prepared you'll feel. That man will close his mouth and never speak again if you told him to. He is begging forgiveness for something that by all accounts was out of his control."

"He could have—"

Nick's brow rose at her hesitation. "You don't know what he could have done, because you don't know what happened. If nothing else, allowing him his story will give you accurate defenses to your ire."

"You won't get me to say you're correct again."

"I wouldn't dream of it."

"Fine. I'll listen." She offered as strong a smile as she could.

His brow furrowed. "Jane?"

The room spun a little as her vision doubled. She knew her feet moved to catch her from what she knew wasn't a fall. Nick guided her to a chair. She felt ridiculous for the catering, especially as it had mostly cleared. Sort of. "I'm fine. My headache got bad quickly this time is all."

"No matter. I'll go get Charles."

"Thank you."

Jane reached for her water while she waited. To ease the tightness of her feet in her shoes, she lifted them onto a chair.

It wasn't a long wait as Charles rushed to her side mere moments later.

He threw open his medical bag. "What is going on?"

"The room spun a little after a headache hit me."

His attention turned to her. "What were you doing?"

"Talking to Nicholas." At his sharp look, she grimaced. "After I'd been pacing and fretting a bit. I also just saw Cole's pa get arrested."

"I see. Have you been drinking water?"

"I've been mostly sleeping since we arrived, so probably not enough."

Charles extracted a large needle from his bag.

"Oh, don't. I'm not that bad off." Jane couldn't be ashamed of the pleading in her tone.

"If it calms—"

"It makes my memories hazy. I hate that. It would make me more stressed than if you gave me nothing."

His lips pursed. "Then laudanum. A few drops in your water."

"Fine."

A clatter behind them startled Jane. Cole rushed to her side, panic creasing his features. "What is it? What's wrong? Is she all right? The baby?"

"I'm fine," Jane answered before Charles could. "My feet are tight in my shoes, and my head is still a little wobbly, but I'm fine."

"That full glass of water, plus two more. If you'd rather it be tea, I'll accept that." Charles pulled a bottle of laudanum from his bag. "Three drops for now. More later if you're still feeling out of sorts."

"Thank you." She met Cole's gaze. "Reassure Cole. He still looks like he might faint."

"This wasn't a severe spell, but I'm concerned that they're still happening. We'll keep a very close eye on you over the coming months." Charlie rose from his crouching position. "Every time one of these happens it could hurt you or the baby, or even both."

"*That* was the opposite of reassuring him." She offered her brother a small glare. "You know I'm being careful as I can. I was recently terrorized for a couple of days, then dragged through the hills on the worlds most uncomfortable wagon."

"Point taken." Charlie kissed her forehead. "Drink, eat, do your best to relax."

"Tell my life to stop trying to destroy me and perhaps I will."

Charlie winked with a grin. "You'd be bored out of your mind with nothing going on but your knitting."

"Go away now before I get riled up, Charles Emerson."

Cole hadn't stopped staring at her for a second. When the door closed, he pointed to her feet on the chair. "May I?"

"Please. My feet swell so. Charles says those with eclampsia often see it." She remained silent while he unbuttoned and removed the shoes.

He set her feet back on the chair, then moved around her. Before she could question why, he set a tray on the table. "Wasn't sure what you wanted. Got a few different dishes there for you."

She plucked at the covers to examine what lay beneath each. She settled on a plate with mutton and potatoes.

Cole lifted her feet again to sit on the chair. He didn't lower her feet to the floor, but started rubbing them. It relaxed her so quick, she forgot to take the bite on her fork. He smirked. "Forgetting something?"

"Hm?" She turned her attention back to her food. "Right. Food."

"You don't mind me doing this, do you?"

"If I did, you'd know it."

"Fair point."

She ate nearly half her mutton before she slowed. Once her hunger had been partly sated, she wiped her mouth. It was now or never. Nicholas was right. She needed to know so she could properly decide how to feel. "What happened to you?"

His hands grew still for several long seconds. Before she could protest, he resumed the massage quietly at first. "Sure you want to hear it now? You didn't want to the whole way here."

"I was in misery, ill, and in the most rickety wagon on the most rickety road known in existence. Of course I didn't want to hear anything then."

"If you're sure."

"Not in the slightest, but it's something I need to hear. I need to know what happened, not the worst case scenarios racing through my brain."

"All right, then. I'll tell you."

The heart has its reasons
which reason knows nothing of.
–Blaise Pascal

Leanne reread Tommy's telegram again as she climbed the steps to the Inn. Having not heard from him in days, she was relieved he'd contacted her. It didn't matter if the missive was short and sweet, at least it was sweet.

Sally's voice paused her progress. "You look happy."

"I am. Tommy's sent a telegram finally. He'll be home in a week."

"That's good. I'd really like to see him."

Leanne sat beside Sally, tucking the note in her pocket. When she focused on the young woman, she frowned slightly. "You, however, do not look at all pleased."

"I am. I'm not. I'm confused." Sally's legs swung forward and back under the bench. Her gaze swept the town back and forth much as Tommy's did at all times. "What's worse is I need a clear head. We're going to speak to a suspect in less than an hour. Molly can hardly be civil to me which makes the trek seem less than a good idea."

"I don't understand."

"Which part?"

"Why wouldn't Molly be civil to you? Last I saw the pair of you, you seemed great friends. Always together drawing the gaze of many a man. Thank you for that, by the way. It helps business immensely."

A soft chuckle trickled from Sally's lips. "I'm glad we could be of assistance."

"What happened, then?"

Sally's lip drew between her teeth. After a minute she released it with a gust of air. "It's complicated."

"Then make it simple."

"I thought it was a dalliance," Sally's tone dropped. She kept searching to be sure they were alone. "Like with Patrick. Molly and I were…"

"No need to elaborate." Leanne could guess by the clues, and the flush coloring Sally's cheeks where she was heading. She shifted closer. "You found it a dalliance. Am I to understand then that she did not?"

"I thought she did. Like you said, we were often together. Our time together included flirting with men, having a good laugh. Much like we both were with Patrick."

"Maybe it started that way for her. However, the wonderful woman you are drew her in."

Sally scoffed, her shoulders drooping. "I don't feel so wonderful. I really hurt her."

"It happens. We often start things with one mind, and circumstances change. I certainly didn't ever intend to settle in with Tommy, much less come to care for him as I do."

"The thing with Matthew was only a flirtation."

Leanne raised her brows in surprise. "Matthew Coleman? The rancher?"

"Yes. It was a mere flirtation. We hardly know each other, but we are getting to know each other. When he kissed me." A soft sigh carried on the light breeze. Sally's features softened. "It was…different."

"Different?"

"With Arthur our kisses were almost perfunctory. Chaste and sweet. There was never any spark of passion or need. With Patrick and Molly it was all passion alone." Sally's blush darkened, spreading toward her chest. "When Matthew kissed me the passion as there, but it was more subtle. It was warmth, not fiery heat. I could have kissed him forever."

"I know that feeling."

"I don't know him well yet, but I like what I do know. Quite a lot." Sally knocked aside a stray curl that dropped onto her forehead. "In exploring a flirtation with him, I'm afraid I hurt Molly."

"You don't feel that close affection with Molly?"

"Not exactly. It's more a deep affection like that of a good friend. Like Ma with you or Kat. Like I told her, I don't know her."

Leanne pondered the statement. "You've been close for months now. I know you've spent many hours together, how do you not know her?"

"I don't even know her real name. Or anything about her beyond being a Pinkerton like Tommy. She's a master at disguising everything about herself, right down to her voice. I like the woman I've been working with, and everything else, but I know nothing about her."

Tommy is a Pinkerton as well. I don't feel that way."

"Because Tommy pulls no punches. You know him. You know his family. You know what he does and even who he was before he was a Pinkerton."

"True enough. He's told me quite a bit about himself, his former wife, and his time in the agency."

"Exactly. I don't know anything about her. We have our lessons together and we play and flirt about town. She knows all about me, and I know nothing about her. I haven't even been granted the kindness of her true name."

"Does she disagree?"

"She says a name is nothing. That I know her, but…oh, I suppose I was cruel. I didn't mean to be, I only meant to be honest. I told her I only knew the face she showed me."

"Perhaps it was cruel in the moment, but it was also truth." Leanne gave a reassuring squeeze to Sally's arm. "I've seen Tommy's other face. You know, when he's not being the sweet, funny, whip smart man we all know. There's a measure of cruelty about him that's tempered with humor."

"I want to remain her friend. I do care for her, but no more than that." Sally sank back against the bench. "When we were interviewing Archie it was like she'd donned another disguise. An angry schoolmarm criticizing all I did."

Leanne did her best to cover her laughter at the insolent tone that matched the pout Sally wore. With the reference of a schoolmarm, the whole thing made her seem like she might have been a child being scolded at school. "That is likely her way of dealing with the hurt."

"It probably is, but if we are going to interview a suspect, she can't do that. We shouldn't be at odds going into the situation."

"Unfortunately, this instance is being forced upon you in a way. Normally I'd tell you to give it some time, but it appears you don't have much."

"I wanted to sit down and talk about what we knew, maybe come up with a solid theory. I didn't want to go in blind like this."

"All you can do is try." Leanne sighed when Sally's frown lingered. "I wish I could help you more than I am. Your ma is much smarter about these things than me."

"I don't think even she could help. Tommy might help, at least he could talk to her, or go with me in her stead." Sally drummed up a smile for Leanne. "Thank you for trying."

"Of course. Now, gather yourself. I see Molly heading our way." Leanne rose. By the time she'd straightened her skirts, Molly had drawn near. "Miss Malone. It's good to see you."

"Miss DuBois." Molly inclined her head.

"I received word from Tommy. They'll be back within the week." Leanne winked at Sally. "Though I may steal him for at least a day once he gets back."

Sally laughed quietly. "You sound like Ma with Pa."

"If you'll excuse us." Molly interrupted Leanne's reply. "Sally and I need to prepare to ride out to a homestead."

Leanne's brows rose, but she nodded. "Of course."

"Stop being so rude." Sally flew to her feet. "I'm beginning to wonder if you should even go. If we can no longer work together, then fine. I'll take David and you can be on your way."

Molly's brow rose. "I'm nothing if I'm not able to complete my duty as assigned."

"Then help me complete it. I relieve you of your duty to teach me anything further." Sally spun and stormed into the Inn.

Leanne cleared her throat, waiting until Molly turned toward her. "A broken heart can ease with time, a broken friendship is far harder to mend."

Molly straightened. "Sally has a big mouth."

"Only with family."

"It still isn't her place to discuss my business."

"She was discussing her own." Leanne set a hand on the woman's shoulder. "Just think about what I said, please."

"I have a job to do. Excuse me."

Leanne sighed as Molly disappeared into the Inn. "Good luck to both of you."

In adversity remember to keep an even mind.
-Horace

Sally urged Agatha out of the corral next to Molly. While preparing to leave they'd managed moderate civility. They hadn't made any progress personally, but had managed to get a semblance of a plan in place. It made her feel better about heading to Jake's knowing they could at least get along for the case.

Molly glanced back toward the jail. "Where's the Sheriff? I thought he was coming with us."

"Unfortunately David's out at he settlement dealing with a dispute at the lodge. One of his deputies will be joining us. Simon."

"Simon?" Molly adjusted in her seat, checking her shoes for her knives.

"Definitely not my first choice." Sally smoothed her hand along Agatha's neck. The horse danced anxiously under her instead of waiting patiently like normal. She tried to soothe the horse while Molly continued checking her weapons. "Simon's not a friendly sort."

"Doesn't he attend that other church?" Molly finally settled back into her saddle properly.

"He does." Sally frowned. She hadn't wanted to bring Simon, but there'd been no other choice unless they wanted to wait for David. She'd rather get this over with. "He is an officer of the law, though. It's not like we can go dig up Uncle Mike to go. He's touch and go with his moods still."

"Can't blame him, I guess." Molly looked toward the jail again. "Here he comes. If our theory holds any merit we should keep an eye on him, too."

"We're only going to talk, but of course we will."

Simon pulled to stop beside Sally. "Sally. Molly."

"Deputy." Molly nodded to him.

"Afternoon, Simon. Are you ready to go?"

"Sure am." He adjusted his hat, the brim low over his eyes. "Where is it you said we were heading to again?"

"Jake Bosen's farm. We had a couple of questions for him is all."

"About what?"

"You let us worry about that." Molly didn't look directly at the man, but Sally noticed her hand twitch toward the knife tucked in her waistband.

"We'd go ourselves, but I promised a friend we'd bring the law." Sally clicked her tongue to get Agatha moving down the street. Soon as they left cobblestone, she spurred on the horse into a faster run.

Snow piled on either side of Tanner Road, but enough people had traversed the path that the road was packed down and smooth. Before they hit the lake, Sally turned Agatha right toward the eastern foothills.

Their passage slowed as the snow was much thicker and higher once they left the road. Only a few trails converged this way. Sally followed them best she could to keep their pace steady. A few miles down she angled north to follow the single horse trail toward Jake's farm.

When the house came in sight, Sally slowed enough so it didn't seem as though they were approaching with too much purpose. Twenty yards from the house the snow eased, trampled down into a sort of yard around the homestead. Out beyond the house the snow sat pure and white, glimmering in the sun.

Sally waited until the other two had joined her in the yard. She didn't approach the house yet, unsure of what they'd find. Unsure if he could hear her from this distance, she tried anyway. "Jake. It's Sally. I wanted to see if we could talk."

"Get off my property," Jake called from within the house. He hadn't bothered to open the door, yet the call was loud and clear.

Sally moved Agatha to the east a bit, eying the windows. The sunshine bounced off the panes on either side of the door. All of them except for one pane in the right window. "He's got a pane knocked out. Be prepared for weapons."

"Always am," muttered Molly. She angled her horse and sat slightly cockeyed, her hand hovering near the rifle in its holster.

"Jake." Sally urged Agatha a bit closer. "We aren't here to cause trouble. I have a couple of questions for you is all. Come on, Jake. You know me."

"If you're not here for trouble, why'd you bring the law?"

"For our protection only. Not because of you. Things have been dangerous in this valley of late, for a great many folk. It's got nothing to do with you." Sally kept a tight hold on her reins, nerves on edge. It took every bit of resolve she had to not set her hand on her own weapon. The last thing she needed was for him to get nervous on the trigger. "Let's just sit down and have a drink, Jake. You can even come to the saloon if you'd rather. I'll cover your drinks."

"You don't fool me."

"I'm not trying to." Pain ripped through her shoulder. She flew back out of her saddle and was halfway to the ground before she ever heard the crack of the gun. The snow did nothing to soften her impact. "Fuck."

Molly screamed something an another crack of fire went off.

Sally blinked against the pain radiating through her chest and arm. She heard sounds around her, but couldn't get her brain back into motion. "Ow."

"Sally!" Molly dropped down in front of her. She ripped aside Sally's coat to check the wound. "Stay down. I got this."

"Wait." Sally grunted when she tried to stand up. "Fuck."

"Hey Sally." Simon's feet came toward her, stopping right next to her.

"Simon." She could hear the sounds of a struggle nearby. Molly must be doing something, and Sally knew she had to help. "Help me up."

"No. I don't think so."

"What?" The word barely made it past her lips before her breath was knocked clean out of her. She doubled over, spotting the man's boot headed for her again. Molly'd been right about watching Simon. She grabbed his ankle and rolled away.

Simon toppled over her. As soon as he hit the ground, Sally struggled to her feet. She slapped Agatha on the rump, "Heim!"

Sally stumbled as the pain from that simple action washed over her. The wave of agony knocked her back down to her knees. She took a few shaky breaths. Right as she began to feel centered, a harsh blow to the back of her head knocked her back into the snow.

Rather than fight back before she was ready, Sally lay there as though unconscious. For a count of one hundred and eighty she took slow, even breaths to focus on pushing the pain away and gathering strength. Through it all a fight raged on nearby, she could hear it all. Hits, grunts, the whistle of a knife cutting through the air.

Sally pushed to her knees, taking in the sight of Molly fighting off both men with her knife. Her moves were quick, elegant, even beautiful. The blows she dealt hit with deadly accuracy. Blood ran along both men's clothes. Sally got to her feet, gathering her own knives.

When Jake spun away from a blow Molly dealt to his shoulder, Sally caught him on the way around with a knife to the gut. "That's for shooting me, you bastard."

He swung, but she ducked out of the way just in time. The injury to her shoulder left her one-handed and slow. But she'd be damned if she would give up without a fight. The glimmer of Jake's own knife swung toward her. She managed to move under the swing, slicing him across the thighs on her way down.

Unfortunately, her body didn't want to get back up and the sharp impact of a knife hit her back. She groaned against the pain. When the knife was ripped out just as quick, the pain doubled so much she let out a yelp.

Sally grabbed her gun from its holster and spun, but Jake was no longer behind her. Molly once again had both men on her.

Sally hefted her weapon toward the closer man and fired a shot. The man dropped like a stone, but a strangled gasp caught Sally's attention.

Molly stood stock still, staring Jake in the face. Confusion flickered through Molly's brows before she dropped to her knees. That's when Sally saw what had stopped her friend cold. A knife stuck out from Molly's chest.

"*Molly.*" Sally turned her weapon on Jake, firing again. She missed. Jake charged toward her. Sally spun on the spot to grab her knife. As his boot came toward her face she rolled under the kicking foot to his standing leg. She sliced right across his Achilles. He crumbled to the ground.

Sally used a heartbeat to get his weapons away from him before rushing toward Molly.

Molly somehow remained upright on her knees. Her gaze fixed on the knife sticking from her chest. A small giggle spilled from her lips. "It has my heartbeat."

When Molly reached for the knife, Sally pushed her arms away. "Don't do that, Molly."

"Sally."

Sally caught her when she crumbled, even though her own shoulder screamed in protest. "No, no, no. Molly, look at me. Don't you dare give up. Andrew will help you."

"He can't." Molly's eyes blinked slow. They didn't seem to register Sally hovering over her. Her gaze was fixed on the blue sky above them. "Molly Malone. My ma's favorite song. She sang it all the time."

"Keep talking, Molly. Please." Darkness seeped at the edge of Sally's vision. She couldn't let go. Not now. Molly had stopped talking, just stared. "Hey, Molly. Talk to me."

Molly took Sally's hand in hers. "Laney. Laney Pierce."

"I prefer Molly."

"So did I."

"Don't talk like that. You're going to be fine. We'll get you back soon. Andrew will help."

"I do love you." Molly's eyes flickered closed. "Sing to me. Sing my song."

Sally blinked against the tears that rushed forward. "Of course."

Quietly Sally sang the familiar shanty about Molly Malone. She hoped and prayed someone had seen her horse and would come looking for them soon. Molly's horse was nearby, but Sally didn't have the strength to get them both into the saddle.

Molly's features grew paler, the flush of life fading with every line of the song. When Sally's tear hit Molly's cheek, her amber eyes opened. She smiled softly. "Sally."

"I'm right here. I'm not going anywhere. I can't, really." Sally tried to laugh at the weak joke. "I sent Agatha home. Someone will come. Don't you worry."

"Not worried. I'm with you. I am tired." The pulse of the knife in her chest had slowed considerably. Her hand drifted toward it. "Take it out."

"No. Andrew will be here."

"Take the knife out. Get yourself home. Let Andrew save you."

"I should have been faster. I could have—"

"Shhh." Molly sighed, her gaze drifting toward the sky again.

"I'm so sorry I hurt you. I never meant to."

Molly blinked slow, a soft smile curving her pale lips.

Sally's head swam, everything growing darker, but she couldn't leave. Not yet. Not with Molly still here. She wouldn't leave her alone.

A yell in the distance caught Sally's attention. Figures headed their way along the horizon. "They're coming, Molly. Hold on."

"Sing to me."

"Molly."

"Please. That's what I want to hear when I go."

Sally clutched Molly's hand to her chest and complied.

*He who demands mercy and shows none
burns bridges over which he himself
must later pass.
–Thomas Adams*

Cole remained silent after he'd finished his story. He couldn't take his eyes off Jane. The turmoil in her features reminded him of the first time they'd split years ago. Back when she'd been pregnant and kept it from him. When she'd loved him, but let him go because he'd been too scared to get in deeper with her.

She poured herself another tea. Her mouth opened as if to speak, but then shut. Brows furrowed, she sipped her tea instead.

He still held his tongue. She needed to do this in her own time in her own way. In his mind he knew he'd not betrayed her for one second. He'd done everything he could think of. If Paul hadn't been there, he'd have gone down the mountain weeks before.

Still, he had sent a divorce decree. No matter that it had killed him to send it, he couldn't think of any other way to reach out to her and have it actually reach her. Even though he'd gotten exactly what he'd hoped out of it, which was for Jane to come, he'd hurt her deeply to do it.

"I need some time." Jane sipped her tea. Her hands shook a little when she set it back down. "I know, in my head, you did what you had to do."

"I don't know. If I'd been cleverer, I might have been able to get out sooner."

"If you were cleverer, you wouldn't be the man I married." An actual hint of a smile crossed her delectable lips. "Also, the man that I married wouldn't abandon a soul for his better good. He proved that with his sisters. It's the who the someone is…"

"That isn't her."

"I know." The smile had faded, the words crisp and cold.

"Sorry."

"Stop. I don't want apologies right now."

"All right. What can I do?"

"Nothing. I told you, I need time."

"You want me to leave?"

"No." For the first time since he'd begun his story she faced him directly. Her eyes were tight, her expression guarded. "You told your story. I suppose it's fair you learn about some of the things that happened back home."

"Gotta admit, I'm curious. I've only gotten bits and pieces. Cora, Archie, Hammy." The mention of the old coot immediately made her eyes shimmer with tears. Once again, she looked away from him. "What is going on back home?"

"Where to start? I suppose with Willow. She fell ill." She reached for the laudanum. Charlie might have ordered her to have a few drops before he'd left, but she apparently thought she'd need them now.

"If it's too hard, you don't have to tell me."

"You need to know. A great many things. There are few happy memories to expound on." She dropped several drops of laudanum into a glass filled with a couple inches of water. Cole knew she despised the stuff, but clearly felt it necessary if she was actually taking it.

"Willow got sick? Was it the asthma?"

"At first, yes. Overall, she's been warming up nicely. I discovered the reason she didn't like Ada finally."

"Really? What was that about?"

"Ada looks like the ma that birthed her. Apparently Willow remembers her white parents, and Ada bears a resemblance."

"She remembers? Never knew that." Their two wards had spent so much time among the Indians, he could hardly imagine that Willow could remember such a thing. Then again, she'd been the twins age when they'd been taken. He had no doubt the twins would remember, but they did seem to have a bit of their Ma's memory.

"Neither did I. We worked on that problem. It still causes her some discomfort, but she's taking her lessons now, and I'm helping her in the evenings. I'm digressing, though. She went with Ma and the twins on a very cold day. The cold caused a severe attack. Charles said he's seen it happen in others with her condition."

"The cold?"

"I know." She sighed softly. "After a few days of treatment she seemed to improve, but in the weeks after she became worse until I had to take her to the clinic. She'd developed pneumonia and had to stay under the doctor's care for days. Thank the heavens Charles and the other doctors were able to help. She came home to us Christmas morning."

"How is she doing now?" He almost hated to admit the worry he felt for the girl. There'd been a heaping helping of hesitation on his part to take the two in. He'd warmed up to them over the past year, and more so since they'd started visiting with Black Moon. Much of the angry behaviors had subsided.

"By the time I left she was back to full function. As long as she stays indoors on the coldest days she'll be fine." Jane returned to her tea. The laudanum had relaxed her shoulders enough she didn't seem nearly as tense. "Of course, there was Cora."

"She got shot, they said?" Cole shook his head. "One of the nicest women I've known, even when she was being mean to me."

"She wasn't being mean, she was being intolerant of you behaving like an ass."

"Not gonna argue with that." He chuckled quietly, glad to see her smile. "I wasn't exactly a good man before you."

"You were always a good man, you just covered it with your rakishness. She saw what you were when you were around Isaac."

"He's a good kid. Wild, but a good kid."

"Still is." Jane straightened. "Sally has a mind the bullet was meant for her."

"Come again?"

"Earlier in the evening Sally was in the apartment with Alma and Arthur, whom Alma had invited over. I guess the dogs started howling, so Sally went to check on them. She thought she saw someone creeping in the shadows. When she was trying to investigate, Arthur surprised her by tapping her on the shoulder. She decked him."

He let out a bark of laughter. "She did? That girl's got fire."

"A little too much. She gave him a concussion." She was laughing as well. "Because she's still kind, despite her fire, she took him to the clinic. When she walked him home she told him she'd be by to check on him in a few hours. Since Cora usually is at the Inn until at least ten-thirty or eleven cleaning her kitchens, Sally wanted to be certain he was doing well under his brothers care."

"I'm sure Isaac enjoyed occupying his brother."

"Sally said he was excited, yes." She took another long sip of tea. "I was feeling restless that night. Worried about you and your lack of communication. I offered to scrub the pots for Cora so she could check on her boy. She agreed, which had her crossing the street before Sally. That's why Sally believes it was her that they meant to shoot."

"You don't seem to think it's too crazy."

"Too much oddness has happened. All of the whores that have been murdered, save for Lucy, were properly murdered. Except Sally. She wonders if maybe they wanted to finish what they started."

Cole shuddered at the idea. "That's grim."

"Grim is a state of being in the town lately. There's been to much death of late." Jane rubbed her hands on her legs. She rose to pace the floor. "The night Cora was shot was the night

I learned I was still pregnant. Ma told me it happened to her twice like this. One baby passed, another survived. I was so happy, but still so sad. It feels wrong to celebrate when another child lays in the ground."

He went to her side. Gently, he set his hand on the swell of the baby. "It's a good thing. I never imagined, I felt so bad about leaving so soon after." His throat closed off, the pain of his departure fresh again now that he'd brought it up.

Her hand settled on top of his. "I couldn't wait to tell you. I knew you'd be excited."

He met her gaze, for the first time since they'd found each other there was no anger there. Her smile was sad, but soft. The deep blue eyes still shimmered with tears. It took all he had not to pull her into a kiss right then. "I missed you so much."

She took a shaky breath. "I missed you too."

A hard pounding at the door startled them both out of the moment as brutal as the knocking itself. Cole groaned out his frustration. "Fucking hell. What now?"

Jane took a step back. The moment was gone far too soon. She sniffled, then went back to the table.

"It's an emergency." For the first time Cole could remember, Tom sounded absolutely panicked. His voice cracked, "Get out here *now*."

Jane's features paled. She rushed to the door, throwing it open. "Thomas?"

"It's…" Tom glanced behind her to Cole. "Make her sit. She needs to…fuck."

Jane touched Tom's arm. "What is it?"

"You need to sit." Tom pushed them back into the room. "Sit."

Jane trembled beside him. "Thomas, you're scaring me."

Cole guided her back to the table, pushing her into a chair. She didn't fight him one bit. Her wide eyes stayed focused on her brother. Cole put a supportive hand on her shoulder. He turned to Tom. "What is it?"

"We aren't staying three days. We're leaving on the first train we get out of here."

"What? Why?" Jane's whole body tensed, her hand grasped Cole's tighter than a vise. "What happened?"

"It's Sally." Tom's head dropped when his voice cracked again. "And Molly."

Jane's nails dug into his hand. "What? Tom, spit it out."

"Molly's gone. Dead." Tom sank into the opposite chair. His head dropped into his hands. "Sally's been shot, stabbed, I don't know. Leanne's telegram wasn't very damn clear."

"Oh no." Jane flew to her feet. She yelped when Cole pushed her back into the chair.

He couldn't risk her getting in another panic. It was his hope that she would still relax so long as she stayed sitting. God willing, the laudanum she'd taken would help, too. He stared at his brother-in-law, trying to get a grasp on what he'd said. Sally shot, or stabbed? Injured, that's all that mattered. It had to be serious for Tom to be so upset. "Sally is—what happened? We need to go back. Now."

"Nick's getting tickets." Tom shook his head in his hands.

Cole knew he'd never once seen Tommy so shaken up. Then again, it was Sally. Since she'd saved Tommy's life, the two had been really close. Cole's heart started to race, worried that if it were dire they'd never make it home in time. "We'll get packed straight away."

"It's my fault. I'm so sorry." Tom lifted his head, looking ten years older in the strain. Actual tears fell as he stared at his sister. "Jane. I thought…I never meant…"

Jane rose much slower this time so Cole let her go. She cupped her brother's cheek, then pulled him into a hug. "There's no way you could have known. Sally wanted to do this. No one could have stopped her. Not with her heart set."

Tom's arm's went around her waist, his face hidden from view against her stomach. When he spoke, his voice trembled. "Leanne said Andrew was operating."

"Should he? I know he's a highly skilled surgeon, but he's also her friend." Jane smoothed her fingers through Tom's hair, then glanced Cole's way. Tears streaked down her cheeks, but she looked the strongest he'd seen her. That alone kept him from going to her side just yet.

"Dr. Noe, too. They're both doing it."

"Are you packed, Thomas?"

"Always."

"All right." She pushed him back to kneel before him. "Let Cole and I get ourselves packed. You eat some of our cold food."

Cole couldn't seem to make his limbs move. He stared at his hands for a long minute. Sally might not have been his kin by blood, but she was better than. Though she'd only started calling him Pa a few months ago, he'd felt like it much longer. He couldn't imagine their home without her. What would he do if she died?

Jane's hands settled in his. Her lip trembled so much he couldn't help himself, he pulled her into a tight hug. For several long minutes she allowed him. He soaked up the warmth of her, praying he was giving as much comfort as he was getting.

He took a shaky breath. "I don't…I don't know what I'd do if she…"

"Andrew is an excellent surgeon." Her voice shook, but she pulled free of his embrace. "We must remember that."

"She's good as my kin, I…" He shook his head again, trying to assemble a clear thought. "She's gotta make it."

"She will. We must believe that." She squeezed his hand. "Let's go home."

"Right. Home."

"The pain still lingers."

At her quiet words, he lifted his gaze. "I know. We're not done."

"Not by a long shot. There's more to tell you, but we have a train ride for that."

He released a shaky breath. "Home, then."

"Home."

"Let's go take care of our girl."

There is no wealth but life.
-John Ruskin

Jane couldn't deny that the closer they got to home, the better she felt. Days of rest on the train, enough food and water to keep her well. The fact that each click of track brought them that much closer to where she longed to be.

Cole's consistent attentions and kindness had softened her toward him as well. She had yet to get over the sting of the divorce papers, for certain. Still, she'd loved the man nearly as long as she'd known him. She imagined it would be sooner rather than later that she'd forgive him.

"Jane?" Charlie stepped into her sleeper car with little more than a soft knock. "Where's Cole gone to?"

"I believe he's trying to reassure the morose one in the next cabin." She offered her brother a smile. "Although I don't think he's getting any more conversation than I would offer him."

"Do you plan to forgive him soon?"

"I've begun to. It'll take time. No matter how much I love the idiot, he hurt me. Even if he did it to try to get my attention, there had to be other ways."

"Have you come up with any?"

She narrowed her eyes at his smug expression. "Shut it."

"'We shall find no fiend in hell can match the fury of a disappointed woman'."

"If you cannot be nice than I don't wish for your words, Mr. Cibber's, or anyone else's." Jane turned her attention back to the window. "Did you receive any word at the last depot?"

"Dr. Noe says Sally still hasn't woken. It was a very long surgery, we don't expect her to wake immediately, even if we hope for it." He reached over to pat her hand. "Andrew is an excellent surgeon. Dr. Noe was extremely complimentary of his skill and speed. He tied off bleeders nearly as quick as they appeared."

"I'm sorry?"

"It means she lost very little blood during surgery."

"But she lost plenty before it."

"It sounds like it."

Jane didn't want to think the worst. She was tired of thinking the worst. It made her upset and needing laudanum to keep her spells away. "Good news? Is there any? I fear I need it."

"I've only received word on Sally. That is our focus and worry at the moment." Charlie leaned forward. "I won't be continuing on home once we reach Denver."

"What? But you have a wife and son to get home to. Not to mention Sally."

"Sally is in excellent hands. I have a patient to get settled in Nebraska."

At the mention of his patient, Jane's heart constricted again. Not once in all of the days she'd known about Ella had she ever been jealous. Now there was a bitter sting at every mention. A sting the woman didn't deserve. She certainly hadn't concocted any sort of plot. She hadn't hid Cole's child from him, nor lied about her death.

"I hope to only be a day or two more, but I'll be traveling on to Lincoln to settle her at the Asylum with a friend of mine. Thankfully, we'll be getting to Denver early tomorrow. I believe I'll be able to make it there and home quickly."

She wanted to express pity for the woman. An asylum was no fit place to go. Cole had once loved the woman, but she'd clearly long ago lost her sanity. Whether it was the baby or being sent to the asylum by her father. Jane made herself face her brother. "She will be cared for? Better than she was, at least."

"Yes. As best as she can be."

"What about her son?"

"She never knew him." Cole voice startled them both. "He made it clear. Richard pulled her from the asylum when the boy was twelve. Guess he looked too much like me for her to realize it was her child. She didn't have Lydia, but couldn't be bothered with James."

"As for what happened to him, we don't know. He must have skipped town with the others." Charles shrugged. "Thomas found Paul, but said he saw no sign of the boy."

"He thought getting my pa was more important at the time. Wouldn't have minded the set. The kid was cruel to his ma, didn't tolerate her one bit, and helping kidnap you? Well, he ain't like nothing I'd imagine Richard would raise." Cole settled onto the seat next to Charlie. "He knows about the money. I imagine he'll turn up one day hoping for some, if he don't get himself killed before then."

Jane frowned at his frank coldness. "He was your son."

"I would've liked to have known him. I would've liked him to be a better man. Unfortunately for all of Richard's influence in his younger years, once Ella came back into his life Richard was too busy caring for her. Paul got his chance to influence the boy, and it looks like he took to it real easy." Cole glanced toward Charlie. "Nick said you're heading to Nebraska, then."

"If there were an asylum in Colorado I'd prefer it. At least I have a friend in Nebraska that I know will see to her care." Charlie stood. "Speaking of, I should head back to my cabin. I'll see you both in the morning when we part ways in Denver."

Jane accepted his kiss to her cheek, then turned her gaze back out the window. She noted Cole slide closer to the window as well. "How is Thomas?"

"Convinced you're gonna hate him forever."

"I don't hate him, not for this. Sally made her choice. I'm terribly worried about her, and yes this was one of my greatest fears when she set on this path, but he didn't force her into it. He gave her the tools she needed to survive and fight as best she could."

"What do you hate him for, then?"

Her anger from before seemed so far away now. "It's complicated. It involves Mr. Hamm."

"Hammy," his voice cracked. "I still can't believe he's really dead."

"When you didn't return after we told you, I knew something was wrong. No matter the papers or your long-standing silence, I knew for that man you'd do anything."

His gaze returned to her, sharp and she dared say angry. "I woulda returned for any of it had I known. Willow, Cora, the baby, any of it. You're my family. You're my home."

The power behind the words had the effect of melting the shard of ice in her heart a little more. She lowered her gaze to hide this fact. There was too much still to explain.

His hand settled on hers and she didn't pull away this time. "They said it happened right in front of you. I'm sorry you had to go through that. That you were there when he died."

"I'm glad I was there when he passed. I don't know if he could hear much by that point, he wasn't talking really. Still, if he could I'd like to think hearing a kind voice when he passed helped ease his pain some."

"It only needed to be your voice and he'd be happy. The old coot loved you."

"So it would seem. What happened after certainly solidified such facts."

"After?"

"You once told me Mr. Hamm loaned you the money to buy the saloon when you got to Dominion Falls."

His brow furrowed at the seeming change of subject. A bit of laughter crept into his tone when he spoke. "Yeah. The old coot had a gold claim worth something. Told me he sold it to Henry and Lil. Made a tidy sum off of it. He was happy to loan it to me, thought I'd be better than the last owner. I paid him back right quick, but never forgot the kindness. Why? What's that got to do with it?"

"Gold claim. Singular? As in, just the one?"

"I don't know. Hammy was pretty tight lipped about the fact he had any money. Might've had a couple of them. I just knew he had some savings and wanted for nothing, so he did what made him happy."

"He certainly wanted for nothing," Jane agreed drolly. A sudden chill coursed through her until she rubbed her hands together. She was dragging this out longer than she should. After everything else telling him about the money shouldn't be such a task. "Truth be told, Mr. Hamm had more than one or two claims. In fact, I believe those that he sold all those years ago to the Daugherty's were starters for them when they first arrived."

"Wait. Before it was a town? I've heard tales of when it was barely a camp. Indians still around, a few holdouts trying to make claims. Word is it wasn't until the Daugherty's came about that anything got organized. Heard it was Henry that got the Army out here for protection."

"I don't doubt it. Henry and Lillian were the sort that were determined to make this area more than a camp. Based on what I've known of Gilbert, he didn't want to do anything so grand as to found an entire town."

"No, he wouldn't like that much. But if he had more than one or two claims…"

"Mr. Hamm had a great many gold claims. As one of the first in the area, I believe he got as many as he could. Newcomers weren't buying from a surveyor so much as from him. The Daugherty's expansions over the years have come after they've purchased claims from him. He had no desire to run the mines or the business of it all, so he held onto them until they were needed."

"How do you know—"

"He owned many continuing North of town, and even some south and east of town as well," Jane interrupted. If she stopped to answer questions, she'd never get through it all before her tears came about. "You know the strange new homestead that was built where I came through the mountains, the one with all of the land behind it?"

"Yeah. I thought it was odd they built right where you came through. Decent farmland in front of it, but they bought behind instead."

"Mr. Hamm owned that land, and the gold claims behind it. The caretaker has no idea the claims exist, though. Thomas apparently found the caretaker for him."

"Is that why you're mad at him?"

"No. Either way, Mr. Hamm was ridiculously wealthy. Likely even more than Henry Daugherty himself. He didn't care to live any different than he did. Although I now suspect he was behind much of the anonymous donations to help the town and its residents."

"You were too," Cole pointed out.

"Yes. I didn't realize Mr. Hamm was as well."

"Wait." He leaned forward, forearms on his knees. His intense gaze locked on her. "Why are you telling me this? Moreso, how do you know?"

"Gilbert—he left everything…to me."

His jaw went slack. After a moment of stunned silence, he shook his head. "Wait-wait-hold on. I'm sorry. Wait."

For the first time in a while Jane had to hold back her amusement. Cole's clear struggle to comprehend what she'd said struck her as amusing. He continued to shake his head. One hand buried in his hair, head still swaying.

"Did you just say that Hammy left all that wealth to *you*?"

"I did. To me."

"I—what?"

"Not the town, not you, not the children, nor anyone else. Me." Her hands shook as her brain struggled over the reality of what she'd said aloud again. She wondered if she'd ever get over the shock of it.

"I always knew he was sweet on you, but I never guessed this."

"I was kind to him is all."

"He loved you, and you treated him like family."

"He was family." She blew some of her nerves out.

"Everything? What about the carpentry business?"

"Everything. The claims, the money, and the businesses. The carpentry business as well as…"

His stunned expression shifted to high alert when she trailed off. "And what?"

"This is the part that involves Thomas." She lifted her gaze, ready for him to get annoyed with her as most of her family was over this. "You know our largest investor?"

"The Armermann Investment Group? Sure."

"Armermann means poor man in German. It was a business Mr. Hamm started himself—with Thomas. They were our investors."

"Tom? Your brother?"

"Yes, that Thomas. Despite knowing I wanted nothing from family, as I'd made explicitly clear to him, he decided to get into this scheme with Mr. Hamm anyway."

Cole sat in silence for so long, Jane couldn't begin to know what he was thinking. "How long are you gonna be mad at Tommy?"

Jane stared at him in surprise. Of that entire story, "That's your question?"

"Just curious. I mean, he did help us do everything we hoped for. We're making money hand over fist, our investors are pretty happy with us. It was a win for him, too. Don't know that I can be mad at him for that."

"*You* don't need to be."

The corner of his lip quirked into a smirk. His eyes were bright with laughter. "Stubborn woman."

"You like that about me."

"Until it's being used against me."

"Suffer."

"Oh, I am." The laughter faded into a pained grimace. He leaned back on the seat with a heavy sigh. His gaze drifted out the window. "That's a lot of money."

"It is. It's all put in a trust and it's mine. I haven't yet decided if you will gain any access."

His brow furrowed again, but his gaze remained outside on the darkening scenery. "We make enough money from our own business ventures. Don't really much care if you ever give me access. That's Hammy's, and I know you'd keep doing good deeds like he did."

The sliver of ice melted a little more. "Really?"

He turned to look at her, his eyes intense even in the fading light of dusk. "All I care about are you, the kids, and our businesses. I never had need for much. Until you, then I needed you. Still didn't care much about things or money."

She allowed a small smile. "Until me, hm?"

"Even when I thought you were better off without me, I still needed you."

Life's a voyage that's homeward bound.
—Herman Miller

Jane stared out the window as the train cleared the mountains and the valley lay wide open before her. She gusted out the relief she felt to finally be home. If she could help it, she'd never travel again.

She'd left their private cabin to come into the passenger car for the last leg of the journey. The cabin felt stuffier and more enclosed the closer they got to home. It didn't help that she was anxious to get to Sally and see how she was doing.

Tom was more of a mess than she'd ever seen him. Even when she herself had been in danger. He'd always had a trick up his sleeve, a plan, a knowledge that it would work out. This time he seemed lost.

He'd really taken Sally under his wing. She knew he cared for her almost like a child. Seeing as he had none of his own, she didn't begrudge him the affection. He wanted the best for her all along. Now he worried he'd ruined her life.

Charlie hadn't joined them on the last part of the trip home. He'd continued on to Nebraska to see to it that Ella was put into an asylum under the care of a friend of his. By all accounts the matter would be quickly handled so he'd be home the next day.

They'd discussed leaving Nick to the task so Charlie could assist with whatever was happening at the clinic. The latest telegram from Andrew had assured Charlie that all that was left to do was wait. Sally would heal in her own time, or she wouldn't.

Cole settled into the seat beside her. Though she'd warmed to him the past few days, he still didn't attempt any affection without permission. She appreciated his continued respect of her wishes. Although this close to home she had the strangest urge to sink into his comfort. They'd be facing what had happened to Sally soon, and their whole family. Their chances to be alone would become fewer.

He stared out the window as well, an almost contented sigh spilling free. "Almost home."

"Almost home," she agreed.

"I never thought I'd be so happy to see this valley."

"Home will do that to a person." Even though she hadn't yet forgiven him enough to take him back in her bed, the past few nights had been some of the most restful she'd had in ages. His mere presence in her cabin, even on the next bed had soothed so many pangs. She wouldn't rush her forgiveness just to revel in the sanctuary of his arms, but she couldn't deny she longed for it again.

"What was that sigh for?"

"Happy to be home is all." She drew nearer the window to catch a glimpse of the approaching town. "Anxious to see Sally. Glad you're home."

She'd thrown in the last comment without thinking about it. It was enough to make him draw nearer. His warmth stayed near her back without touching her. "I'm not leaving you again. Not for nothing or nobody. The world could burn and I wouldn't care. I'm staying right where I belong."

"I'm sorry." No matter what she'd been through, he'd been through so much as well. Still was, in some respects. "That she must go to such an awful place. Even with Charles' friend watching over her, I know you never wanted such a fate for her."

"There's a lot I never wanted for her. This is just one more thing." He leaned forward on his knees. "I used to think I let her down, was convinced of it. Seeing her this past month proved that isn't true. She was lost from the day Lydia died. There was no saving her."

Tears warped her vision of the town. She cleared her throat and blinked them away.

"It'll be good to be home. Even better to see the kids."

"They missed you terribly."

"And I missed them."

She set her hand on his. The simple touch brought his sharp gaze on her. "You'll have to tell Leanne about Paul. I don't think Thomas is in any fit state right now."

"He sure isn't." His fingers tightened around hers.

"Or I can tell her."

"I'll do it." He placed his other hand on top of hers. "Charlie and Nick already know what she and Alma are to me."

"All of our secrets are unraveling."

"Guess that's what happens."

The brakes squealed as they closed in on the town. Nick took the seat across from him. He adjusted his vest before he leaned his arms on his knees. "Thomas is waiting at the door."

"It isn't his fault. He must know that." Jane straightened to a proper sitting position, adjusting her skirts as she moved. "Besides, last we heard she isn't even awake."

"He's still going to blame himself. However, I believe it's about more than Sally. He held some affection for Molly as well. I get the impression he trained her, and she excelled well beyond him. He was proud of her." Nick studied Jane intently. "You are appearing much better than you have of late."

"It's amazing what a good night's sleep can do for one's disposition. What's more, I've now had three of them. I'm terribly worried about Sally, of course, but I no longer feel like my brain is going to seep out of my skull under the pressure."

Cole quirked a brow. "What's that now?"

"You heard me." She touched a finger to her head. "I still have a headache, it never seems to fully go away, but it isn't so bad I fear the worst."

"Charles won't be satisfied," Nick pointed out. "He'll want to continue to keep an eye on you. Based on what he told me on the journey west this has killed women, even as it's seemed to go away."

Nick's words had the effect of Cole grasping her hand tight. "Killed them?"

"Charles likes to panic pregnant women." Jane patted Cole's hand. "Remember how he did so when we learned it was twins. I have excellent doctors, and a wonderful midwife. We must have faith in them."

"As well as your disposition improving with your husband around." Nick nodded to them both. "It has helped immensely."

The train slowed even more. The whistle announced their approach to the depot. Despite what she'd said, a nervous hum of energy began to zip along under her skin now that they were so close. "I do pray she's all right. I couldn't bear it if she wasn't."

"Dr. Cross is an excellent surgeon. Charles said he outstrips him in skill. I'm certain Sally will come out the other side." Nick patted her hand. "I'll try to go temper our brother. Take your time and don't overdo it."

"You're not my doctor."

"Thank goodness for that. I'm certain I'd kill you if I had to treat all of your maladies, seeing as you hardly ever listen. Dealing with your legal matters is far less annoying." Nick kissed her cheek, strolling back down the aisle.

Cole's fingers tapped anxiously on his thighs. "Sally's a strong girl. A lot like her ma."

Jane flushed at the compliment. "Though not by blood. Yes, I hear that quite a bit."

"A stranger would never know she isn't your blood. It's odd how much she's come to look like you."

"You exaggerate, sir."

"Do not. I told you, I'm not a liar."

"Yes, you did." She took a deep breath when the train came to a stop. "Let's go."

He helped her to her feet. The moment they departed the train, they were swarmed with friends giving greetings of care and support.

Kat swept her into a tight hug. When she released Jane, she cupped her face. "What on earth happened out there? Charlie's missive was so vague. Oh, Jane. I'm so sorry about Sally. I have no idea what happened."

"Katherine, please." Jane clasped her friends' hands. She was about to dismiss her when she noticed Cole pulling Leanne off to a quiet corner of the platform. She fixed her attention back on her friend. "I have much to tell you, and it's all horrible and wonderful. The important thing is Cole is back where he belongs. Now I need to see all of my children before I can begin to explain it all."

"Take your time. You know where to find me." Kat kissed Jane's cheek before shooing her on.

Cole approached the second she left Kat. Without her having to ask, he answered, "I told her she doesn't have to worry about him ever again. Said I'd explain everything later."

"Considering she thought he was dead didn't that confuse her?"

"A little. Come on."

Jane let him usher her off the crowded platform to the street. They made it to the clinic quick as possible as many greetings were called to them both. She pushed open the door to find Andrew sitting at the desk staring at a medical text. Far as she could tell he wasn't seeing the page at all. His eyes were glazed over.

"Dr. Cross?"

"Hm?" He lifted his head, then shot to his feet at the sight of her. "Jane!"

"How is she?"

"She's still holding on." Andrew nodded to Cole. "Welcome back."

"Thanks. What's that mean?" Cole's hand found its way to Jane's waist without permission. His hold was secure rather than comforting, like he thought she might faint. "Holding on?"

"The bullet to her shoulder nicked an artery. She lost quite a bit of blood before I could get to her. I also had to take a kidney. She's lucky to be alive." His carefully schooled expression crumbled. "I worked as fast as I could. She wanted me to save Molly, but there was nothing to be done for her."

Jane reached out when the young doctor's head drooped. She squeezed his hand gently. "Thank you, Andrew. I know you did everything you could. I know you care for her, she's your friend. Thank you for being there when we were so far away."

Andrew sniffled. After a short nod, he cleared his throat. "I apologize. That was unprofessional of me."

"Like I said, you care about her. You've been a wonderful friend. Can we see her?"

"Room three. I know it's your favorite." Andrew sank back into his seat. "I believe Mr. Coleman is with her now, and your brother barged up there a few minutes ago."

"Sorry, did you say Mr. Coleman?" Jane glanced at Cole, unsure how that had happened.

Cole shrugged. "You'd know better than me."

"Apparently I wouldn't." Jane headed for the stairs with Cole at her side. She tried to ignore the shaking of her hands as it grasped the railing. The door to room three sat wide open. Tom knelt next to the bed, his forehead on the mattress. Across from him sat Matthew, Sally's hand in his. His other arm reached up where his fingers ran gently along her forehead.

Sally lay silent, pale as a ghost. The sight ripped through Jane until she had to gasp for air. She grasped Cole's hand to steady herself. He pulled her close to him, holding her tight. "She's gonna be fine. She's just waiting to make a dramatic return."

Jane laughed weakly, smacking him lightly on the chest. "Thank you, you oaf."

"Any time."

She approached the bed. Unable to find words at first, she set her hand on Tommy's shoulder. "Tom?"

He snorted, sniffled, then scooted down the bed without lifting his head.

"Right, then. Mr. Coleman. It's good to see you." Jane leaned down to kiss Sally's forehead. She remained close, brushing her fingers along the curls that fringed her face. "Sally, you can't do this. Remember the baby doesn't like when I'm upset."

Matthew cleared his throat slightly. Both of his hands now held Sally's to allow Jane her concern. "Jane, Cole. Welcome back. Andrew hopes she'll wake soon."

"I didn't know you two were friendly." Jane perched on the edge of the bed while Cole leaned over Sally and kissed her forehead.

"Just recent is all." Matthew turned his gaze back to Sally.

"Does anyone know what happened?" Cole took the seat by the bed. His hand rested on Jane's, then squeezed tightly.

"Not entirely sure. I think Miss DuBois said she was going to talk to Jake about something or other. I was picking Stephen up from school when that horse of hers came tearing through town. She leaped right over your fence into the corral."

"Home," Cole said quietly.

"What?" Jane turned to Cole.

"Last summer she asked me to help her teach Agatha to go home on command. It was Tommy's suggestion to use the German word, Heim." Cole stared at Sally. "Didn't take Agatha long to learn. Sally isn't half bad at training her."

"Oh. Then, what happened, next?" Jane wondered at Sally's idea to train her horse to do such a thing.

Matthew's hand ran along Sally's. "I managed to wrangle the horse back out and got the sheriff. When we got out to Jakes she was still talking. Singing, really."

"Singing?" Jane studied Sally's pale features.

"Molly Malone. Barley making a peep, too. The second I touched her shoulder she done collapsed. Molly was already gone. Knife to the heart." Matthew leaned forward again to smooth a finger along Sally's cheek. "Deputy was dead, shot in the head. Jake's the worse for wear. He got stabbed a few times, and cut on his ankle."

"Ankle?" Tom's head lifted. "What sort of cut?"

"Right across the back, deep too." Matthew turned his attention toward Tom. "Why?"

"That's a disabling wound. Surefire way to get a man to stop." Tom still didn't look at any of them. Not even Sally.

"That means Sally or Molly got him. He was supposed to go down, maybe not get up."

"Well." Jane brushed her hand along Sally's arm gently, being careful not to disturb too much as it was propped in a sling. "We'll have to wait for Sally to awaken and tell us what happened."

"It may be a bit." Matthew met Jane's gaze. "Andrew said it could be days. If you want to see your other kids I don't mind staying."

"That's very kind, Matthew. Thank you. Thomas?"

"Not moving." Tom had dropped his head back to the bed.

"When you do I expect your things back in your room." She kissed his temple. "That's an order."

His grumbled reply was lost to the bedding.

Jane straightened. "Matthew, will you send someone if she wakes before we have a chance to return?"

"I'll send Bonnie." Matthew had resumed smoothing his fingers along Sally's forehead.

"Thanks." Cole pulled her from the room. He closed the door behind him only to droop against the wall beside it. His features were pale, eyes haunted. "She don't look good."

"No, she doesn't. She'll pull through. You said so yourself, and you don't lie."

He tugged her into a brutal kiss so fast she yelped. When he released her, he kissed her forehead. "We're not losing anything else. I won't let us."

"What a lovely sentiment. How do you propose to stop it?"

"Sheer force of will."

The ordinary acts we practice every day
at home are of more importance to the soul
than their simplicity might suggest.
—Thomas Moore

If it weren't for the fact they needed to go see Sally again soon, Cole would be content to stay right where he was for as long as possible. When they'd arrived at the Inn they were again bombarded by family.

The best part by far had been the kids.

Clara shrieked so loud half the restaurant covered their ears. She'd climbed into Cole's arms and refused to let go even to say hello to Jane. Because of the chaos and general merriment it took nearly half an hour to get the kids back to their apartment.

With all of their kids and wards, and even Lizzie on hand, the apartment was crowded in a way Cole reveled in. For far too long he'd been essentially alone in quiet. The only sound he'd had was Ella's frantic, desperate searches for a child long dead.

Clara lay curled against him dead asleep after her frantic excitement. Colton curled up next to her much the same, his little arm stretched to rest his hand on Cole's. Jesse, Lizzie, Cindy, and Jay all huddled around the table playing a fierce game of checkers.

Jane sat on the settee with Willow in quiet conversation. She held some papers Willow had brought to her and spoke to the girl with a gentle smile. Cole watched her lips intently as she spoke. He pulled his gaze away when she stood.

Alma sat bouncing at the piano as she had been since they'd come home. The moment he'd entered the apartment she'd let out a squeal and bounced in her seat, her hands flapping furiously. Then she'd raced toward him and thrown her arms around him repeating his name over and over. Once she'd finally released him to return to her seat she hadn't played. She still didn't play now as her excitement kept her bouncing and rocking.

Thankfully, Jane had dismissed Ada the moment they'd come home. That meant he had the kids, and Jane, all to himself. He could revel in this blissful moment of return forever if life would let him.

The gentle rattle of the teapot drew his gaze back to Jane. He found himself entranced by the act of her moving about to set up her tea. Every simple movement was like a soothing balm for his soul. A twitch of her fingers as she considered which tea, deciding as always on her favorite orange.

The swish of her skirts as she turned to grab the decanter of whiskey to set on the tray alongside her teacups. Her waist as she bent to add a few pieces of coal to the stove. The way her hand kept returning to slip along the swell of the baby.

The familiarity and ease was rich with a comfort he'd longed for. So much so he wanted her to understand how much it meant. He didn't want her to continue to worry, fear, or doubt he'd for one moment longed for Ella. That love had been his youth, a different life, a different man. A man who had no idea the sort of connection he could find with a woman.

When she turned toward him, tray in hand, she paused. The hint of a coy smile drew the corner of her delicious lips upward. She set down the tray before she settled in beside him. "You're staring."

"Can't help it." He caressed her cheekbone. Her deep blue eyes never left his for a second. The coldness of their days in California, which had lingered on the train, had softened. She was still guarded, though. He wanted to wipe those doubts away so she felt as at peace as he did in this moment. "This is what I dreamed of every night. It's what kept me up at night."

"This? Me?"

"Yes, you. The kids. You." He held her gaze so she'd know he meant every word. "Just you. Being you."

Her brow furrowed, a playful smile on her lips despite her apparent confusion. "You're making little sense."

"I'm making all the sense in the world. I missed you. Not just the sex, though with the book you sent, that was plenty enough."

A warm flush flooded her cheeks. "For me too."

"It was you. Every day. In everything. With the kids, making the tea, running the casino floor, beating me at checkers. All of it."

"I beat you at checkers because you're easy to distract. I wear a low-cut dress or my robe to reveal my bosom and you can't help yourself." The flush kept her cheeks rosy under his continued intensity. The bit of hesitation faded as her shoulders relaxed. Her hand settled on his shoulder. "This is what I missed, too. Seeing you with the children. With me. Running numbers in the ledger. The way your nose crinkles when you're adding a long list of numbers."

"It doesn't." He wrinkled his nose at the insinuation. "I don't do that."

"You do. It's rather adorable."

"I'm not adorable."

"Oh, but you are. A sweet, cuddly—" She shrieked when he snaked his arm around her waist to tickle her.

Clara and Colton startled awake. Cole's leg kicked when both Jane and the twins tried to get him. The tray rattled loudly, nearly falling right off the table.

"Hold it." Jane still wore a smile, though her tone held enough command to still even the excited children. She bent to move the tray. A deep sigh emerged when the dogs began howling outside. "Jesse, Jay. Would you get the beasts and let them in?"

"Sure thing, Ma. You still gonna let them sleep in the bed now that Pa's home?" Jesse practically skipped to the door.

Jane blushed deep red, clearing her throat at Cole's look. "Just get the rotten beasts. It happened just as I suspected all along. Cole swore he'd train them up right and then I was left to deal with it all by myself."

"Wait." Cole stood beside her. Much as he wanted to pull her close, he hesitated. Unsure how forgiven he was, he didn't dare push her. He couldn't believe his ears after all her scolding and complaining about the hounds. "You let Whiskey and Bourbon sleep in our bed with you?"

"It was cold. Don't look so pleased with yourself. I also allowed all of the children, and occasionally Leanne to sleep with me."

"Is that so?"

"Ma, look!" Jesse burst back in a second later. Whiskey bound past him, jumping right on Cole's injured leg. "Whiskey, stop."

Cole ground his teeth together to keep from kicking the dog away. The enthusiastic pup didn't know he was injured. "Damn."

Jane kept her concerned gaze on him when he sat back down. "What exactly am I looking at, Jesse?"

"The pups were howling because of him." Jesse swung his arms with flair toward his uncle.

"Michael!" Jane left Cole's side to greet her brother.

He ignored their reunion to gather himself from the flash of pain. He scratched Whiskey behind the ear, then urged him toward his brother. By the time he was able to stand again, Jane led Mike to the settee. Cole extended his hand. "Glad they got you out."

"Thanks." Mike accepted the handshake. "Jane says the two of you have been married for a while now. I guess belated congratulations are in order."

Cole chuckled low. "Over three years. It was nice to keep it quite a while, but I guess we're done with that."

"We are," Jane agreed. "Secrets are spilling everywhere. Can I get you something to drink, Michael?"

"I wouldn't mind some whiskey." Mike took a seat.

"Me either." Leanne appeared at the foot of the steps. "I hope you don't mind a visit so soon after you got home. Tommy isn't in any fit state for company right now."

"Did he come home?" Jane poured the drinks after a quick glance at Leanne. "He shouldn't malinger. It'll do neither him nor Sally any good."

"No. He's still there." Leanne took her drink, then paused. She set it down to face Cole. "Could you explain what you told me at the station?"

"Before I do." Speaking of secrets being spilled, it was time for more. Cole turned his attention to Mike. "Your brothers already know, it's only fair you do too. Leanne and Alma are sisters, and they're both *my* sisters. Half, anyway. We had the same pa."

Mike sat with his glass hovering near his lips. The glass lowered slowly. He opened his mouth, then closed it.

Leanne hadn't moved, her hand still on Cole's arm. Her eyes were wide, fingers tight on his forearm. Then a ridiculously bright smile spread across her face. He recognized it as a sign of coming trouble. Before he could step back she threw her arms around him, kissing him soundly on the cheek. "You dear, sweet, oh my. Why didn't you say we were telling people?"

"I didn't know until I did." Cole peeled her off him. His nose wrinkled when she planted another kiss on his cheek. "Stop it."

"There's plenty you don't know about what happened in California." Jane handed Leanne her whiskey. "Although such things are best told in select company."

"Plenty happened here, too." Mike's hand shook when he lifted it to his lips again. "Things you should probably know. You probably saw the rubble and have questions."

"Rubble?" Jane's brow furrowed. She turned her attention to Cole. When he shook his head, she turned back to Mike. "No. We went straight to the clinic, and back here. We had a bit of tunnel vision."

"Oh." Leanne gasped. "You don't know?"

"Know what?"

Cole eyed Leanne, then Mike. "What happened?"

"There was an explosion." Leanne spoke quiet, her eyes lowered. "At the undertakers, and it hit the cooper shop, as well. Kendrick is dead."

Jane's hands flew to her lips. Her whole body swayed. "Oh no. Graham. Is he…"

"He's alive. Still unconscious. Doubt he'll want to be alive when he wakes." Mike's hand continued to shake so hard, Leanne pulled the drink from his hands. She wrapped her arm around his shoulder.

When Mike shook his head, Leanne lifted her gaze. "Graham had taken Joshua to work with him that day. He was killed in the explosion."

Cole's body went numb, and he couldn't help but turn to stare at the twins where they played. Joshua hadn't been much older than them. "No."

"What about Linh?" Jane's voice was strained, her hands wringing together. "Her and the baby? Are they all right?"

"Linh had the baby two days ago. She's distraught, but Jun has helped." Leanne took a shaky breath. "Poor Mike found Joshua in the mess."

"Oh. Oh dear." Jane sank to the couch. Her fingers pressed to her forehead. "When he wakes the first thing he should see is that baby. He'll be sorely tempted to return to drinking after this. He'll…oh dear."

"Jane." Cole sat beside her, panicked at how pale she'd become. "You need to relax."

"Trying." She leaned into him. The simple, natural reaction warmed his heart even amidst the turmoil of the news. "They'll never be the same. Graham may go back to what he was. We have no way to help. There is no cure for this sort of pain."

Cole kissed her temple. "We'll do what we can."

"I know."

*One word frees us of all the weight
and pain of life.
That word is love.
-Sophocles*

Jane leaned on the doorframe of the twins' room. In a near mirror scene to the night before he left, Cole sat on the floor beside Clara's bed. The pair carried on a deep conversation. Colton curled in his lap, dozing against his chest.

Her heart swelled to see him with them, as it had all day since their return home. The way he'd taken time with each of their children and wards. The pure joy on his face when Clara had climbed him like a tree when she'd seen him. The true pain at seeing Sally in her condition. Tiny little moments like this one where he listened to his daughter as though the story she told was the most important thing in the world.

What he'd told her earlier, before her brother's arrival, she had to admit it had nearly completely melted the sliver of ice in her heart. To know he'd missed her in those little moments as well. The intensity of his gaze when he'd said it left no room for doubt he meant every word.

A smile like she hadn't felt in weeks settled into place. There was plenty of trouble and worry all around them, but her heart was full for the first time in weeks.

She slipped away, heading through the quiet apartment. All of the older children were watching the Burlesque in their booth. Her parents minded the hotel. For the rest of the evening they would have blissful quiet.

Jane stoked the fire in their room. The idea of a bath after her travels sounded appealing, but the comfort of the bed drew her stronger. In the end, she thought the comfort of her husband would be the most soothing balm of all.

One by one she pulled the pins from her hair until the locks fell free down her back. She ran her brush through the tangle of curls. She took her time, knowing full well Cole would linger with the twins until Clara settled to sleep.

Their first day back had been filled with the children, their friends and family, and spending time at the clinic with those injured. They'd spent more time with Sally, some with Graham, as well as Linh. She'd sat with Archie for quite some time as he'd told her what he'd told Sally before she went out to Jake's.

After she'd relayed the information to Tom, and insisted he go rest with Leanne, Patrick had arrived to spend some time with Sally. She'd been surprised to see him, as he'd been marked as checked out from the Inn in the registration book.

Apparently he'd planned to leave the day before, but Sally's predicament had him delaying two more days in hopes she'd wake. After that, he had no choice but to leave. After over six months in their town, she imagined he had plenty to attend to in St. Louis.

As for her and Cole, they'd spent the past several days talking. All their conversations hadn't softened her to him as much as that day had. Now, being back in their room where she'd spent hours without him, longing for him. Her resolve was weakened.

Even so, right at that moment she knew things weren't entirely better. What she needed more than anything was his reassurance. She wanted to lie in his arms and remember what a good, deep sleep felt like. She wanted to reconnect with him on a deeper level before they resumed their bedroom activities.

Like when they'd first met. They'd spent months connecting as friends, and more, before they finally made their way into bed together. She wanted, maybe even needed, to know that connection still existed. Damaged and wounded as they'd both been by the past few weeks.

The door closed softly, the click of the lock sealed them into the quiet room. She lifted her gaze to find him in the mirror. A soft smile lingered on his features. "Clara finally went to sleep. Your ma is out there now."

"She wore herself out. I'd wager a guess that little girl would have talked herself hoarse just to keep your attention."

"She didn't need to talk to keep my attention. I sat in there watching her sleep for five minutes before your ma came in." His eyes caught hers in the mirror. "Seeing them…all of them…I…"

Jane lowered her gaze when he got too emotional to speak. "I'm glad to know you missed them, because they were all missing you terribly."

"Of course I missed them."

"You didn't mention them." She closed her eyes against her own sharp tone. Where on earth had that come from? She thought she was getting close to forgiveness. "Sorry. That was uncalled for. I don't…I'm not certain where it came from."

His hands settled on her shoulders, a gentle touch. Hesitant. A hesitation well earned after her tone. "I didn't dare mention them. I didn't want him to know we had kids and wards, and definitely not about Alma. It was bad enough he knew about you."

"If you tried to send telegrams, how could he not know about the children?"

"You didn't answer after my first telegram. I thought it was strange but didn't know the reason. I didn't mention the kids because I didn't know what was going on. Not sure what made me keep my mouth shut on them, I just knew something wasn't right. Then Paul showed up, and I started to get an idea."

"What about Richard? You said Paul or James went through his stuff. Wouldn't he have known?"

He sank onto the end of the bed. "Honestly, I haven't written Richard in years. I had a pretty damn good life. I didn't ever want to look back; I sure didn't want to go back."

"Why a divorce?"

"I told you. I had no other way to get word out, short of running off. I didn't know what he'd do if I did that. I knew he'd let me send that damned decree if it said I got all the money. I hoped you'd know I'd never willingly do that."

"Never is a dangerous word." She tried to let go of the unrelenting pain of the moment she'd first seen the papers.

She might have thought she was better, but it was stubborn. All the melting his actions had done that day evaporated with the renewed pain.

"I also knew that even if you did believe, you'd never stand for it. You'd make sure I got nothing."

"I told James and Nicholas to make you bleed."

"I saw the papers. They listened."

"I know. They're very good. I told you my lawyer was better than yours." When she met his gaze, his pain was as visible as hers felt. She'd hurt him by attacking him again. Out of the blue, after such a peaceful day. "I'm trying. I don't know why I brought it back up."

"I know. You're hurting. You're not the only one." He extended his hand toward her. Brows turned down, he silently pleaded for her to take it. When she did, he pulled her closer. "We do better together."

"I know. My trust is thin right now. I trusted you more than anyone."

"I didn't betray you. Sending them papers about broke me. I gave up. I no longer cared. I was willing to steal a horse to get the hell out, no matter the cost. I sat and drank, waiting in hopes you'd turn up. The next time Ella wandered, I let her go…and Paul took her." He shook his head, his eyes closing. "I kept seeing you everywhere. I was losing my mind. The day you came, I was ready to go. Then Paul showed up with Ella. Shoved her off his horse. You saw how fragile she was."

"That's why you called out to her. She ran right into your arms."

"I thought I'd seen you right before he showed up with her. Once I saw she wasn't injured, I looked for you again, but you weren't there."

"No. Your pa was kidnapping me."

He pulled her closer until they were nose to nose, forehead to forehead. "I didn't betray you. I was shocked to see Ella, to see the boy, but my first thought was to send you a telegram. I asked for you to come out with Nick. I didn't know what was going on, but I knew I needed help. I couldn't do it myself."

"Clearly."

"All I wanted was you and our kids. All of 'em. Being here, having them around, having you right here. I don't want anything else."

"I need you to do something for me." She hadn't lied, her trust was razor thin. Still, there'd be no healing if she kept punishing him.

"Anything."

"I want to sleep in your arms tonight. Only sleep."

"That's the best idea I've heard in a long time." His finger tucked under her chin. Slowly he drew her gaze to his. "Are you sure? I know you're angry still. Hurt."

"Buddha tells us that 'holding onto anger is like grasping onto a hot coal with the intent of throwing it at someone else. You are the one that gets burned'. I'm tired of hurting us both. I'm only asking to sleep in my husband's arms. We'll get to the rest later."

"There's no rush. I'm home now, and just having you here is enough for me. I love you, Jane."

"I love you, too."

"Wasn't sure I'd ever hear that again."

"I only hurt so bad because I do love you. It's also the only reason I came to find you."

"Long as you still love me, we'll work out the rest."

Ask me no reason why I love you;
for though Love use Reason for his physician,
he admits him not for his counsellor.
—William Shakespeare

Jane sat at her table in the restaurant. Her tea sat before her growing cold. She couldn't seem to tear her eyes from the goings on across the restaurant. Cole once again stood surrounded by children, much as he had been since their return the day before. Though Colton and Clara were back in the apartment with Ada, the rest of their brood were listening to his animated story with intensity.

She could tell by the glimpses she was catching, the tale he told them of his journey held a great many discrepancies from the truth. It was a fantastical story that she could have sworn she heard mention of a snow monster in.

Cindy sat perched on the registration desk, interpreting his story for Lizzie. Jane would have expected Jesse to be doing the interpreting, but her eldest was far too caught up in the story. With Jay and Isaac at his side, the boys were hanging on Cole's every word. Even Alma was listening, though from a seat nearby. You could really only tell she was listening by her gasps and twitters at the right places along with the others.

"Well." Katherine plopped into the seat beside her. "I'm guessing by the look you're giving your husband right now that you won't be joining us for tea this afternoon."

"There's no look," Jane protested.

"There is a look. Adoration and lust. I stand corrected, it's two looks."

"It is not."

Kat gave her a pointed look.

"We won't be retiring to the bedroom." Jane felt the heat of a blush rising. "As we haven't yet, I doubt it will happen this minute. Besides, he's enjoying himself."

"Hold on a moment." Kat leaned forward. "What on earth do you mean you haven't yet?"

"I mean we haven't resumed our usual amorous activities."

"Jane."

"What?"

"You found him days ago. You had several days' worth of journeying by train in a private sleeper car."

"I'm quite aware."

Kat's brow furrowed, her hand settling on Jane. "Don't tell me Charlie said you couldn't due to your illnesses?"

"No, although immediately after my ordeal I was in no fit state."

"I'll need more information on this ordeal, but that's changing the subject. If not under orders, then what?"

"I'm finding it difficult to get over my hurt." Jane stared at her cold tea rather than face her friend. "Every time I think I might, it returns again."

"Because of the divorce?"

Jane nodded meekly. Unable to tell the rest of the story, she avoided speaking at all.

"You said yourself yesterday he didn't want to send that. His hand was forced. Granted, you haven't expounded on how or why, you did utter those words from your very mouth."

"Because I'm aware of the facts. My brain and my heart are entangled in a bit of a battle."

"Your libido isn't."

Jane couldn't help but join her friends giggling. "I doubt there's been a day that hasn't been an issue for me."

"Then if your other parts are battling, why not let that lead the way?" Kat leaned in close. "It hasn't steered the two of you wrong yet."

"You don't have some sort of wager going on our reconnecting as husband and wife or something do you?" Jane cast her friend a sideways glance. In the past when her and Cole had been arguing, their friends had been known to bet on when they would make up again.

"I didn't even know you two hadn't reaffirmed your marriage yet, how would I know to bet on such a thing?"

"I suppose that's true."

"Very much so. Oh, well, speak of the devil. Good afternoon, Cole."

"Kathy." He nodded to her.

Jane leaned over to see the children clamoring for their coats. "What's this?"

"Your brother James is taking them sledding. Said he'd do it soon as I finished my story. They're heading to Nick's office now to force him to make good on his promise."

"That poor man has no idea what he's getting himself into." Kathy shook her head. "That lot will cause havoc when there's several of us watching them. He's daring to do this himself?"

"I told him he was crazy. He just laughed and said he'd be fine." Cole shrugged. He glanced at Jane. "I'm gonna check on the horses. I haven't been out to the barn yet."

"Make certain Tempest isn't going too stir-crazy. I haven't been able to take her on a ride in ages. It's the worst part of being pregnant." Both Cole and Kat gave Jane exasperated looks. "What?"

"You've been terribly ill these past weeks and not being able to ride is the worst thing about being pregnant?" Kat chuckled. "Oh, Jane."

"What? Going for rides is relaxing. I'd wager to bet I'd feel better if I could ride."

"That's not all that's relaxing," Cole muttered.

Heat rose to Jane's cheeks so fast, she had to duck her head. She rarely got embarrassed by his innuendos. Their lack of intimacy really had her off-center.

"That's what Jane always says," Kat chimed in without any censor. The woman was bound and determined to push the issue.

When Jane managed to lift her head, Cole offered a wink. "See you soon."

Jane only nodded her agreement. As Cole walked away from the table, she smacked Kat's hand. "You're not helping."

"Oh, please. You've always been quite vocal about how relaxing you find your marital relations. You've got no reason to be mad."

"Katherine. I can't just…"

"You can. The only way past trouble is through. You spent weeks missing your husband. Why continue to deny how much you love him now that he's here and present?"

"I'll not deny it's been truly wonderful to see him with the children. He's so happy to be among them again."

"And you."

"Hm?"

"He's happy to be with you again. You aren't the only one casting longing looks at your spouse. His is more desperate longing, your is a bit more hesitant, but still present."

Jane eyed the doorway he'd passed through moments before. "The only way past is through, you say?"

"I sincerely doubt you'll regret it. You never have." Kat set her hand on Jane's. "You love him. You have for years."

"Yes. He still hurt me."

"The way you were looking at him just now when he was regaling the children with his tale of daring? That is the feeling you should cling to when that hurt creeps in."

"He has been working overtime to prove this is what he's wanted and missed. He's used so many words."

"Then he means business." Kat met Jane's smile easily. "The more words he uses, the more he means it."

Jane couldn't deny the attentiveness he'd shown her and the children had warmed her heart so much in the past day. The wounds had put a metaphorical bundling board between them, and it seemed time to remove it.

Her love for him hadn't faded, Katherine had a point there. They'd always worked through their troubles best together rather than apart. Apart was when disaster happened. The love and affection she'd felt in his actions of the past few days should take precedence.

"Thank you." Jane squeezed Kat's hand. "I think I'll retire for a couple hours. I don't know if I'll make it to tea this afternoon."

"I'll make your excuses. Go on." Kat winked. "Get some good relaxation in. We'll have tea tomorrow and you can finish telling me the whole story."

"I'll see you later." Jane made her way through the casino to their apartment. Fortunately, Ada was already gathering the twins to head to the restaurant. With the apartment clear, Jane hastened to the bedroom to make herself presentable.

An odd sprinkling of nerves revealed itself through a slight shaking of her hands as she dabbed a little perfume on. She freshened the linens though they'd only slept in them one night. In the closet she removed her layers to don her dressing gown.

She tugged the pins from her hair until it cascaded down her back. Never before had she felt nervous to proposition Cole in any way. After weeks of missing him, followed by weeks of pain and fear, this time things were different.

The back door closed. It was now or never.

"Hello?" Cole called to the otherwise empty apartment.

"In here," Jane responded. She didn't yet leave the closet, her rear seemingly rooted to vanity stool.

"Jane? I thought you were eating with Kathy." Cole's voice drew closer. "Where you at?"

"Right here." She pushed to her feet, pausing at the closet door. "Ada took the twins to the restaurant."

His brows rose as he looked her up and down. "Were you planning to sleep?"

"No." She drew closer. "I thought, perhaps, we could try some relaxation."

His throat bobbed under the force of a big swallow. When he spoke his voice was hoarse, "Jane. Don't tease me. I don't got the strength."

"Speak like my Cole."

"Sorry. You caught me off-guard. I don't have the strength."

She lifted her gaze to his. Her breath caught at the heat of lust in his eyes. "The only way past the pain is through."

"Doesn't mean we've got to force it."

"Being home, more than anything, has shown me where your heart is." She set her hand over his heart. The rapid beat warmed her own heart even more. His hand closed over hers. "The pain may linger, but I still love you. I've missed you."

His fingers brushed over her cheek. "I've missed you, too."

"We've always gotten past our pains better together."

"When we don't, disaster happens."

She chuckled. "That was my exact thought only a little while ago. Like my concussion."

"The horses trampling me."

"A madman nearly killing me."

"My Pa nearly killing us both." His arms went around her at her shiver. "Together."

"Together."

He brushed his lips across hers gently. "Are you sure? I don't want to force it."

"You never have. You chased my skirts for two months before we ever discovered the wonders of the bedroom."

"It was worth every second."

"It also meant we nearly starved ourselves locked in that room for over a day."

He chuckled, his grin crinkling his eyes. "It was a very good day."

"It certainly was. Our obligations no longer allow for such luxuries."

"Maybe we've got a couple hours now before all the kids come back."

"Then we best make haste, my husband."

"Whatever you say, my wife."

*There is a fullness of all things,
even sleep and love.
—Homer*

Cole leaned back against the door he'd just closed, caught by the sight before him. When he'd slipped from bed to make his morning constitutional Jane had been curled tight against him. He'd wanted to delay his departure from the bed because of her closeness. He'd missed it so much, but nature had demanded his departure.

If this was his reward, it was well worth it.

In the few minutes he'd been in the water closet she'd rolled to her other side. The thin muslin sheet draped across her curves like a fabric wave. One creamy leg remained exposed. The sheet slipped along her thigh, over her hip, and swooped along the baby bump. Her breasts were covered as the fabric gathered in the hand she had across her chest.

Blessedly, her shoulder and the sloping curve of her spine remained exposed. Right down to the sensitive dip at the small of her back.

Even in sleep she was sublime.

Every nerve ending fired to life, ordering him back to her side to resume the pleasure they'd basked in the night before. After over a month of desperately missing her, two nights in excruciating worry, followed by days of inexhaustible discussion—they'd done nothing but reconnect until the wee hours of the morning.

As to that, he should let her sleep. They had plenty to do that day, and she'd more than earned the rest.

A soft sigh whispered through the air. She shifted enough that the sheet pulled away from her ass. His cock twitched to attention without any further prompting.

He crawled across the bed slow as possible to avoid waking her yet. A gentle touch to her hip brought only another sigh. A small shift of her body drew her the tiniest bit closer. He swirled his tongue around the dip in the small of her back.

Her back arched under her next sigh. Once again he teased the spot. He trailed a finger up her spine. As always, her body responded to the slight touch. Her back curved like a cat to follow his touch.

Slowly he kissed a trail to follow his finger until his body was flush against hers. Her ass twitched against his hard-on. A low groan carried through his kiss to her neck. He didn't stop his trail of kisses, delivering more along the soft skin of her shoulder.

She turned toward him. A sleepy, yet incredibly sexy smile curved her lips. Eyes hooded, her fingers already danced along his arm. "You couldn't let me sleep?"

"Not looking like that, I couldn't." He brushed his lips across hers. "One look and you got me going all over again. You're going to leave me aching."

"If I responded every time you got going we'd never leave this room."

"I'd be fine with that."

A throaty chuckle shook through her. With a gentle push she rolled them until he was on his back. Before he could grab her, she'd already swung her leg over to straddle him. "I'm well aware you would."

"That mean you're leaving me like this?"

"I could." Her breasts pillowed against his chest when she leaned forward. "However…"

"I like that however."

Soft lips brushed his, then his chin, his throat. "However, we've been apart for over a month. That's such a long, long time."

"You don't have to tell me." He wanted nothing more than to grab her to him, but he really liked the path she was on. Slowly her body moved down his, her lips dancing along his flesh. Unlike the hesitancy of the first time they'd reconnected yesterday afternoon, the night before had proven much more in line with how they'd always been with each other. What Jane was doing now was about to drive him crazy.

"We have a lot of lost time to make up for." Fingernails scraped along his thighs.

His eyes closed at the rush of excitement that spiked through him so fast he almost jolted from the bed. A low rumble echoed through his chest before he fairly growled, "Jane."

"Hm?"

The sudden lack of any touch had hm reluctant to open his eyes. If she'd left the bed, he'd be far too miserable for words. The whisper soft touch of hair at his thigh gave him hope. He opened his eyes to find her staring him down. "Jane."

"Yes?" Her tongue flicked out to catch the tip of his cock.

He gripped the sheets as his hips bucked at the suddenness of her touch after she'd stopped. "Fuck."

"We'll get there."

He groaned at her laughter. Before he could protest, her lips closed around his length.

The bell above their head rang harsh into the moment. The moist heat of her mouth disappeared. She glared at the bell, then his way.

"You're not."

"Shh." She crawled back up his body, her legs still straddling. The heat of her core pressed into his length. "Maybe they'll stop."

"What if they don't?"

"Then they'll have to wait." Her hands pressed into his chest. Once she sat straight, she shifted her hips against his. The bell rang again. Disappointment twisted her lips. "Well, I guess we'll have to be quick about it then."

"What—"

Her body lifted and she sank down onto him. His full length wrapped in delicious heat. After a moment of stillness she began to move above him.

He'd already been raring to go. His end would come quick. Unwilling to leave her unsatisfied, he slipped his hand between them to tease her clit. A deep moan came from her. Heat spread through him, every muscle tensing for release.

The pleasure exploded through him, sending shudders along every muscle. Jane didn't stop, still moving above him, milking the moment longer. He sat quick, increasing the pace of his teasing finger. He caught a nipple in his mouth, suckling it.

Nails dug into his shoulder moments before he felt the impact of her orgasm. He continued to tease her until the last shudders coursed through her. Her lips captured his, holding him in the kiss, drawing him deeper into her.

When she finally pulled back, her face was flushed, lips swollen. He didn't let her move when she tried to. "Let 'em keep waiting.

She laughed softly. The shudder of her body ran along his to tease him again. "No. We've already overslept. Don't forget, we have plenty of time now."

"It's not enough. Never enough."

"You're telling me." She brushed her lips across his. "You go see who it is. I'll be right out."

He groaned when she slid off him and disappeared into the closet. "You don't play fair."

"Never have."

There was no way to argue with that, so he left it alone. He grabbed a pair of trouser to throw on. He'd get properly dressed later. First, he had to see who had rung the bell.

In their living room Ada sat with Jay. Willow sat at the desk, her tongue stuck out as she wrote on a piece of paper. Cole found Charlie standing near the stove, sipping from a mug. "Charlie. You made it back."

"Just now. You were taking a while, so I made some coffee." Charlie took another drink. He glanced toward the bedroom. "Where's Jane?"

"Getting ready. Why?"

Charlie gestured him closer. His tone dropped low to keep any of the others in the room from hearing, even though they were far enough away. Cole appreciated the thought, especially considering the subject he broached. "I wanted to tell you that Ella is in the care of my friend Dr. Clease. He's a good man and will give her the best care possible."

There was something in Charlie's tone that raised the hair on the back of Cole's neck. "What is it, Charlie?"

"I don't think she has long. She's been malnourished for a long time." He took another sip before clearing his throat. "In Holle Creek, and on the train, during my exams I thought I noticed something. With Dr. Clease to assist we were able to perform a more thorough exam."

"And?"

"She has cancer, Cole. We detected multiple tumors."

What might have devastated him if Charlie had been talking about Jane, only brought a bitter sense of pity. The Ella he'd once known deserved better. Now after all of her suffering he only hoped it meant a quick end for her. "How long?"

"We can't know that. We don't even know how long she's been this ill."

"Don't take it wrong, but I hope it takes her quick. That woman's suffered too much already."

"Do you want to know when it happens?"

Cole pondered the question. With Nick's help he'd set up an account to handle payments for her care. He'd left that in the hands of Nick, not wanting to deal with it. He'd moved on from Ella long ago, and only hoped she'd be taken care of now. "No. Ella's been gone a long time. I mourned her a good long time. Nick's got the account. When it happens, see she gets a proper burial. Then Nick'll get the money funneled back into our accounts."

"Then that's what we'll do." Charlie's gave shifted when they heard the bedroom door open. He smiled warmly. "Good morning, Jane. You're looking well."

"Being home with my husband will do that." Jane crossed the room to them. Her arm immediately went around Cole's waist. "To what do we owe this visit?"

"I got in an hour ago. Stopped by the clinic to see what patients we have since my absence."

"Wait." Jane left Cole's side to stand directly in front of her brother. Her hands settled on her hips. A scowl furrowed her brow. "You've just arrived home, you went to the clinic, then came to see us?"

"Yes." Charlie matched Jane's frown. "What?"

"Charles Emerson Young. Go home and see your wife and child." Jane pointed to the door. "The rest can wait. You haven't seen them in nearly two weeks. Believe me, I know what it is to miss your spouse and family. Go."

"But Jane—"

"Go."

Charlie set down his coffee and put his hands on her shoulders. "If I promise to go straight away, will you let me tell you why I came by?"

After a moment, Jane nodded. "Fine. Make it quick."

"Sally is beginning to wake. The moments she is awake she's distraught and mildly incoherent, but she is returning to us."

There is no remedy for love but to love more.
-Henry David Thoreau

While Jane had shooed her brother out the door, Cole went into the bedroom to change. He made quick work of it, seeing as they were going to go see Sally. He knew Jane would be anxious to get going, no matter if her brother said she wasn't fully with it yet.

When he left the bedroom, Jane was leaning over the desk talking quietly with Willow. Because of her own hurry to leave the bedroom, her hair hung loose.

Unlike the wild, untamable curls of her best friend, Kat, Jane's were smooth and silky. They cascaded down her side like a waterfall of pure sunshine. Her features were soft, calm like they hadn't been since before they'd lost the baby. A delicate smile lingered on her lips as she demonstrated something for Willow.

When Willow took the pencil from her, Jane's deep blue eyes rose to meet his. An almost embarrassed, possibly pleased smile lit her features along with a blush.

He grinned in response, then nodded to the door. "Seeing as your brother said she ain't fully with us yet, I thought I'd see to the horses before we go. That all right?"

"Certainly. Based on what Charles said we should give Sally some time to come to herself before we go barging in."

Willow paused what she was doing. She bit her lip, fidgeting with her pencil. "Can I go?"

"I have no doubt Sally would be pleased to know you were eager to see her." Jane hugged Willow gently. "Why don't Cole and I see how she's doing? I don't want to overwhelm her right away. We'll let her know you want to see her, and soon as she's up to it we'll let you have a chance to see her."

Willow appeared to think about it for a minute. Then she nodded and went back to her writing with a quiet, "All right."

Jane offered Cole a warm smile. "I'll be ready when you're finished."

Cole threw on his coat. First he went to do as he'd said he would. The Inn's horses came first. He only gave them a passing look over. They were usually well cared for by the stable hand. In their personal half of the barn he checked on all of their horses again.

First the twins' ponies, then Willow and Jays. Then he checked on Brag and Bluff, both of whom seemed happy to see him.

When he made it to Sally's horse, Agatha, he found her still a bit anxious. She hadn't let anyone but the Coleman kid near her for days. He spent a little extra time on her again. After a couple of carrots and an extra brushing, Agatha definitely seemed calmer.

When he left the stall the two remaining horses both stomped and snorted impatiently. Jane's horse, Tempest, nickered at his approach. He brushed his hand along her nose. "I know you're impatient to get moving again. Jane hasn't been well enough, but I'll take you out tomorrow. Get that blood flowing."

His shoulder got nudged when his own horse, Faro, stuck his nose out. Faro blew a huff of air against him.

Cole chuckled. "I haven't forgotten you. Let me say hello to Tempest first, eh?"

Faro nudged him again, nipping at his hair. His feet stomped forcefully. He whuffled at Cole with his lips, then nickered as well.

"Bully." Cole offered Tempest a carrot so he could move on to Faro. "Don't you worry, you demanding beast. I'll get you out for a run this afternoon."

Faro lowered his head to Cole's waist. He nudged at the coat where the carrots were hidden.

"You want a carrot? After bullying me, you think you deserve such a treat?" The horse nudged Cole hard enough to make him stumble a step. He chuckled low. "Fine, fine. You're lucky I've got better things to do. Here, you rotten beast."

Soon as Faro had eaten his carrots, Cole moved to the ladder beside his stall. He climbed quickly up to the hay loft. Though the maze of small haystacks he wove the familiar path to the small room tucked in the back. They stored a few items in this room, mostly their travel trunks.

He popped open his trunk to find the boxes inside. He might have missed Christmas, but Jane still needed her presents. The three smaller packages got stuffed in his pockets. The unwieldly larger boxes were more of a challenge. He made it back to the ladder more on memory than sight.

By the time he managed to get the boxes down the ladder and return inside Jane was indeed done getting ready. She leaned on the desk, her back to the door. Her hair had been arranged so several curls still danced down her back.

He rushed into the bedroom to set down the boxes before he raced back out to her. Since she still leaned over the desk, he bent down to place a gentle kiss to her neck. Though in conversation with Ada, Jane tilted her neck for him. He took the chance to apply several more kisses.

"Are you ready, then?" Jane turned to face him.

"Almost. You need to come with me first."

She tugged backwards a bit when he pulled her toward the bedroom. "Oh no, Mr. Mitchell. We must leave this apartment today."

"I'll behave."

Her lips twisted into a smirk. The light of laughter danced in her blue eyes. "Really?"

"Promise."

A low hum of doubt was her only protest.

"I wouldn't keep you from seeing Sally. I want to see her, too." He tugged her toward their room again. This time she followed.

She gasped as soon as she'd crossed the threshold. "What's this?"

"I missed Christmas. Wanted to see you got your gifts."

Rather than the protest he expected, she rushed toward the boxes. The top flipped off the first box. With a rustle of paper she pulled an elaborate cape from the box. "Oh my."

With great care she laid the cape across the bed. Her fingers trailed along the black details, then along the deep blue fabric. She opened it to inspect the warm flannel lining.

"It's beautiful, Cole. Far too fancy for every day, but absolutely stunning."

"There's a matching dress on hold at the shop you like in Denver for when you're back in your corset."

"By the time I'm able to wear it, it'll be next season. They might have to adjust the style."

"Nah. Winters last forever here. You'll find reason before the snow melts."

A warm flush flooded her cheeks. She made no protest to his point. When she flipped open the next box, she smiled brightly. "A fur cape and muff? This will be wonderful for every day."

He pulled aside the boxes to give her room to lay out the pieces. "Leanne told me you wouldn't wear the other one every day. Thought you should have one for that."

Her fingers slipped through the soft fur. After a moments hesitation, she repeated the motion. "Wait. I know hare, beaver, and even wolf. This is none of those."

"Sure isn't." He'd spent a small fortune on the two capes alone. It wasn't like they didn't have it, but she'd frown at the expense. It didn't matter. He'd wanted to spoil her after she'd come up with the idea for the brothel.

"What is—wait." She straightened to face him. "What is it?"

"Ermine."

"You spent far too much."

"Too bad. You came up with the idea for the brothel and that made us flush. I wanted to treat you with something special. You did a good thing for us." He leaned closer. "It's not like we can't afford it."

The delicious blush returned to his cheeks. She poked him in the chest. "I am *no* Krenshaw. I do not ever plan to flaunt my wealth. And for the moment it is *I* who can afford it. We haven't set anything legal with my inheritance."

"Jane. You've been running the books the past two months. Do you think we can't afford it without that hunk of money from Hammy?"

"I suppose you do have a point. We were stunningly well off without it."

"Exactly. Now finish opening."

She turned to the two smaller boxes. The first revealed a hair pin she exclaimed over. She accused him of using Leanne to get it. After his denials, she turned to the smallest box. Inside sat a long pin with nine sapphires across the front, a pearl between each. "Cole. It's lovely."

"Nine stones for each of the kids."

Her fingers danced along the stones for a moment. She turned to brush her lips across his. "Thank you."

"I thought you'd yell at me for more jewelry."

"This I'll get plenty use out of."

"You'd get less if you stopped wearing your collars so high."

"You poor soul."

The moment she replaced the pin in its box, he pulled the last gift from his coat. He held it out to her. "One more."

"What? Cole, no." She eyed the box he held. Lips pursed, she narrowed her eyes. "What do you think you're doing?"

"Open the damn gift, woman."

She set the box gently on the bed. Her hands hesitated from pulling off the paper. "If this is what I think it is, Cole."

"Open it."

When she'd unwrapped it she didn't yell or complain. She surprised him with a loud bark of a laugh. "You have got to be kidding me. Thomas must have been dying."

"What?"

She disappeared into the closet without another word. A few bumps and some shuffling echoed from the small room. Then she emerged with a very similar box. "This was one of your gifts."

Cole set it next to hers, opening the box slowly. As it revealed a Colt Peacemaker nearly identical to the one he'd just given her, he laughed outright. "Well at least for once we've got matching guns. You can't complain I got one better."

"You still have the Walker." Her finger danced along the grip of the weapon she mentioned. She leaned enticingly closer. "Don't you worry, there's a matching holster for your new Colt to match your current one."

"Wasn't worried." He tugged her flush against him. "But I do want to thank you."

"No, no, no." Her finger pressed to his lips. "I told you, we have places to be."

"We always have places to be. I've got something I need right now."

"Need, hm?"

"I always need you."

"You don't play fair."

*Well it has been said that there is no grief
like the grief which does not speak.
-Henry Wadsworth Longfellow*

Jane stood in the doorway to Sally's room, unable to yet breach the threshold. Cole remained behind her, his quiet support showing in the hand at the small of her back.

From where they stood she couldn't tell if Sally was awake or asleep. Sally's face turned toward the window, her breathing steady and even. Months ago when Sally had been attacked, when she'd emerged from that horror she'd seemed stronger. More assertive, more certain of where she needed to be, what she needed to be doing.

Though she couldn't even see Sally right now, the impact of how diminished she seemed hit her heart like an arrow. Something in the air sang of deep sorrow so strong, Jane's heart clenched. She put a hand to her mouth to stop the sob from emerging.

No one remained in the room with her now. Tommy was gone. Even Matthew had left his bedside vigil. Andrew had told them that she'd sent them away. She'd even shooed Andrew off.

Cole's quiet support gave her reassurance and strength. Jane could only imagine how Sally must feel now that she was awake. While there'd been deaths at the hands of the man once intent on killing her, none of them had felt as close to Jane as Molly had been to Sally.

After a deep breath to steady her own internal demons and memories, Jane tapped lightly on the door. Sally stirred at the noise. Jane took that to mean the girl was awake. She crossed to the other side of the bed. There she found Sally's eyes open, staring at the balcony doors.

Jane took a seat in the chair. "Sally?"

"Ma?" Sally blinked a few times. When she turned her gaze from the window, her eyes widened. "Pa? You're back."

"I am. Your ma came to rescue me." Cole sat on the edge of the bed. "Guess she got tired of having to be rescued and needed to be the rescuer."

Jane smiled despite her concern over Sally. "He's not wrong."

"You—you needed rescuing?" Sally flinched when she tried to move.

"It's quite a tale to be told. If we let Cole do it, there may be mention of snow monsters."

Cole smirked. "Heard that did you?"

"I caught bits and pieces of the tall tales you shared with the children, yes." Jane took Sally's hand in hers. "I'm not certain you have the stamina for the full story. Right now, we're worried about you."

Tears flooded Sally's eyes. One fell, and they began to stream down her cheeks in earnest. "Ma—I—Molly. Oh, it's all too much."

Jane leaned forward to brush her hand soothingly along Sally's forehead. "I know it all seems that way now. It's so new and so very painful."

"It was a mistake. It was all such a—I'm so sorry."

"Shhh." Jane brushed tears from Sally's cheeks. "You did nothing wrong."

Sally scoffed through a hiccup. "I did."

"Investigating is a tricky thing. Heaven knows I took enough wrong turnings trying to figure out the mystery of Clara's doings. You had no idea Jake would—"

"Simon." Sally gulped on the word. Her hand tightened on Jane's. "He helped Jake. It was them against Molly. I had to shoot him."

"Easy. Slow down. Take a breath. That's good." Jane was surprised by the admission. So was Cole by the way he rose to pace. "We'll get it all figured out. You're not by yourself now. Thomas is hardly sleeping he's so busy working and worrying about you."

Sally sobbed. She yanked her hand free from Jane's to cover her face.

"You just woke up, you're only coming back to yourself. We can talk about something else instead, if that will help."

Sally nodded weakly.

"How about I get you some tea and something to eat? Cole can begin the tale about his time in California. If you're still up to it when I get back, we can talk about what happened to me there."

Sally used the palm of her hand to swipe away tears. She sniffled. "All right."

Jane kissed her forehead. "I'll be back in a few minutes."

Cole took Jane's seat. He kept his gaze on her as she left. Even so, by the time she'd pulled the door partially closed he'd begun his story.

Jane didn't have to go far. Andrew climbed the stairs with a tray of tea and stew. She smiled at the young doctor. "I was just about to come down and get something for Sally."

"That's who this is for. How is she doing?" Andrew reached the top by the time he'd finished his question. Following Jane's lead, he stopped where he was. He settled the tray on the banister. "She didn't kick you out. Is that a good sign?"

"I don't think it's a sign of anything. She's not doing well." Jane sighed. "Physically I think she'll recover nicely. You and Dr. Noe did an excellent job, I have no doubt. It's her spirit I worry about."

"Me as well. I know Molly was a dear friend."

"She most certainly was dear to Sally." Jane knew Andrew didn't know the half of it.

"I hate that they fought before they went out to Jake's to question him. Sally was quite troubled by their argument."

"I imagine that's part of what has her so distraught right now. It's never a good thing to lose someone after there's been trouble. There are things you never get to say."

Andrew's gaze drifted off. Lines of sorrow creased his young features in a way Jane had never seen on the young man. "I know how it can trouble someone to have your last words be in anger."

It seemed as though he knew trouble better than Jane ever suspected. When he lingered in whatever memory had him trapped for several minutes, Jane set her hand on his arm. "Andrew?"

"Sorry." Andrew gave a quick shake to his shoulders. "My sister and my father's last words to each other were said in anger. She's not been the same since he passed."

"I'm so sorry."

He offered a smile marred by sadness. "The concern now is Sally. I can do little for my sister from here, but I can do what needs done to help Sally."

She sighed deeply. "I don't believe she wants help right now. Perhaps with time we'll get through to her, help her see she did nothing wrong. More importantly, that she isn't alone in these feelings."

"We'll be there for her when she needs us." Andrew picked up the tray. "Shall we?"

"Yes. I imagine Cole is being cautious with the depth of his story, so it'll likely be close to finished by now. Even if it isn't, she's probably tiring easily." Jane pushed the door back open. "Sally, look who I found on my way to get tea."

"Good afternoon, Sally." Andrew set the tray down on the table. "I brought up some tea and stew. Your ma has said that Cora's stew fixes near any woe."

"It certainly does. I don't know what she does, but Cora's stew is nearly magic." Jane stood beside Cole. His arm immediately went around her waist to pull her tight against him. Sally barely looked up, but she also didn't balk at Andrew's presence. Her features were already drawn, dark circles under her eyes. "You're looking tired, Sally."

"I am." Sally picked at her quilt. "I'd like to hear what happened to you, though."

"You will. I'll return in a few hours to finish Cole's story." Jane squeezed Cole's shoulder for support. Sally's lack of fire worried her more than the physical injuries. "We'll give you some time to eat and sleep before you hear the rest. I've no doubt your doctor will tell you that you require sleep to help your body heal."

"She's not wrong." Andrew's voice was cheerful, but the gaze he cast on Sally was fraught with concern.

Sally offered another weak nod.

Jane sat on the edge of the bed. She cupped Sally's cheek to get her attention. With a shaky breath she leaned forward until their foreheads touched. "There is only one thing I want to say. I know you won't believe it now, but you need to hear it."

"Don't, Ma."

"It isn't your fault. It's the fault of the bad men that thought they had the right to hurt people."

"But—"

"I know you have every reason in the world to believe it's your fault, that you could have done more. I also know I can't convince you otherwise until you're ready to accept it. Believe me, I understand more than you could realize." Jane kissed Sally's forehead. "Now, spend time with your friend and get some rest. I'll return in a few hours."

"If you say so." Sally didn't smile. She remained staring at her hand where it continued to play with a loose thread on the quilt.

Cole wrapped his arm around Jane's waist as they walked from the room. He closed the door, and stood there staring at the door as though he could see through it. "That ain't Sally. She barely reacted to my story at all. Didn't have a thousand questions at every sentence."

"No. It's not her at all. She's been broken. Now she needs time to put herself back together."

Cole turned to face her. Worry creased his features. "What?"

"I've seen lots of broken women in my time. Not all of them put themselves back together the way you do."

"Then we'll have to hope that Sally is as much like me as everyone says she is."

*Death is nothing;
but to live defeated and inglorious
is to die daily.
-Napoleon Bonaparte*

Sally stared at the window curtain. Every bit of concentration had to go into watching the faint twitch of motion that belied the incomplete seal of the window behind. The little flicker of curtain was all that kept her mind occupied. Anything to stop thinking, to stop remembering.

Having company made matters worse. The sorrow, pity, guilt, and comfort they all brought in only made the black hole in her heart widen. She wanted none of it. Deserved none of it.

Molly lay dead in the icehouse behind the remains of the undertakers.

Dead.

Never again would Sally hear the familiar laughter. The way she could change her voice and used the gift to trick and tease so many. The smile Sally now knew she'd had only for he.

Sally balled her hand into a fist so tight her nails dug into her palm. The pain momentarily swept away the thoughts and memories. She returned her attention to the curtain. In careful, measured seconds, she counted the space of time between the flutters.

A knock came on the door. Sally chose to ignore it.

"Sally?" Andrew's voice carried over his soft footsteps. "I need to check your injuries."

"If you must," she whispered. It was cold. She knew. Andrew had been her friend, he'd fought to save her life. He'd be better off without a friend like her. Look what had happened to Molly.

"I must." He slipped the sling over her head. As he peeled back the bandages, he didn't comment on her small flinch from the movement. "It's healing well."

Sally grunted when he gently palpated the area. She didn't complain, and he didn't apologize as he had in previous days. Her heart gave a pang of regret over the loss of the easy friendship they'd shared. It was better this way, that's what she had to keep telling herself.

"Once we get this back on you, we'll have to sit you up to look at your back."

"Fine."

"Sally." Andrew remained silent until she finally turned toward him. His deep grey eyes were pinched in concern. "A great part of healing is wanting to get better."

"Then I guess I'm in trouble." Tears rushed forward so fast she turned her head back to the window to hide them. The suddenness of the movement made her shoulder smart. She hissed at the pain.

"Your family wants you to get better, and so do your friends."

Sally shook her head. "I'm no good as a friend."

"As your friend, I disagree." He sat beside her. His hand closed over hers, giving it a gentle squeeze. "I admit I didn't know Molly well, but I doubt—"

"Don't speak for her." Sally closed her eyes.

"Fine, then I'll speak for myself. Whatever it is you think you're punishing yourself for? It wasn't worth this."

"What?"

"You're pushing everyone away. You don't deserve such loneliness."

"I'm not pushing."

"You sent Patrick off without a bye or leave. Your mother says he was quite upset. He extended his stay to see you lived. He wanted to see you before he went home."

"He knew I lived. That's all that matters."

"It isn't. Not to a true friend."

Sally's heart choked her words off for a minute. The pain in Andrew's voice, the hurt she imagined Patrick had expressed. It was best. It had to be. She only hurt those that loved her. She wasn't worthy of such caring. "Check my wounds if you must, then leave me be."

He sat in silence for several minutes. After a hefty sigh, he lifted the sling back over her head. He touched her shoulder gently. "I'll help you sit."

She bit her lips between her teeth to keep from crying out in pain as she sat. Her breathing grew rapid to try to burn off the pain before it erupted. When he finally finished and helped her to lie back, her hand gripped the quilt. Tremors of buried tears coursed through her.

"I'll get you something for the pain. With time, the pain will lessen." His voice remained kind, soft. One last squeeze to her hand and he rose. "You have a visitor, if you'd like."

"I don't want to see anyone."

"It's Matthew."

Like the bullet had skimmed her heart again, an ache dove through her to her soul. Matthew was the reason she and Molly had fought. She'd begun to care for him, but no. In the end it had ruined everything. Her selfishness had destroyed everything. "No."

"He's been here every day."

"No."

"Fine." Andrew sighed again. "I'll send him away for now."

"Forever."

"I won't do that. If you want to do it, you'll do it yourself."

Sally closed her eyes as his footsteps faded away. After a few deep breaths as she tried to focus on the curtain again. The tears still wavering in her eyes made seeing the movement impossible. "Damn it."

The sound of footfalls much heavier than Andrew's approached her room. Sally shut her eyes before he could knock or speak. "Go away, Tommy."

"I don't think so. I'm done coddling you." The creak of the chair told her he sat in front of her. "We're gonna talk about this."

"No." She tried to will away the sting of tears before she opened her eyes. The last thing she needed was for him to see her upset. Hell, she expected to see his anger with her. Molly had been his protégé, too. Sally had caused her death. "I don't want to talk. Not with you."

"Too bad. I'm here and we're talking."

"You told me I was ready. That I was good, smart, capable clever. You told me I could handle this. That I had everything well in hand." Her voice rose in pitch before she could stop it. She opened her eyes to glare at him. "You were *wrong*."

"I did tell you all of those things." Tommy didn't balk under her glare. He held her gaze calm as anything. "And I was not wrong."

"Molly is *dead*. She's dead because I wasn't clever enough to figure this out. She's dead because I went with Simon instead of waiting for David. She's dead because I rushed it so she wouldn't have to be around me any longer than necessary. She's dead because of *me*. I caused her distraction. I caused it all."

"Pinkerton's get—"

"I'm not a Pinkerton. I never will be."

Tommy leaned forward, slate blue eyes focused hard on her. "Mistakes happen."

Sally scoffed. "That's all I am is one big mistake. For everyone."

"You aren't."

She shook her head. He didn't understand. It's all she'd ever been. She'd been delusional to think she could be more. Too much time around Jane had given her a higher opinion of herself than she deserved to have. "She's dead and we still don't have answers. She'd be alive if it wasn't for me."

"Molly died doing what she loved doing. Doesn't matter if you two fought or fucked, she would have gone into that with the same clear head she always did. Molly was no fool. Neither are you."

She ripped her gaze away to stare at the curtain again. Her jaw clenched against the urge to cry. "Take it."

"What?"

With a vague gesture to the table she repeated, "Take it. My notebook. I don't want it any longer. Never again."

"Sally Ann."

"Take it and go." She couldn't stomach the idea of continuing. So many mistakes had been made. So many lives lost. She wasn't clever, she wasn't smart. She was a fool. "While I pittered away the time in fun and games and hurting people, over a dozen people were left to die or be gravely injured. I want no part of it any longer."

"You have to finish the job."

"Molly is dead. The job is done."

"I haven't been as involved in this for weeks. I don't know the case like you did. I can't do it without you."

"That's why you need to take the notebook. I can't—I won't—do it anymore."

He lingered in silence for a long time. She lost track of the seconds she counted after five minutes. Sally refused to look his way or give in to whatever technique he was trying. He didn't get it. No one could understand.

When he spoke again, his voice was soft, kind. It killed her even more that he thought he had to talk to her like a fragile doll. Even worse that she felt like one. "Did I ever tell you about—"

"I don't want to hear about how you went through the same thing."

"I didn't ask if you wanted to hear it. I asked if I ever told you about when Clara disappeared. When she took off without a trace, lost for seven years only to return as Jane."

That got her attention. Her body tensed in her sudden curiosity. She forced it to relax, keeping her focus on the curtains. Rather than answer, she held her silence.

"Mike contacted me straight away when she didn't show at his place. He told me everything, even though Clara made him swear not to. I was in the middle of a tricky job, one that was going to pay good money. I abandoned it to go on my own search for her. Took me near about two years to find her."

She almost opened her mouth in her utter shock. He couldn't have said what he'd just said. He'd found Clara?

"Bingham, not that I knew his name back then, but he had her working in a brothel in some town out in Nebraska. Hair dark as night, face full of coal, turning tricks. She was a popular whore, she was. Raking in the money hand over fist."

Though she still refused to speak, he had her full attention.

"Clara couldn't stand me. Not a bit. She was nothing like Jane, and our relationship was nothing like what we've got now. Even in Jane's worst fits of temper she couldn't compare to how much Clara hated me for nosing in where I didn't belong. I tried to get her out of there. I tried my damnedest, but the woman wouldn't budge."

Sally made the uncomfortable work of adjusting her position to semi sit against her pillows. Tommy didn't make one offer to help her. She stared at the notebook on her table with unnecessary intensity.

Tommy cleared his throat. "I found her twice more after that. Every time I found her she got that man to take her away. Even when she was miserable and wanted nothing more than to leave, she refused to leave with *me*. The last time I think I got through, though. Based on her letters anyway, it seems I did."

She bit her tongue against the hundreds of questions in her head. Her curiosity had failed her, tossed her life upside down. Still, she couldn't help wondering at how anyone would prefer the life Clara was living to leaving with her actual family.

"That third time she was living quite the high life. In some fancy house with servants and all. I had a time sneaking into that place. One scream and she could've had me arrested, not that it would've stuck. I got her to keep quiet by reminding her of the baby she'd been carrying when she left. Jesse. That's when she started thinking right and figuring out how to get away. Not that she did, not until she became Jane."

Tommy shifted, leaning forward on his knees. "I only ever found them because of Clara. Bingham, he was like smoke on the wind. Evil. Clever. Better at changing who he was than Clara ever could be. She left bread crumbs everywhere she went. Because of that bastard, I couldn't find the kid no matter how hard I tried. After that last time I even lost track of Clara. I failed to save my own sister. She suffered for years because I couldn't get her away. Her son suffered for years."

She wanted to point out where Jane was now, the life she had, but she kept her mouth shut tight. She didn't dare let him know the crack in her armor he'd caused. The stirring of curiosity awakened somewhere under the chasm. It was a stirring she didn't dare chase. She'd rather sink into the hole and remain where it was safe. Alone.

"I say it was my job, and Lincoln's assassination that led to the death of my marriage, but it wasn't. It was my singular focus on Clara. I worked jobs that followed along her trail. I ignored jobs closer to home with better pay, because I wanted to bring her home. I went after it like it was my only job. In the end I failed because Clara died anyway. I lost my marriage, my relationship with my family suffered. Until Jane showed up in Dominion Falls I'd all but quit working. I gave up."

Sally held her breath, unsure if he was going to try to bully her again. She didn't think she had the strength to argue again. To tell him that all she wanted to do was disappear into the hole in her chest and hide away from it all.

He took the notebook she'd been staring at. "I'll give you some time. You've just started, and it's your first real hit. I'll do what I can and hope you return to finish the job. Or even after. I still believe you've got what it takes. When you're ready, we'll get back to work together."

She sagged against the pillows. Her eyes closed when he kissed her temple.

"Any woman tough enough to drag my ass from a fire is tough enough to get through this. You've just got to believe you can."

"I don't."

"You will."

*He that is busy is tempted by but one devil;
he that is idle, by a legion.
—Thomas Fuller*

Cole stood at the top of the steps to the casino pit. Though he'd been back for several days already, tonight was their first night back on the floor. They'd used the days after their return to be around their kids as much as possible. With James set to return to Buffalo, and Jane's parents not far behind, it was time to return to their life in full.

Jane already bustled about behind the bar. The bright smile she wore didn't completely hide her exhaustion. Only the fact she kept returning to a stool kept him from heading her way to holler at her.

The casino floor hummed with activity. The gambling tables were surrounded, the bar full as well as the tables scattering the floor. Though there was no burlesque that night, Dale sat at the piano beating out a lively tune that had a few folks dancing where chairs normally sat during the shows.

It was a relief to see that their business hadn't suffered even if he'd been gone, and the town had been facing such turmoil. Despite the cold weather, their low patronage for the hotel, and the chaos with all of the deaths, the casino wasn't faltering. The reports he'd gotten from Wil suggested the brothel was booming as well.

Cole descended the steps into the crowd. He made his way toward the roulette wheel to check on Cuddy. He exchanged greetings along the way, stopping right beside Henry Daugherty as the man placed a bet.

Henry extended a hand. "Cole. Good to have you back in town."

"It's good to be back." Cole shook the man's hand. "It looks like you're cleaning up tonight. Save a little for the house, would you?"

"I'll do my best, but no promises." Henry grinned as he turned back to the table.

Cole took his time as he continued to wend his way through the floor. Greetings were exchanged with every face that turned his way. He paused to chat with every dealer around the floor. While he chatted with Edgar, something caught his eye. Unsurprisingly, it was Jane.

Her bright smile faded suddenly, crumpling into sorrow. She sank into the chair, closing her eyes.

Panicked something was wrong with the baby, Cole excused himself to rush to her side. "Jane? What is it? What's wrong?"

"Nothing." She lifted her gaze to his. A watery smile crossed her features. "Really."

"Something's wrong."

"I left to come find you quite soon after his death. The lack of Mr. Hamm's presence hit me rather suddenly is all. This is the first night I've worked any length of time since his passing."

He squeezed her shoulder. His gaze swept the floor as hers did. "It won't ever be the same around here, I don't think."

"It certainly won't." Her hands drifted along her stomach. "I've been thinking."

"Yeah? How much is it gonna cost me?"

She smacked his arm, laughing lightly. "Not about any schemes, you louse."

"I don't know, the last scheme earned us a pretty penny, so I don't mind. Just like to know what it's going to cost to get started."

"No schemes. Names."

"Ah. What were you thinking, then?"

"Perhaps Charles Gilbert, or Gilbert Nicholas."

"I like them both, but Charles? Thought he annoyed you most."

"He does, but I've grown fonder of him of late, I suppose."

"Think you should use either of your brothers' names? The remaining ones might get jealous."

"I already have Jesse Michael and Colton Thomas."

"Are we gonna have another couple to get your other brothers in?"

"No. Not on your life. We are *done*. Nine is plenty of children." She poked her finger into his chest. Her lips pursed, brows furrowed. She looked ready to scold him. "Don't say it, don't even think it. I am done dealing with this."

"I was teasing." He captured her finger, laughing at the scowl she continued to give. "No more. I'm with you. Don't like how sick you've been this time, we won't risk it. Does that mean you won't take in any more strays, either?"

"Nine is more than enough. This pregnancy has done me in. Not again. No strays. We'll find homes for them before we take in another."

"I'll remind you of that the next time a stray comes along."

"Fat lot of good it'll do you, too." A wink preceded her grin.

"Now it's you that best be teasing."

"Maybe." Her gaze drifted back toward the floor. "It's nice to see the casino so busy. With all that's been going on, coupled with our not being here, I was worried. Ma and Pa did a good job keeping our business going."

"They did. Your ma kept the books neat as a pin, too."

"She runs the finances for both farms in Buffalo. I would hope she would."

"I didn't know that."

"I didn't either until—well, Charles. What happened to you?"

Charlie took a seat across the bar, his head lowered. Cole couldn't see what Jane had commented on. Charlie rubbed his hand over his face. "Graham woke up."

"Oh no. Did you have the baby there?" Jane rose from her stool. She circled the bar to her brother. Her gasp sounded over the noise of the bar as she lifted his hat. "Charles."

"We had to sedate him." Charlie winced when she touched the growing bruise under his eye.

"You're going to be concussed from this. Graham packs a hell of a wallop. Fran." Jane stopped a passing waitress. "Will you be so kind as to get some ice in a towel, please. Thank you."

Cole leaned on the bar, eying Charlie. The bruise shadowing his eye was already a deep purple. "You definitely got the worst of it."

"I know, and we haven't even told him about Joshua yet. He woke up ready for a fight. I believe he was merely surprised is all. Confused. I don't think he even remembers what happened yet. He simply woke in a strange place and in pain." Charlie winced when Jane examined the spot once again. "Stop that. I'm the doctor here."

"I'm well aware of that fact. Cole, please get Charles' favorite brandy."

Cole knelt to open the cabinet with their best liquor. By the time he'd poured the drink, Jane had ice pressed against her brother's eye.

"You'll need someone with you tonight to be sure you don't fall asleep," she said. "What about Millie and George? It'll give you an excuse to spend more time with them."

"No good. George has a cold. I can't have him around the clinic with the injured." Charlie took over hold of the ice. "I'll be fine. I'm manning the clinic tonight anyway."

"Charles Emerson." Jane took the seat beside him. "Don't make me call Ma."

"Fine, fine. No need to get nasty." Charlie glared at his sister with his good eye. "Nick or Tom'll be there, I'm sure. Tom hasn't stayed here because he's keeping a close eye on Sally. I think he keeps hoping she'll come out of her melancholy."

"Don't we all," Cole muttered. Sally had barely gotten out of bed. She'd shown some interest in his and Jane's stories, but immediately fallen back into her moping state after. Nothing seemed to be getting through to her. He was worried she wouldn't recover. She'd be another broken women like so many he'd seen before. It wasn't something he wanted for her.

"Very much so," agreed Jane. "As long as you'll have someone keeping an eye on you, Charles. We mustn't have the only doctor in the family being a difficult patient."

"That's rich, coming from you." Charlie chuckled, wincing through his own laughter. "Blast that man hits hard. Fist like a boulder."

"Don't I know it." Cole wrinkled his nose. "I'm glad to have only been on the receiving end of it once or twice. It's much better to have him fighting for me than fighting me."

"I only hope that our town isn't down a mayor. If we lose who Graham's become in the past few years, he won't do us any good as mayor, or anything really." Jane sighed. "Well, if you gentlemen will excuse me, I have work to do."

"Not too much," Charlie called to her retreating back.

Cole shook his head when Charlie turned to him. "Don't worry too much. I've been watching her. She's sitting as much as I've ever seen her sit. I don't think she's feeling up to snuff. Not as bad as she was, but not good."

"Definitely not. You don't simply recover from eclampsia, even if your stresses are moderately alleviated."

"Huh?" Why did all the Young's have to be so long-winded?

"Your return to her side isn't going to fix her medical issues."

"Ah." Cole kept an eye on Jane as she wandered the crowd. As always, her cheerful smile and conversation carried a wave of increased volume and cash flow behind it. His woman was pure magic on the floor, but it didn't prevent what Charlie was talking about. Plus, there were so many other troubles right now in the town, even if the floor showed happiness right then. There was also the matter of Sally. "That isn't all my being home can't solve."

"Unfortunately not. I think we all wish the problems were resolved by now. The past year hasn't been easy."

"Sally won't get fixed so easy, either. If at all."

"Perhaps she will. It's going to take time, though."

"I hope you're right."

When sorrows come,
they come not single spies,
but in battalions.
—William Shakespeare

Jane knocked gently on the door.

Linh sat in the rocking chair by the window, baby Jun in her arms. Graham remained asleep on the bed. It was amazing to Jane ow even a locomotive of a man like Graham could look small in the beds of the clinic. She'd checked with Dr. Noe before coming upstairs, and Graham hadn't woken since he'd punched Charlie the day before.

Linh offered a small nod to Jane, then waved her inside. She gestured to the bed. "He sleeps again. When he wakes, it is brief and scared."

"Dr. Noe said he hadn't woken since last night." Jane drew closer to see the baby. She smiled down at the small figure, brushing her finger along her cheek.

"It was once. He realized his fingers were gone." Linh closed her eyes. "He doesn't know about Joshua."

"That's what I was afraid of. We'll see that he learns. If you don't mind me helping."

"No. I don't know how…it is difficult."

"You're mourning in the midst of having great joy. No one knows how to do that."

A tear slipped down Linh's cheek. "I am happy she is here, but I am sad. I am…"

Jane sat in the chair near Linh. She set a hand on Linh's and gave it a small squeeze. "You feel guilty for being happy. It's to be expected, though it's probably very confusing."

"Yes. Very. I worry for how he will be. He might be angry with me. I made him take Joshua that day. I had work to do, but so did he, and then…"

"It isn't your fault. It isn't Graham's. It's the awful soul that did this."

Linh's gaze hardened, a darkness in her gaze Jane found surprising. She'd only ever seen Linh as kind, soft-spoken. Now in her anger, there was something rather dark and determined in her gaze. "They must pay."

"Thomas is working on that. We'll find out who, and see they pay for their crimes."

Linh's expression returned to an almost innocence when she focused on her child again. "She will never know her brother."

"She will. You'll tell her about him, and so will Graham."

"Not if he is angry."

"He will be angry, but not at you. You must be there for him when he wakes. You and this little one. He must remember what he needs to live for. He must remember that even in this awful pain, there is joy to be found."

"Sometimes it feels not enough." Tears slipped down Linh's cheeks again. "I sound cruel."

"No. Not cruel. You're mourning. Like I said, it's confusing to say and to feel; but you're allowed to feel sad even at the same time as you feel happy. Such happiness reminds us of our losses."

Linh stared down at her little one. "Jun is happy. Quiet. It is good."

"Yes it is." A noise from the bed drew Jane's attention.

Graham grunted. His body twitched, then flailed. With a vast snort, he woke. "What—"

"Graham." Jane kept her voice soft, calm. It would do no good to startle him in this state. She'd seen what had happened to Charlie when he did. Approaching the foot of the bed with great care to remain out of reach, she met the eyes of the confused man. "Please remain calm. I'm pregnant, remember? If you hit me, Cole will see you properly punished."

"Janey?" Graham blinked a few times. He shook his head, glancing around the room. "What's going on?"

"The first thing you need to worry about is right over here. Linh?" Jane urged Linh forward. Once the petite woman had reached Graham's line of sight, Jane guided her to the side of the bed. "Look, Graham. Your daughter is here."

"Jun," Linh said in an undertone. "She is here. She is a good baby."

Graham's eyes widened. "Wait. You had the baby? When? How? I…" His words failed as he stared at the infant in Linh's arms.

Linh offered the baby to him.

Graham took the offered child, pulling her close. When he lifted his bandaged hand to touch her face, he stopped. He stared at the appendage with obvious confusion. The two missing fingers were obvious even with the bandages. "What the devil?"

"Focus on your daughter, Graham. Look at Jun." Jane needed the man to keep calm, especially with Jun and Linh so close. She circled the bed opposite his wife.

Linh shook her head, the tears falling free now. She buried her face in her hands, sobbing strongly.

"What is it?" Graham glanced at his wife in concern. He wrapped an arm around her shoulder to draw her close. "Linh. What's wrong?"

"How much do you remember?" Jane moved closer, relieved he was focusing on his family. She set a reassuring hand on his shoulder. "Or rather, what's the last thing you remember?"

"I—I don't know. Let me think." His forehead wrinkled in concentration. "I was at the office. I had to prep that cowboy for storage. I was complaining that the icehouse was getting full."

"Anything else?"

"Not that I can recall. It's all fuzzy. Why is that?"

"It's probably for the best. I imagine the memory is painful, as are your injuries."

"What memory? Janey, what the hell happened?"

"There was an explosion. Someone set off dynamite at your place. We aren't certain how much, but they say there were two blasts. Your office and Kendrick's Cooper shop were destroyed. Kendrick didn't make it out alive."

He stared at Jane for several quiet minutes. His head turned to look at the bandage on his hand. "That's why I—am I missing fingers?"

"Two, I'm told."

"Two. Kendrick is dead. An explosion? Dynamite? Why? Who would…"

Jane's heart panged as his expression changed dramatically. "Graham."

"Wait." He sat straighter, hissing in pain at the movement. "I remember—I took Joshua to work with me. Linh had—Linh?"

Linh had let out another loud sob at the mention of their son.

"Yes. You did take him to work with you." Jane swallowed against the lump in her throat. She twitched her nose against the tears threatening to erupt. "I'm so sorry, Graham. Joshua—he was killed in the explosion."

"*What?*" The baby startled at Graham's explosive shout. Jun let out a loud wail in response.

"Try to focus on Jun, and on Linh. They need you. I know it's worse than—"

"What the hell do you know? You don't know nothing about it. All your kids are alive."

Jane fought the urge to remind him she had children in the ground. Though she'd mourned deeply, neither pain was comparable to the other.

"Joshua." Graham's voice cracked.

Jane smoothed her hand over Graham's bald head when his features crumbled. "I can't begin to imagine how I would feel if this had happened to any of my children. I do understand the pain of loss, though. I know you must cling to what you do have with you. You will help each other in time. Cling to them, Graham. To your wife, your daughter."

"I will kill whoever did this."

"We'll make certain they're brought to justice." Jane let out a shaky breath.

"Linh," Graham whispered.

Jane took a step back when Linh curled against her husband. "I'll let you two have some time. I'll see that Bonnie brings you some food in a little while."

Graham nodded, pulling Linh even closer.

Jane closed the door softly. She leaned against the door frame with a heavy sigh. It was unclear whether the double vision was real or the warping of everything from the tears that burned her eyes. She closed her eyes to settle the feeling. Her fingers danced over her belly. There was no pain, no headache at the moment. She took comfort in that.

"Jane?" Andrew's quiet voice broke through her attempt to relax. "Are you feeling well?"

"Tired. Worried. Interminably sad." Jane opened her eyes, relieved to find the world righted again. "Graham is awake. I've told him about Joshua."

"How is he?" He glanced at the closed door. "Do I need to get a sedative?"

"Not at the moment. He has a very good sedative in the form of his daughter and wife right now." She turned her gaze down the hall where Sally's room sat. The door stood cracked open, but from where she stood Jane couldn't see the bed.

He followed her gaze. "I'm concerned for her recovery. With the melancholy, I fear she won't heal properly. I'd hoped to send her home in a few days to finish recuperating, but I worry it will hinder her further without her doctors reminding her to move."

"Perhaps. Perhaps not. I wonder if being around the children and Alma wouldn't help her find a way out of the melancholy. You'd be welcome to visit as often as necessary, or more than if you want to visit as a friend instead of her doctor." Jane turned her gaze back to the young doctor. "If you're agreeable to her going home in a few days, that is."

"If she shows improvement, we'll try it." Andrew paused at the sound of footsteps heading up the stairs.

Jane frowned when the person made their way to the top of the steps. She carefully forced away her frown to offer a neutral nod to the man. "Pastor Eckles."

"Mrs. Mitchell." Eckle gave her a look up and down. "At least that's what was told to me. You are in fact married now."

"Yes. We have been for some time. Your complaints that my children were bastards were for nothing. Not one of them was born out of wedlock."

Andrew's eyes widened at her comment. He didn't make a comment, staring at Jane in surprise.

"I would never call a child such a thing," Eckles protested in a sickly saccharine tone. "The children are gifts from the Lord."

"You appear to have forgotten I have ears. You also forget to ensure your surroundings are free of listeners before you try to preach. I've heard those words out of your lips myself, which means my children also have." Jane smoothed her hand over her stomach. "Besides, whether or not we had been married at the time of their birth, all of my children are deeply loved."

"The sins of the father are often cruelly bestowed upon the children. Look at young Joshua. It is the deepest of tragedies, but—"

"Excuse me?" Jane snapped to standing. Andrew's head whipped around to face the preacher as well.

"You cannot possibly mean that a good and just God saw fit to kill a child because of Graham?" The cruel statement had apparently startled Andrew out of silence. "I've only known him to be a good man, and a fair mayor."

"He ran a den of iniquity, just as Mrs. Mitchell here." Eckles eyed Jane. "No child should ever die in such a way, and the one that caused this should see his comeuppance for a horrible act upon an innocent. However, you yourself know that Mr. Cooke was not a 'good man'."

"I won't deny Graham had his struggles. There isn't a soul that doesn't. I imagine your life isn't free from sin itself, Pastor. Every man that strives to better himself is a better man for it. Graham worked hard, prayed hard, and in turn has become a good and just man of God."

"But is his wife a believer? Or a heathen like her people?"

Jane's jaw clenched. Anger coursed through her nerves like molten lava. A headache bloomed out of her sudden tension. "Perhaps you'd best be on to visit whomever you were set to visit, Pastor. I'd like to not say something I'd regret."

"We cannot change who we are at our core, Mrs. Mitchell. Thank you for giving evidence to my point. Pardon me, then. I'll go see Mr. Bosen." Eckles walked between them toward the patient room. He entered after a brief knock.

"That self-righteous prick," Jane spat before she could stop herself.

"I'd heard tell that Pastor Eckles took a harsh view on sinners. I never knew it was quite so blatant." Andrew set a hand on her arm. "I'll ask again. Are you well?"

"I was. I'm not any longer. I believe I need a lie down until I can calm myself properly."

"Then let's see to helping you lie down. This way."

"Maybe I should retire at home so Cole won't have a need to search for me."

"I'll assist you there."

"Thank you, Andrew."

*And for the season it was winter,
and they that know the winters of that country
know them to be sharp and violent,
and subject to cruel and fierce storms.
-William Bradford*

The wind hit the windows with a bold harshness that startled Jane back a step. She'd know the storm was coming. The entire town had watched it bearing down on them. The snow whipped past the windows until you could see nothing but white.

Jane paced in the nearly empty restaurant. Her hands clenched together to try to relieve some of her taut nerves. Cole had gone to help Andrew batten down the clinic. He'd not arrived back to the Inn before the storm hit.

"Have some tea." Cora set down a tray laden with tea and cakes. "We might as well use these up. They'll go to waste if we don't."

"They'll hardly go to waste with so many people here." Normally excited at the prospect of cakes, Jane sat automatically. She kept her gaze on the windows, though she'd never be able to see a thing through the blizzard.

"He'll make it home eventually." Cora poured them both tea.

"I know."

Cora set her hand on Jane's. "He'll make it home. If he was at the clinic, I'm certain he'll find a way to make himself at home until the storm lightens enough to attempt the trek home. At least this time you know where he is."

"True." Jane sipped her tea. Cora had a point. It wasn't like he was in an unknowable situation again. He was at the clinic. Sally was there, so was Graham. Though neither were in sparkling moods, at least he'd not be alone. "You're right. Thank you."

"I've no doubt it's difficult to be separated again so soon, even for however long this blizzard lasts."

"I've barely had him back a week. It's been so wonderful seeing him back doing all the things he does best."

"Including you." Cora blushed at her own statement.

Jane snorted, nearly spilling her tea in the process. "Cora Turner. That's the first time I've heard you make an inappropriate joke without prompting. Perhaps the tales of your rather vibrant courting aren't deception after all."

Cora didn't answer. Her brows rose as she sipped her tea. While her eyes were diverted, a rather secretive smile graced her lips.

"Oh, you have a little wicked in you for certain. You need to show it more often."

"I believe all of these years around you and Kat have been a bad influence."

"No, I don't believe that. I believe we've inspired you to remember what fun it is to be unfettered. You spent far too much time around Martha trying to behave."

"Speaking of Martha." Cora pulled a cake onto her plate. "I heard from her last month."

"You did? I didn't think anyone had heard from her in years, not even her own mother."

"Is that so surprising?"

"I suppose not. She didn't leave this town on happy turns, accused of treason, giving the dynamite to the Renegades. I've no doubt her relationship with her mother was never repaired as it has been for Kat."

"Precisely." Cora glanced around them for prying ears. The restaurant sat as quiet as it had since the storm hit. "She's had another child. According to the letter, she and Lewis really enjoy living their life among the tribe."

"Having only known the pious Martha that judged my choices, I find it hard to believe. However, I've heard nearly as many stories about her as I have you. The stories make it seem less impossible to find Martha enjoying daily life among Indians."

"Honestly, her relationship with Lewis was a surprise to us all." Cora's features softened as she spoke of the past. "Lewis was Kelly's best friend along with David. The three of them went around these hills all the time. No corner of the valley was safe."

Jane smiled at the idea of David running around the hills as a slightly wild young man. "David caused trouble?"

"All three of them. It's like Jesse, Isaac, and Jay about ten years from now. If you could imagine that."

"Clara's David? Sheriff David? No. I can't." Jane chuckled.

"He was great fun. At the time we thought Lewis was the odd man out. David and Martha courted for nearly two years, and Kelly and I were quite close right from the start." Cora sighed, a dreamy smile on her features. It got swept away almost as quick. "To this day I can't tell you when Martha started going around behind David's back. It was a shock even to me, and we were really close, I thought."

"You really had no idea?"

"None. It had to have been happening for months, probably longer, because Martha was showing within weeks of when they turned up married and pregnant. Poor David. I've never seen a man so heartbroken. At least until he came back and found you."

"David has mastered the sad puppy look." Jane tried to hide her smile. "It's a shame he had to learn it through multiple heartbreaks. I'm relieved he's found Lee. I don't think he'll have to face such heartbreak again."

"It took him far too long to find his happiness. He's a good man. Always was, too. Although when he was younger he had a certain measure of wickedness with his kindness."

"He still has it, he's simply an expert at hiding it. I've seen it a time or two." Jane's appetite had returned at the pleasant conversation. Though still worried about Cole not making it home, she at least knew he was safe, as Cora had said. She grabbed a cake from the tray. "Come to think of it, where are the boys?"

"They're making use of the third floor seeing as its empty. They're playing whatever games they can come up with, I imagine." Cora selected another cake before she refreshed both of their teas. "I'm certain they'll be down soon as it cools off. With no fires lit I don't imagine it will take too long."

In the interest of preserving coal and containing the heat, they'd closed off the third floor once their patronage had lessened after Christmas. They'd reopen it at the first sign of thaw. "I thought I'd locked that floor."

"Jesse is a sneaky, clever young man."

"Don't remind me—or rather, don't remind David." Jane laughed softly.

"I wouldn't. Though Jesse is much like he once was, he doesn't care for such reminders."

"At least David and Lee knew he was staying here tonight anyway so they needn't worry about him. Sally is safe in the clinic with Dr. Cross and Bonnie, and perhaps Cole."

"We're all safe and warm. We saw this storm coming for miles."

"That sense of quiet the town had as we all held our breath waiting for it to hit was nice." Jane grabbed another cake. "Although after being apart from Cole for over a month, the idea of being separated even a few days seems more than I can bear. That cold bed is unpleasant."

"I know the feeling." Cora leaned back in her seat. "You said we have four guests total remaining?"

"Yes. Four, all of whom are on the second floor. Then there's my brood, Michael, Nicholas, as well as my parents. James left on yesterday's train. Hopefully he didn't meet the storm on his way east. I'd hate to be stranded in a train car."

"It wouldn't be pleasant," Cora agreed. Her brow furrowed. "Why didn't Mike head to his own hotel? He had time."

"We weren't certain he would have the time. There was no way of knowing the storm would wait near forty-five minutes to hit. The last one slammed into us within ten minutes. We nearly lost a half-dozen people trying to make it home in time."

"True enough."

"I believe Nicholas wanted to stay so he wouldn't be in his home alone for the length of the storm. Much as he prefers to be alone to his own devices, he likes interaction and conversation from time to time."

"You mean he gets lonely."

"Yes." Jane soaked in the sweetness of her cake for a few moments. Though Cora appeared to be done, Jane snuck another onto her plate. "I imagine you get lonely as well."

"It's been almost four years since my Kelly passed, but yes. Especially these past months that Arthur has been off to college much of the time. Why do you think I spend so many hours here?"

"You love chaos? You did raise Isaac, after all."

Cora laughed warmly. "He is chaos in the body of a young man, for certain."

"You must be talking about Isaac." Mike approached the table with a warm smile. "For certain you aren't speaking of my nephews."

Jane tilted her head to accept his kiss to her cheek. "Jesse and Jay are plenty chaos when they get around Isaac. I worry for my third floor with those three running lose."

"Worry for the hotel. That tornado we had last summer has nothing on that trio." He gave Cora's shoulder a squeeze before he took a seat. "Where's Cole?"

"He went to help Andrew batten down the clinic. It appears he didn't make it home before the storm hit, unfortunately for me." Jane sighed deep as she could. "He does always help keep me plenty warm in a storm."

"Jane," Cora half-chided. Now that they were with another person, her wicked smile was accompanied by a delicate blush.

Mike leaned closer to Cora. "I do believe she says those things just to see if she can still make you blush. It's a game for her, and a pleasure for those that get to see you blush."

Jane cut her brother a look at the near-flirtatious comment. His expression remained neutral while he poured a cup of tea. Jane had noticed an uptick in his mood since her return from California. The bright moments such as these were few, though. To that end, she chose not to wonder at it too much, instead she'd enjoy it. She sipped her own tea. "Either way, I believe we'll gather in my living quarters for popcorn tonight. Popcorn and stories. The children say my pa has some of the best tales."

"They're mostly tall tales, but yes they are fun." Mike took a big bite of cake, then paused. A low moan rumbled from him. "This is delicious, Cora."

"It's an old family recipe." Cora's blush deepened with the aid of the compliment. "I have a secret that goes in it. I only lament I never had a girl to pass these recipes onto."

"Katherine says Cindy has been expressing interest in cooking and baking. Perhaps you can take her under your wing." Jane leaned forward. "You never know. Perhaps my Clara will be keener on cooking than I ever was."

"The world can only hope." Mike ducked from her swatting hand. "What? You forget I was on hand for your disastrous attempts at cooking."

Cora laughed when Mike gave a full-body shiver. "It can't have been that bad. You exaggerate to embarrass her."

"I wish that were true.. He embellishes nothing." Jane wrinkled her nose. "Those eggs were like shoe leather. My attempt at biscuits nearly burned down the homestead."

"Thankfully we were able to put the fire out quickly," Mike said through his laughter. "The look on Jane's face. I've never seen such defeat. She battled a madman but couldn't conquer flour and eggs."

Cora was laughing outright by then. "Oh no."

"It's true." Jane chuckled, remembering all to clear the utter dismay she'd felt. "Why else would I rely solely on your delicious cooking and not have a kitchen in my own apartment? I simply can't do it. I must accept my limitations, and cooking is one of them."

"You'll starve if left to your own devices?" Cora shook head. "What if I'd decided to remain at home for the storm?"

"I'd be in real trouble if neither you or Ma were here. You can't ever leave, Cora. I don't know what I'd do without your good food."

"Luckily I have no intention of leaving. I've no doubt you'd find someone to replace me, though. I don't think you'd ever truly starve." Cora rose as she polished off her tea. "Speaking of, I should get started on supper. I've got a lot to cook for."

"Let me help." Mike gathered the tray.

Jane furrowed her brow at her brother. "You're going to cook?"

"What of it?" Mike set his own cup on the tray.

"Ma will be here in about fifteen minutes. She said she wasn't going to let Cora feed this army on her own."

"Then I'll assist her in cleaning up." He swiped the cake from her hands and stuffed it in his mouth.

"Michael!" Jane rose to go after him, but the baby made her too slow to get anywhere near him. "I'll get you for that."

The door clattered, startling a small shriek from her. Fearing something had been blown into the door, she moved closer. Another clatter shook the door on its hinges. Then it burst open, and someone burst inside. The heaved the door closed so hard it slammed back in place.

Jane stared at the snow-covered person turning the locks. "Cole?"

He turned to face her. Ice and snow covered him from head to foot until his black coat appeared white.

She rushed forward to peel the muffler form his face. "My goodness. I'd made my peace with believing you'd remain at the clinic until the storm lightened."

"And m-miss a chance t-t-to keep you warm?" His teeth chattered through his wicked grin. Snow clung to his eyebrows and eyelashes.

"It looks like it'll be me warming you up, Mr. Mitchell."

"B-b-bully for m-me."

The foolish man wonders at the unusual,
but the wise man at the usual.
—Ralph Waldo Emerson

Cole stood in the doorway of the Inn. He was supposed to be keeping an eye out for riders returning from the searches of the surrounding area. While he was keeping one eye outside, the rest of his attention focused on the antics inside the lobby.

Somehow Jane had managed to get all the tables and chairs out of the way. The restaurant and lobby area sat completely clear. Then she'd roped the entire family, all their guests, plus Cora and her boy into a rather large game of Blind Man's Bluff.

At the moment Jane herself had the blindfold on and tried to tag anyone that passed near. He chuckled low as Jesse, Willow, and Jay all managed to escape her reaching hands while darting close enough to hit her skirts.

The blizzard had blown over during the night. The sudden silence woke them out of a dead sleep. That morning he'd met with David and many of the men in town to set up search teams. After every storm they liked to ensure everyone had made it through the storm all right.

Due to his lingering leg injury, Cole got volunteered to remain in town to take census as the search teams came back in from the surrounding valley. He didn't mind so much. Although working with Davie had been an odd thing for him. He still didn't like the goody-two-shoes all that much. Still, with Graham laid up in the clinic Cole felt he should step up in the absence of the mayor.

In fact, he'd been gathering his coat before Jane could even make the suggestion. The look she'd given him when he told her where he was going had made him want to stay to take full advantage of her affections.

Instead, he'd followed through with his plans. He contented himself with the fact he'd get his reward soon enough. Jane would see to it, she always had.

He chuckled under his breath when Eunice tagged the back of Jane's skirts before getting away from her spinning daughter. If it weren't for the pure joy and laughter on her face, he'd worry about her keeping her strength up during the activity.

Her face flushed, a smile wide as it ever was, and her laughter kept him where he stood. He knew Eunice would let Jane win if she began to get tired.

He glanced out the door again for sign of someone approaching. The waiting game might be a necessary part, but it annoyed him. He'd rather be out there doing the searching.

The disappearance of the blizzard had left behind unseasonably warm weather. That made many folks eager to get out and about, but until the search parties were back it was best to stay in once place.

Jane had concocted the giant game that took over their lobby to do just that.

Cole turned at the sound of a whistle. A cutter slid smooth along Main to a stop in front of the Inn. Zeb hopped out with his nephew, Ian. "The ranches are intact. All hands accounted for. Marv Keenan said they lost some cattle, but Coleman is in the clear. Asked about his sister. I told him everyone at the clinic was doing fine."

"Thanks, Zeb." Cole checked the ranches off his list. Considering the losses both ranches had suffered the past year, it was good to know they'd weathered the storm well enough. "Still waiting on a few more reports. Can you take the cutter back to Henry's place? I'm sure his hands will get it put up proper."

"Will do. Ian, go open the shop. People'll be out and about in no time, especially seeing as they're clearin' the streets." Zeb hopped back into the cutter. He raced back down Main toward Fourth.

Sure enough down on Miner's Row a team of men worked on clearing the streets of snow. A great new plan of Jane and her ladies that was double edged. Great for the townsfolk who walked everywhere or used horses. Not as good for those from the outer areas like the settlement and the homesteads they were checking. If they used cutters or sleighs, they had to stop at the meadow and continue on foot.

Still, Cole appreciated it. Made it easier for the locals to get to the casino for gambling. Depending on how fast the team worked, the cutters wouldn't make it to the Inn's porch.

The next two cutters rode up together. Teddy didn't bother getting out of his cutter. "Settlement is clear. Those in the lodge were more than ready to get out for some fresh air, but everyone is accounted for."

"Thanks, Teddy. We still got a few teams out, but that's our biggest worry. Appreciate the help." Coel nodded to the next cutter. Inside was one of the stable hands from the Inn. He'd been filling in for Archie since he was injured. Jane had even hired someone to replace him, expecting him to help Archie indefinitely. "Noah. You'll get these two cutters put up at the livery?"

"Sure thing. I gotta get to work anyway. Horses need cared for." Noah let out a whistle and both cutters turned to head down Main toward the livery.

A hand touched his back. Jane leaned over his arm to glance at his list before she lifted her gaze to his. "I finally managed to catch Ma. Although I believe she took pity on me."

"Maybe she thought you looked tired and needed to sit." Cole leaned down to meet her kiss. The happiness remained in her eyes, but her features were drawn now that she wasn't in the middle of the game. "Because you do."

"I've done nothing but laze around the apartment for days."

"That ain't all."

Pink dotted her cheeks, her gaze locked with his. "True. I did enjoy keeping my husband warm as well."

"He enjoyed keeping you warm."

"I'm quite aware." She leaned closer. "Shame it's so warm today."

"We'll leave the stove off tonight so we need to warm each other."

"I doubt we'll need to do such a thing. We'll make do nicely enjoying each other's company, no need to freeze ourselves."

"So long as we're enjoying ourselves, I'll take it."

"We will. I have no doubt." She leaned against the wall beside him. "My point being, I have been very well behaved as of late. A little game of Blind Man's Bluff isn't going to hurt."

"Little game? That's no little game."

"I honestly didn't expect every single person in the Inn to participate. It's rather fun, and surprisingly challenging with so many players." Jane's gaze drifted over his shoulder. "It would appear the Sheriff has returned."

Sure enough, David and Mike approached in one of the wagons that had been fitted with runners like a sleigh. Neither man appeared particularly happy. Cole moved onto the porch so the men wouldn't have to shout. "They were checking the eastern homesteads. Don't look none too happy, do they?"

"No. They certainly don't." Jane joined Cole on the steps when the wagon drew near. "Good morning, David. Michael."

Cole eyed the blanket in the back. It was clearly bodies. "Who'd you find?"

"They Lyman's. They were out in the storm." David's brow furrowed. "It was odd."

"How so?" Jane's hand tightened on Cole's arm. "People get lost in storms."

"Thing is, they weren't lost at all." David's back hunched as he fiddled with the reins. "They were sitting outside their own homestead, less than a foot from the door. They definitely weren't confused by the storm, their backs were to the homestead like they just sat there waiting for the storm to hit."

"What?" Jane's hand flew to her chest. "Why in heavens would they do that?"

"No idea. I'm taking them to the clinic. They're frozen stiff." David winced.

"I doubt there's anything the doctor's can do, but we've seen people recover from being frozen back in New York. When we were kids they got one out of the river frozen near solid. The man went on to live another twenty years once he thawed out proper."

"From being frozen?" Cole's stomach churned at the idea. "Really?"

"Really. I guess the body goes to some lengths to protect itself. It doesn't happen often, but once in a while one of them comes back. Charles will know what to do if there's anything to be done." Mike glanced in the back. "In good news, the children weren't there. We found them at a neighbor's, the Sanders. Said Fred and Betty dropped the children off when they first saw the storm coming."

"How incredibly strange." Jane approached the wagon bed. "They sent their children off and then sat outside their homestead? What on earth?"

"Leave the wondering to your brother." David squeezed Jane's shoulder. "When he gets back, of course."

"Of course." Jane backed up the steps to Cole's side. Her hand resumed its tight hold of his arm.

"What about the rest of the homesteads?" Cole glanced east where the two men had been searching. "Did you get through them all?

"We did. All six families accounted for. The only ones that had any trouble were these two." David straightened, reins in hand. "I'll get them to the clinic and come back here to double check our list."

"So far everyone's reporting back that everyone is safe. We had plenty of time before the storm hit, so that's a blessing." Cole waved them off as the wagon slid across the street.

Jane wrapped her arm around his waist, her gaze on the wagon as it pulled to a stop in front of the clinic. "Why on earth would someone willingly sit out in such a storm. I mean, certainly they had to have been unable to find the door. Right?"

"One would think." Cole ran his hand along her back. He hoped the small reassurance helped keep her calm. She was already tired, he didn't want her getting ill on top of it. "Why don't you sit down? You look a little pale."

"It's just shock." She sat on a bench despite her protest. "At least so far everyone else is safe. Let's hope it stays that way."

"It will." Cole took a seat beside her, stretching out his injured leg. "We had near an hour warning before the blizzard really hit. No way people weren't prepared."

"People new to the area might not have been. They might not have had enough supplies or coal to sustain them."

"Who's new enough around here to not know?"

"The Filch's south of town. They just moved here this past summer and come from Texas. They don't have any experience with true winters."

"Tommy's checking on the southern homesteads. We'll know soon enough if they made it, and if they need supplies. I'm sure that's your burning question."

"I'm going to assist if I can."

"You always do."

Time will explain it all.
He is a talker, and needs
no questioning before he speaks.
—Euripides

Jane stood on porch of the mercantile. Observing the town while she leaned on the railing. The unseasonably warm weather had continued in the few days since the blizzard to the point where nearly all the snow had melted. The ache in her ankle told her winter wasn't done with them, but she was going to enjoy the weather while it lasted.

Based on the bustle of folks moving through town, she wasn't the only one determined to enjoy the weather. People long hidden away in the snow and darkness of the winter months wandered the streets.

A large crowd of men that worked for Hammy before his demise now moved through the destruction of the undertakers and cooper shop. Teddy led the group to clean up the mess as well as Hammy ever had.

Jane remained content to allow the entire town believe he'd fully taken over the business, for that was her plan. For a year he'd run under her to be sure he could handle the business aspect as well as the actual construction work. She planned at that point to sign it over to him for mere pennies. Until then she ran the books and suggested order of projects but left Teddy to the rest of it.

They hoped to clean away all of the rubble from the explosion and the church fire before the next storm hit. If it went to plan they would begin construction on all three buildings at the first true spring. There was so much work to be done in the town, Jane had encouraged Teddy to look for more workers in the spring. Even if they were only temporary, they'd need the help.

The church and undertakers would take precedence as essential businesses in the town. Whether or not Graham returned to his work remained to be seen, but if he didn't they'd find someone else to deal with the backup of burials. Including Hammy's.

Jane's next perusal of the street found a familiar face climbing the steps to the mercantile. She smiled her greeting. "Reverend Greene."

"Jane. It's good to see you out and about."

"It's good to be seen. I don't care for being cooped up," she leaned in to mutter an aside, "or being ordered to do nothing by doctors."

"You never did like sitting still. It's a good day for exploring."

"It certainly is a most beautiful day. Most of the town appears to feel the same."

"For certain. My walk here took quite a bit longer than expected. I've been stopped no less than ten times by parishioners that have been hiding away in the winter weather."

"At least they haven't forgotten in their hibernation."

He nodded. "It is a blessing to have a wonderful congregation to tend to."

"Where would Reverend Lyons be? I'd expect him to be enjoying the sounds and scents of the town come to life. Moreso, it isn't often I see you around with Eli close at hand."

"Eli chose to visit those of our congregation in the clinic. He's assured me he could make it from room to room. I'm not one to hinder his steps toward independence."

Jane was delighted to hear it. "I'm so glad he's adjusting to his loss of sight so well."

"More in some ways than others. He's taking steps. It's quite pleasing. His favorite time is reading the bible together. I start a passage, and he attempts to finish. I believe he wishes for your memory in those times."

"I believe many wish the same. If I could explain how I do it, I would."

"No explanation necessary. It's a gift from God."

"Ah yes, but it's a little double edged. There are some things I wish I could forget, and others I wish I could remember." Jane sighed softly. "I have resigned myself to the fact that such memories will never return."

"Because many blessings came with the loss."

"A great many." She glanced back to the mercantile. "Shopping today?"

"I agreed to come get some necessities for our home and the church."

She glanced at him in surprise. "Church?"

"Yes. Another reason I'm glad I ran into you. Teddy has offered us use of the new cooper shop he and Hammy were building on Fourth Street. It's right next to the home we've been using. It wasn't designed as a church, but it will suffice for its purpose as a temporary home."

"Well, I admit I'll miss only having to step out my door to get to your service." Jane grinned at his chuckle. Ever since Christmas they'd been using the casino as a church, which meant Jane only had to leave her apartment to get to service. "It has made this tired and lazy pregnant woman quite happy to not have to go far for services."

"You are anything but lazy, Jane."

"Perhaps. I've felt it of late. I do know that you'll feel better having a place that is solely for services."

"You've been very generous to allow us use of the casino these past several weeks."

"It's hardly generous. We don't use the casino on Sundays, so it was no trouble at all."

"I thank you anyhow."

"You're quite welcome." Jane glanced back toward the bustling, shouting crowd of workers. "I imagine this corner and the church will be cleaned before it snows again."

"You think winter will return?"

She massaged her leg as the ache flared again. "With another blizzard if my ankle is any indication. I only hope we get as much warning this time."

"It was pleasant to know everyone had time to make it to shelter."

"Yes it was." She spotted Cole limping his way to the clinic. "I'll let you get to your shopping. I should go see how Cole's leg is healing."

"Our prayers are with him."

"Thank you." She hightailed it to the clinic fast as she could. Unfortunately, many calls of greeting delayed her passage long enough that by the time she got inside the clinic there was no sign of call. All of the exam room doors were closed. "Blast it."

Rather than interrupt exams that might not be her husband's, she took a seat in the waiting area. She hoped Charlie would get Cole just right so he'd yell. Then she'd be able to find him easily. Then again, she didn't want him hurting that badly. Maybe only a little badly.

The front door slammed open. A man so filthy she barely recognized him filled the frame. He barely glanced at her before he opened his mouth to yell, "*Doc*! There's a cave-in."

Jane jumped to her feet as every exam room door flew open.

Charlie rushed out of one room, bag in hand. "We'll need all hands—"

"Nah. Just one of ya," Benji argued. "One man in the mine. Buried himself."

"*What*?" Jane stepped toward where Cole hovered in a doorway. "What do you mean?"

"Excuse me." Charlie bustled past Benji to head to the mines.

"We was leavin' for lunch. Near 'bout everybody was out but Ronnie, me and Joe. Joe and I was leaving, but Ronnie didn't come. I was askin' him why when he took a sledgehammer to the support. Joe and I barely got out."

Cole's hand encompassed Jane's. He gave it a squeeze. "You said he knocked out the support? On purpose?"

"Sure as shittin' did."

"Benji, do you need checked by the doctor? You're bleeding." Jane glanced back to where Andrew, Bonnie, and Lydia remained standing at their doors.

"Nah. Was a small rock that hit me. Mostly stopped now. I ain't no more right in the head than I was before." Benji waved and disappeared from the doorway.

Jane turned to Cole. "Your leg."

"It'll wait. I'll come by after lunch." Cole nodded to the others. "They'll send someone if Charlie needs help."

Jane leaned into him when his arm slipped around her waist. All three doors closed, leaving them alone. She took a shaky breath. "On purpose?"

"I'm guessing you'll want to talk to Tommy now."

"He should know what's happened. Hopefully Andrew will tell Sally."

"Tom'll do it. Anything to get her back moving again." Cole's features sank into a frown. He glanced toward the stairs before guiding Jane to the door. "She's still got no fight."

"There are times when she almost does, but then it fades away. I keep hoping her natural curiosity will bring her back out of where she's hiding in herself. It's not happened yet." Jane shook her head. "Between the Lyman's odd incident and this with Ron, perhaps she'll stir to life once again."

He paused on the porch alongside her. Both of them stared into the distant hills where the mining equipment kept running, though the swarm of people had come to a standstill.

"Jane," Tommy called as he rounded the corner. "Shouldn't you be resting?"

"I'm fine. I was out enjoying the day." Jane turned to face him. "We were on our way to look for you."

"I was at the brothel. Garit has to leave town for a couple weeks so Wil and I were working out a schedule." Tom pulled out a cigar, holding it out to Cole. "From Wil. Says it's his last until Garit returns from his trip."

"Thanks." Cole tucked it in his pocket. At Jane's curious look, he winked. "Can't get them outside of New York. My guess is Garit is heading east to visit family and picking more up."

"Ah." Jane turned her attention back to Tommy. "How long will Garit be gone if he's going all the way back east?"

"Likely two weeks, maybe longer. His pa fell sick." Tom raised a brow. "Now, what is it you wanted to find me for?"

"Another oddity has happened." She looked back toward the west. "At the mines."

"Oddity? I don't like the sound of that."

"You shouldn't." Cole's frown deepened. "According to Benji, Ronnie Jones knocked out a support. Caved in the mine on himself when everyone left for lunch?"

"Come again?"

"It sounds as though Ronald Jones just killed himself." Jane turned back to her brother. "Much as it appears the Lyman's did the same, although Betty still lingers in between death and life."

"And unwilling to explain what happened as of yet." Tommy shook his head. "Excuse me."

Jane sighed as he barreled into the clinic. "Well then, Sally should know in short order."

"Think it'll help?"
"We can only hope."

What is called resignation
is confirmed desperation.
—Henry David Thoreau

Sally half rose from the bed when she heard the miner shout about a cave-in. Her body moved stiff and sore, but she made it to her feet. The burst of energy and curiosity both quickly faded once standing.

She settled back into the bed. The stack of books Jane had brought her remained untouched. The fresh notebook and journal she'd also brought had met the same fate. They all sat at her bedside unopened. Not one pencil mark in either.

She couldn't bring herself to resume her activities from before. Every time she even thought about it, Molly immediately sprang to mind. The cost was too high. So many people had died, including one that had trusted her to have her back.

The sounds of the clinic quickly returned to normal quiet activity in no time. Sally sank deeper into her covers, pulling them high as possible.

Heavy footsteps pounded up the stairs a few minutes later. Tommy entered her room without so much as a knock. He didn't say a word to her. His features were furrowed in anger as he paced the length of her room. Quiet mutterings she could make no sense of filled the air.

He paused at the foot of her bed. Mouth open as if to speak, but he clamped it shut instead. The pacing resumed. Back and forth, and again.

Sally couldn't deny the spark of curiosity that rose at this abnormal behavior from him. Rather than give voice to it, for curiosity was dangerous, she drew her gaze away from the man wearing a hole in her floor.

Earlier in the day Andrew had opened the curtains to reveal the bright, sunny day outside. He'd told her it was rather warm out, and tried to get her to the balcony.

Part of her hated how she'd been treating her friend of late. He remained determined to help, but she didn't want any assistance. Perhaps she should, but something was missing.

"We cleaned out Molly's room." Tommy's voice was gravelly with an emotion she couldn't place. The admittance drove the knife of pain deeper in her chest. Like a Pinkerton in no time it was like she had never existed. Perhaps because for all the rest of the world knew, Molly Malone hadn't existed.

Laney was a real person. Someone out there would care. Sally wondered if anyone had bothered to tell her true family. If she had any. Her heart lodged in her throat again at the renewed acknowledgement that she hadn't truly known Molly. The protest that cleaning out Molly's room happened too soon faded before she could form it.

"I sent her personals to her aunt. That woman was the only family she had left, besides us." Tommy leaned on the footboard. "I kept her wigs and incidentals. They've been put in storage for the time being."

Molly had an aunt. Some real family. That was more than Sally had ever known.

"Her ma got killed right in front of her. She was young, maybe ten, twelve at best. Did you know that?"

"I didn't know anything," Sally whispered. "Nothing at all. She never told me anything of import. Not even that she had an aunt somewhere."

"That's how we live, Sally. The only reason anyone around here knows me is because my family is here. We're meant to forget who we were. I never was good at that part." Tommy didn't look up from his hard gaze on his own hands. They gripped the footboard so tight his knuckles were white. "Do you really think I told everyone I met about me?"

"She—" She pinched her lips together to silence the argument. Nothing she said would make a difference. He didn't understand. She had known all of that, and in the end it hadn't mattered. Her inability to know more about Molly had been their downfall. She hadn't been able to believe Molly had feelings about her, and in the end it had killed her, and Sally's spirit right along with it. "It doesn't matter."

"Obviously it matters to you."

"It doesn't matter." Now that she had enough strength and range of motion to do so, she turned on her side to avoid looking at him. "Not anymore."

He growled in frustration. The bed shook when he pushed away from it to resume his pacing. Back and forth again and again until he dropped into he chair right in her line of vision. "It seems Ron Jones killed himself."

This time she couldn't shove aside her curiosity. Why on earth would he kill himself? How? Did this have something to do with the miner shouting about the cave-in? She stared at Tommy in disbelief. "What?"

"You heard me right."

"But—why—what?"

"Word is he made sure the mine was nearly empty for lunch. Then he went and knocked out the support beam beside him. We might not have known what happened, but there was a witness."

A witness. Something they hadn't had yet for the oddities of Miss Bee or the most recent event of the Lyman's. Sally pushed herself back to sitting. That meant the past few deaths had been suicides, not murders. "Why?"

"No idea. Strange though, isn't it?"

Unbidden, her mind raced over the past year. The bulk of her notes ran through her head as easily as if she'd read them mere hours ago. Probably because she'd been running through them over and over for weeks.

The only connections she'd come up with had been whores and the good men of God from their church. Those connections no longer made sense. The Lyman's and Ron all went to Glorious Valley church, much like Miss Bee had. If they were dying, things made even less sense than they had before.

She'd been right. She wasn't any good at this. Defeat dragged her back down into the bed. "Strange as anything else that's happened. No more, no less."

"Sure it is."

"I know what you're trying to do. It won't work. I don't care."

"I need your help on this. Even more than I did before."

"No. You don't. You work alone. Always have."

"Sally."

"Stop it." Her voice cracked at the strength of her protest. "I don't care."

"Whoever did this tried to kill you, remember?" Tommy leaned closer. "They did kill Daisy. Worse, they killed Joshua, an innocent child. They killed Molly."

"Get out of my face."

"No."

Sally screwed her eyes shut rather than look at him any longer. She didn't think could bear to witness his disappointment in her. Every inch of her body ached, but the worst ache of all remained in her heart. "Please."

"Sally." Disappointment dragged all energy from his tone. He sighed heavily. A warm hand settled on her cold one. "I don't know how to help you out of this if you won't let me."

"Maybe I don't want out."

"You will. You'll become bored and get tired of this nothingness. Eventually you'll need more." He squeezed her hand gently. "You said you would help me in figuring out your notes. Will you at least do that?"

"Please go away." Sally pried her hand free of his. "Please."

A gentle knock interrupted whatever Tommy might have said. Another voice she didn't care to hear right then spoke instead, "Sally? Oh, Mr. Young."

"Call me Tommy, Matthew. Come in. Sally's not much in the visiting mood, but she should know we're here anyway." Tommy ignored the glare she gave him. He smiled bright as anything when he stood to shake hands with her newest guest. As if he hadn't just been partially scolding her, partially worrying over her. "She'll probably be nasty to you. I hope you can handle that."

"Have you met my sister?" Matthew came into her line of sight as he shook Tommy's hand. He grinned as well, a bit of a wicked gleam to his eye that reminded Sally why she'd been so attracted to him. "She's got a heck of a nasty temper on her when she's of a mind. I think I can handle it. I've not come to see her because she's had the doctors send me away. This time there wasn't anyone downstairs to stop me. I imagine she'll be plenty upset I'm here."

"I'm right here," Sally grumbled. Much as she wasn't in the mood for company, she didn't appreciate being spoken about as if she wasn't right in front of them.

"She speaks." Matthew turned his full attention on her. "I've been worried about you."

"Nothing to worry about." Sally dragged her gaze away from his intense stare. Much like the shock of the news of Ron, Matthew seemed able to awaken parts of her she'd rather remain quiet. It was because of those feelings she'd fought with Molly. "You have more important things to worry about."

"Think I should be the judge of what's important enough to worry about." Matthew took the seat Tommy had abandoned. He smirked as Tommy chuckled behind him. "But thank you for your opinion."

Sally rolled to her back. She'd rather stare at the ceiling than face the two men determined to drag her out of her melancholy. "You've seen me. I'm well enough. You can go about your business now."

"My schedule is clear the next couple of hours. My foreman is minding the ranch and Stephen is at school." Matthew didn't rise at her dismissal. He settled into the chair more comfortably. The quick glance she took proved he stared intently at her, even though his words were directed at Tommy. "Quite a bustle around town right now. Heard talk of a mine cave-in?"

"Minor one," Tommy confirmed. "One man trapped, seems as though he wanted to be."

"Wanted to be?" That drew Matthew's intense gaze away.

"He knocked out the support beam himself."

"Desperate men will do desperate things." Matthew turned back to her. His expression wavered in a confusing mix of anger and grief. Sally had to fight the urge to reach toward him. "Wonder what could have made him so desperate."

"Grief," Sally whispered without meaning to. "Or guilt."

Tommy didn't seem to hear her. "Could have been a lot of things."

Matthew, on the other hand, stared her down. The breathtaking pale green eyes softened. He offered her a sad smile.

"I'll have to look into his situation. Maybe he had some debts he couldn't pay." Tommy resumed pacing behind Matthew.

Matthew's fingers brushed the back of her hand, then reached out to touch the apple of her cheek. That's when she realized her cheek was damp from tears. He brushed along her cheek twice more before he pulled back as though he hadn't touched her. All the while Tommy talked out loud, jotting notes in his notebook. Matthew cleared his throat. "Are you hungry, Sally?"

"No." It was a flat out lie, and soon as she'd said it her stomach rumbled in protest.

Matthew chuckled low. The sound warmed a little of the cold around her heart. "Are ya sure about that?"

"No."

Tommy slapped his notebook shut. "I'll go get some grub. Do you think you can get the lazy one out of bed so she can eat like a human?"

"I'll do my best." Matthew nodded to Tommy as he left. Once he was gone, Matthew slid from the chair to kneel in front of her. His head tilted to be the same angle as hers. Once again his fingers brushed along her cheek. "Just tell me one thing."

"What?"

"Are you that desperate?"

Sally's eyes tightened in the fight against fresh tears. The lump in her throat hardened until she had to swallow against it. Her grief seemed unending, the joy she'd found in life for the past year seemed so far. Still, she hadn't truly thought about ending it all as Ron had. Passing thoughts had happened, sure, but to truly think of ending it? Her stomach churned, but she shook her head.

"Promise me you aren't."

"Why?"

"Please, Sally. I'll let ya keep telling them to send me away all ya want, but I need to know you ain't that desperate."

She closed her eyes against the flood of tears. They trickle along her face anyway. "I'm not…most of the time."

"Sometimes you are."

"Sometimes." She'd never admit it to Tommy, or Ma. Something in the look Matthew had given her after she'd given reason told her he'd understand somehow.

His hand rested on hers. "Then let me check on ya. Every day. I don't gotta stay long, but I need to know you ain't that desperate. I've seen it before, and I don't ever wanna see it again."

Her eyes fluttered open to meet his. "You have? Who?"

"You don't get that story until ya start letting me be your friend again."

"I can't."

"You can. And ya will. That's my promise."

"You can't promise that."

"I just did."

Hope is necessary in every condition.
–Samuel Johnson

Jane rocked in the chair, knitting needles flying. It annoyed her to no end that of all things her mother had tried to teach her she'd picked up on this instead of cooking. However, when she'd been ordered to sit as much as possible this had been her mother's solution. Knowing she'd hate being still, Eunice had urged her toward knitting. It seemed Clara had been terrible at it. Of course, it figured Jane would be able to pick it up.

Perhaps it was the precision needed to maintain the pattern and tension, or the mere fact she could memorize the pattern with a simple read-through.

Either way, she'd found it a good way to keep moving while being still. Reading was always preferred, but she found she could do both if she propped her book properly. At the moment she had no book, only the quiet room and Sally's sullen company.

Though Andrew had cleared Sally to go home so long as they could follow instructions, Sally refused to leave. It surprised Jane. She thought in her current mood Sally would prefer to lock herself in her room and refuse all company.

According to Andrew and Tommy, Matthew Coleman had been consistently by every day since the cave-in. Rather, since Sally's injury, but she'd stopped turning him away after Ron Jones death. He never stayed long, only a few minutes each day. At least Sally had ceased refusing his visits.

The sheets rustled at a moment from Sally. She turned to lie on her back, staring at the ceiling. A silent sigh made her chest rise and fall.

Jane paused her knitting to study the young woman she felt as close to as if she were her own daughter. She gathered her knitting to set in the basket beside her. Without a word she got herself to her feet. She moved to the bed quietly.

The swell of her belly gave her some difficulty in stretching out beside Sally. Jane persisted until she'd pulled Sally into her arms. When Sally curled into her, Jane held her quietly. She didn't push Sally to speak, explain or defend herself. That wasn't what she needed.

For a good ten minutes Jane held her, stroking her hair gently. It wasn't her place to break the silence. Sally's struggles were forefront now, and Jane imposing herself on the girl would have her retreating even further. Tommy's attempts had proven as much.

Sally broke the silence with a quiet, "Ma?"

"Yes, Sally?"

"How did you do it?"

Jane pondered the question. There were many things that could be the root of it. "Do what?"

"Keep going? I mean, all you went through…"

"I've had dark times, if that's what you mean."

"And then some."

Jane chuckled softly. "I suppose you're right. Dark times is an understatement. I did die once or came as close as was possible."

"Not that."

Jane thought back on her living memory. "I suppose you're right. Those weren't my darkest moments. When I lost my baby the first time, I didn't want to come back. I struggled greatly when the saloon burned as well."

"Your brother was killed—because of you."

She sighed deeply. That particular situation was not in her list of darkest moments, she hated to say. "Unfortunately as cold as it sounds, that wasn't difficult for me. I never knew George so I didn't have the sense of loss as I would have had it been Michael, or any other brother these days. That isn't to say I don't feel deep guilt for it."

"How did you do it? Go on."

"I don't know that there is a *how* to it. Life wasn't going to stop moving forward simply because I didn't want it to. I had to learn how to live past what had happened. I clung to whatever bit of life I could. No matter what it was. Katherine came into my life soon after I lost the baby. She was of great help and comfort to me."

"And George?"

"I suppose getting vengeance was what drove me then. That and seeing Cole again. When I was left in that cellar I thought it was over, done with. I tried for hours to escape, but I couldn't make the door budge. I believe that's the first time

I truly gave up. Then Thomas arrived and I was able to fight again."

"Vengeance?"

"Yes, vengeance. Not revenge." Jane didn't cease offering comfort by stroking Sally's hair. "That's an important distinction."

"How so?"

"Revenge would have been solely for what was done to me. I wanted the chance to make things right for everyone in the best way I could. I couldn't ever give Jesse back the years he lost, nor David. I couldn't return George to his family, but I could help to see that no one else would be in danger again. I learned to rely on those around me, and we took care of it."

"It doesn't seem worth it. After everything is lost."

"I wasn't fast enough to save George, or that vagrant Bingham murdered, but I still fought. I had to see it finished. Same with the Inn. We didn't figure out what was going on in time to save Mel, the saloon, or even what happened to you and Thomas."

Sally sniffled, wiping her tears on Jane's bodice.

"The people of this town were what gave me hope then. *You* gave me hope by rescuing Thomas at risk to yourself. You proved you were a fighter. You *are* a fighter. I know it feels as though your world is crumbling and every decision you've ever made was wrong. There are only two paths here now. You can let them win, or you can fight harder."

"She told me she loved me."

"Molly did?"

Sally nodded, burying her face in Jane's shoulder.

Jane sighed softly, resting her cheek on Sally's head. It was making a little more sense now. But why would Matthew be coming by? Why did she find him at Sally's bedside upon her return home? "And what happened then?"

"I didn't know her. How could I have…"

"You told her you didn't feel the same?"

"How-how could I?"

"The young man visiting you?"

Sally sobbed into Jane's shoulder. It was several minutes before she managed to speak again. "She…Molly…jealous."

"I see. That's what you fought about?" Jane didn't press further when Sally only nodded. The young woman continued crying against Jane. "My dear girl. You're not at fault for not sharing the same love. You did love her, perhaps only as a friend, much like Katherine and myself. Not loving someone in the same way doesn't make you an awful person."

"We fought—and she went—hurting—and I was cruel—she died." Each short phrase was punctuated by a hiccup.

"It's tragic you didn't get to find resolution. I'm so sorry for that loss, but you mustn't forget you and Molly shared a dear friendship. It was a kinship that gave you much laughter, joy, and even love. You can be grateful for that."

"My fault."

"No, Sally. It isn't your fault. The men that killed her, it's their fault. Not yours. From what Thomas tells me, Molly excelled at her job. He told me she was one of the best fighters he'd seen until you."

"It was…like a dance." Sally sniffled. Her tears slowed as she settled more calmly against Jane's shoulder. "She fought both of them at once. It was beautiful until…"

"I've seen you fight. I can well imagine it was like a dance." Jane followed Sally's gaze to the window. This was a pain she couldn't take from Sally, though she wished she could. The best she could do was to try to help her through. "What happened was infinitely tragic, especially with its timing, but what happened between you and Molly does not make her death your fault."

"It feels like it is."

"That's a feeling that's difficult to get past, but in time you will. You have plenty of life left here, and you must choose what to do with it. You have time to consider what your future might hold. For now, you must choose what to do about the case you dropped in Thomas' lap."

"I don't think I can. I wasn't quick enough and they're all dead."

"You aren't dead. They tried to kill you. Twice."

"I didn't die."

"No, you didn't. So will you choose to live?"

Toward no crime have men shown themselves so cold-bloodedly cruel as in punishing differences of belief.
-Russell Lowell

"I think, maybe, she'll come home in a few days." Jane turned to face Cole. "It would seem she actually appreciates the visits from Mr. Coleman and doesn't think they'll remain the same when she returns to the chaos of home."

Cole spotted the young man she'd just mentioned leaving the clinic. The cowboy raked his fingers through his hair before he replaced his hat on his head. He leapt onto his horse and rode off around the corner toward his ranch. "There something between 'em?"

"I believe perhaps there could be. At the moment Sally's too overwhelmed with what happened to Molly to face any such thing. She feelings guilty about having any feelings for him." She pressed into him in a way designed to distract him completely. "Must you work at the brothel tonight?"

He groaned low at the sight before him. Her blue eyes set up toward him through her lashes. She'd graced him with the pleasure of wearing a low-cut dress so her breasts swelled as she leaned into him. He tugged her close. "You don't play fair. You know it's my turn. Tommy's been over there the past two nights."

"If there's a bright side, it's that there will be no more charade of you getting cozy with the beautiful young Buttercup when you're there."

"Only one I'm getting cozy with is you." He tapped a finger under her chin. When she lifted her gaze, he brushed his lips across hers. "No more pretending, Mrs. Mithell."

"No more pretending. I rather like it."

"Also means less scandal."

"And so you went and ruined it." She sighed softly, arching until her breasts pillowed against him again. "I suppose I should return inside."

"Evil woman."

"Evil man." She smiled wickedly. The distraction of her breasts had kept him from realizing how she'd been maneuvering. Her fingers danced along his length. Tingles of excitement coursed through him. He'd already been hard, and she had to go making things worse. "I can feel you though my layers. It's a shame you have to head across the street."

"We've both got work, but if it helps I'd rather take you into the office to have my way with you a few times."

She groaned low. "That makes it worse, because I'd rather you did as well."

"Mrs. Mitchell." Parker Krenshaw's voice delayed Cole's urge to do as he'd said despite their need to get to work. The dandy reached the top of the steps next to them. He inclined his head to Jane, then to Cole. "Mr. Mitchell."

"Mr. Krenshaw." Jane withdrew from Cole's arms to face the new arrival. "You're early this evening. Betting doesn't begin for another twenty minutes."

"I prefer being early to being late." Parker offered a friendly smile. The man didn't have nearly the oily air his uncle had. Cole still didn't care for him, but at least he could tolerate him. He certainly could tolerate taking the man's money every month. "I had actually stopped by the clinic to visit Linh. She still isn't up for much visiting, so I took my leave earlier than anticipated."

"Yes, I can understand. Linh and Graham do prefer privacy right now. Who could blame them?" Jane laced her arm through Parker's. "Let's see to getting you settled then, shall we? I imagine the rest of our Gold Gamblers will be along shortly. Have a good evening, Cole."

"I'll have a better night at home after work." He winked when she tossed a wicked grin his way on her way through the door. He adjusted himself to ease the discomfort of an unsatisfied libido before heading to the saloon.

Inside he found the saloon bustling with activity. Loud shouts, off-key singing, and raucous gambling at the nickel-ante made the noise level as loud as he'd ever heard it. It was good to see and hear, especially seeing as it was regular townsfolk. No cowboys would be through for a few months now.

Wil stood behind the bar shooting the shit with customers. Even through his laughter and conversation, he made a practiced sweep of the bar every few minutes. Much as Cole always had when he'd had the saloon in the early days. At Cole's approach, he nodded. "Good weather means good business."

"So does cold weather. They like keeping warm."

"Ah, but those further out don't make the drive as often. Think half the territory is in here tonight. Not that I'm complaining." Wil's gaze swept the bar again. He lingered near the stairs with a frown before returning to Cole. "Thought Tommy was coming back tonight."

"Nah. I gave him a break. I haven't been on duty since I got back, figured I'd take a turn. Let him have a night to his thoughts."

"Or his woman."

"Or both." Cole chuckled. He gave the bar a once-over. He spotted many familiar patrons littering the tables. "The girls keeping up?"

"Sure are. It's the best batch of whores I've managed. Got four in rooms right now. The rest are working the floor like champs. Ain't no one lingering with the gamblers."

Buttercup strode through the crowd with purpose. She leaned on the counter. "Need three gins, a bourbon, two beers."

Cole raised a brow. The woman had a purpose about her that seemed a bit familiar. To be honest, it reminded him a bit of Jane. "Didn't see ya talk to no one on your way up here."

"The gins are for the poker game. Carl, Benny, and Gene are playing too good. They can't hold their gin like they do beer. It'll throw them off their game a bit."

He nodded, impressed with the assessment. "The others?"

"The beer is for Clive. He's working up the gumption to ask for Narcisse. Had his eye on her for awhile, but always settles for Poppy."

"I see." Cole set the bourbon on the tray. "And the bourbon?"

"Scott." Buttercup glanced over her shoulder toward the stairs. Right where Wil had frowned earlier.

"Watch it with him." Wil's expression was dark. He leaned on the counter. "He's been nervous tonight."

"I noticed. That's why I'm taking him the bourbon." Buttercup rearranged the drinks on the tray for easier dispersement.

"You've got a good eye. Ever thought about coming to the casino? Jane would appreciate another sharp eye on the floor." Cole knew Jane would like the way Buttercup read the customers near as good as Jane always had. Maybe he'd mention it. They could put her in charge of the whores in time, if nothing else.

"I like what I do, but thanks." Buttercup lifted the tray and began to work her way through the room.

"Stealing my whores?" Wil's lip lifted in a smirk.

"I'm pretty sure they're my whores." Cole chuckled low. He turned his attention to the men at the bar. As he dispersed drinks, he checked out the man Buttercup and Wil had mentioned. "What's this about Scott being nervous?"

"Atcheson, over there by the stairs. Been keeping an eye on him tonight. He's been fidgety and nervous like I ain't ever seen. Talking to himself a lot." Wil turned to rearrange the bottles on the shelf behind the bar. "Seems calmer now, but don't know what had him that way."

Cole had to agree. Though Scott appeared relatively calm, his knee bobbed in a rapid beat. "What do we know about him?'

"Miner. Was friends with that Ronnie fella. Figured maybe that's what got him out of sorts. Seeing as his friend just killed himself, I didn't figure I'd try my luck." Wil wiped his hands on his apron. He bent to grab a bundle of glasses from behind the bar. "We're running low."

"I'll get some from the storeroom. A couple bottles of whiskey, too." Cole stopped to thump on the beer barrels. "We're gonna need to replace a barrel by the end of the night, too."

"I've got one left. Three are supposed to arrive on tomorrow's train, don't ya worry."

"Wasn't worried." Cole tossed his towel over his shoulder on his way to the storeroom. The clutter inside had him taking several minutes to figure out where everything was. Jane would have a fit to see the storeroom like it was.

He grabbed an empty crate to load some glasses in. Soon as it was full, he found another to add whiskey to. He stacked the crates to carry back out to the bar. When he passed, Wil stood still, searching the room more intently. Cole set the crates on the back counter. "What's wrong?"

"Where the devil did they go?"

"Who?"

"Buttercup and Atcheson. I had to go deal with an argument at Billy's table. It took a few minutes to resolve. When I finished, the pair of them disappeared."

Cole waved over Poppy. "Where'd Buttercup go off to?"

"Scottie took her upstairs." Poppy glanced toward a room on the upper level across from the bar. "She didn't look too happy about it, but he pays real good."

"Damn it." Wil threw his towel down. Without another word, he bolted for the stairs.

A high-pitched scream tore through the cheerful chaos of the saloon. All action stilled at the sound, several men rose to look around curiously.

Cole met Wil's gaze. Both of them raced into action at once. Wil finished climbing the stairs and turned left to race around the balcony the long way.

"*Whore.*" The door of room seven broke open, Buttercup landed hard with the remains. Cole froze at the top of the steps. He noticed Wil had slowed his pace, his gaze intent on the room across the way.

Buttercup stirred, struggling to her elbows. Another scream ripped from her lips. A gunshot went off and the girl collapsed back to the ground, silent.

Scott stepped into view of the doorway, and that's when Cole saw what had the whore screaming. Two sticks of dynamite sat clutched in the man's left hand, a long length of fuse trailed behind him into the room. If it was lit, they were all screwed.

"*Everyone out.*" Cole stayed where he was, trying to keep an eye on Scott as well as Wil, who kept moving along the opposite end of the balcony. "*Dynamite.*"

That got the room below scattering faster than anything. Wil even paused his trek. The manager's gaze remained fixed on the young whore sprawled on the floor.

Scott laughed maniacally. "You're all going to *burn.*"

"Scott." Cole tried to distract the man while Wil continued to creep along the balcony closer to the whore "What the fuck are you doing?"

Scott lifted the dynamite high in his hand so they could see the sparking end of the fuse dancing closer to the sticks of TNT. "We're *all* going to burn! Sinners! Succubi! *Denizens of hell.*"

Cole took another step closer. "Scott. You don't have to—"

Scott raised his gun, aiming straight for Cole's head. "Depart from me, ye cursed into everlasting fire, prepared for the devil and his angels."

Cole felt the sting of pain along his ribs same time as he heard the shot. A glance down told him the bullet had merely skimmed his ribs.

The distraction had been enough that Wil had nearly arrived at Buttercup. Unfortunately, the fuse was almost at the dynamite.

"Wil, *move.*"

Buttercup shifted with Wil's tug. Scott spun around at the interruption, his weapon firing again. Wil stumbled, but managed to haul Buttercup into his arms a moment before the concussion hit.

Cole's arms flew up to protect his face as his entire body flew backwards. Something caught him in his ribs, and then he was falling, rolling, thumping down. His ears rang, his body protested any movement.

He managed to groan a curse before black fell over him.

*Scorching my seared heart with a pain,
not hell shall make me fear again.
-Edgar Allen Poe*

Jane stopped her conversation with the young Reverend Lyons as loud noises filtered toward the Inn. She excused herself to head outside. Panicked screams and yells from Main Street drew her around the corner.

A crowd streamed from the saloon into the street. The whores screamed, men yelled, all of them running fast on the cobbled street. The chaos coupled with her bad ear made it difficult to figure out what they were saying.

She rushed into the street among the crowd. Bit by bit the words coalesced in her brain.

Dynamite.

Jane grabbed her skirts to run. A moment later the explosion hit. She stumbled back onto her rump. People ran around her away from the sound. She scrambled to her feet.

Before she got to the steps of the saloon arms circled her waist to hold her back. "No you don't, young lady."

"Pa, let me go. Cole."

"We'll get him. You need to stay put. We don't know if there's more. There were two at the undertakers, remember?" John spun her to face him so quick, she got a little dizzy. He held her shoulders firm. "Let the law do their job. Cole will be found."

"What if…what…oh, no." Jane sank to the ground soon as her pa released her shoulders. Tears slipped free. This couldn't be happening. Another set of arms circled her as Kat sat on the street beside her.

"Breathe, Jane. Breathe," Kat murmured, holding Jane close. "Remember the baby."

Jane released a shaky breath. It wouldn't do her any favors to get overwrought now. She needed the doctors to be focused on whomever was inside, not her. "I know. I'm trying."

"Good. You sound better."

"It was a shock. It still is. I…" Jane surveyed the crowd still filling the street. "Cole isn't out here, which means he was in there. Oh, Kat. I just got him back."

"That's right, you did. He's not about to leave you now." Kat urged Jane to stand. "Get up. They're bringing someone out."

Jane leaned into Kat as the litter drew close. The familiar visage of Wil come into view. Blood covered most of his face. His leg contorted at an odd angle. "Oh, Wil. Is he alive?"

"He's alive. Barely." Andrew gazed at her over the top of the litter. "I need to get him to surgery immediately if we want to keep it that way."

"Of course." Jane took a step back. Through her panic and worry over Cole, another thought flared. She squeezed

Kat's hand. "I'll be fine, Katherine. I need you to send a telegram to Garit immediately. He'll want to know."

"Now? But you're…"

"The initial shock is passed." Jane turned to face her friend, needing her to understand the urgency without worrying her more about Jane's state of mind. She knew Garit and Wil might be called closer than friends, but it wasn't something for anyone and everyone to hear. It wasn't Kat's current worry, though. "Truly. I'm of clearer head now. I'm insanely worried, but I won't do anything rash. Please, send the telegram. Garit is—well, he and Wil are close as family. He needs to know what happened."

"If you're certain you'll be all right." Kat clung to her hands, concern lining her features. "Are you having any pains?"

"No more than usual. I promise. You can join me at the clinic when you're done if you're worried. I certainly wouldn't mind the company."

"I'll see you there."

Jane turned away as her friend took off to see another litter being carried outside. Dr. Noe strode alongside it, her features grim. Jane could only gasp as Buttercup got carried past. The beautiful young whore's body lay contorted as Wil's had, blood soaking her clothes. "Oh, Buttercup."

This time she didn't pause the litter to question if the girl lived. She'd seen Buttercup blinking weakly. Horror balled in her belly until she felt a little sick. She turned back toward the saloon. Slow and steady she crept forward through the crowd until she drew close to the steps. Several whores huddled together, staring at the open doors to the saloon.

Jane counted eight whores. That meant two were still missing along with Cole.

A shout went up from inside. She fought not to hold her breath when little more was heard right away. Nearly ten agonizing minutes later a third litter emerged with Charlie beside it. When her brother met her gaze, she moved to meet the litter at the base of the steps.

Cole lay unconscious on the litter. A strange sucking sound accompanied each breath. "Charles?"

"Lung collapsed, dislocated shoulder, definite concussion, perhaps bleeding on his brain. I need to examine him better in the clinic. I'll do everything I can, Jane." Charlie moved swiftly alongside the litter. He didn't complain when Jane did the same. The entire time his focus remained on the man being carried.

"I know you will." Jane clung to Cole's hand as they walked. When they got to the clinic, she released the hand so Charles could get to work. She didn't dare interrupt him or fight to get in. She knew he needed to focus on Cole in order to save him. He'd said he'd do everything he could, which meant the situation could well be dire.

For several minutes she stood in the door of the clinic. The last place she'd touched Cole. Her feet needed to move, but she couldn't seem to make them.

"Jane, dear." Lillian wrapped an arm around her, guiding her through the doors. "Come inside. Let's make you comfortable. Your Ma is seeing to the Inn, and your brother came from his own hotel to help with yours. You'll stay here."

"How did—"

"You should know best of all how fast news travels in this town." Lillian situated her in a chair in the small kitchen at the back of the clinic. How she'd gotten Jane there, she couldn't remember. Time was acting funny. Lillian set a teapot on the stove. "Leanne, Cora, and Katherine will be along soon enough to attend to you."

"Leanne will need attending to. He's her brother." Jane uttered the words before she could remember she ought to school them. Her brothers knew, of course, but she didn't know if anyone else was supposed to.

Lillian glanced her way, an amused twitch to her lips. "That explains it, then. I always thought he treated her different than the other whores. That would be why."

"They're half-siblings. They share the same horrible pa." Why couldn't she shut up? She really should stop running her mouth.

"We aren't all blessed with parents like yours, I'm afraid." Lillian set the teapot on the table. A clatter sounded down the hall behind Jane. Though Jane thought perhaps they'd found one of the missing whores, Lillian smiled. "Ah. There's the very woman we speak of now."

Leanne rushed forward to Jane. She swept Jane in a hug so fast, Jane could hardly breathe for the intensity of it. "Is he going to be all right? What happened? Where is he?"

"Slow down, Leanne. Jane is in as much shock as you. Come, sit. Have some tea. I'm certain we'll receive an update on your brother in short order." Lillian set teacups in front of Leanne and Jane. "Cora and Katherine will be joining us soon."

"Charles said his lung collapsed. A dislocated shoulder. There's a head injury. I don't know what else. Wil and

Buttercup are in terrible shape as well. I don't know what happened except I heard the crowd calling about dynamite." Jane's hand shook so hard the cup rattled in its saucer.

"Ma?" Sally leaned against the wall as she made her way slowly down the steps. Her features were strained with pain, but she made it to the kitchen. "Ma, what's happened?"

Jane's eyes filled with tears before she could say a word. She buried her face in her hands.

Lillian explained to Sally in hushed tones as she led the young woman to the table. "We're all going to be here for a while. I'm going to send for Trixie to take care of food and drink. Cora doesn't need to be bustling about the kitchen when her friends need her."

"You don't need to call your cook," Leanne protested.

"I didn't say I needed to, I said I was going to. That's all there is to it." Lillian set a warm hand on Jane's shoulder. "Try to have some tea. I'll send for Trixie and we'll pretend as though this is our weekly tea. I'll also see if we can get Faith over here. All of your friends should be here for you both."

"Thank you." Jane set her hand on Lillian's.

"No thanks needed."

Jane turned her attention to Leanne when Lillian left the kitchen. She set a shaking hand on Leanne's. "Charles will see to it he comes through."

"I know." Leanne sniffled. She dabbed her eyes with a kerchief she'd procured from her belt. "You told Lillian I am his sister."

"You're his what?" Sally's eyes grew wide.

"Leanne is Cole's half-sister, as is Alma." Somewhere from the depths of her worry, a smile formed as she faced

Sally. "I'd planned to tell you myself soon, but the opportunity hasn't presented itself."

"Alma, too?" Sally shook her head. "That's why he took her in."

"He took her in because he has a big heart he didn't want anyone to know about. I came along and ruined it all for him." Jane squeezed Sally's hand. "Cole was almost killed, Sally."

"I know, Ma." Tears filled Sally's eyes. "I'm sorry."

"Don't be sorry." Jane leaned forward. She pinched Sally's chin to hold her gaze firm where it was. Her own desperation might have made the hold harder than it needed to be. "Be strong."

"I'm going to try."

"That's all I ask."

Sally sighed softly, staring at the silent form on the bed. "Well, we'll have similar scars Wil. Your beard's going to be messed up for a while."

Wil remained still and silent. Eyes closed. No reaction at all. From the reports of those still clearing out of the saloon when the blast hit, Will had practically leaped off the balcony to get Buttercup away from the explosion. He'd taken the brunt of the fall.

Andrew said the most concerning injuries were his back and his head. He'd had to actually put holes in Wil's skull. The hope remained for him to wake in a few days. If he did, the prognosis was good. If he didn't, well…

"I'm not losing two friends within a month, Wil. Wake your stubborn ass up." Sally pushed herself to her feet. Everything still ached, but she forced herself past the pain.

She leaned down over him to kiss his cheek. "I'll be back. I need to check on Ma. She wasn't doing so well."

When she rose, she found Matthew staring into the room. His features twisted in a perplexed grimace. "Sally?"

"Matthew." She made her way to the door annoyingly slow. It would be a relief when she could move normal again. "I'm sorry. I lost track of time with everything going on. I wanted to check on Wil, then Ma and Pa before you got here."

He studied her in silence for a long time. So long she had to fight the urge to squirm under his intense gaze. He finally spoke, "You're feeling better."

"I don't know that I am." She hesitated a moment before she took his hand. The flicker of happiness that crossed his features sparked something in her heart. A foreign something after her weeks of misery. Something she felt the strongest urge to shove down. It didn't go anywhere despite that urge. A small flame of life glimmered in her heart.

"You don't know?" His fingers brushed along her cheek. Those remarkable green eyes searched hers. "You're more alive than I've seen ya lately."

"It's anger. Pure, steaming anger."

"Guess that's better than desperation."

"I don't know that it is. Anger burns fast. It's not something you can hold onto for long. Buddha likens it to holding a hot coal to throw, you're the one that gets burned." Sally blinked a few times. What she'd done had been so like her ma, it caught her off-guard. She wasn't great at remembering phrases like she did. "How did I remember that?"

A smile tweaked the corners of Matthew's lips into an adorable grin. "Sally?"

"Sorry. I reminded myself of Ma for a minute."

"That ain't a bad thing. Your ma is a good woman."

"She really is." It dawned on her she still held his hand. For some reason the realization didn't make her withdraw it quite yet. "I fear it won't last long, but for now anger will drive me forward."

"Then I'll keep checking on ya." He pulled her closer, so close he could have kissed her. The idea sparked a weird mix of excitement and worry. Instead he placed kiss to her forehead. "If you'll let me."

"Yes. I will." She met his gaze quietly. "I'm sorry."

"Don't be." He winked. "I'll let ya get to your parents. I'll see you tomorrow."

"Tomorrow," she agreed. Sally could have cursed the fact she realized part of her wished he'd kissed her properly. The way her hand felt cold when he took his away added to the disappointment. It wasn't right for such feelings, not so soon after Molly. Besides, he was a good man. He didn't need the mess that was her.

With a heavy sigh she turned back down the hall to get to Cole's room. Inside she found Jane sound asleep with her head pillowed on Cole's chest. By some miracle Cole wasn't asleep. With his head injury, among others, it was amazing how quick he'd woken.

Andrew had explained that there was still risk of his lung collapsing again, and a brain bleed that was slower than Wil's had been. They were watching him carefully for any sign of danger. So far, he'd done really well. Though very sore, he was awake and semi-functioning.

He turned his head and offered her a nod.

"Sorry," Sally whispered. "I wanted to see how you were doing."

"Hurt like hell. Got shot and broke several ribs when I hit the stairs. Leastwise my head ain't more messed up than usual." He tapped a finger to his temple. "Bad headache still. Charlie says they're watching for a few days to make sure it isn't bleeding like Wil's."

"You don't need any more holes in your head." Sally's cheeks warmed when Cole quirked a brow at her joke. She was surprised herself she'd made it. When was the last time she'd made a joke? "Sorry."

"No. Don't you dare be sorry. That was funny."

"Maybe a little uncalled for."

"That's what made it funny. I'm glad to see you joking. How's Wil? Buttercup?"

"Wil's still unconscious. Andrew said if he doesn't wake in a few days it may be more than they can fix. The leg'll heal in time but brains are tricky."

"That's what Charlie told me. It's why he wants to keep me trapped in here."

"I think we all want you well, Pa. Andrew said your lung could collapse again, too."

"So far, so good on that front. I'm not moving much, though."

"Good. You need to let it heal."

He wrinkled his nose. "Stop fussing and doctoring. Neither you or your ma listen to doctors, but you expect me to."

She chuckled softly, nodding. "Fair enough."

"What about Buttercup?"

"She's awake, but in considerable pain. They keep plying her with morphine. Wil protected her from the worst of the blast, but she's also got a broken leg, and arm, along with the bullet in her shoulder." Sally rubbed her own shoulder at the mention of the wound. Buttercup's had been in her right shoulder, but the reminder made her own wound burn. "Even with a limp she'll still be the prettiest whore thanks to Wil."

"She'll be relieved. Said she likes doing what she does right before it happened."

"What did happen?"

"Scottie."

"Atcheson?" Sally reached for her notebook instinctively. It wasn't on her person any longer. She'd given it to Tommy. Would those instincts fade with time? Rather than face questions she didn't want answers to, she turned to the matter at hand. "He did this?"

"Sure did. Wil said he was acting all nervous. Figured since he was a friend of Ronnie's, that had him riled. Wil was keeping an eye on him. Buttercup took him a drink to try to calm him down some more. I was in the storeroom and Wil was dealing with an issue at the nickel ante when they both disappeared."

"Why Buttercup?"

"Don't know. She did approach him, so maybe she was just there." Cole shrugged, wincing at the action. "Damn."

"This makes no sense."

"You're telling me. We heard her scream. The damn crazy bastard threw her right through a door. Right after he shot her I saw the dynamite and yelled for everyone to get out. He started yelling something about us burning in hell. An everlasting…"

"'Depart from me, ye cursed'." This from Jane. She hadn't stirred from her rest. Still, she spoke quietly into the conversation. "'into everlasting fire, prepared for the devil and his angels'. You might recognize it, Sally. It's from the book of Matthew."

Sally plumbed the depths of her memory. Chapter and verse were difficult for her. The verse was oddly familiar, though. After a few minutes, the memory came forward. "Chapter twenty-five. Verse forty-one."

"Very good." Jane yawned. Her eyes remained closed, her body relaxed. "I recognized it when your pa said something about everlasting fire."

"Ma. Shouldn't you be at home? I heard Bonnie say you'd been bleeding."

"I've been ordered to be off my feet every minute I can. I am off my feet." Jane's eyes drew open. She nestled closer into Cole, her gaze on Sally. Sally thought there was a bit of reproach in her tone for Sally's meddling. "I am off my feet. Seeing as Cole is doing relatively well, all things considered, I'll head home at supper where Ma will force me to lie down the rest of the night. I'm disobeying no orders. I promise."

"Sorry." Sally's cheeks warmed again at the admonition. She could feel the tingle spread down her chest. "I'm just worried is all."

"We all are," Cole assured her. "Your ma is most worried of us all. She fought hard to keep this baby right where it is. Last thing she's gonna do is ruin it now."

"I know she won't." Saly's hand settled where her reticule would sit on a proper dress. Since she still wore her nightgown, it was nowhere to be found. Not to mention once again she'd been reaching for the notebook she no longer had in her possession. "I need to go check on something."

"When you find Thomas, it's on page twenty. Miss Bee's kitchen." Jane's eyes drifted closed again.

"How'd you know?"

Jane's eyes flew open to meet Sally's with surprising intensity. "Because I recognized it immediately. I told you as much."

"Right. Of course. Memory."

"You might ask Thomas about the Lyman's kitchen while you're at it."

"I will, Ma."

The greatest test of courage on earth is
to bear defeat without losing heart.
-Robert Ingersoll

Sally stood on the balcony outside her room. A cool wind blew through town, harkening the return of winter soon. The clean, cold scent hinted an approaching storm to bring winter back to its rightful place.

She studied the hole in the side of the saloon. Men clamored around the hole trying to close it off before the storm hit. Without a doubt they worked fast so their drinking and whoring wouldn't be interrupted. Tommy would have to man the place along with the men they'd hired as more dealers until Garit returned.

Down the street to the east sat the empty lots where Graham's place one stood alongside the cooper shop. This had to end. Now. Before any more lives were destroyed by this evil.

She didn't know if she felt strong enough to help it reach that end. Her heart still ached every time the anger abated for a moment. Her head still swam with doubts alongside thoughts of the root cause of such terror.

It was an ugly mess in her heart and head right now. How on earth could she gather herself to return to aiding Tommy?

At the very least, she'd promised Jane she'd try. To do that, she needed to see Tommy.

"Sally?" Andrew knocked on the door to her room. "Sally, where are you?"

She moved back toward the balcony door. "I'm right here."

"Come back inside. You're going to catch your death standing out there. The weather is taking a turn." He rushed to her side to help her back to the bed.

Sally sank onto the bed, rubbing her cold fingers along her thighs. The cold had been somewhat good to shake some of the cobwebs away. Her confusion and melancholy hadn't abated by any means, but there was a stirring of life. "I'm feeling a little stronger now. I wanted some fresh air."

"Fresh air?" He pulled the chair closer to the bed to sit before her. "That cold air is coming back with a vengeance. If you desire fresh air, I must insist you dress appropriately to meet it. Your body is still healing. I don't want to see you fall ill."

"Yes, sir." She offered him a mock salute.

His lips twisted in a smirk. For a moment he looked like he was going to scold her some more. Then he chuckled quietly. "I'm glad to see your spunk is returning."

"I'm trying, at least." Sally rubbed her bad shoulder. It took some effort not to wince at the movement. "Not sure I'll ever feel normal again."

"It's going to take some time. Your body went through quite the trauma." He peeled her hand away from her shoulder. He lifted the bandage to check the wound. She looked away from it as she always had. When he'd finished, he settled back in his chair. "Your shoulder looks good. Your back looked well yesterday so I won't check it today."

"Seeing Buttercup's injury made mine ache worse."

"It simply reminded you is all. You're healing remarkably well. I said you could return to your home several days ago. Why haven't you?"

She didn't want to admit it was because she looked forward to Matthew's daily visits to check on her. That's all it had been at first, along with the melancholy that she didn't think would withstand the persistence of her family. She searched for a better reason. It wasn't difficult to find. "Ma isn't doing well. There's Alma, and all the children. Mams and Paps, Tommy, and now even Mike are all there helping. I don't want to give them all one more thing to worry about and watch over."

"I don't believe they'd mind. You are family." Andrew took her hand in his. "Your ma says there's a blizzard coming. Perhaps you should be home before it hits. Be with your family."

"Cole is here. If Ma is home before the storm hits, I should be here. She wouldn't like for him to be alone." Sally smiled weakly. "I have some thinking to do anyway. I need to see Tommy. Then I'll need Bonnie to help me get dressed."

He straightened. A smile returned to his features. "Get dressed? That's a good sign."

"I told you I was trying. I'm angry right now, and that's helping. Unfortunately, I'm still dreadfully sad and that isn't."

"I'm happy for whatever keeps you going, whatever helps bring that spunk back. If it happens to be anger, I'll take it. I can fetch Bonnie for you. As for your uncle Tommy, I don't know where he's at right now."

"I'm right here." Tommy leaned on the door frame. "I came to visit our people and Cole. I wasn't sure you wanted to see me yet."

"I did." Sally squeezed Andrew's hands. "You'll get Bonnie?"

"I'll send her up in a few minutes." Andrew kissed her forehead on the way to standing.

"Thank you."

Tommy cleared the doorway so Andrew could pass. He entered the room slowly. A wary eye on her, he leaned on the back of the chair Andrew had abandoned. "What did you need?"

She hesitated, unable to swallow the lump that had formed in her throat. This was proving difficult, even with the anger aiding her along.

"Sally?"

She glanced at the wall that separated her room from Cole's. "My notebook."

"What about it?"

"I think I'd like it back. For now."

"Is that so?"

"I can't—I don't—no promises."

Tommy settled into the chair finally. He didn't free her notebook, didn't offer comfort or seem glad at all. "Why the change?"

"I'm angry."

"Anger is good so long as you remember it should be about vengeance, not revenge."

"I want it all to stop. I *need* it all to stop. Molly died. Joshua. Cole could have died, Wil still could. I need it all to stop. I need…"

Tommy moved to the bed when she sobbed. He folded her into his arms, running his hand along her back. "If you work with me, I know we can figure this out. I think you and Molly were onto something, you just weren't sure about it."

Sally sniffed when he placed the familiar form of her notebook in her hands. The weight felt comfortable and familiar. A chill still ran down her spine. If she was wrong, so much more could be lost. If she was right, maybe it could finally all come to an end After a few blinks, she wiped away her tears. "Miss Bee."

"Yes."

"I need to…I need to go back over everything. I—Ma told me to ask about the Lyman's kitchen. Was there a bible?"

"There was."

"Open to the book of Matthew?"

"Yes."

"Chapter twenty-five?"

"No."

"What?" Sally fully expected him to answer in the affirmative based on Jane's suggestion. Why did Jane want her to ask, then?

"Chapter thirteen."

Sally's mind raced over the chapter he mentioned. Her mind faltered on the phrases. They kept crossing with other chapters and books until her mind spun. She closed her eyes against her whirling thoughts. "Damn it. What I wouldn't give for Ma's memory."

"Stop pushing so hard. Jane would tell you to relax. Like she did when she taught you to shoot, or when you were trying to remember your first burned notebook."

"Chapter thirteen," Sally repeated.

"Verse—"

"Don't. Let me try." She took a deep breath, then released it. After a few minutes it was almost as if she could see a picture of the bible pages in front of her. She even held out her hands like it rested there. "Verses forty-one through forty-three seem along the right lines."

"How so?"

"They mention gathering all the things that offend, that do iniquity, and casting them into the furnace of fire. After which, and I quote, 'then shall the righteous shine forth as the sun in the kingdom of their father'."

"Very good."

Sally flipped through her notebook, staring at the pages of notes as they flew past. Tommy already had all of the information. He'd figure it out without her. "Then maybe you don't need me at all."

"I do. Believe me. Take your time, go over everything again. The new perspective you have might just help. There's a storm coming in and I think we'll be safe through it. When it's over we'll talk and head out to deal with the situation."

"You've already got it figured, I knew it. You did it without me."

"I don't have it figured out completely. I have a strong suspicion, and I think you do too. I want to know they both line up. You knew more about the case than I did. Plus, your notes are written in your own style. I can't make heads or tails of some of your symbols."

"Tommy."

"Yeah?"

"I only want to finish this. I don't know that I ever want to do it again."

"You won't know that until you get a win."

"I don't know that it could ever be called a win. Too much has been lost."

This is the true nature of home –
it is the place of Peace:
the shelter, not only from injury, but from
all terror, doubt and division.
–John Ruskin

Jane snuggled Colton closer to her. She quietly soothed his whimpers at the storm raging outside. The blizzard had hit with more than ample warning once again. She'd made it home safe, and most of her family was in the Inn with her.

Cole and Sally remained at the clinic with Charlie and his family. Andrew and Lydia had opted to stay there as well. Bonnie had to returned to the ranch with her brothers. Dr. Noe had also returned to her small homestead.

Charles had hinted toward staying at the Inn to monitor Jane. Only the reassurance of Eunice that she'd had plenty of children and could mind her own daughter had swayed him. She thought her own request that he monitor Cole had also had some impact.

For the moment she was content. Cole continued to display no signs of any brain injury. His remaining at the clinic for observation during the storm would reassure them all he would heal rather well. Sore, but alive, thankfully.

Alma settled in on the couch reading quietly. Jay and Willow entertained Clara across the room. Jane had an inkling the two were teaching the girl to speak Ute. She might have protested giving the child new ways to trick her ma, but she was too pleased to see them growing closer to the other children to complain.

The storm had already been raging for over a day. Jane hoped it would break in time for them to attend church on Sunday. With any luck, this would be a shorter storm and end the next day so they might go in two days time.

John set a cup of tea on the table beside the settee. "Eunice will return shortly with supper for you. We'll take the children to eat in the restaurant with the others."

"You should take them first, I'm not terribly hungry at the moment." Jane would have rubbed her stomach, but her son lay flush against it. His head buried in her shoulder, his small little fists clinging tight to her dress. He showed no sign of letting her go, or relaxing. "You might need to bring some food for this little man as well. I don't think he's releasing me any time soon."

"The winds are far worse this time. I hope there isn't too much damage from the storm." John gazed out the window. "At least we know the farm back home is all right. James says the storms have been easy this winter out east."

Jane sipped her tea with some difficulty. Colton's shoulder sat right under her chin, making it difficult to move proper. "When do you think you'll be heading back to New York?"

"Seeing as the situation has changed somewhat, we'll be here a while longer."

"How, exactly, has the situation changed?"

"Due to Cole's long absence and your trip out west, we're now quite close to you having that baby. I believe your ma is determined to remain until he's born. With James and our foreman manning both farms, we have some time."

"You've already been here for months," Jane tried to protest.

Her father cut her a look. "We're aware."

She cut her protest short at his look. "If you're certain."

"We don't ever do anything we aren't certain of. Don't you worry about us." John sat on the edge of the settee. He eyed the child sprawled across her. "Some would say you're coddling."

"I don't mollycoddle any of my children."

"We all do sometimes." John rubbed his hand soothingly along the boy's back. "Hey there, little cowboy."

Colton's eyes opened to stare at his grandpa. His thumb remained firm in his mouth. The boy's free hand continued to squeeze and release Jane's arm. Fat tears clung to his lashes, though he no longer sobbed.

Jane sighed softly, brushing a few tears from his cheeks. "I believe it was the tornado that got him so scared of storms. He wasn't before."

"To be fair, the tornado was awful scary." John lifted Colton from her stomach. The boy held onto her arm for a minute but released it to curl into his grandpa.

Jane smiled warmly at the two. "Short of Cole, I don't think anyone else would have been successful at prying him away. Now the challenge is to get him to eat in the restaurant with all of those windows."

John winked. "I know the secret."

"Do you now?"

"What do you say to some supper, Colton? Mams made something delicious, I bet. I heard talk of sourmilk biscuits." John grinned wickedly at Jane. "And possibly a pie using some of the preserves."

Colton smiled around his thumb at the mention of pie.

Jane laughed softly. Her pa hadn't been wrong. "I think you definitely won him over with talk of a pie."

"It always works. I'll take the children up front. We'll see to it someone brings you some supper as well."

"I can—"

"You're to lie down as much as possible. There's no need to head down the hall for supper when someone will not only bring you some, but also keep you company while you eat."

"Fine." Jane knew when an argument would work. This wasn't one of those times. She settled back to finish her tea.

John went to round up the rest of the children. They all made quite a loud show of heading out of the apartment. Even Alma talked excitedly to whomever would listen. Jane could hear them talking back and forth the whole way down the hall toward the restaurant.

Jane rubbed her hands over her stomach. She closed her eyes against the ache that seemed to have settled permanently in place. An underlying feeling that something was on the verge of going terribly wrong had her following orders with little argument.

Even though she'd managed to calm quickly the day the saloon blew up, she'd developed some bleeding. Though it had mostly slowed to almost nothing, both Bonnie and Charlie were deeply concerned. She couldn't deny she was as well. Cole wasn't much better, though in his current state he wasn't in much position to push the issue.

Her own concerns kept her off her feet whenever possible. She rested to the point of boredom. Even her books were brought to her as she asked for them. It was all quite annoying.

She felt like a spoiled queen on a throne having everything done for her.

Still, she hoped her good behavior would allow her to go to church on Sunday. She didn't like missing the sermons.

Plates rattled near the door. Nick maneuvered into the room with a tray nearly overflowing with food. He balanced it precariously while closing the door. "How on earth Ma expects us to eat all of this, I have no idea."

Jane tried to keep her smile restrained while he carried the overfilled tray to the table. When he set it down, all laughter faded. Biscuits, beans, smoked ham, and fried potatoes were only the start. Several pieces of pie sat on another plate as well. "Is our mother insane?"

"I believe she expects you to eat quite a lot." He rested his hands on his hips, studying the tray with a frown. "We'll do our best and toss the rest to the hounds. She'll never know."

"She always knows, but I'm not opposed to the suggestion. I hardly have the appetite for even a small plate, much less a feast."

"You're right. She does always know." Nick handed her a plate. He took his own in the desk chair beside her. "How are you feeling?"

"I'm quite tired of being waited on, frustrated, worrying about Cole, aching, but overall I'm surprisingly well." Jane took a bite of food. She paused to enjoy the rich flavors her mother had managed to impart. She wished she could learn to cook, she did enjoy eating.

"That's good to hear. Everything sounds as expected."

"I'm also hoping this storm ends tomorrow so we might go to services at the new temporary location for the church."

"Do you truly believe Ma is going to allow you to walk all the way to the church?" Nick eyed her quietly. "I wish you luck convincing her of that. You can study your bible just as well where you're at, not that you need the studying."

"Precisely. I have the book memorized. I prefer to hear the sermons from Eli and Mark. They're always quite comforting, and my soul needs the comfort."

"I suppose that's as good an argument as any."

"It most certainly is." Jane enjoyed a few more bites as comfortable silence lingered between them. Once she felt satisfied, she wiped her mouth with a napkin. "Why are you here, Nicholas?"

"I live here." His gaze drifted back to her, a suspicious glint in his eyes.

"That isn't what I meant, and you know it."

"You should always be precise with a lawyer."

"Fine. I meant why are you here at the Inn? Why are you weathering the storm here rather than in your own homestead?" Jane set her plate down to let the food she'd eaten settle before she tried again. "You were here for the last storm as well."

"I wanted to be of assistance. Seeing as how you're restricted in activity, it seemed logical to come assist where I could."

"Logic. Of course. It isn't because you're lonely."

"Jane."

"I'm allowed to worry for you, am I not?"

"You have no need for concern. I'm quite content."

"I don't know that you are."

His eyes tightened. His napkin swiped across his mouth. She couldn't detect any other change in expression, she had an inkling that he hid a grimace.

"Nicholas?"

"I enjoy conversation. The homestead is rather quiet, especially during storms."

"You desire companionship. There's nothing wrong with that." She set her hand on his. To broach the next subject often brought the conversation to an abrupt end. She hoped having him alone with her incapacitated self would allow it to continue for once. "You were married once."

"That marriage came to a disastrous end. I have no need for romance or deep love in my life, Jane. There are— things—that would make another marriage impossible."

Jane could guess at what such things were. In her short life she'd seen more than her share of horrors. So had Nick. Great losses in the war had forever changed him. "The nightmares?"

His eyes cut to hers with a sharp, accusatory rawness.

"I have them," she admitted. Though she hated having them, and talking about them, it seemed like something she needed to share with Nick. Out of all of her brothers, she felt he could relate most of all. He kept things tight to himself, and that meant it would have to show in other ways. Nightmares made sense. "After what I've been through, they're inevitable I suppose. I assumed after what you'd been through you might have the same."

"You do?"

"Yes. They've faded somewhat to become less frequent, but no less violent. They get worse in times of stress, or when history repeats such as when Mac tried to kill me. Cole has suffered some black eyes in his attempts to pull me out of them." Jane fiddled with her napkin. "But he understands. He hates them, wishes he could take them away, but he understands. His support helps them fade and makes them easier to come out of."

"I'm not looking for someone to ease them. I've told you, I don't expect to ever have a great love like you and Cole have."

"You must stop punishing yourself. What happened in the war was tragic for everyone. I know in your case you feel responsible for what happened to your friends. How long can you keep punishing yourself?"

"For as long as necessary."

Jane sighed, lifting her gaze to meet her brothers. "Rochefoucauld, on repentance."

His brow furrowed. "I haven't your inclination."

"Somehow I think you know this one."

He stared down at his plate. After a shaky breath, he nodded. "'Our repentance is not so much regret for the ill we have done as fear of the ill that may happen to us in consequence'."

"You've suffered a great deal more consequence than was earned, most by your own hand. If you don't seek great love, fine. Please, perhaps, seek companionship. You don't deserve to be alone in this world. I don't believe you enjoy it as you once did. That's why you come for companionship now. You know you don't deserve to be alone any longer."

"I will consider it."

"I do hope so." Jane squeezed his hand. "It's time to stop watching in fear of consequences, and time to start watching for happiness."

"Happiness may be a stretch."

"Contentment, then."

"Contentment."

In case of dissension,
never dare to judge
till you've heard the other side.
—Euripides

Sally carried her carpet bag to the bed. She still didn't have enough strength to carry anything heavy. It would be easier to fill the bag with her books at the bed. Tommy was supposed to be coming by that evening to take her home.

The storm had faded away during the early morning hours. A cold wind still whipped through the streets of town, but the snow and bluster were gone. On his way to help run checks on the surrounding homesteads to ensure everyone was safe from the storm, Tom had stopped by to offer to take her home.

Rather than try to rush home, she wanted to give the town, and her family, time to et everything settled after the storm. After all, she was in no rush to leave the clinic. It would be nice to be home, for certain, but she hated leaving Cole there without family.

Perhaps Jane would return again that night to keep him company.

Sally set the last book in the bag, then proceeded to add the journals. She stopped at her notebook. It still lay open to the notes on the scene at Miss Bee's place. She closed it with a finger. The familiar fear trickled back until her belly twisted in a knot.

The desperation and fear in her Ma's eyes when the saloon was attacked flared in her mind again. She'd promised to try. Before Molly it was all she'd wanted to do. That surety, that drive, that excitement seemed so far away now.

Sally exhaled slow to steady herself. At the very least she could finish this. She needed this done as much as anyone else. After that, maybe she'd find something to do with herself again.

She slipped the notebook into her reticule. Despite the doubts pressing down on her, the returned weight felt comfortable and almost comforting. She moved to the armoire to remove the few items of clothes Mams had brought over for her.

A muffled voice carried into her room through the partially open door. At first she assumed it to be one of the doctors or nurses tending to a patient. The longer the voice hit her ears, the more she realized it wasn't one of them. She listened harder. Words emerged from the muffled tone. Sin, Lord, repent among them.

Sally edged toward her door to hear better. Her ears strained to hear more clearly, and to figure out where it was coming from.

"'The soul that sinneth it shall die. The son shall not bear the iniquity of the father'." Though still muffled, the words came clearer now she paid attention. A weeping protest followed behind the words quoted from the bible. "It matters not, Jacob."

Sally finally recognized the voice. It was a man she hardly spoke to if she could help it. Plenty of people had heard his preaching against their will. Pastor Eckles. Whatever was said next came too quiet for her to make sense of. She edged into the hall. If she were to be caught trying to listen, she would use the excuse of heading toward Cole's room.

"'Wages of sin is death'," Eckles muffled voice carried a note of finality. "Let us pray together."

Sally's fingers twitched toward her notebook. She couldn't tear her eyes away from Jake's door. Though certain it was Eckles inside, she wanted to see first-hand it was truly him. Why, she didn't know.

By the sound of it, Eckles counseled Jake no further. The wages of sin being death sounded more like a dismissal. Either way, it was nothing like what the Reverends Greene or Lyons would ever say when counseling a sinner.

Footsteps sounded in the room Sally stared at, so she turned to head neared to Cole's room. The door opened behind her, leading her to pause. She glanced over her shoulder to find Eckles eying her coolly. She offered a small nod, speaking quietly, "Pastor."

"Miss Spencer."

"It's Mitchell, actually. My parents are married, after all."

"Two wrongs don't make a right, they say."

Sally's brow furrowed at his words. The man's contempt for her mother had always been clear, even when he put on a nice face in public. She chose to ignore his comment. "Is Jake improving?"

"As the one that swung the sword, do you care?"

"If I had swung to kill, he would be dead." Sally intentionally didn't mention the bullet that hadn't made its target due to her carelessness. If it had hit her target, the man would be dead. Then again, if he were dead they wouldn't be able to question him.

"Cold words. I should expect no less?"

"You find my words cold?"

"I do."

"Funny. You're the one that likes to quote Romans six, verse twenty-three. The one that reminds us all that the cost of sin is death. Your parishioners must fear death at every turn. Tell me, did you counsel Mac before his death?"

"Mr. McElroy was a member of my congregation if that's what you're asking. He made a great effort to turn his life around. To fight the good fight."

Eckles eyes narrowed. A cold smile bloomed. "Only warriors of God can offer such punishment to a sinner."

"Sinner? Ma is a good Christian who has helped those in need from the moment she had the capability. She's been married for three years, not one of her children was born out of wedlock. Or is it that she speaks her mind and is a woman of business?"

"Those businesses include gambling and whoring."

"And thus she deserves punishment according to your choice scriptures."

He stepped closer. "According to our Lord God."

"That punishment could have killed her unborn child, and possibly led to her losing one of those children. What does God have to say about that?"

"If you would come to God, perhaps you would learn."

"Sally?" Cole's voice surprised Sally so that she jumped.

"Pa!" Sally spun to find him standing in his doorway. She'd been too intent on her argument with the Pastor to hear him moving. "What are you doing out of bed?"

His gaze lingered on Eckles, a dark fury drawing his brows close together. He finally turned his attention to her. "I thought I heard your voice."

"Let's get you back in bed." She moved forward. It took some effort, and true pushing her tired body didn't care for to get him inside. With every step, his gaze remained fixed on the door until she managed to get it closed.

"Sally? What are you thinking?" He glared over her shoulder at the shut door. "Was it Eckles? Is that—"

"I only have a working theory, Pa. There's a lot I need to go over with Tommy, and then we'll deal with it. I couldn't pass up an opportunity to get some questions in when I saw him." Sally wished they hadn't been interrupted, but it was what it was. She managed to get Cole to sit. Her muscles were sore for the effort she'd put in. She sat in the chair with a low groan. "Why'd you have to fight me?"

"You're not up to dealing with nothing. What are you planning?"

"Nothing yet. I told you I have to meet with Tommy and go over this working theory."

Cole's gaze settled on the door again. "You were provoking."

"Needling, perhaps."

"Provoking."

"Pa, are you even supposed to be out of bed?"

"Going home Monday. I can be up and walking. You're changing the subject."

"Yes I am." Sally set her hand on his. "You're poorly, ma is very poorly. Let Tommy and I worry about the rest please."

"You're poorly, too."

"Yes, but I'm more healed than either of you. Tommy and I will handle things."

"You'd best be careful. There's enough of us not doing well, and you aren't healed much."

"I promise. I'll go to great lengths to remain intact."

"You'd better. Don't want to lose ya."

"Me either, Pa."

Nothing contributes so much to tranquilizing the mind as a steady purpose – a point on which the soul may fix its intellectual eye.
–Mary Wollstonecraft Shelley

Sally remained at Cole's bedside. He'd fallen asleep about half an hour before. While he slept, she attempted to settle her mind with a book. The encounter with Eckles continued to race through her mind. Though she didn't trust her mind to settle the mystery, she couldn't make it sit still.

She set the book aside, staring at the curtained windows. In the past couple of weeks all of her original theories crumbled to dust. Along with Molly, they'd thought it might be something to do with their church.

All the men were good men of God. The women all had either been whores, or likened to one, and yet all were accepted at the church here in town. Welcomed, even. At first Miss Bee's death had been an oddity among them.

Now there was the Lyman's and Ronnie. If it had been about their church, why would those that attend Glorious

Valley be dying? Moreso, why would they be dying intentionally?

Pastor Eckles had always unsettled her and Ma but appeared to have a strong following of like-minded souls. The idea that one solitary man could commit so many murders and attacks didn't seem possible. Especially when you added in the fact that Sally herself had been attacked by two people, neither of which had been Eckles. Tully and his whores had been set upon by a group of men.

Could Eckles have set others to do his bidding? In the name of the Lord?

If so, why were they now killing themselves? It didn't make sense at all.

Sally rubbed her forehead. A headache pounded against her skull in time with her swirling thoughts. She needed the assistance of Tommy to go over this all. Not only could she make no sense of it, her confidence was too shaken to trust her own mind.

She had to put it aside with some busy work. There wasn't any left to her right then. She'd managed to finish packing her things that morning. After that she'd had a pleasant lunch with Cole. They'd spent the morning waiting for the men to finish checking the surrounding area after the storm.

The problem was, what to do while she waited? She found it difficult to occupy her mind without someone to talk to. The book she'd been trying to read certainly wasn't cutting it.

"Everything all right in here?" Bonnie poked her head in the room.

Grateful for the distraction, Sally drew closer so they wouldn't wake Cole. "Yes. Cole's resting for now. I expect Ma will be by soon to sit with him if she can get someone to help her over here. I think Paps and my uncles are helping with the checks."

"It was your Paps that checked on the ranches. He brought me in this morning. Matthew's checking on the cattle. He said he'd stop by to see you this afternoon."

"He's kind to keep checking on me." Sally did her best to keep the heat of embarrassment from flooding her face. The kindness Matthew showed her was little more than friendship. She had to have hurt him when she turned him away, and she didn't blame him one bit for that.

"My brother is a good man. Of course he'll check on you. Besides, he fancies you."

"He might have once, but I've been cold. Besides, I'm not certain I'm up for any sort of fancying any longer."

"You were hurt. He knows that."

"What of Andrew?" Sally knew no better way to turn the embarrassment off herself then to reflect it back to the source. "He fancies you."

"He's merely kind." The light of embarrassment deepened in Bonnie's cheeks. On her it was a beautiful sight.

"And so is your brother."

"Oh, you."

Sally laughed outright, stopping herself to check and see she hadn't woken Cole. "Thank you for checking on us."

"Making the rounds. Mrs. Lyman is awake now. Seems out of sorts, but that's to be expected, I suppose. Graham is doing well, I caught him actually laughing."

"You don't say? That's wonderful. Perhaps he'll come out as good a man as he's been."

"I do hope so." Bonnie nodded to her. "I'll be on my way. More patients to check on."

"Talk to you later."

"Sally." Cole's voice sounded from the bed, gruff with sleep.

"Pa." Sally returned to her chair by the bed. "I'm sorry I woke you."

"Losing someone don't mean you can't move on." His voice remained quiet. His eyes were closed. "Don't let it ruin ya."

"Pa. You don't understand."

"I do. Better than you know."

Sally's further protest drowned under a shriek from down the hall. She rushed fast as she could to the door.

"Dr. Noe. It's Jake!" Bonnie ducked back into the room where Jake had been recuperating. The same room Pastor Eckles had left that morning.

Sally moved slow down the hall to allow Dr. Noe time to pass her. By the time Sally got there, Dr. Noe was pulling down Jake's lids. Sally turned from the sight; not out of disgust or fear, but to examine the room.

Jake's body lay on the bed, no sign of struggle or distress marred the muslin around him. From the doorway she thought she detected a stain on his lips. A bible sat on the table, open wide. She would wager a bet it sat open to the book of Roman's.

She stepped further into the room to get a better look. On the floor sat a bottle that Dr. Noe bent to pick up. She barked, "Don't."

Dr. Noe straightened to her full height. She studied Sally for a moment, her brows lifted. "Excuse me?"

"Sorry. I'm not being impertinent. I think we need to be careful. Andrew should test whatever is left in that bottle." Sally's suspicions rose as she spotted the stain of red lingering at the corner of Jake's mouth.

Bonnie had the sheet half pulled over Jake. "What? Why?"

Dr. Noe folded her arms across her chest. "What are you talking about? This man succumbed to his injuries. We were afraid—"

"He was getting better, wasn't he?" Sally interrupted. She didn't have a problem with the new doctor, but the woman was unfamiliar with the situation's full extent. The doctor stepped in front of her to block her path, Sally didn't back down. "I heard him talking this morning. He carried on a full conversation."

"You're the one that sta—"

"And he's the one that shot me. I said it earlier, and I'll say it again. If I wanted him dead, he would've been. He wasn't. In fact, he was getting better. Tommy and I had designs on questioning him this afternoon."

Bonnie tucked the blankets around the body. Rather than acknowledge the two women having a bit of a contest of wills, she went around the bed to the bottle. She crouched down beside it. "There's a little left, but not much. It appears that some spilled on the floor."

"Please pick it up carefully so no more spills. Hopefully it's enough for Andrew to test." Sally met the doctor's gaze. She wouldn't back down, but she hoped to appear mildly contrite. "I'm sorry, Doctor. Jake was a suspect in at least one of the attacks this past year. The fact that he died is suspicious, even with his injuries."

"That man's bowel was nicked. The poison of his own making got into his body. These things happen in cases like his." Dr. Noe's brow furrowed.

"Wouldn't he have died sooner if that were his cause of death? And Andrew is the one who repaired his bowel, and I can personally attest to his skills." Sally smiled at Bonnie as she set the bottle on the table with care. "Thank you."

"Andrew's skills are impeccable, but these things can still happen." Dr. Noe's hard edges softened.

"I'm not saying they can't." Sally glanced toward the body. "Why don't we let Andrew do an autopsy? If I'm mistaken, you'll have my sincerest apologies for interrupting."

"An autopsy would be perfectly acceptable." Dr. Noe sighed. "Much as I hate to admit it, Jake was showing signs of great improvement. I don't like to believe someone was murdered in my own clinic."

"I don't think Uncle Charlie would care much to know it, either." Sally glanced to the bed. "I only hope that Mrs. Lyman is mildly lucid then, for otherwise we have no other witnesses."

"Miss Sally," Dr. Noe's voice softened in kindness. "You're looking pale. You should sit down."

"I think I will." Sally followed them both from the room. Once the door was closed, she leaned against the wall. "I don't have the stamina for much right now. This will do me no good for what needs to be done."

"You have to let your body heal." Dr. Noe guided her back to her room. "Impatience is not the friend of healing."

"It isn't, but it's all I have right now." Sally sank into a chair. "Will you check on my pa? I woke him up, I want to be sure he's doing all right."

"I'll check on him, if you rest."

"I promise." Sally settled back in the rocking chair. Though she had the biggest urge to move closer to the window, she remained resting as she'd been ordered.

A throat cleared, then the familiar, friendly voice of Matthew spoke, "Good afternoon, Sally."

"Matthew." She smiled as he entered the room. "You shouldn't have come today. I'm sure after that storm there's plenty to deal with at your ranch. Although I was glad to hear you all made it through well enough."

"Already checked my cattle. Stephen wanted to come into town to play with his friends. I can't be sure, but I think he, Isaac, and your brothers are planning some sort of mischief."

"I wouldn't put it past them."

"I don't think anyone with a brain would." He laughed softly as he pulled a chair up closer to hers. "How are you doing today?"

"Honest?"

"Honest."

"Tired. The desperation lingers, but it is quiet for now. I have things to attend to before I can deal with it."

"Then you have a purpose."

"For now."

"And what after that purpose is completed?"

"I have no idea."

"I guess we'll have to find you a new purpose." He smiled softly, his hand settling on hers. "Whatever keeps the desperation quiet."

"What if I can't find one?"

"I'll help you."

*The belief in a supernatural source of evil
is not necessary;
men alone
are quite capable of every wickedness.
-Joseph Conrad*

Sally tried to be discreet in her eying of Jane. Despite all reports that she rested often, and the checks on the baby were good, dark circles lingered under Jane's eyes. She looked drawn and tired even more than when Cole had been gone.

"Stop worrying so," Jane scolded quietly. She nestled in close to Cole. Even in his sleep, his arm went around her.

"Sorry. You don't look well, Ma." Sally helped get the blankets settled around Jane while Cole dozed on.

"Funny enough, I have several doctors and a midwife worrying over my state of being. Not to mention Ma, Pa, and Cole." Jane levelled her blue eyes at Sally. "You have more than enough to be getting on with. Worrying about me should be the lowest of your priorities at the moment."

"How can it be? You're my ma."

"True enough. However, there is little you can do about my ailments. That is up to your little brother in here, and my doctor's. This is not something you can control or do. What you can do is continue with what you're doing."

Sally fussed with straightening the books on the table beside Jane rather than admit the exceedingly familiar doubts creeping back. Though mere hours since they'd discovered Jake, she already second-guessed everything she'd done. If she could make the impact needed.

"Tell me."

Sally jumped at the words. She found Jane's sharp gaze on her. Damn if her ma didn't miss a trick. "Tell you what?"

"What was the first thing you did when you went into Jake's room? Without regard to your own strength or healing, what did you do?"

Head bowed, Sally did her best to not mumble her reply. "Looked for clues."

Jane's hand clasped Sally's. Surprising warmth and strength radiated in the hold. "This is a part of you. It hasn't left you unwounded and you'll have time to lick those wounds soon, but it is part of who you are now."

"Maybe it shouldn't be. Look what happened—"

"What happened was a tragedy, but you cannot continue using it to excuse your own fears. If you wish to malaise and mope and doubt, you may do so when you have seen this through. If you stop now, you'll never forgive yourself."

"I'm already there," Sally mumbled.

"Then that is a problem. One you have little time to overcome, because you have a job to finish." Jane drew Sally's hand close to her chest. "You have strength in you that you haven't realized. It's all right you haven't figured it out yet, or that you don't believe it. I'll believe it enough for you until you're ready."

The warmth and belief in Jane's tone warmed Sally's heart. A spark of hope flared again. She couldn't seem to keep that spark burning into a true flame any longer, but she'd give it a go.

"I need to rest, and there's no need for you to sit and watch us sleep. I believe you had plans with the young doctor, did you not?"

Sally glanced toward the clock on the dresser. Who knew how far Andrew had gotten in the several hours she'd spent with her family. "I'm likely too late by now."

"You'll never know unless you go. It's fine. Cole and I have survived more than a quiet afternoon in the clinic on our own." Jane smiled warmly, winking at Sally. "Go see what your friend has made of the situation."

"I will, Ma." Sally made her way to the door. By the time she got there, Jane's eyes were closed and she snuggled close against Cole. Sally smiled at the sight before turning away.

She hoped against hope Andrew had waited some for her to be able to be in on part of the autopsy. Then again, she'd expressed some urgency in the matter. She knocked on the door to the autopsy room.

"Who is it?"

"Sally."

"Come on in," Andrew called back.

She stepped into the room. Her smile sank when she spotted Jake on the autopsy table, already open. "Oh, I did miss it. Darn."

"You indicated urgency. I anticipated you down here much sooner." Andrew scribbled notes as he eyed the heart lying on a scale.

"They brought Ma over, so I spent some time with her and Pa since I'm going back home tonight." Sally grabbed the large apron from its hook to throw it on. She did her best to not wince when she reached behind her back to tie it off. "Did I miss everything?"

"Of the physical autopsy, yes. I did leave the stomach for the end, though."

"Oh, wonderful. I'm most interested in that, as well as the bottle." Now that she was in the room and faced with the possibility of real answers, the nagging doubt stayed well back. She stepped closer as he jotted his final notes on the heart. "What does it look like? Was Dr. Noe correct that this was natural after the injuries?"

"You'll be pleased to know his intestines remained intact. My repair on them didn't fail." He guided her over to the body. The spot on the intestines was clear without his assisting point. "You can see the stitches there. No sign of tearing or leakage."

"Well, that is good news. I'd hate to think your stitches could fail."

"If it helps more, I took greater care on yours than his." He winked to cover his joking tone before moving over to the table on which the stomach sat in a bowl. "Would you like to do the honors?"

A good part of her wanted to. She deferred with a shake of her head. "I'll accede to your expertise."

"Modesty doesn't become you, Sally." Andrew made his incision quick and clean. The contents spilled into the bowl.

Rather than the usual stench and mess of rotted food, a sweet-smelling liquid took up the bulk of the contents.

She moved closer to observe the dark liquid swirling about. No bits of food to be found. Though unusual in most autopsies, Jake had also been unconscious for some time, being spoon fed broth and water as they could. "How long had he been awake?"

"A day at most. We were supplying him with liquids only until we could be certain he could handle more. We offer a rich bone broth, as you know, not wine." He lifted his gaze to hers. "Which would you like? The wine or the blood?"

She already had a suspicion of what the cause could be. Fast as the death would be, she doubted it would appear in the blood. Though fairly certain, she needed confirmation. "Tell me, Dr. Cross."

"Oh. Well." He folded his hands in front of him. His body straightened, eyebrows raised as though to give her his fullest attention. "Yes, Miss Mitchell?"

She couldn't help but laugh at his tone of propriety. In response, she curtsied low. "If you would please, sir. Would you tell me without testing the wine, or noting the contents of the stomach, what does it appear his cause of death is?"

"Ignoring those rather key factors? Why?"

"I have a suspicion."

"Before I opened the stomach I would have suspected a heart attack."

"What hides well in sweet wine, Andrew?"

"We both already know the answer to that. It has killed kings and commoners alike."

Sally moved to the dark bottle. She picked it up and turned it in her hands. A sniff only gave notes of fermented blackberries and possibly oak. "In wine it's impossible to detect by scent. Is there a test for Belladonna among your many tricks and chemicals?"

"Not precisely. I can certainly rule out other poisons. If it had been foxglove I could have. Belladonna, no."

She strode back to the bowl, glaring at the dark contents. "If only he'd eaten the leaves instead. We'd have proof then."

A knock on the door pulled her from the disappointing bowl of empty proof. When the door opened to reveal Tommy, she offered a wan smile. "In good news, we think we know what killed Jake. In bad news, we don't know how to prove it."

"How's that?" Tommy nodded to Andrew. "Doc."

"Mr. Young. Sorry, Tommy." Andrew joined them near the bowl of Jake's stomach contents. "It appears all he has ingested was a sweet wine. Then, he died of an apparent heart attack."

"Ah. Tricky." Tommy's gaze landed on Sally. "And?"

"The king killer. Belladonna."

"Funnily enough you know that black nightshade grows wild around these parts."

"Black nightshade isn't poisonous and differs from Belladonna," Andrew objected. His brows furrowed. "Belladonna could be grown here in the right conditions, I suppose."

"How? Sally racked her brain for answers. When Chauncey had died she'd studied Belladonna. "That's why I found it odd that Ma believed Chauncey died from Belladonna. Where would whomever gave it to him get it? Are there wild patches of belladonna around here?"

"Black Moon says several new patches of the plant showed up throughout the hills south of here. They're all thriving, too." Tommy folded his arms across his chest. "He's had to change the routes of his mountain tours to avoid them. Kids think they're sweet berries, and they look similar to black nightshade."

Andrew frowned. "If he knows they're there, why doesn't he remove them?"

"Once it starts, it grows like a weed. Hard to remove and irritating to the skin. He's been making some effort with winter set in to rid us of some of the patches." Tommy leaned over the bowl with Jake's stomach. "Sally?"

"Right." Sally brought her attention back to the matter at hand. "Eckles visited Jake this morning. I heard him talking to him. It didn't have the sound of the sort of supportive counsel we'd receive from Reverend Greene. He mentioned that the son should not bear the iniquity of the father, and Jake was sobbing. Whatever Jake said, Eckles told him it didn't matter. Then I heard him mention Romans six, twenty-three about the cost of sin."

"Death," Tommy finished. "Anything else?"

"He confirmed Mac was a member of his congregation, said that he was fighting the good fight. I asked him about Ma, and he told me only a warrior of God could offer such punishment to a sinner. I was going to question him more, but Pa overheard me."

"What's your conclusion?"

"I think we need to see what Pastor Eckles' Sunday sermons are like and question him appropriately." Sally leaned back against the table where Jake's body lay. Tommy's approving nod helped keep the nerves at bay. It was amazing how actually being in the midst of it made everything else seem far away.

"Questioning yes, we definitely do need to do that." Tommy rubbed his hand along his chin. "Now that we have a minute, tell me it all."

"The first to be attacked or killed were all good, loyal members of Reverend Greene's congregation. The men were vocal about their support of the existing church—the women all…"

"Former whores, except Jane of course," Tommy finished with a nod. "Although she was a sinner by all accounts. All of the women were well-accepted and supported in Greene's church despite the black mark of sin on their souls."

"I know something to do with the church was your working theory, Sally." Andrew's brows knit together. "Are you saying this was some sort of holy war?"

"To Eckles point of view, yes." Sally began to pace while she thought. "It was all our congregation except for Mac. He killed himself after a visit from Eckles, as well."

"Why? If he was doing God's work?" Tommy didn't look nearly as confused as Andrew. If anything, Sally would almost say he looked proud.

"Ma was pregnant." Sally stopped short. "The news came out after his attack on her, she'd just learned that day. Then Miss Bee. She's the abnormality."

"How?"

"She was killed with no precipitating event. Maybe she was going to talk. I need to put her aside because I'm not certain why her death came."

Tommy nodded. "Then go on. Why the others?"

"Joshua. The iniquities of the father should not be visited on the son. Joshua was killed in the explosion that nearly killed Graham—not just a good man of our church, but the mayor. The Lyman's—they killed themselves. How could he convince these people to take their own lives?"

"The same way he convinced them to rid the town of its evil." Tommy leaned on the table, his gaze on the dark window. "First thing in the morning we're heading out to hear a sermon at Glorious Valley, Sally."

"I'll be ready."

Faith, noun.
Belief without evidence in what is told by
one who speaks without knowledge,
of things without parallel.
—Ambrose Bierce

Sally slowed Agatha as they came within sight of the candlelit church. Tommy pulled to a stop beside her. His horse's last footstep crunched away into silence. A light, cold breeze dusted across the icy snow cover, making no dent on the surface.

The sun had just begun to peek over the eastern mountains to their left. Services for their own church wouldn't begin until nearly eight. Eckles had always run a much longer sermon that began around six-thirty.

Cutters and wagons sat all around the church, each connected to a horse or horses. The horses stood mostly quiet, their breath expelled into the cold air like smoke in the bitter cold morning air.

Despite the hour, there didn't appear to be a soul moving in the church. Candle light flickered in the windows. The few pews she could see appeared empty. The entire area was eerily quiet thanks to the lack of wind.

Tom's horse stamped against the frozen snow. Brag let out a snort of protest to their stillness. Sally herself was already sore from the long ride. She didn't dare complain, not when there were more important matters to deal with.

She slid her hand under her cape to free her gun. When she rested it on her thigh, Tommy nodded his approval. In moments he'd done the same.

The surface of the snow remained unblemished. Not one track showed despite the fact several people and families had gone to the church. Not even the weight of a horse or wagon had left a mark. That meant no human would, either. "If they've gone anywhere we won't be able to track a thing. The snow is hard as stone after last night."

"There doesn't appear to be anyone inside, either."

"I think we'd hear the sermon from here if there was. I remember Eckles being rather loud when he got fired up during the brief time he worked with Reverend Greene."

"He sure did. It was a marked difference from Mark's quiet tones. Startled many a parishioner." Tommy adjusted the reins in his hands. "Let's head in. Keep an eye out and your gun at the ready."

"I will." She urged Agatha to walk beside Brag toward the church. The whole way there she kept her eyes peeled on the surrounding area. The valley lay sheer white with snow. Not one sign of movement anywhere. The nearby tree cover of the foothills lingered with shadows thanks to the late sunrise and cloud cover. Nothing in the shadows seemed to be moving.

She swung off Agatha. Despite her attempts to keep it at bay, a grunt of pain escaped on landing. For a moment she leaned into the saddle to let it subside.

"You good?" The question came in a mere whisper.

"Yes," she responded in the same undertone. The flash of pain eased into the familiar dull ache she'd been living with of late. With one more deep breath she was able to straighten. While she tied off Agatha, Tommy used gestures to show she should go to the front while he took the back of the church.

Sally nodded her understanding. She edged along the front of the building toward the open door. By now she definitely should be hearing something of Eckle's preaching. At most she thought she caught a whisper or two.

The soft noises ratcheted tension through her. She lifted her weapon to the ready. Each step was taken slow as possible to avoid making noise. She edged through the vestibule which sat devoid of all but a few coats too small for adults. Brow furrowed, she worked her way toward the main portion of the building.

When she got to the main door, she hovered in the shadows. She peeked into the candlelit room. The was no sign of life in the pews to the left. Not one soul to be seen.

She crept to the other side of the vestibule, training her weapon in preparation for a surprise. At first, none came. The pews on the right also sat empty.

Whispers dusted the silent church like gentle snowflakes. Soft, tiny voices. Almost like those of children.

Sally stared at the small coats hanging in the vestibule. Whatever Eckles had done, had he left the children alone in the silent, cold church? The door sat wide open, allowing cold air to creep into the building.

She edged through the door, her weapon still raised in fear of duplicity. Soon as she cleared the door she found five children huddled around the stove. They stared at her with wide eyes as her weapon focused on them. The smaller children whimpered and scooted closer to the older ones. One boy, clearly the eldest, stared at her with his chin raised in defiance.

"My goodness." Sally sank against the wall. Her weapon didn't drop, but she turned it toward the seemingly empty church. She took a chance to speak to the oldest of the children. His glare gave her little hope of a reply. "Kyle Ross. Is there anyone else here?"

"Pastor said you would come, and you would hurt us."

"I'm not going to hurt you, or any of the children, Kyle." Sally's stomach turned at the suggestion. "Where is Pastor Eckles? Where are your parents?"

"Went out back. Near an hour ago. Told us to hold tight. Warned us about you."

She wondered at how they hadn't all left, but obedience was a big thing with Eckles. Unfortunately she believed that though he didn't believe children should suffer for their parents, he likely also believed in not sparing the rod to keep obedience.

"Stay there," she urged them, hoping they wouldn't take a chance to escape now that she was there with a gun. "It's brutal cold out, stay warm by the stove."

Sally moved faster now, rushing through the open church toward the back. Behind the pulpit was a small room, closed and locked tight. Sally took a deep breath to gather her strength for what she had to do. She kicked the door hard. It splintered open, revealing Eckles' living space. She crept in, searching every corner for a sign of movement.

Empty.

She released a breath of relief, then scanned the walls quietly. Most of the shelves sat empty, save for a few books, several large bibles, and three bottles like the one they'd found in Jake's room. The shelf was large, and dust circles gave evidence of the large number of bottles missing.

She took down one of the remaining bottles to study. Like the one in Jake's room, there was no markings or any indication of what the bottle held. She slipped it into her pocket before leaving the room.

The children had miraculously stayed where she'd told them to. It was then she noticed several cups sitting on the floor. Panicked, she raced toward the children. They all scampered into the corner at her approach.

She lifted the cups to sniff the contents. It didn't smell like wine. "What was in these?"

"Water. I melted some snow." Kyle glared at her gun.

"Oh, thank goodness. Pastor didn't give you anything to eat or drink, did he?" Sally searched the faces of each young child. When they'd shaken their heads, she sighed her relief. Though she knew it would ease their minds to put it away, she kept her weapon at her side.

The back door rattled before it flung open. Sally spun, raising her gun toward the sound. When Tommy entered, she lowered the weapon to her side. "Pastor left the children here. Kyle says they all left near an hour ago. He's been taking good care of the little ones since."

"I found the women and ten men." Tommy's features were grim. He approached with barely a glance to the children. "It seems the Pastor offered them all some sweet wine."

"I found a few bottles in his room, with a wide shelf now empty which appeared to have been full not long ago." She tapped her gun against the bottle in her pocket. For the moment she tried to push aside the fact that a good number of people lay dead behind the church somewhere. "The question remains, where is the good Pastor and any others not accounted for?"

"I don't know the size of his flock, so I'm not sure how many that would be."

Sally released a slow breath in an effort to remain calm. If the Pastor hadn't joined the rest of his flock in drinking the wine, what was he up to? An uneasy feeling settled in her stomach. "We should get the children back to town. I'm certain the Women's League can help figure out somewhere for them to stay and locate any family they may have outside the territory."

Tommy studied the children again. "There's a wagon out there. The snow is hard enough we should be able to get you all into town safe enough."

Kyle stood, straightening his shoulders. The thirteen-year-old tried to look every bit a man, though his gangly limbs and smattering of acne ruined the effect. "Pastor told us to stay here. Our parents—"

"Are dead." Tommy didn't bother beating around the bush. "You're all orphans now. I saw your parents, Kyle. And the parents of all these young ones. They're all dead out in the woods. We need to get you back to town where we can see you get food and warmth."

"Pastor said we would see them soon." Kyle gathered two younger boys closer to him.

"You will, in a pine box, once we can return for them. Lucky it's cold enough they shouldn't give off any scent to attract wildlife." Tommy moved toward the children, but several scooted back away from him.

"Tommy." Sally moved closer to them, sliding her gun back in its holster now that she had Tommy close by. She knelt by the two youngest ones, smiling softly. "Lila, Mary, do you remember me from the library?"

Both girls nodded wide-eyed.

Sally turned toward the two clinging to Kyle. "Miles, you know my brother Jesse. Chris, I'm afraid I've only seen you around town. Lastly, the young master Phil Harmon. You were part of the group that attacked me with snowballs."

Phil flushed under the accusation, but nodded with a small grin.

"We aren't going to hurt you, but it is bitterly cold and this fire is already faltering. We're going to take you all into town where you can have a nice, hot meal at the restaurant. We'll see to it you all have a place to sleep tonight. No one is going to hurt you, I promise."

Kyle glared at her, keeping the two boys close against him. "Your promises mean nothing. You're a sinner."

"We are all sinners. It is the grace of God that saves us." Sally rose back to her feet, eye-to-eye with Kyle. "You already lost your brother this last year. I know that's when your parents started coming to this church. I can't imagine how tough this is, but we aren't here to hurt you. We're going to take you to town and get you fed."

Kyle paused for a minute, then looked down at the kids. Finally he nodded. "Fine."

"Good. Will you help me bundle up the children? Tommy, will you guide back Agatha, and I'll drive the children?" She thought another horseback ride would hurt quite a bit.

"I'd best drive the wagon." Tommy moved with her, a distrustful gaze on Kyle. "I know you're hurting, but it's best I go in the wagon."

Sally knew better than to complain, she merely nodded. "Whatever you think is best."

"Then let's move."

They worked quickly to get the children wrapped in coats, mufflers, and mittens. As Tommy worked to lift them all into the wagon alongside Kyle, Sally moved to gather the horses. She paused, her gaze focused on the town so far in the distance it seemed a dark shadow across the land.

The dazzling morning sunlight tried to blind her as it bounced off the snow. She lifted her hand, focusing on something she thought she'd seen. "Tommy?"

"Just get the horses."

"Tommy, look. What's that?"

Tommy stepped up beside her, shielding his eyes as well. "What?"

"That—" Sally pointed toward the dark blur almost like a cloud. "Right there."

"Smoke." Tom turned to head back to the wagon, then paused, turning back. "That's a *lot* of smoke."

"You don't think…"

"Let's move."

"Let's move."

While I was musing the fire burned.
–Psalms 39:3

The unfinished cooper shop showed all evidence of its hasty conversion into a church. On short notice and with a rush on several other projects, Teddy hadn't been able to do the job up to the usual standard. Two of the only windows sat tall up in the rafters for ventilation due to the abnormally large brick fireplace.

The remaining two meager windows sat on the walls along the back of the building. The rest had yet to be installed. As they planned on building a new church once the winter ended, placing windows hadn't been a priority. That left the only cool air in the crowded room to come through the unfinished walls. Though it was bitterly cold out, there was no breeze to push it through.

Reverend Greene had lit a fire out of kindness due to the freezing morning, and though he'd extinguished it as the room filled, the room now sat stifling. A huge crowd had turned out for service, and they barely had seats for everyone.

Despite all of that, the mood in the church remained jovial. Friendly greetings had been exchanged throughout the room before service started. A pleasant quiet had settled over the group at the first indication of prayer. Now they all sat listening to a sermon focused on healing from painful difficulties, the value of their community, and how they had come together in these hard times.

Jane closed her eyes, her hand running along the swell of her abdomen. Though she tried with all her might to focus on the sermon, which was the whole reason for her leaving Cole's side that morning, she couldn't seem to concentrate. An ache in her back refused to go away no matter how she repositioned herself.

A hand settled on her arm, pulling her from her quiet discomfort in surprise. Jesse gestured upward and rose to sing with the rest of the congregation. Jane couldn't begin to think of rising, so she remained in her seat When her mother cast a concerned look her way, Jane offered a weak smile.

The hymn came to an end and the congregation sat again. Jane shushed her mother when she leaned toward her to question her. Reverend Lyons had just risen to offer a prayer. Jane closed her eyes, folding her hands in front of her to join. With effort she focused on Eli's prayer.

"Amen," she murmured with everyone else. When she lifted her gaze, she realized Eli hadn't left the pulpit.

His head tilted a small amount, his nostrils flared. "Do you smell that?"

Jane glanced over toward Nicholas on her other side, confused. A murmur went through the church, expressing the same confusion plaguing Jane.

Nick half-rose, but Reverend Greene got to Eli's side first. When he tried to usher away the young minister, Reverend Lyons held on for an extra moment before he let go. Eli shook his head. "Sorry. I thought I smelled—never mind."

When Nick returned to his seat, Jane took his hand. A gush of moisture caught her so off-guard, she squeezed his hand hard. She thought perhaps her waters had broke. She sat in silence, trying to grasp what was happening. It was too soon for the child to come. The pain of a contraction stretched across her stomach and she squeezed Nick's hand even harder. "Oh no."

He leaned close, "What's wrong?"

"I—I believe I need Bonnie, or Charles. I don't feel so— what's that?" A whisp of movement caught Jane's eye. Along the floorboards a sort of fog floated. She rose from her seat slow, ignorant of the whispered urgings to get down.

"Jane." Nick grabbed her arm. He followed her gaze. "What?"

Jane moved closer to the pulpit, her hand still laced with Nick's as she stared at the floor. The smoke lingered, and in a crack between the floorboards she saw a flash of orange light. "It's—*fire*."

"*Fire*," came a scream near the doors at the same time as Jane's.

Jane's head flew up. Flames licked at the front doors. "Dear God in heaven."

Panic rippled through the room like a tidal wave. People scrambled toward the flaming doors, then back. Smoke filtered into the room as flames appeared under the windows along the back of the building, then along the walls.

The crash of broken glass introduced a gust of flames into the building near the back.

"It's everywhere," she whispered. Smoke cut off her words and she dissolved into a coughing fit.

Nick's arm circled her, dragging her toward the fireplace. David called for calm, trying to usher everyone toward the one place where brick covered the wood below and around them, the fireplace. Most people protested at ow it would trap them, and Jane could see their point. Still, the fire was even under their feet.

Jane's lungs tightened under the smoke. In a panic she pulled the knife from her reticule. She cut at her skirts, ripping off the cloth in strips, then cut them into triangles as best she could. She called for the twins and Jesse, tying them on soon as her children gathered close by.

Nick and her pa took her cue and began to call over others to do the same. Once all of her children had something covering their faces, she gathered them close. She didn't know what good the cotton covering would do, but it was her only hope. She backed up with them closer to the fireplace.

Flames licked higher on the walls, some of them reaching the ceiling.

The twins screamed, clinging to her skirts. Panic filled her as people began to drop to the ground from the thick smoke. Jane's own lungs felt tighter than a drum.

Everyone huddled close together. Jane found herself packed in by David.

"We can't bust out the walls, the ceiling will cave in," he yelled at someone.

"Where's the water?" someone else yelled.

"We're all here. Who's gonna save us?"

A brutal pain stretched across Jane's belly. The scream that tore out of her was so primal it caught her off-guard. She clung to an arm, hearing David's voice in her ear trying to reassure he in some way.

"Something's…" Jane gripped her stomach as pain wrenched through her. She collapsed to the ground, her hand slipping in a thick dark liquid. Blood. Dark red blood. "*Charles.*"

Another pain stabbed her so hard she screamed again.

Charlie appeared in front of her, his entire visage covered in soot. "Jane. Breathe."

"Somethings," coughs wracked through her, "Wrong. Blood."

Charlie's eyes widened. "We've got to get this baby of her now or we'll lose them both. We have to find a way out of here."

Jane screamed again, collapsing to the brick floor.

From outside a familiar voice yelled back, "*Jane!!*"

Fire is the test of gold;
adversity, of strong men.
—Seneca

Cole shrugged into his coat. He wanted to go onto the balcony for a few minutes to get some fresh air. He'd been stuck inside too long. Jane had left an hour ago with the help of Nick to make it to church for services. He didn't mind missing them, he only went to church on occasion.

He wanted nothing more than to head home to finish recuperating there. Jane had made him promise to stay in the clinic under observation for another day.

After she'd left for church, Cole had stopped by Graham's room to check on him and his family. The man was healing well physically. His spirits were far better than Cole had expected. Most likely his attitude had plenty to do with the healthy baby he'd been holding.

Cole was relieved his friend was doing well. He worried the tides would turn when Graham left the clinic to return home. At home he'd be faced with many reminders of his son.

Cole hoped Jun and Linh would be able to keep Graham on a good path.

He shook off his concerns to head outside. Cold air hit him hard. He drew in a deep breath in response. His ribs smarted at the action, but he inhaled again anyway.

Then paused.

Instead of the familiar crisp, cold air of winter he'd expected, he got a nose full of something else. Smoke.

Cole turned up and down Main Street to find the source. Nothing caught his eye. He strode to the end of the balcony where it jutted out from the end of the building to accommodate the stairs to check the next street.

That's when he saw the fire blazing up the sides of the temporary church.

His heart stopped dead. His hand gripped the railing. His entire family was in that building. Jane. The twins. Alma, Sally, Cindy. He wanted to run, but his feet wouldn't move. An attempt at a yell ended with a garbled cry.

In one heartbeat, reality crashed down on him so hard his knees buckled. The heart that had stopped began to race fast. He screamed out *fire* even though he had no idea if there was anyone in town outside of the church. He rushed into the clinic and pounded on Graham's door. "There's a fire at the church!"

Without waiting for a reply, he tore down the stairs so fast he skipped half the steps. He yelled at Lydia to get to the emergency bell in hopes it would draw someone to help. There were hundreds of miners that didn't attend services.

He slid over the slick snow through the streets and down alleys until he got to Fourth Street. Across the street from the building he skidded to a stop.

Screams and yells echoed from inside. One brutal scream ripped his heart right out of his chest. The familiar voice echoed with pain and terror. "*Jane.*"

The emergency bell clanged through town, jolting through Cole's soul like a death knell. Fear gripped him in place, unsure what to do as he was one man against a blazing fire. A portion of the roof cracked, then fell into the building to renewed screams.

Cole rushed forward to the spigot and filled a bucket of water. He raced back to the building, pausing at the entrance. A metal bar had been lodged into the handles of the wide doors. He poured water over the metal.

He peeled off his coat and grabbed the iron stake. He tugged hard to free it. Shouts echoed around him as men ran toward the fire to help. Heat blazed through his coat to scald his hands. He gave another brutal tug to the metal. His ribs protested the sudden harsh movement. Water sprayed around him, dousing him as much as the building, but he didn't stop until the bar came free.

With a harsh kick the doors burst open to reveal chunks of ceiling. He could hear no more screaming from Jane. "Jane! Colton! Clara!"

Water dripped from his hair, freezing as it dribbled along his flesh. As the fire died under the onslaught of water, a figure emerged through the smoke. Nick's features were grim as he carried Jane. Blood soaked her skirts.

"Jane," the word choked in his throat. He couldn't move, even as Nick raced past with Charlie hot on his heels. Only knowing she'd be cared for kept him from racing after them. He had more family to find.

A strong hand landed on his shoulder. Graham's voice was gruff. "We'll get your family."

"No." Cole pushed into the building, climbing over rubble even as bits of wood and water rained down on him. "Colton! Clara! Cindy!"

Forms scrambled over the destruction, familiar faces of friends. Cora passed him with Isaac, both coughing heartily, soot streaming along the freezing water that dripped along their hair and faces. Cole could hear Graham shouting at everyone to meet at the clinic where they'd get warmth and food while they waited for medical care.

Cole lofted himself over a fallen beam and found the crowd gathered around the fireplace. He spotted the twins and raced toward them quickly. He gathered them both close as he stared up at his mother-in-law. "Where's Alma? Sally?"

Eunice coughed a few times, then shook her head. "Not here. Alma stayed home with Willow and Jay. Arthur stayed with the lot of them. Alma was too upset—about you. Sally left before dawn with Tommy."

Cole searched the crowd. "Jesse! Cindy! Lizzie!"

Jesse and Lizzie were by David and several huddled forms on the floor. Kat lifted her head from the group, nodding to Cole. Cindy lay in her arms, a cut bleeding on her cheek, but she was awake and moving.

"Go to Jane." Eunice coughed again. "I'll be right behind. John will get the twins there."

Cole hesitated, then rose. Clara continued to hang onto his neck, Colton his leg. The weight of Clara's clinging made pain stretch across his ribs, but he didn't complain. "We need to do—"

"You need to go to Jane. Immediately. It seems the mayor is taking charge. Go." John peeled Clara from Cole's neck. "Be quick. Go on, Eunice. I have them."

Though he wanted to protest, the urgency in John's voice spurred him forward. He climbed back over the dripping, hot rubble. With every step he helped Eunice best as he could. He urged her to avoid the hot spots, and got her out safely.

Once they were free of the still smoldering church, he bolted for the clinic. Inside he rushed through toward the one closed room. He burst in to find Charlie standing with a scalpel over Jane's stomach. "You're not cuttin' on her!"

"I have to, Cole. Or they'll both die."

Cole's eyes fell on Jane's still features. Soot streaked every inch of her face, turning her hair black. His heart stopped again. "No."

"Here." Nick urged him up to Jane's head. "Clean her up. It'll give you something to do while Charlie works."

Jane's body jerked and the smallest of winces puckered her brow before she stilled. Cole did as he was told, using water to remove the soot from her face. With every swipe he realized how pale she'd become. Her lips held a faint hit of blue.

"Come on, Jane. Don't do this to me. Stay with me."

What we call despair is often only the painful eagerness of unfed hope.
—George Eliot

Cole kept his focus on Jane as much as possible. He'd cleaned the soot from her face and neck already. That left him with little to do but watch her pale face. Her head flopped to the side as her whole body moved a shifted with whatever Charlie did.

For all that Charlie did to her, she didn't whimper or even wince. Maybe it was a blessing that she was so weak. She couldn't feel whatever was happening to her. The flip side being, she might be close to death.

Cole pulled her hand to him, kissing the back of it. He held on tight to her hand. In her ear he whispered low, asking her to not leave him dond the kids. In desperation he prayed that God would be in his favor for once.

"Baby's out. Ma, get her going for me. I've got to stop this bleeding." Charlie's voice was taut with tension, and

Cole suspected fear. Based on Jane's continued lack of response, he could imagine why.

"I've got her. Save that one, I'll save this one." Eunice's normally bright and kind voice held the same note of stress in it. Cole had no idea when she'd entered the room. He'd been too wrapped up in Jane to notice anything. That, and he didn't want to see what Charlie was doing. He suspected it would make everything worse.

Cole swallowed against the lump in his throat. The baby hadn't made a sound. Then Charlie's words hit him. Tears burned his eyes, his nose ached from needing to release them. Charlie and Eunice had both said 'her'. The baby was a girl. "Did you hear that, Jane? It's a girl. You were wrong. Wake up so I can tell you. I don't get to say it often."

"I need more to soak this up. Cole. In the cabinet. Grab every bit of cotton you can find and bring it to me. Gauze, towels, it doesn't matter at this point." Charlie was elbow deep in Jane's belly, his hands moving constantly. "If I can't stop this bleeding I'm going to have to extirpate the uterus."

Cole rushed to the cabinet and threw open the doors. He grabbed a stack of cloth piled there in his arms. Before he'd even set them down, Charlie was grabbing some from the top. Cole backed up as Charlie shoved the cotton into the open wound by the handful. Unable to watch any longer, he turned to Eunice. The woman stood there rubbing the baby vigorously.

In the midst of the utter chaos a weak cry emerged from the baby before it fell silent again. The room spun under the rush of relief that tore through Cole. He gripped the edge of the table to steady himself.

"I'm going to need to try a transfusion. She's lost far too much blood." Charlie still worked on the wound. The pile of fabric Cole had brought now gone.

"A what?"

"Get me more, Cole. Now."

Cole rushed back to the cabinet. "What did you say you need to try?"

"I said a transfusion. I have to replace the blood she's lost."

Another pile of fabric in hand, Cole returned to the table. "Then take mine. All of it. Whatever you need."

"We've found them to have greater success when it's family, or of the same sex. It's risky and could kill her as easily as it could cure her." Charlie puled out a large bloody mass of fabric from Jane's belly. The cloth flopped to the floor with a wet *slop*.

"I'll do it." Eunice continued working on the baby, who hadn't made another cry since the first one minutes before.

"I'll do it." Sally stood in the doorway; her eyes wide on Jane. She paled as she watched Charlie working furiously. "I don't know nothing about taking care of a baby, Mams. You do. I'll do it. What do I need to do?"

"Give me a minute." Charlie shoved more gauze into Jane's belly. "I'll get you set up soon. The bleeding has slowed."

Another cry came from the baby. Still feeble, but this time she didn't stop. She was the smallest baby he'd ever seen.

Sally's hand settled on Cole's arm. She smiled at the baby. "Mams will take care of her, Pa. Let's take care of Ma.

Charlie said we need another table for me to lie down on. Can you help me move the recovery bed?"

Cole nodded automatically, not really hearing her at first. His whole body felt numb. Crossed between relief that the baby was crying, and fear over Jane kept him trapped in place. He couldn't seem to let go of Jane's hand.

Sally gently pulled him free, then over to the recovery table. "Pa. If you don't help me, I can't help her."

Cole startled out of his own thoughts. He helped Sally draw the second bed close to Jane. It took all of his effort not to lose it when he took note of the amount of blood staining the floor. He moved back to Jane, kissing her forehead gently. "You didn't ever tell me a girl name. You gotta come back and tell me what we're gonna call her."

The room continued to bustle with activity around him. Cole ignored it all to focus strictly on Jane. He brushed his hand along her soot-stained hair. His eyes closed against the sight of her continuing pale features. He pressed his forehead to hers, whispering prayers in her ear. The small cries of the baby continued nearby, giving him some reassurance at the same time as Jane's continuing stillness ripped at his heart.

It seemed like hours passed before someone touched his shoulder. Charlie's voice strained from exhaustion. "I've got the bleeding stopped, I think. I'm only letting Sally go for a little longer, then Ma is going to give Jane some blood."

Cole lifted his head to meet his brother-in-law's gaze. "Will she make it?"

"I don't know." Charlie's features showed lines of strain. "Ma. Bring him the baby."

Eunice stepped into view with a small bundle in her arms. Cole lifted his arms instinctively. She placed the tiny infant in his arms gently. "She's holding on good and strong now. You'll need a name."

"We only talked about a boy's name. Jane was sure it would be a boy." Cole ran his finger along the baby's tiny cheek. She squirmed, then let out a squeak of a sigh. One more fidget and she suckled on the heel of her hand. "Is she hungry?"

"She's tired. She'll be hungry in a while, but this young they don't need much." Eunice stroked the infant's forehead a moment, then straightened. "All right, Charles. Let's let Sally recuperate and get me set up."

Cole couldn't tear his gaze from his new daughter, even with the renewed bustle of activity in the room. The only time he looked away from the babe was to check on Jane. After a while he took notice of the dampness on his cheeks from tears he hadn't realized had come free. He swiped at them gently before resting his head on the table beside Jane's.

"Bonnie was helping," Sally's quiet tone reached Cole. "Matthew got a few burns, so did Stephen, along with a broken arm. The twins are doing well with Pops. They were hanging out with Linh and Jun upstairs, keeping out of the way."

"What about Jesse?" Charlie inquired.

"He's coughing a lot. There's a big bruise across his back. When he was protecting Lizzie, he got hit by some roof. Cindy has a bad cut on her face, and is also coughing really bad. Kat said she's had a few contractions, but nothing that had her too worried. I think Bonnie was going to check her to be certain. That's all I had time to check. When I heard about Ma, I came here quick as I could."

"Thank you, Sally. Where were you? We expected you at service."

"Tommy and I had something to do." Sally's voice drew closer. "Pa."

"Yeah?" Cole couldn't bear to lift his head any longer. He feared seeing Jane not improving. Too often he'd seen the image of her near death. He couldn't bear it again.

"We know who did this. Soon as we find him, we'll make him pay."

Cole managed to pull his head up for that bit of news. He found Sally staring at him, still pale as she'd been. Her eyes were as fierce and dark as Jane's got when she meant business. He nodded. "You'd better."

"We will." She sank into a chair. The fierceness faded leaving her weak as the babe in his arms. Her hand drifted to her forehead. "Woah. That took a lot out of me."

"Sit and rest until you feel stronger." Charlie came around to Cole's line of sight. "I'm going to get cleaned up and see if I can't help our other patients. Sally, I showed you want to do. Unhook Ma in no more than an hour."

"I will." Sally turned her attention to the baby. "Well, look at her."

"She's smaller than the twins were." Cole cleared his throat against the lump that seemed lodged there permanently.

"Beautiful, though." Sally brushed a finger along the babe's cheek.

"She is. Just like her ma."

"Ma will make it."

"She has to."

There is a sacredness in tears.
They are not a mark of weakness,
but of power.
-Washington Irving

The water from the wash tub fell in freezing sparkles to the snow. Sally stood in the doorway, washtub still in her hands from tossing out the water. The freezing air prickled her skin. After the heat of the over-full clinic it felt like a blessing.

She had no idea how they'd managed to feed every soul in the clinic. Somehow they'd managed to make a good show of it, and every soul had been fed.

The clinic was full to bursting. Even as Charlie had allowed the families that lived close enough to be checked on easily to return to their homes; like Kat, Norman, and their children as well as Cora and Isaac. So many remained in the clinic rooms with their injuries. From burns to the effects of breathing in so much smoke, nearly every room had multiple families in them.

Pops had gone home to the Inn to see to Alma, Jay, and Willow. With it being Sunday, the casino hadn't been open. That gave them the night at least before they had to deal with staffing the floor and restaurant.

She put away the washtub. Her energy already drained after that action, she leaned on the counter. The day had been so long, she hadn't rested but for the hour after she'd given her ma the blood.

Her nerves still felt raw after the events of the day. Between what they'd found at Glorious Valley, the fire, and Jane. Everything seemed far too much on top of Molly. She didn't have the strength for this.

A shudder ran through her from head to foot. Tears clogged her throat and nose. Four people had died in the fire, three had suffered severe burns that still might not make it. Every person in the church had been injured in some fashion.

"We'll head out in the morning to gather the bodies," Tommy's voice reached her before he stepped into the small kitchen with Nick.

Sally gathered her emotions back in tight at the sight of her uncles. Though she felt fit to burst, the last thing she wanted was for Tommy to see it. He'd be so ashamed of her for not being able to handle it all. Truth be told, she'd barely thought of those bodies or the children they'd found since she'd learned of Jane's predicament. Somehow she found her voice. "What of the children of those people?"

"Amazingly despite her own injuries, Lillian has already begun to make arrangements for all of them. At least temporary ones until we can find their families, or permanent homes." Tommy's face drooped with tiredness. He seemed to be every bit as exhausted as she felt. "Fanny says they're all in good health."

Sally furrowed her brow. The name was unfamiliar to her. "I'm sorry. Fanny?"

"Dr. Noe," Nick supplied before Tom could answer.

"Oh." Sally rubbed her hand over her face. Of course Dr. Noe had a first name. She just hadn't thought to learn it yet. "I'm going to check on Ma."

"You did a good thing today." Tom's gaze fixed on her with the sort of intensity he usually reserved for his suspects. Her skin crawled under the weight of it. "Good thing it somehow worked. Charlie tells me they don't know what makes those transfusions fail or succeed."

"Just dumb luck, I guess. Not that we've had too much of that lately." Sally pushed off the counter. As she passed her uncles, a hand touched her arm. She paused in surprise to face Nick.

"Are you all right, Sally?" Nick's features maintained their standard eerie stillness. Behind the stoic features there lingered a gentleness in his gaze to match his kind tone. "You've had a go of it lately, and your body is still healing."

"I'm tired is all. I did a lot today, and I don't think my body was ready. I'm fine. Really." Sally brushed him off to dart from the small kitchen before her tears could reform. She did her best to ignore the murmurs from her uncles until she'd gotten far enough to no longer hear them.

At the top of the stairs their discussion got lost in the quiet murmurs from the rooms around her. Sally moved quiet as possible down the hall past doors both closed and open. The door to Jane's room sat half open. The chatter of the twins who should have long ago been in bed stretched out of the room.

Eunice tried to hush the children, her quiet admonishments not cutting through the young ones exuberant replies. Sally leaned on the doorframe to find Clara protesting she wanted to be near the baby. If Pa had the infant, she wanted to be with Pa. Eunice's amused frustration creased her face into lines of laughter.

To avoid being seen, she edged to the other side of the door where she could see Jane and Cole on the bed. Jane's features had a little more color to them, though she remained unconscious. Cole held the small bundle in his arms. With nearly every breath he alternated from staring at the baby with near-reverence, and at Jane with tense lines of fear. His head had to be spinning as much as Sally's.

If she went into the room, there would surely be even more chaos. Her heart and brain could take no more. She turned away to lean against the wall. It would be best to go home now and return in the morning to continue helping. The last thing she wanted to do was go hunt down the dead bodies Tommy had found behind that church.

If Jane woke, much of the burden of fear would be relieved. Perhaps then Sally would be up to such a journey. That wasn't how a detective was supposed to think, much less a Pinkerton. She should be ready to go no matter what. Her insides twisted so much she only wanted to crawl in bed and never get out.

A door opened somewhere in the hall, then closed. Sally drew her eyes open to over assistance to whomever needed it only to find Matthew heading her way.

Matthew peeked over her head into the room before lowering his gaze to hers. "How is she?"

"I don't know." Sally's lip trembled embarrassingly. She managed to hold the tears back, at least. She searched the lines of Matthew's face to see the damage done by the fire. Blisters lit along his hairline and down his neck. Her gaze fell to his bandaged arm.

"Doc says it isn't so bad. I should heal all right, just some scars. Like yours." His fingers grazed along the scars at her temple. When she cringed at the touch, he took her hand in his. "They aren't something bad. They're a sign of strength, not an ugly mark."

"That's what they keep telling me." Her brain told her to pull her hand free. Her blasted heart refused. The warmth of the simple touch, felt like a soothing balm after the horrors of the day. She didn't dare meet his eyes, though. The tears would surely break free if she did. She cleared her throat against the emotions threatening to clog her speech. "How's Stephen?"

"Good. Don't think that broken arm's gonna keep him down long. Bonnie's with him. I had to get out of that room for a while."

"I know the feeling."

A gentle touch to her chin drew her gaze up to his. Concern puckered his brow. His pale green eyes were soft with worry. "How are you?"

"Fine." The word cracked under the weight of buried emotion. She shook her head. "Everyone could have died. Ma, the twins, my uncles, you…"

The sweetest smile crossed his lips when she included him in the mix. His thumb brushed along her cheek. He drew her close, wrapping her in a strong yet gentle hug.

The fight she'd had a split-second thought to give collapsed under the warmth of his comfort. She clung to his shirt, to him. The tears still refused to fall. She didn't dare within earshot of her family.

"Come with me." It wasn't a request. He took her hand in his, pulling her down the hall toward the stairs.

Sally followed without argument. She allowed him to lead her all the way down the stairs to the kitchen. Though they had no coats, she didn't protest when he led her right out the back door onto the porch. They moved a little fast in the cold until they reached the barn behind the clinic.

Light filtered in from the distant streetlamps to give the barn a faint glow. The cold wasn't as bad inside with the heat of the horses. After a flick of a match, a lamp came to life.

Matthew moved around the barn as if he knew it. Unsure what he was doing, Sally stood with her arms crossed against the chill that grew. Then Matthew flung a heavy blanket around her shoulders. He pulled her to a bale of hay where he pushed her to sit.

A few minutes and two lamps later he sat beside her. His arms circled her to pull her close against him. "There ya go. Ain't no one here but the horses and me."

It was all the permission she needed. She curled into him. The first tears flowed free at his reassurance. Within the comfort of his arms she cried until she thought her eyes were dry. Then she just rested her head against his shoulder. Part of her wondered when he'd pulled her into his lap, the rest didn't care.

His cheek rested against the top of her head, one hand gently ran along her arm. Every bit of her relaxed until sleep crept in. When she squirmed against the urge to sleep, he hushed her gently. "When's the last time ya slept for real?"

"Before Molly," she admitted against her better judgment.

"Then sleep."

"It's inappropriate."

"Didn't think ya cared about such things." A soft laugh softened his words. "You were causing grief all over town a few weeks ago."

"That was a few weeks ago."

"The world can change overnight. Don't mean you ain't still you."

"I don't know who I am. I don't think I ever did."

"You'll figure it out in time."

"Will I?" She lifted her gaze to meet his. "Do I even want to?"

"I think you will. Whether ya want to—well, that's up to you. We can all hope ya do all we want, but it's all up to you."

"We?"

He smiled softly. "I may not be your family, but I am your friend."

"I don't know why."

"Friendship is funny that way. Now rest your head, get some sleep. I ain't tired. Slept most of the day."

"I should go home." She tucked her head into his shoulder again.

"Sure. That's why you're moving." He chuckled under his breath. "Get some sleep."

"I'll try."

A low, soft song washed over her. She smiled as he remembered when they'd sung to Alma together. Before she knew it, her body relaxed further.

Sleep finally washed over her and took hold.

If it were not for hope, the heart would break.
-Thomas Fuller

Cole startled awake at a tiny cry. He immediately sat to scoop the baby out of the basket he'd put next to the bed. The twins still lay in the trundle beds by Eunice. Eunice rose slower than he did at the cry. She moved slower than usual, likely every bit as tired as Cole.

Though Cole walked and bounced the baby, her little cries didn't stop. He glanced at Eunice. "I think she's hungry."

"I'll change her diaper first. While I do that, you try to sit Jane up. We'll see if she's still got milk after that mess. If not we may have to ask Linh if she'll nursemaid for us." Eunice took the baby from his arms.

Cole turned his attention to Jane. He moved to her side and brushed a finger along her forehead. She didn't stir at all at his touch. The lack of any reaction made his heart ache. What if she was forever damaged by what had happened?

He did his best to push aside those fears. She was here and alive. He'd have to focus on that. In an effort to keep the twins asleep, he spoke low, "I gotta move you, Jane. It might hurt. Sorry."

He peeled back the covers so he could move her whole body instead of just her upper half. With great care, he scooped her into his arms. Though his ribs protested the movement, he managed to keep his reaction to the flash of pain to the smallest of curses.

He set her gently into a sitting position and rearranged her blankets. Before Eunice could bring the baby, the door opened with a small knock. Cole set his finger to his lips to keep the man that entered quiet.

Charlie nodded his acknowledgement and closed the door quietly. He waved to his mother before moving to the bed. "I need to examine her."

"Your ma was gonna try to see if she could feed the baby."

"No name yet?" Charlie pulled the blankets back down. He lifted the chemise to check the incision.

"She only picked a boys name last we talked. I got no idea what to name a girl." Cole frowned when Charlie pressed hard into Jane's stomach. He moved forward, about to stop the man. "What the hell are you doing?"

"I have to see if the uterus is getting smaller. With the trauma—"

Jane whimpered.

Both men froze to stare at her. Her eyelids fluttered open the briefest moment before closing again. Charlie sighed. "That's a good sign. She's coming back to us. Jane?"

Jane's brow puckered. Her eyes remained closed this time.

Cole brushed his hand over her hair. "Jane."

Charlie pressed on her belly again. Jane's eyes immediately flew open. Pain creased her forehead and the corners of her eyes. She blinked slow a few times. Her gaze fell on Cole, her brow creased in confusion. Then her eyes widened. Her hand tensed in his before going lax again. "Something's…wrong…the baby."

"Shhhh. The baby's just fine. Your ma has her." Cole couldn't stop touching her now that she was awake. His hand rested on her head, his thumb running along the creases of pain on her forehead. "She's just fine. I promise. Tiny, but good."

Her gaze fell to her stomach as Charlie returned the blankets to their place. When the baby cried again, her eyes lifted to find the source. Her lip trembled. "Oh. No."

Cole jumped when her head fell to her chest. Gently he lifted it back up, but her eyes had closed again. He released a shaky breath before he kissed her forehead. "That mean she's going to live?"

"She's got a much better chance now. Everything seems to be healing well enough." Charlie stood. "Go ahead, Ma. I've got more patients to check in on. Let Bonnie or myself know how it goes with the feeding. I spoke to Linh last night and she agreed to assist if it was needed."

"Thank you, Charlie." Eunice glanced up from her task.

"Pa?" Colton sat in his trundle bed, rubbing his eyes. A big yawn cracked his young face.

Cole kissed Jane's forehead again before moving to the twins trundles. Eunice used Cole's departure to take the baby to Jane's side. That allowed Cole to turn his full attention to his little boy more easily. "Hey, Colton."

Colton climbed into Cole's arms, resting his head against his shoulder. His small breaths puffed against Cole's neck. His fist clenched Cole's shirt. "Want…Mama."

"Mama's sleeping." Cole rubbed Colton's back. "You can see her when she's up later, all right? Hey."

Clara had blinked awake. She yawned wide as anything before turning back to her side and drifting right back to sleep.

Cole chuckled softly. Clara loved sleep as much as play when she had a mind for it. He rose with Colton to carry him to the rocking chair. Once settled in, he rocked his son slowly with one eye on Eunice and Jane. Despite the baby being at her chest, Jane's eyes didn't even flutter.

He closed his eyes against the sight. If Jane were awake, she'd be giving every bit of her attention to the baby. Most likely to the twins as well, which would be hard on her exhausted body.

Cole continued to rock Colton slow and steady. His eyes drifted closed as they moved.

A hand touched his shoulder. Eunice smiled down at him. "You fell asleep."

"You look like you could, too. How'd the baby do?"

"It seems she got some food, if not at least comfort. Jane's body knows what to do even if she's not fully back to herself. The baby is settled back in her basket fast asleep."

"Good." Cole rose slow and steady. It wasn't slow enough to keep Colton asleep. The boy raised his head to look at Cole sleepily. "You ready to go lay back down with your sister?"

Colton shook his head before he dropped it back to Cole's shoulder. His thumb slipped into his mouth. "Mama."

"She's still sleeping."

"Mama," Colton whimpered. "Want mama."

"Why don't we try to go get some food? I bet we can scrounge up some grub."

"Nonsense," Eunice interjected. "I'll get something made for us. You lie back down. If the little cowboy can be still, he can join you. Might do Jane some good to have her boy close."

Cole would have protested. The look on Eunice's face, and the fact he'd never been good at making food won out. He'd survived on tinned goods alone in California. At Eunice's urging, Cole returned to the bed to lie down beside Jane.

Colton lay sprawled across his chest, asleep within seconds. Cole focused on the rise and fall of Jane's chest. The simple act of her breathing gave him some reassurance. It wasn't her awake, but at least she was alive and breathing. He'd hold onto the hope of her brief moment of alertness until the next one came.

A few minutes later small footsteps rushed toward the bed. Clara climbed onto the bed, crawled up along Cole's legs, then flopped between him and Jane. She latched onto Cole's free arm, nestling in the crook of his elbow. Within minutes she fell asleep as well.

With the warmth of the two children on him, Cole soon found himself dozing along with them. It wasn't until the smell of eggs and coffee hit his nose that he woke again. Eunice bustled about the room. She threw open the curtains before setting a couple of chairs at the small table. Soon as she'd set out plates she moved to the bedside.

"Clara, sweetheart. Come with me." Eunice picked up the child to carry her to the table. "Come along, Cole. You need sustenance. I brought some bone broth for Jane if we can get her to wake again. It'll keep warm on the stove."

Cole didn't have a thought to protest. His stomach rumbled at the smell of eggs. "You'll have half the clinic jealous over the smell of fresh food."

"My first concern is you and these children. Lydia was working on a large batch of food for the other patients. I heard mention of Lillian sending some of her staff to help with the clinic and the restaurant. The others will be fed."

"You are a good woman, Eunice."

"I told you. It's Ma."

"Yes, Ma."

Sally's whole body ached. Nevertheless, she fought waking from the slumber she basked in. She hadn't slept so deeply since she'd woken after the trouble at Jake's homestead. Despite her desperate attempts to remain asleep wakefulness edged its way through her.

She shifted to stretch, then froze. Her movements were restricted.

Now she knew the reason she was so warm. Another body curled against hers. Strong, warm, lean.

Matthew.

Sally's eyes flew open when her memory caught up to her current situation. The horse stalls lined along the walls came into focus. The hay bale they curled on edged into vision, as well as Matthew's hand stretched into the cold of the morning. Her head lay pillowed on the arm attached to that hand.

His other arm draped across her waist. Surprise caused her fingers to flex when she realized they were laced with his. She released the hold, bracing her hand against the hay to push to sit. Matthew grunted behind her. His hold tightened before his motion stilled.

A loud snort signaled his waking. He sat so fast he toppled right off the hay bale. His bottom hit the floor with a solid *thump*. "Ow."

Sally couldn't help herself. She laughed out loud at the sight of him sprawled on the hay-strewn floor. His hair stuck out at odd angles, as did his legs. She covered her mouth when he half-glared at her, unable to quell her deepening laughter.

After a moment, he joined her amusement. Low chuckles carried on the cold air. He ran his hand through the unruly mop of brown hair. "Well."

"You said you weren't tired." Sally kept the blanket wrapped around her to cover how cold she'd become with the absence of him curled against her. The barn was far from warm, even with the horses. "I thought you were a man of your word. Yet here you are, fast asleep instead of keeping an eye on me."

"I had more than my eye on you." Soon as he said it, his ears turned pink with embarrassment.

Sally guffawed, kicking his boot. "Matthew Coleman! You give off the air of a decent gentleman. Turns out you're nothing but a rotten scoundrel."

"I didn't—I meant—oh, stop laughing at me." He gathered his long legs together and hopped to his feet. His laughter joined hers as he plopped onto the hay beside her. "You know I meant that—oh, forget it."

She tried her best to stop laughing and appear reticent for her continued mirth. His shove proved she wasn't entirely successful. A laugh lingered in her voice, "Oh, my. I haven't laughed like that in a while."

"Glad I could help you out. Now give me some of that. It's damn cold." He pulled the blanket over his lap. A shiver shook through him. He raised his hands to blow on them. "Sorry. Really thought I could stay awake. I was trying to keep ya comfortable. Guess I got too comfortable myself."

"I was comfortable. Mostly. I don't think a hay bale makes as good a bed as a straw tick. My back is a bit sore." She scooped his hat off the floor to hand to him. "I won't deny I was nice and warm, though. Also slept really well. Thank you."

"Glad I could help."

"I'm glad you could, too." For some reason she couldn't quite place, her nerves began to race a bit. She rubbed her hands on her thighs as if to warm them.

He took her hand in his. When her eyes found his, they were soft and kind. No heat, no need, just simple affection. "That's all I want to do."

"I know." Her heart panged in response to the fondness. She longed for it, but didn't feel deserving of it. "I don't know if you are."

"How's that?"

She leaned closer to press her lips to his in a soft kiss. His arms circled her, erasing some of the morning chill. The warmth of his responding kiss carried through her. Their lips danced together as they had weeks before, warming her soul more than her body. For a moment it seemed the chasm that had taken over her heart shrank in size.

Molly's face flashed across Sally's mind.

With a gasp, she pulled back. Her legs scrambled her a distance of a few feet away. The cold of the morning soaked back into her bones. Like ice in a cracked glass, the disappointment in his features shuddered the chasm wider again.

When he stood, she shook her head. "Don't."

"Sally. It's—"

"No. I'm sorry."

"Sally, wait."

She didn't give him the chance to finish the thought. Rather than race back to the clinic, she tore around it to get to the Inn. Through the restaurant, casino, and into the apartment she barely breathed.

How could she have been so stupid as to kiss him? How could she have let him comfort her? How dare she give him false hope! She couldn't love. Her love hurt.

"Oof." Sally hit a solid wall hard enough to crash back onto her rump. Pain echoed back through her wounds.

Tommy's brows rose as he turned to face her. "What the devil, girl?"

"Sorry. I wasn't watching. Ow." She groaned as her back smarted on her return to her feet. "That hurt."

"I imagine so." His piercing gaze looked her over. He paused at her hair and his brow furrowed. "Where have you been? I checked your room for you. Is that hay?"

"I, um…what did you need, Tommy?" She wasn't about to tell him where she'd been, or who she'd been with. It didn't matter. Such a thing would never happen again.

"Sally, we really should talk."

"I don't want to talk anymore. I want to finish this. I want it to be over. I need it to be. I want to go on with my life and pretend this never happened."

"That won't ever happen."

"It will because I'm done. I want to see Eckles pay and that's it. No more."

"Sally."

"Tell me what you needed, please. I need to go get cleaned up. I'm still covered in soot from yesterday."

"I noticed." His consternation lingered in his furrowed brow. He apparently decided not to argue, because he only shook his head. "We were heading south to gather the bodies from Glorious Valley. I thought we'd see if Eckles is around there anywhere."

"All right. And?"

"Are you coming?"

"I can't. I need to get cleaned up, and I need to help Mams and Pops. Half the staff was in the fire. We need all hands on deck."

"Didn't you just say you wanted to finish this?"

"I do. I also don't want Ma and Pa's businesses to fail."

"Fine. Do what you will, Sally. I'll give you a full report when we get back if you care to hear it." He stormed down the hall without another word.

Guilt nagged her for being so brusque, but her mind raced and heart squeezed in a tight knot so she couldn't think or dare to feel. She didn't know which way was up any longer. What was she doing with herself?

"Sally!" Alma rushed forward soon as the door opened. She grasped Sally's cold hands in her warm ones. Her blue eyes were moist. "Sally. Sally. Sally. Cole."

"He's across the street with Ma and the new baby. I bet Pops will take you to see them if you'd like to." Sally put every effort into keeping her own nerves out of her tone with Alma. The woman was a bundle of nerves enough as it was. She didn't need the addition of Sally's. "Isn't that right, Pops?"

"Mams sent word a little while ago that Jane had woken for a few minutes. She's disoriented, but at least she's making an improvement." Pops was struggling to get the pups to sit still while Jay ran around the apartment with Clara's bird on a string.

"Whiskey, Bourbon, *sit*," Sally snapped. The dogs plopped their rears down in unison. She sighed in relief.. That morning she felt much like Alma likely did all of the time. There was too much chaos in everything, everywhere, including her own mind. She wanted it all to stop.

"Thank you, Sally." Pops settled back at the desk.

"I'm glad to hear Ma woke. Thanks for telling me. Alma, I need to get cleaned up and dressed for the day. Do you want to help me choose a dress?"

Alma nodded, turning for the steps.

Sally paused at the bottom of the stairs. "Sorry, Pops. I'm a little sore today."

"That's to be expected. Take your time. Ada should arrive soon to help with Jay and Willow. Then I'll be able to take Alma across the way."

"Thanks." Sally climbed the steps. At least for a little while she could distract herself with Alma.

Then she would have to deal with herself. Eventually. Not for as long as she could avoid it.

Maybe this was why Clara had run away. When things got this messy, it seemed a much easier thought. Perhaps she could go visit Patrick. Get away from everything for a while.

Then again, Patrick would remind her of Molly.

Sally paused at her doorway. Alma riffled through the line of dresses in Sally's closet. She ran her fingers along every piece as though testing the feel of the fabric, which she probably was.

Sally closed her eyes a moment. The last thing she needed to think about was Molly. Molly was a big part of the problem. She'd done wrong, and now couldn't ever make it right. No one could.

Certainly not Matthew.

Even if it felt like maybe he could help her make things seem right again. He didn't deserve the mess that she was. A mess that didn't even know if she could love. A mess that didn't know her own mind. A mess that didn't even know her own heart.

Not anymore.

Men never do evil so completely and cheerfully as when they do it from religious conviction.
—Blaise Pascal

Tommy stood to the side as the group of men carried the bodies, one-by-one, to the wagon. Andrew made his way among the bodies performing a cursory exam of each before he allowed them to be carried away. Five more male bodies had appeared in the woods since he'd been there the day before. Apparently they'd used the distraction of the church fire to complete the job.

Or perhaps the five men had been the ones to set the fire in the first place. He recognized a few of the faces as being part of the group helping to put out the flames—if that's what they'd been actually doing.

A child had died in the fire, as well as three adults. Dozens suffered the effects of breathing in smoke, burns, as well as injuries from the roof collapsing. He wondered at the purpose of setting the church fire if Eckles was so opposed to children suffering for their parents. Perhaps that was why the whole flock appeared to have ingested the wine.

Despite the numerous bodies littering the forest floor, not one of them was the man himself. Eckles remained hidden in the wintery landscape somewhere. Worse, Tommy didn't know how big his congregation had been. Therefore, who knew if there would be more problems in town? What other horrors could he have planned? Or would he know he was caught and disappear?

Andrew finished checking on the last body, then came to Tommy's side. "Not one of them has any sign of injury. No broken teeth to indicate they were forced to ingest the wine. I'll know more once I finish the autopsies, but on the surface it appears this was voluntary."

"I'd bet my stake in The Hangman's Inn that it was."

"Then you're convinced."

"I am. I don't know how he managed to manipulate so many to his cause, much less to end their own lives. The man has always made my skin crawl. He was booted from Reverend Greene's tutelage for being too extreme."

"People gravitate toward what they want to hear, often to their own detriment. Still, I can't imagine going to this extreme." Andrew shook his head. He turned his attention from the bodies to face Tommy. "On a different subject. I'm rather concerned about Sally."

"You're not the only one." Tommy watched them carry Collin Oates away. The man had been in Sally's notes as having been in the saloon the night Cora was shot. For that matter, so had Jake. The girl had been onto something. She just hadn't put it all together.

"I know Molly was a dear friend to her, but she's taking her loss very hard."

"She blames herself."

"She was shot," Andrew protested. "She was losing a lot of blood at the time. I'm surprised she managed all that she did to stop those men."

"Not just for that, although that's enough."

Andrew's brow furrowed as he turned back toward the bodies. "This is Eckles. Not her."

"She doesn't think she was fast enough." Tommy gestured toward the bodies. "To stop this, to save Joshua, to have stopped the fire, or to save Molly. She suspected for some time it was connected to the church, but bucked her instincts to let Simon join them to go talk to Jake."

"It isn't her fault that the world is damaged."

"No, it's not. You can't tell her that, though. She wouldn't listen."

"Then we keep telling her."

"You tell her stubborn self anything and see how far it gets you."

Andrew gusted out another sigh of frustration.

"She needed evidence to move forward with any suspicions. Evidence she lacked until Archie recalled hearing Jake's voice. Then the evidence started to present itself, but too late to stop everything from happening. It happens sometimes, and it's not anything you can stop. It's always a blow. For it to be her first case…"

Andrew remained silent when Tommy let his sentence trail off.

Tommy's own guilt crept forward. Sally had shown such promise and now it was all collapsing around her. She didn't have the will to pick herself back up yet. "She may never be able to become a detective after this."

"I'm not concerned about her vocation. I'm concerned about her spirit." Andrew's gaze turned north, though they couldn't see the town from the trees. "She has been a good and fast friend for me in this town. I've enjoyed our time together. Since she has woken from her injuries there's been a change."

"I'm aware." Tommy's stomach twisted in a knot. Everyone had noticed the change, and no one had made an impact to stop it. "I thought it was mostly me she was angry at."

"I don't think it was ever you specifically." Andrew's lip twitched into a frown. "She's been quite brusque. Cold. For a little while she'll be as she always was, then it's as if she remembers what happened and she gets angry all over again. Angry with herself for allowing herself to be happy."

"Grief is ugly."

"Life is ugly. I thought she knew that. Look at what she's been through before. Life hasn't been kind to her until she met your family. Perhaps she got too comfortable in the ease, but this blow really has struck her hard." Andrew sighed as they gathered the last body. "They'll be taking them to the clinic. We'll store them in the lean-to, out of sight."

"I'm going to search the church again. Sally didn't have much time with them kids right there to do a proper search."

"Would you like someone to stay behind in case of trouble?"

Tommy couldn't help but grin at the idea of the doctor staying behind to assist. The man still had trouble getting in and out of a saddle. Tommy doubted Andrew would know the first thing to do with a gun. "Who? You?"

"No. Definitely not." Andrew's crooked grin proved the man at least had a sense of humor over his abilities, or lack thereof.

"Don't worry. I'll bet Nick planned on staying behind anyhow. David will guard you and the wagons on the way back."

"Then good luck." Andrew tipped his head in acknowledgment before heading out of the woods.

Tommy stared at the ground where the bodies had been. The fact that Sally had been acting different for Andrew as well was concerning. The melancholy when she'd first woken was one thing. To be treating someone he knew was a dear friend with the same snappish behavior was another thing all together.

He didn't have the faintest idea how to deal with it, how to snap her out of it. Especially since she hardly wanted to be around him anymore. He was the one that had introduced her to Molly, he supposed he couldn't blame her.

A twig snapped, preceding Nick making his way toward him. He knew Nick had stepped on the twig on purpose to make him aware of his approach. The man could be silent as Tommy when he wanted to be. Tommy wiped the consternation from his face as best as he could with a swipe of his hand. He nodded to his brother. "Are they gone?"

"On their way back to town. Where are you starting? Out here?"

"No. I was just thinking."

"About?"

"Sally."

"You're not worried she spent the night in the barn with that Coleman kid, are you?"

"She what?"

Nick's brows rose. His goatee twitched in what Tom suspected to be hidden laughter as he stared his brother down. "I saw them head out there after we bumped into her in the kitchen. When I went to get my horse this morning they were sound asleep on the hay. Fully clothed, but comfortable by the looks of it."

"Is that so?" Tommy wondered at her mood when he'd seen her that morning, then. Far as he knew, she was rather sweet on the young rancher. Of course, according to Jane that had been the cause of her fight with Molly.

"Thomas?"

"Right. The church. I'd like to take a look around the pastor's room."

"Change of subject it is, then. Do you think he actually left anything behind?"

"He left some bottles of his special wine, so there might be something else to be found."

"That's a big maybe."

"I'm aware."

A good man would prefer to be defeated than to defeat injustice by evil means.
—Sallust

Sally took the baby Eunice handed her. She smiled when the little one's eyes opened briefly before shutting again. Tiny though she was, her little features were a perfect miniature of Jane's, with a hint of Cole in the mouth. "You said Ma gave her a name?"

"Sorry you've missed her waking twice now." Cole sat on the floor with the twins. A game of jackstones in the middle of them. Colton bounced the ball, scooping up near all the jackstones with surprising speed. Cole applauded his son before continuing, "She was up for near five minutes this time. Talked to us all. Willow and Jay were here, Alma too."

"I'm sorry I missed it, too. I was starving. I had to eat something. I'm mad I missed her." She glanced toward Jane's sleeping form on the bed. "It's good to hear she's doing better, though."

"It certainly is good news. We're all quite relieved. Good news is much welcomed these days." Eunice took a seat. Her features were drawn in tired lines. "Anyhow, she suggested the name Evelyn Leanne. I believe the Evelyn is significant to Cole."

"My ma's name." Cole's gaze remained fixed on the game in front of him. An odd tension lingered in his tone. "I don't have no objections to it. My ma was a good woman. So's Leanne."

"Evelyn." Sally kissed the baby's forehead. "A beautiful name for a beautiful girl. You are very lucky, little one. This is a good family to be born into. The best one, really."

Eunice chuckled softly. The light of laughter eased some of the tiredness from her features. Her gaze had settled on Sally, a curious light of sadness behind them despite her laughter. "Some other families might object to that suggestion."

"Well, it is. There's lot of love and plenty of family to fight for you." Sally didn't have time to question Mams on what might be bothering her, as Cole rose right then. She handed off Evelyn easily. She dismissed her momentary questions, seeing as there was plenty for her Mams to be concerned over. "I'm going to go check on Wil, then head to the library."

"I went and saw Wil myself right before Garit got here. He's awake." Though he spoke to Sally, Cole's full focus remained on the infant in his arms. His tone was soft and light as though to keep from upsetting her. "Garit arrived right before I left. He was relieved to find Wil awake."

"I'd heard Garit arrived, and that Wil was awake. Dr. Noe told me on my way through the lobby. That's why I wanted to look in on him."

"I told him I'd visit again when I could." Cole's gaze fell on the baby when her eyes opened again. "Hello, Evie. I hope you're not hungry again. I'd rather your ma was awake when you're feeding next."

"She's fed twice with Jane asleep, I've got no doubt the third time will be the charm." Eunice nodded to Sally. "I do hope you'll join us for supper. We haven't seen enough of you these past few days."

"I have every intention of being around for supper. I haven't been able to see my siblings much, either." Sally kissed Eunice on the cheek. "Try to get some rest in the mean time, Mams. You look tired."

"We all do."

Sally paused to place another kiss to Evie's forehead before slipping from the room. Bits of conversation filtered out from the rooms she passed. Now that it was daytime most of the doors sat open allowing visitors in, and patients to visit each other.

The room at the end of the hall where Wil had been cloistered all week remained closed. Sally knocked quick and sharp before pushing the door open. "Good morning—oh my."

She immediately stepped back out of the room and shut the door firmly. Of all the things she'd expected to see, Wil and Garit wrapped in a passionate embrace to rival her parents hadn't been a thought. She spun on her heel, then stood there dumbfounded. What should she do?

Walk away and pretend she'd seen nothing seemed the best option. When Wil was feeling better they could talk, but she didn't figure Garit cared for friendly conversation.

Then again, perhaps she should reassure them their secret was safe with her. The last thing she needed was added tension.

The door flew open behind her. Without ceremony or apology she was yanked backward by her collar. Her yelp cut off quick when she was spun and pushed into the door. Garit's pale gray eyes flashed with a hardness she'd never seen, even in his angriest moments at the saloon. His lips curled in a snarl. His hand dangerously close to encircling her throat. "You'd better not tell anyone what you saw."

Sally stared at him unmoving for nearly a minute. His anger was defense, it was clear to her. She relaxed despite his dangerous stance. After a moment she offered a smile she prayed came across as reassuring rather than anything else. "Believe me, Garit. I'm the last person you need to worry about blabbing about this."

"If you do—"

"Garit," Wil's voice was uneven, rough. "Sie wird es nicht sagen. Molly war ihre Geliebte."

Sally flinched at the mention of Molly. Still, she didn't back down from Garit's continued hard stare. She set a hand on the wrist still quite near her throat. "He's right. I won't tell. Molly was my lover."

Garit pushed back from the door, eying her quietly. "You speak German."

"Some. Molly was teaching me, and my Uncle Nick has been as well. My understanding is rough, but I know enough." She took a shaky breath. "For what it's worth, I'm happy for you both. Truly. Everyone should have someone they care about that much."

Garit's eyes narrowed. "Most would find us—"

"I'm not most people."

"I guess not."

She turned her attention from the angry German to face the bed, and Wil. He appeared tired, bruised, and burned. Much like most of the clientele of the clinic in the surrounding rooms. He had the added trauma of some bound limbs and what she understood to be a damaged back as well.

She drew closer to the bed, offering a smile. "You look like hell, but you're alive. I'm so relieved. The Golden Touch wouldn't be the same if it was only Garit. He's not nearly as friendly, the place isn't as cheerful when he's in charge."

Wil offered a weak smile. "I'll try to be less friendly."

"Or Garit could try to be friendlier."

"It ain't in him. He's a cold bastard." Wil closed his eyes, wincing at some unseen pain. "Worse when he's scared."

"You scared me enough. No more of this." Garit sat in the chair opposite where Sally stood. "Left my dying Vater to come home."

"Home?" Wil opened his eyes at that.

"Ja. Home."

The look of adoration that crossed between the men tugged at Sally's fragile heart. Rather than let any of it show, she shoved it down to bury it again. She bent to grasp Wil's hand. "I'll give you both some time. It doesn't look like you're going to be awake much longer. I know you've only been awake a short time and likely have questions, but you don't need to worry over any of it."

Garit frowned. "I still want them answered."

"I know, and we will. All you need to know now is that we're going to take care of it. We know who started it all. He'll pay. Don't you worry." She kissed his cheek. "I'll be back later. Garit, lock the door next time."

"Ein stinkender Fisch."

"I don't know that one." Sally glanced toward Wil for help.

Wil chuckled low. "It's like—rakefire."

"Well, I suppose that's my cue to leave." Sally backed to the door. On her way out she paused long enough to lock the door before she shut it completely.

With a heavy sigh, Sally made her way downstairs. She hesitated in the lobby, unsure what to do next. She expected Tommy and the men to be a while longer. She didn't want to linger in the clinic where she'd run the risk of running into Matthew right then.

Her wondering flew out the door that flung open to reveal a panicked Reverend Greene. He made a beeline for Sally. "Where's your uncle?"

"My—which one? Why?"

"Tommy. Eli is missing."

"*What*?" Sally gripped his shaking hands. His eyes darted around the lobby as though he might see the missing man or Tommy. His nerves were rattled. She tried to redirect his attention, and to soothe with a calm tone. "Reverend."

"What?"

"Reverend Greene. Come. Sit." She pulled him some nearby chairs. Her hands didn't leave his, giving him a gentle squeeze. "Tell me what happened as you remember it?"

"I came here this morning to visit with the wounded." He took a shaky breath. A crack of guilt had slipped into his words.

Sally knew the congregation had worked hard to protect the ministers as best they could, and that's how several had gotten injured. "I know they appreciate the visits. Didn't Eli join you?"

"Eli remained at the house to rest. He's not recovering as fast as I am."

"Which is normal. Some of the patients are recovering much faster than others. Uncle Charlie says it's in a person's composition. Nothing that is their fault."

"I saw it in the epidemic," Mark conceded.

"We all did. How was Eli doing when you left?"

"Well. He was sitting near the stove for warmth, listening to the sounds of the town passing by. He says they soothe him." The reverend shook his head. "I was here for a few hours. When I returned home, he wasn't there."

"Could he have gone for a walk? I know he's been attempting more independence."

"No. I looked. He wouldn't go far if he did that. Only up and down the street." Mark frowned. "I searched all through the shops on our street, and he wasn't to be found."

"I'll go see what I can find out. We'll find him, Reverend."

"Please. Even a faith as strong as his can't survive much more turmoil."

"Even faith strong as yours would be shaken." Sally gave him a quick hug before grabbing her coat. She rushed through the alleys toward Fourth Street where the remains of the temporary church sat. Right next to it was the home the Reverend's had been using.

Sally made her way up and down the street speaking to everyone she passed to find out if anyone had seen Reverend Lyons leave his home. Finally, after nearly half an hour someone said they'd seen him speaking to Roland Hill, a large beast of a miner that liked to partake in the boxing matches the Inn sponsored.

When pushed further, they said they both got into a wagon with Reverend Eckles.

Sally ran to the Inn's barn in a blind panic. She saddled up Agatha, and climbed into the saddle. Far as she knew, Roland lived in the long-houses for the miners. He had no family to speak of. The last place they'd go was there.

Sally paused at the edge of town, considering a north or south route. In the distance she could see several wagons heading in from the south. "North, then. They wouldn't risk being seen by those bringing back the bodies."

She turned Agatha north, riding along the road. She turned to head to the Lyman's home first since it was closest. With no evidence of them there, she continued on toward Jake's homestead. Her nerves rattled at returning to the spot where Molly had been killed, but she had to find Reverend Lyons. For that matter, she had to find Eckles.

She leaned down over Agatha's neck, urging her into a dead run. Somewhere along the line her hat flew off, but she didn't stop. As she drew near to the homestead, she didn't slow, racing around it toward the back where a wagon sat against the homestead.

She tore around the building again, swinging half out of the saddle while Agatha kept running around the building.

When they turned the corner to head back south toward down, she called *Heim* to the horse. She dropped to the ground and let Agatha keep running.

The soreness in her kidneys smarted at the brutal landing, but she managed to keep her footing. She crept along the edge of the house.

A crunch of snow behind her was just enough warning to duck and roll. Roland's punch landed against the hard side of the house rather than her head.

Sally sprung to her feet. Crouched and ready for the next attack, she eyed Roland carefully. "You have brawn, but it doesn't match for skill, Roland."

"Jake bested you. I can too." He smiled coldly, rolling up his sleeves. When he lunged forward, she ducked around him.

The gun in her holster was a tempting idea, but she wasn't good enough of a shot. Her last fight had proven it. She moved to avoid another punch, rolling away. Before she got to her feet, she slid one of her knives from its boot holster, spinning as he approached again to slice along his arm on her way past.

Blood squirted over the snow. She'd managed to cut deep, but not deep enough to fell him yet She moved several feet away, planning her next attack. No longer did she have the stamina for a long fight. She had to make this quick.

Before he could lunge again she let loose the knife. It made its mark, landing right in his throat.

There was no time for celebration as a crack rented the air and pain burned through her side. Sally stared down in surprise at the hole in her coat. She pushed it aside to reveal a wound that began to trickle blood. "Damn it."

"A prostitute is a deep pit." Eckles held his weapon steady on her. "Come inside, harlot. There's plenty of room."

"I'd rather not."

"You can die out here in the cold, or in there in the warmth. Eli and I were having a nice chat before you interrupted."

Only the idea of getting Eli free held any attraction for her. She stared down the barrel of his gun, lifting her chin. "You're so fond of punishment, Pastor. What of Leviticus?"

"Come inside, we'll discuss matters like civil folk."

"While I slowly bleed to death?"

"That is the plan."

He wears his faith,
but as the fashion of a hat.
-William Shakespeare

Tommy stood in the center of the cold church. The coal stove in the corner sat long extinguished. The pews sat in neat rows on either side of him. Rather than tall airy windows like the town's original church which had burned down months before, short windows scattered along the walls in uneven increments.

Paintings hung between the icy windows depicted punishments of sin rather than any beautiful images of Jesus or heaven. Dark crimson cloth the color the blood draped the pulpit. A carpet of the same color covered the floor underneath.

He wrinkled his nose against the darkness that seemed to seep into every corner of the church. The Pastor certainly did like his fire and brimstone.

Nick stepped into the church, shutting the door with a firm snap. He glanced around the sanctuary before approaching Tom. "Are you finding many clues standing in the middle of the church?"

"I'm just taking in the man's aesthetic. You can't understand a man until you see where he lives, what he does, what he believes."

"If you say so. Can we get a move on?"

Tommy ignored Nick's tone to focus on the interior of the church again. The place clearly hadn't been built with Hammy's careful hand and keen eye. Eckles must have used the labor of his own congregation to get it built.

He walked up the aisle slow and steady. Every painting, every unevenly placed window met his calculated gaze. Rather than deal with the pulpit, he figured he'd save it for last. Instead, he circled behind the dais to where the pastor's living quarters sat. The door remained wide open from where Sally had kicked it open the day before. Nothing appeared disturbed even though several more men had returned to the area to add their bodies to the rest.

In the back of the room sat a small kitchen area with shelves lined with tinned goods and its own small stove. Several small barrels lined the back wall. Tommy grabbed a glass and opened the spigot on one barrel. A rich, dark liquid poured out.

He lifted the cup to his nose. Elderberry. Mostly juice at that point, likely early on in the fermentation process. Unsure if the belladonna had already been added, Tommy merely set the glass on top of the barrel.

He continued to move through the room, taking in every small detail along the way. A handful of books sat on a shelf above the desk. Below those a shelf sagged with bibles. He pulled one off the shelf to find it covered in dust. Clearly Eckles hadn't touched those bibles in a while.

He moved to the bible sitting on the desk, a notepad beside it. The top sheet remained blank, as did every page beneath it. The bible didn't have any markings either.

A glint distracted him from his search. He reached to get the frame from the recesses of the shelf at table level. It rattled with the movement.

Eckles stood in the picture, several years younger than he was now. The man beside him held some similarity in echoes. More like an uncle, or perhaps a grandfather, rather than a father. Based on the age difference between the two, he'd guess grandfather. The older man held a thick bible in one arm. His other hand rested on Eckle's shoulder. No, not rested. It was more of a tight grip.

Tommy flipped the frame over, removing the back with care. A nickel dropped onto the desk, rattling and rolling to a rest as it hit the bible. A second picture sat in the frame, facing its back. Several whores stared grim faced into the camera. In the top left of the image one woman caught his attention.

A strong nose, beady eyes, and a lack of a chin. Just like Eckles. "Huh."

The woman had to be Eckles' mother. His mother had been a whore, a nickel one if the coin was any indication. By the looks of the grandfather, he would have disowned her for such a sin. So how did Eckles come to be with the dour man in the frame?

Tommy pulled the image free, but there was nothing else in the frame. He turned his attention to the bibles lining the shelf. One appeared the oldest, and as large as the one in the photograph with the older man.

He slid the bible free from the shelf and wiped the dust from the cover. A faded gold-embossed name sat in the lower corner. *Anton Eckles*. Anton. Same as Eckles.

Inside the front cover he found a short letter, worn with time. The scribbles were barely decipherable. He drew closer to the window to see all the faded words.

Mr. Eckles,

This is your grandson, Walter. He's now near six years old. I cared for him for Delia all these six years. She has died in an accident. Without the funds she provided to feed and clothe him, I can't take care of him any longer.

He is a good boy. Quiet. Causes no trouble.

Best,

Eliza Potter

Tom folded the letter and replaced it in the bible. He gathered the pictures and the nickel, adding them to the front of the bible with the letter. He flipped a few pages in the bible and spotted some phrases along the lines of Eckles' sermons on the pages alongside passages.

"Thomas. I do hate to interrupt your nosing around in there, but perhaps you should see this." Nick didn't bother to come to the door. Instead, he called loudly from the chapel.

"Be there in second." Tom grabbed his finds to take with him from the room. He headed back out to where his brother stood at the pulpit. "What is it?"

"Look at these notes." Nick stared at the bible, flipping back and forth between pages.

"I was going to get around to the bible. I was saving it for last."

"Maybe you should have looked here first."

Tom glared at his brother, who ignored him in turn. He turned his attention to the large bible lying on the pulpit. Unlike the bible on the desk, in this one the pages were littered with notes. Passages had large circles around them with lines toward those notes. Some were clearly messages to be delivered in sermons. Others were, "Names."

"A list of sinners, demagogues, whores, and thieves. To name a few. I am named among the demagogues. You're an instigator. I believe we know where our sister and niece fall in the line of things."

"Cora?"

"I haven't finished going through the whole book, as it is a bible and therefore quite long. However, I haven't seen mention of her. Mike was a libertine, destined to face judgment for lying with a whore."

"We'll take this with us, too. There's a lot to figure out, and I'm not sure Eckles will do much talking when we get our hands on him."

"When? Don't you mean if? No one has seen him."

"We'll find him." Tommy slammed the bible shut. "Don't doubt me on that."

"What else did you find, then?"

Tom withdrew the pictures. "They were back-to-back in a frame. The picture with Eckles and his grandfather was facing out, the whores to the wall."

"Back left?"

"Unmistakable, right?"

"Mirror image, almost."

"In this bible is a letter from a woman that raised Eckles until he was six. Then his ma died, and she shipped him off to his grandfather."

"I'm surprised he wasn't immediately sent to an orphanage considering his origin."

"Me, too. Based on the picture, and the few notes I managed to glimpse in the old man's bible, I am too. Guess he figured he'd make a righteous man out of him, or he followed that the son shouldn't bear the sins of the father." Tommy's head shot up when he heard hooves pounding outside, drawing ever closer. He pulled out his weapon and ran to the entryway, holding it up as he flung open the door.

David drew to a stop in front of the church, his horse dancing beneath him. "Tommy. We need you back in town. Quickly."

"What is it?"

"Reverend Lyons is missing. Sally went to find him near two hours ago and hasn't returned. Reverend Greene doesn't know where she went, except she said she'd find Lyons."

"Damn it. Sally. Nick, get the book. We gotta go, *now*."

Glory built on selfish principles
is shame and guilt.
-William Cowper

Sally had other knives hidden on her person, but Eckles had a gun. What was more, she didn't know if there was anyone else in the house guarding the reverend. Blood trickled along her skin. Inch by inch her dress began to darken with red. She couldn't begin to calculate how long it would be before it would be too much. If she was bleeding in her belly, the time would be less.

Whether out of her own stubbornness, adrenaline, or the grace of God, the pain was minimal. She gathered her skirts in her hands and walked to the house without another word of argument.

She was relieved to find the home empty, save for Eli. That meant it was down to just her and Eckles. The one-room homestead held no hiding places for anyone else.

In a chair, unbound, sat Reverend Lyons. She rushed toward him to grasp his hands. They were cold, but strong in their return hold. "Reverend. Have you been harmed?"

"Sally? No, I haven't been injured. Have you? Is that blood I smell?" His grasp on her hands grew stronger.

"Your nose is getting quite sharp, Reverend." Sally rose when Eckles footsteps drew near. "I'm so glad you're unharmed."

"Let's have a seat now." Eckles poked the gun into her back.

Sally considered fighting him off right then, even with the gun pressed against her. After all, how long could her strength last?

In the end pure curiosity had her comply with his request. She wondered how everything had happened. The whole thing was a puzzle that she had all the pieces to, but she was struggling to fit them all together.

She took a seat, putting her arms behind the chair so he could tied them. While he wrapped the rope around her wrists, she held the cuffs of her coat by her fingertips. With the thick wool coat on, he didn't notice the leather straps around her wrists holding two of her knives around her wrists. It was a good thing she had returned to wearing them daily when she'd decided to finish the job. She'd always been better with a knife than a gun.

The whole time Eckles worked on tying her, he mumbled to himself. All about sin, the devil, hell, and more. Sally ignored his rambling to focus on the man beside her. "Reverend Lyons."

"It's Eli, please." Eli turned in his seat to face her. Though he couldn't see her, his gaze fell in nearly the right spot. A soft smile lit his features. The concern for their situation only showed through a tensing around his pale eyes. "Given our situation propriety seems to be overrated."

"Eli. I'm afraid I just had to kill Roland. I hope I'll be forgiven, but it was him or me."

"God knows your heart, Sally."

"Thank you. I regret that I'm likely going to have to hurt Pastor Eckles as well. He's the one behind all of the murders in town this year. Aren't you, Pastor?"

Eckles seemed to be finished with what he clearly thought was a thorough tying of her wrists. "You'll be quiet, harlot."

"No. I don't think I will. You saw to having good, decent men murdered. Keller, Ellis, Chauncey, Keenan? All were honorable men, who went to church every week and had a relationship with God." Sally released her hold on her sleeves. With Eckle's back turned, she shrugged her shoulders to lift one hand through the rope. It was tight, but thanks to the coat she was certain she could pull free. "And us women."

"You're all whores, the lot of you. You'll all burn for what you did."

"Leviticus, Chapter 24. 'If anyone injures his neighbor, whatever he has done must be done to him'. After what you've done, what will your fate be?" Sally grabbed the edge of her right sleeve with her left hand. As she pulled on it, her hand crept through the rope slow in hopes she wouldn't attract attention. "Cora wasn't a whore."

"That should have been you. You can't see fit to die." Eckles moved to hover over her.

She stilled her efforts to free herself to face him dead on. "Daisy. You saw to it she died. She was a doctor, Pastor. She cared for the injured and sick without a thought to who they were, or what they had done. Often without care of payment for those too poor to pay. She also went to church every Sunday. Prayed for forgiveness often."

"She's the one that chose to become a whore. You all did."

"Choice? You call that a choice? Women have very few choices in life, Pastor. Perhaps we did choose to become whores, but it was because we had few options. A woman marries, becomes a secretary, or a whore. Daisy had lost everything dear to her, including her husband, whom it's told she loved a great deal. Becoming a whore gave her a chance to keep doctoring, saving people's lives."

Eckles eyes flashed. "Whores are the poison that rots this earth. Men's souls are taken by your wanton lust."

"It isn't the men's souls that are taken. It's the women's. I had no choice when I became a whore. I didn't know or understand what I was getting into, but I had to survive."

"You did not keep your father's command, you forsook your mother's teaching."

"I had no father." Sally's heart lurched at the admittance. "None that I knew. My mother told me he died when I was a babe. He wasn't ever around anyhow. As for her teaching, she didn't bother with much. She didn't want me, told me so often enough."

"Sally," Eli said quietly. "You've never said such a thing before."

"Jane, she's my real ma. Soon as she saw what I was, she took me under her wing. Loved and supported me. The ma that birthed me didn't bother none. Other than to keep telling me I was an obligation. She was only doing it because she promised. Who she promised, I don't know. My pa, God, she didn't follow through. Wanted me to be something I never was. I hated her much as she hated me."

"You would hate your own parents, so you turned to whoring, pedaling your flesh." Eckles' nose wrinkled. "Tempting good men from God."

"If it weren't for men, there would be no whores. They're the ones that have declared they *need* pleasures of the flesh, would likely die without." Sally freed her hand, then held still. "They seek it before marriage, after, during, it matters not so long as they can keep from the discomfort of their pricks not being in a pussy. Sorry, Eli."

"We'll pray for your forgiveness soon enough, Sally." Eli almost sounded amused.

"The men in your own congregation would frequent the brothels. Married men, unmarried men, widowers and bachelors alike. They all crossed our threshold and sought those pleasures, even under your brand of preaching, Pastor. Jake, Reuben, Ron, Fred, and even Roland out there. Is that how you so easily convinced them to drink your poisoned wine? Did you tell them there was no hope for their sins? Or was it because children were dying, or near dying like Ma's babies?"

"The war was never supposed to take the innocent."

"That's when Mac died. When you found out Ma was with child. Jake because of Joshua? What else did Jake do besides the explosion? Who was it that attacked me? It was a couple. Perhaps it was the Ross's? Or maybe the Lymans?" Sally kept a firm grip on the wrist of her coat to keep the rope from falling. She was set to attack at a moment's notice now. "None of it really matters, I suppose. They're all dead now. I am curious about one of the deaths from your congregation. Miss Bee. She was a terrible dressmaker, but I don't understand what prompted her death. No children died before she was killed. Was it her gossiping? Did you fear she'd tell the world what you'd done?"

Eckles sighed heavily and rose. He slipped a bandana from his pocket as he rose. "Yes. Now I'm growing tired of this. Reverend Lyons and I were having a conversation before you arrived. I need you to be quiet so we can finish."

"That's too bad. I don't do well with quiet." Soon as he got close, she kicked her leg out at his knee.

He doubled over, the gun in his hand firing before she kicked it away. She pulled her arm free and shimmied out of her coat.

Eckles tried to rise but she didn't give him a chance. She grabbed a knife from her wrist, driving it into his hand where he pressed it into the table for support. She turned to kick the gun all the way out the door.

That's when she noticed the blood on Eli's leg. "Reverend. Are you all right?"

"It's just my leg." Eli's voice was strained, but clear. "I'll be fine."

"That's good." She rushed toward him. The world spun before she got there. Her legs crumbled under her, and she landed on the floor with a grunt. *Great*. Whatever had been keeping her going was wearing off. She suddenly felt weaker than a kitten.

"Sally?"

"Just a minute." Sally took several bracing breaths. Her hand hovered over the wound on her stomach. She opened her eyes to search the room for anything that would help. A muffler hung on a peg by the door. That would do.

Ignoring Eckles' cries of pain and protest, she pushed herself back to her feet to grab the muffler. She wrapped it around her waist a couple times, then pulled it tight as possible. Pain flashed through her as the knot she tied pressed hard into the wound. It wouldn't save her, but it might give her enough time to get back to town.

She grabbed the bandana from the floor and used it to gag Eckles cries. "That's better. You should always be muzzled. Now, Eli. I need to tie up Eckles and get him into the wagon. I'll need your help to get him there, seeing as he has a very bad knee. Not to mention we're both injured. I think if we work together, we can manage."

Sally used the roped he'd tied her with to tie his wrists with greater care than hers had been tied. It took a great deal of maneuvering, but they got the man to the wagon outside. She would have simply knocked him out, but dead weight was even harder than struggling weight to carry.

Soon as she'd helped Eli into the wagon, she went back for her coat. She took a few minutes to look down at her wound. Blood now rather thoroughly soaked a trail down her skirts. With how lightheaded she felt, she imagined she was bleeding inside as well.

She made it out to the wagon and managed to haul herself into the seat.

"Sally? Are you well?"

"Enough for this, Eli. I'll get us home, don't you worry. Eckles will go to jail, and hopefully hang for his crimes."

Sally slapped the reins to get the wagon going fast as possible toward town. Her brain felt foggy, but the road home was straight enough, she hoped.

After several miles figures came into view in the distance. She pulled on the reins to get the horses to stop, but they kept going. With a shaky breath, she set the reins in Eli's hands. "Pull on those. Someone's coming."

A rider broke from the pack, tearing toward them. Tommy stopped beside the wagon as Eli got the horses to a stop. "Sally."

"Tommy. I got him." The world dimmed, and the ground raced toward her with brutal expediency.

The bravest are surely those who have the clearest vision of what is before them, glory and danger alike, and yet notwithstanding, go out to meet it.
—Thucydides

Cole did his best to eat some of the food Eunice had brought. It was a simple meal, meant to be filling, he knew. His distraction kept him from focusing on the food. One eye remained on Alma the whole time she held Evie. When Eunice had come by with the food she'd brought Alma to visit and taken the twins home.

Alma had asked to hold the baby, and Cole didn't mind letting her while he ate. She'd always been good with the twins, he certainly wasn't worried about her dropping the infant. In fact, the only reason he watched so carefully was because he enjoyed seeing her with the babies. For some reason around the infants, she seemed at her calmest.

"Cole." Jane's voice sounded from the bed, rough with sleep. "Is that—food?"

"Yeah. Your ma brought you a plate if you're up to it." Cole set aside his fork to care for her. He wasn't really hungry anyway, and she needed to eat to get stronger quick as she could.

Her eyes landed on him with more clarity than he'd seen in the handful of times she'd woken so far that day. The familiar strength added a spark of life to her gaze he'd missed. A soft smile graced her lips. "If Evie isn't hungry, I am."

"She's sleeping right now. Alma's got her. Come here." Before she could dare to protest, he flung aside the covers. With her awake and showing some spark of life he wanted to get her up out of the bed. Picking her up made his ribs hurt like the devil, but he spoke over her protests. "I'm carrying you. That's final."

"Boor." For all her protest, she laid against his chest willingly. She remained quiet until he'd set her in a seat close to Alma. Once there, she leaned close to the pair. She brushed her fingers along the baby's cheek. "She's being very good. She must like her Aunt Alma."

Alma lifted her gaze to Jane. Confusion puckered her delicate brow. "Aunt?"

"Yes. You are hr aunt, just as you are with Colton and Clara. You're Cole's sister, right?"

Alma's brow furrowed further. Her gaze darted around the room, settling on Cole when she found no one else. "No tell."

"We can tell now," Jane reassured Alma in a warm tone.

"But, no tell. Cole doesn't like it."

"He doesn't mind anymore. You and Leanne are his sisters, and it's time people knew it, and all he's done for you." Jane winked at him. "Isn't that right?"

"That's right," Cole agreed. He gave Alma a reassuring nod. When his sister turned back to the baby, he pushed a plate of food toward Jane. "Eat. You must be hungry after all that baby making and blood losing."

"I feel as though I've been trampled by a stampede." She gathered some potatoes on her fork. Soon as she took a bite her eyes fluttered close. A low hum of delight crossed her lips.

Cole couldn't help himself, he leaned in to kiss her gently. He tugged her chair closer so he could press his forehead to hers. "No more. You're not allowed to scare me like that again. We're done. No more babies. No more strays."

"Strays don't almost kill me, but yes." She set her hand on his wrist. "We are in agreement, Mr. Mitchell. I've been far too friendly with death more than enough times for my taste. I won't risk it again."

"Mean it?"

"Do you? This one was all your idea, remember?" She kissed him softly. "Now let me eat."

"Fine. So long as you're really doing better, and you promise not to do it again."

"Both are true." Jane turned back to her feed. She ate slow, but with enthusiasm. Halfway through the meal, her pace slowed. "It's delicious, but I don't want to overdo it."

"Then back to bed."

"No."

"Jane."

"Please. I'm feeling better than I have. I'd like to sit somewhere other than the bed I've been languishing in."

He didn't want to point out how tired she looked. If push came to shove, he had to admit she did look like she felt better, even if she was tired. "You're supposed to rest."

"I will, but I don't want to go back to sleep yet. When Evie wakes, I want to be awake. I'd like to feed her myself without someone helping. Would you get me to the rocking chair? It'll be more comfortable than this chair." She tried to stand on her own before he could help.

He immediately moved to help her to her feet. "Stubborn woman."

"You wouldn't love me if I wasn't."

"Fair point." He guided her to the rocking chair a few feet away. Before she could ask for it, he grabbed a blanket to drape over her legs. Then he went to stoke the fire a little higher. By the time that was done, Evie started fussing.

Alma carried the baby to Jane. "She's a good niece."

"Yes, she does seem to be a very good baby. It's a good thing, too. Cole would be in a frightful state if he had to worry over a cranky baby as well as myself." Jane set the baby up for feeding. "I do still tire very easily, Alma. I do hope you'll do me the kindness of holding Evie again when she's done eating."

"Yes. Yes." Alma's bright smile had returned as she took her seat.

Cole leaned down to kiss the top of Jane's head, but a harsh rattling wagon pulled his attention to the window. Tommy's shouts for the doctor drew him outside to the balcony. He peered over the railing to find Tommy gather Sally in his arms and carry her inside.

Jane's sharp gaze focused on him as he closed the door on the rising shouts outside. "What's happened?"

"Can't rightly say seeing as I've been in here for days. It looks like the little Pink got herself wounded, though." He didn't say Sally out of respect of Alma's presence. The last thing he wanted to do was destroy her current calm state. Despite his caginess, or maybe because of it, he noticed that Alma's ear had tilted his way despite the book in her hand. "Saw two men of God in the wagon, one in knots."

"I see." Jane turned her attention to the babe nestled at her breast. Though he couldn't see her features, he imagined her mind was racing. He only hoped Evie would distract her from getting too tense. "Then I imagine we'll get a report soon enough, unless you care to go find out for yourself."

He knew the suggestion was made as much for her own curiosity as his. Still, he didn't like leaving her this weak I she wasn't in bed. "I don't know."

"Alma is here to aide me with Evie. I already told you I feel stronger than I have. The food really helped. Go on ahead. Tell Thomas to come visit once matters are settled somewhat."

"I'll be back quick as a wink."

"I sincerely doubt it. It's of no matter, I'll be here. I'll doze if I need to." She turned her head up to accept his kiss. The only sign of how troubled she was reflected in the way her blue eyes had darkened.

He wanted to get her answers, and he wanted those answers himself. To that end, he raced down the stairs to the lobby. Tom stood in a doorway, unmoving. Cole approached in just a few strides. "What happened?"

"I don't know the whole story." Tommy's gaze didn't flicker from the room where Dr. Noe and Bonnie cut the clothes from Sally. When they got to her corset layer, Tom turned his back to the room. "Reverend Lyons says Eckles shot her, then they had an argument and Sally—the girl turned tables on Eckles."

"You said she was good."

"She is. Too bad, too."

"How's that?"

"Don't think she'll keep on after this with her attitude lately. I thought it would be an easy case to work her in on when we started with Keller. The whole matter turned out to be a lot messier than I ever thought it would. Too messy." Tommy brushed his hand over his face and along his beard. "Lyons took a hit in the leg. Charlie's in with him now. Fanny?"

"Just a moment please," Dr. Noe called from the room behind them.

"Eckles did all of this?" Cole's temper rose at the realization. "All of the deaths?"

"All of them. He manipulated his congregation into doing dastardly deeds in his quest to rid the earth of sin. When children started to get hurt, it was his congregations turn to die."

"Sally—she was asking Eckles about Jane's attack. When Mac got her."

"Not surprising. I've still got some questions for him, but I'll get the answers soon. Lyons says Sally got herself a few answers before she turned the tables. Eckles is on his way to jail for now. He'll get his medical care when we get around to it. I'm tempted to offer him some of his own wine."

"What?" Cole glanced at Tommy. Wine? What did that have to do with anything? "I missed a lot, didn't I?"

"Yes."

"Gentlemen." Dr. Noe stepped between them. She wiped blood from her hands as she leveled her gaze at them. She was an attractive woman; strawberry blonde hair curled into an elegant twist on her head, sparkling brown eyes. Single at what would normally be considered spinster age in her hometown of Boston. Cole wondered how she'd escaped marriage with her looks and wealthy family.

Tommy wasn't in the least bit distracted. He stared the doctor down. "What's the word, Fanny?"

"I won't know more until I'm in there operating. The bullet went in her side, nicked a rib. I think it lodged in her liver. I don't think her recovery would be too bad, except she's still recovering from her last attack." She focused on Cole. "You might see if Eunice up to helping with some blood. There's a fair amount in her belly, so I don't know how much she's lost. I'll have Dr. Young do the procedure. He's more practiced than I am."

"Thought that didn't always work too good." Cole turned to look in the room where Sally lay, now covered in a sheet. Pale, but not sheet white as Jane had been. Bonnie worked without ceasing, spraying something on Sally's belly.

"Both Sally and Eunice gave blood to Jane without incident. It stands to reason that it has a very good chance of working. Now excuse me, I should begin." Dr. Noe moved through them again and shut the door in Cole's face.

Cole leaned against the frame with a sigh. "Are we sure we got the right man? There can't be any more of this."

"I'm sure. Now we nail him to the wall."

"Sure wish we hadn't become a state."

"How's that?" Tommy stirred from his dark stare at the closed door.

"I'd like a little law of the land dealing with that bastard."

"Wouldn't we all?"

The natural healing force in each
one of us is the greatest force in getting well.
—Hippocrates

"You're not killing him," David said by way of greeting. He didn't rise from his chair as if to stop Tommy or make any move that indicated he'd enforce his decree. "Charlie's in dealing with his wounds now. Marshal should be here in three days barring any further storms."

"He'd already be dead if I planned on killing him," Tommy pointed out. He took a seat opposite the sheriff. One quick glance around the room told him the pastor wasn't in one of the holding cells on the first floor. "You put him upstairs?"

"There's plenty that want him dead. I figured having to go through two of us would make it more challenging. Plus, Jesse comes to visit. I didn't want him seeing that man. How's Sally?"

"She came through surgery fine. They gave her some blood from Ma. Fanny expects she'll wake tonight or tomorrow."

"Glad to hear it. I heard word Jane is awake and moving again, too. I'd planned to stop by and see her tomorrow."

"They're putting Sally in Jane's room when she's ready. You should be able to talk to her then." Tommy leaned back in his seat, propping his legs on the desk. "It's going to take a lot for the town to recover from all of this."

"I know." David ran his hands through his hair. The past year had aged him as much as the rest of them. Lines had appeared on the man's youthful forehead. "Lee is a wreck. She's so worried about Jesse and Marjorie, not that Marjorie will remember."

"They'll come through all right. Jesse's already chatting it up with Stephen, plotting their next great adventure to cause chaos and destruction. It's the adults that are going to suffer the longest. Trust was broken. People they thought were friends did all of this. Mike says Cora is afraid to leave her kitchen now."

"Maybe once that maniac is dealt with everyone can begin to heal."

"Easier said than done. Jane still isn't healed from her past. Cole says she still has nightmares. Charlie witnessed some on their trip out west."

Footsteps on the stairs broke off the conversation. Charlie settled his bowler on his head as he came into view. "He'll live to see his hanging."

"Hanging's too good for him." This, surprisingly, from David.

Tommy nodded in agreement. He'd had the same thought himself. "It definitely is. Cole was lamenting the territory becoming a state. He's wishing for a little law of the land to deal with this situation."

"I doubt he's the only one." Charlie approached the pair. "If the marshal is getting here as quick as you say, he shouldn't require any further medical treatment in the interim. I'll come by when Lewis arrives to answer any questions."

"Lewis was just here a few weeks ago." David sighed. "I didn't expect to have to see him again so soon."

"Well, he's just happy he's not being called to find a dead woman walking anymore." Tommy hopped to his feet. "I'll walk back with you, Charlie."

"You're not going to talk to him?" Charlie slipped into his coat. The gaze he settled on Tommy was suspicious. "Seems unlikely."

"Nah. I'll come by later. Maybe I'll get to talk to Sally first, which I'd prefer. I just came to see if he was going to live long enough to die." Tommy nodded to David. "I'll be back maybe tonight to talk to him, but definitely for my shift in the morning."

"I've got Artie and Hank working overnight. Glad you'll be here tomorrow. Lee will be happy to have me home during the day for a change."

"Artie and Hank?" Tommy paused at that news. He'd hoped for better guards. Then again, he wouldn't trust Mike to guard the man after what he'd been through, not that Mike had returned to deputy duties yet. "They're not used to the job. Are we sure they won't nod off."

"I'm hoping with two on duty, that won't happen. I've been picking from the men I know of decent repute. None of them are skilled lawmen. I wouldn't mind taking on a few more experienced hands, if you have a mind." David nodded to him. "Seems as though it wouldn't be a bad idea anymore. What with recent events, and word of several drives coming through at first melt."

"I'll reach out to some of my contacts, see what I can find." Tommy put his hat back on, then headed outside after Charlie. "Don't act so surprised I know how to behave, Charlie. I want this done right or I would have finished him just for what was done to Jane and Sally."

"David was there. You couldn't have." Charlie adjusted his bag to hold it under his arm while he slipped on his gloves. "I'm not certain anyone in this town would have begrudged you for it, though. He's done a lot of damage. I'm going to have to send a telegram to a friend of mine. He'd be very interested in the psychology of this. Then again, there aren't many survivors from his church to interview."

"Not a one that I know of. Apparently a handful of miners went to that church as well. I doubt at this point any of them would admit it if they were still alive."

"Not unless they like the idea of a lynch mob at their door."

Tommy grunted his agreement to the statement. "I'm going to stop in and see Jane and the baby before I head to the Inn to man the place. Ma and Pa deserve a night off from working the floor after all they've done."

"They deserve much more than that. They've been saints staying on here so long."

"Ma isn't complaining one bit. She got to be here for her grandchild's birth. Then again, that wasn't pleasant and happy either."

"To say the least." Charlie held the door open for him. While they removed their hats and coats, he glanced around the empty lobby. "Everything looks settled for the moment. I'll come with you to check on Jane. Hopefully she's still awake."

"I hope so. I haven't been able to see her since before yesterday. I haven't even seen the baby yet."

"The baby has a name. It's Evelyn."

"I know that." Tom knocked briefly on the door before entering. He found Jane at the table setting out the dominoes he'd found in Molly's hotel room. "Dominoes?"

"I planned on teaching Cole." Jane's attention moved to the bed that had been squeezed in near the stove. "Sally still hasn't woken, so I thought we'd play a game while we waited. Cole went to get some food and drinks."

"I'll take that as a good sign you're feeling better. Wanting to occupy yourself, to eat and drink, all are good signs." Charlie kissed her on the cheek.

"I'm feeling stronger every minute," Jane confirmed. She frowned when Charlie knelt beside her chair. "Must you?"

"You know I have to check to see how you're healing." Charlie smirked. "I promise to not pester you again tonight."

"Please be quick about it, then. I don't want you ruining my pleasant mood—and don't you dare wake that baby, Thomas."

"I wasn't going to, sheesh." Tommy leaned over the basket she'd set the baby in. "She is beautiful. Favors you both."

"She does seem to, doesn't she? My nose, his chin, eyes are like yours, though." Jane grunted quietly. "Ow."

"Sorry. Almost done." Charlie adjusted the blanket back over her lap a moment later. "You're doing well. Have you been able to walk on your own?"

"It's easier with assistance, but I've managed a few steps." Jane turned her attention back to Tommy where he remained hovering over the baby. "I haven't seen you since before I nearly died, and you give all the attention to the baby."

"Well, I never do know what your temper will be with me. Nearly killed me for helping you out of a tight spot but hugged me when Sally got near dead. Now that she's been hurt again, I didn't know which Jane I'd find." Tommy kissed her temple. "Glad to see you're in fighting mode again, Jane."

"Glad to be in it. I'm rather tired of shaking death's hand. It's getting tedious."

Charlie snorted, settling into a chair. "We're all getting rather tired of it, Jane."

Tommy took another seat. "You know how to play this game, Jane?"

"I've never played it as myself, but I recall the rules rather clearly." She rearranged the tiles around the table. "Do you know how?"

"I do. Charles?"

"I'm unfamiliar with the game, myself." Charles straightened. "Once you go over the rules with me, I should be fine."

"Then we'll team up, one experienced player with a novice. I'll take Charles." Jane grinned at Tommy. "You take Cole."

"Sure, you take the one with the memory as close to yours as we can get."

"That is the idea."

To the soul, there is hardly anything
more healing than friendship.
-Thomas Moore

Jane took a seat beside Graham and Linh's bed. The couple remained huddled close with baby Jun wrapped in Linh's arms. For his part, despite the fresh bandages from the fire, Graham had a robust, healthy appearance again. "You're looking much better, Graham."

"Feeling better. Mighta been able to go home already, but after helping out at the fire they wanted to keep me around a few more days. Feel bad about that, it's been real crowded in here."

"I wouldn't worry much about that. Spirits have been pretty good as families all gathered in rooms together." Jane offered a smile. "Plus, it gives Charles further excuse to cement his plans for a full hospital."

"Never thought we much needed one before this year." Graham adjusted himself with a wince of pain.

"Neither did most of us. The town is growing, though. Even without the events of this past year, we would need one soon." Jane glanced toward the mother and daughter curled against Graham. "It'll be good you'll all get to leave this place soon. It's difficult to heal anything but physical wounds in here."

Graham ran a finger along his daughter's cheek. "Don't know how we can go home to that house now after Joshua."

Linh made a whimper of a sound, followed by a harsh word. Jane didn't know any Chinese, but she wagered a guess it had been a curse.

"Sally seems to think it was Jake that set the explosion at your place, based on what Eckles said to him before he drank the poison. Eckles himself will be facing the marshal in another day or two." Jane set her hand gently on Graham's. "You'll focus on each other, on Jun, and your future children. You won't ever forget Joshua, but with time you'll learn how to live without him. I'm truly sorry for your loss."

"Still don't seem real most days. Think it will be when we get home."

"I'm afraid that's likely to be true. Once home where you were a family, you'll be dealing with the reality in a new way." Jane sighed softly. "Thank you for helping with the fire. You have stepped up in ways I once didn't think possible."

"I hate that someone else lost a child." Graham's voice grew thick with emotion. "It's not right. No one should. That man should burn like he wanted all of us to."

"That would be a fitting end, but I believe he'll have a hanging in his future."

"Not enough," Linh whispered. "Not for him."

"I don't think there's a soul that would disagree with that. Unfortunately, our laws are not an eye for an eye." Jane turned at the knock on the door. She smiled at her husband as he entered. "I wondered where you'd wandered off to."

"Stopped to see Wil and Archie. You saw them earlier today while I was working." The blasted man had gone back to work despite Charlie's admonitions not to. He was worried about the businesses, especially with word of what had happened in Dominion Falls reaching newspapers as far as Chicago. Cole nodded to the pair on the bed. "Good afternoon, Graham. Linh."

Graham returned the nod. "Working already?"

"Better than you, lazy sod. All you did was lose a couple of fingers and get some big slivers in your back." Cole grinned when Graham laughed at his teasing. "I don't got the excuse of the cold keeping the bodies frozen to save my neck."

"Well, you do got the fact that you're as wealthy as the Daugherty's these days to rest on," Graham teased right back. "'Specially now that Janey's got a handful of gold claims at the tips of her fingers by all accounts."

"The claims are mine, not his." The public ones were, at least. Jane knew word had gotten out about some of her claims. The rest were under a false name and now in both her and Cole's names despite her plans to keep them in her own before California. She'd had the mind to keep the known ones in hers in case they ever longed for a bit of scandal again. "That means he needs to keep working. The money for those is in my name, not his."

"Oh-ho-ho. I thought you were married. Doesn't that give him rightful claim?" Graham's grin took on a familiar wicked bent. "He could toss you in an asylum and take it all. No one would argue that you were one crazy lady."

"My lawyer is better than his—"

"Her lawyer is better than mine—"

They'd spoken at the same time. Jane laughed along with Cole. She winked up at him. "He already knows I'd make him bleed if he tried to leave me for real. He saw the papers."

"I did. She's evil." Cole kissed the top of her head. "We should get back to the room. Sally's getting restless. Wants to get out of here."

"She's hardly healed. Then again, neither are you and you're going out and working." Jane half rose, but paused to kiss Graham on the cheek. "When you get home it'll get much more difficult to fight the urge to drink again. Be careful for me, will you?"

"I'll do my best, Janey. I've got Linh and Jun here to help."

"And me to beat you about the head if you slip." Jane squeezed his shoulder. She offered a teasing wink. "I know how much you always did love my nagging."

"Sure did. Just like a nail though the skull." Graham's expression was more serious than his jesting words. His next came out deep and warm. "Thank you, Jane."

Jane circled the chair to take Cole's arm. She could make the walk on her own, but it would be much easier on his arm. Once outside the room, she released a long breath. "I do hope he continues to cope this well at home. I'm worried for him."

"That's still a strange thing to hear from your mouth."

"I'm aware. It feels strange to say it."

He pushed open the door to their room. Sally sat on her bed, nose in a book, Evie in the basket at her feet. "Sally. How's the baby?"

"Slept the whole time." Sally didn't even look up from her book.

Jane took in the cover in confusion. "*Lorna Doone*? That isn't your usual sort of book, Sally."

"So?"

Jane frowned. "You are aware I finally got the new *Monsieur Lecoq* book over from Europe. *Le Petite Vieux des Batingoles.*"

"I am. I appreciate it, but we should put it in the library. I don't think I'll read it."

Rather than argue, Jane picked up the baby and carried her over to the rocking chair. She wasn't crying for food yet, but the time was coming. "I also have *L'Homme qui rit* or *Les Chants de Maldoror* for something a little more exciting, or in the case of Maldoror, rather challenging."

"This is fine, Ma. Really, I chose it off of the stack on the table. I saw all the books and picked this one, may I finish?"

Jane turned her attention to Evie after Sally's peevish tone. Cole gave her a concerned look, but at the shake of her head, left it alone. "Eunice said she'd be by with supper and Willow and Jay. Seems they're a little jealous that the twins have been able to spend so much time over here."

"They aren't fans of the clinic, so I'm surprised. Especially seeing as we're going home tomorrow finally."

"We're going home, but you're taking it easy. Let Tommy and I work. Garit has the main handle on the saloon, but Tommy and I will fill in."

"There's so much to be done," Jane protested heavily. Spring would arrive in short order, and there were numerous preparations she'd planned to do before they would have a full hotel again. "February will be our worst month client-wise, seeing as we are usually snowed in for most of it. If I promise to behave, can I see to arranging some cleaning and rearranging? I think we could make the pit flow better."

"Is that a promise you intend to keep?"

"Of course."

"I've heard that before." The hint of humor in his tone sparkled in his eyes. He leaned in to brush his lips across hers. "So long as it's your brain working, not your body, I don't got no complaints."

"The brothel won't slow like the hotel. You and Thomas will need to cover it more until Wil is back up to working, which could be a while. I'd suggest another manager for the brothel, but I don't think Garit or Wil need the intrusion. They've run it fine until Wil got hurt."

"We'll see if we can dig up another manager for the Inn."

"The Inn? But—" she stopped her protest when his finger pressed to her lips.

"We were busy this last year, despite it all. Word is spreading, and I expect it's not gonna change anytime soon." He leaned on the arms of her chair, keeping his gaze level with hers.

"I suppose. According to some scientific journals there's a big event going to happen next year right around here. I've already taken one reservation from an astrophysicist out of New York."

Sally's book thumped to her lap. Cole's jaw dropped, confusion pinching his brows. He gaped for several long minutes. Sally spoke first. "An actual astrophysicist?"

"What the hell is that?" Cole glanced toward Sally. "You know what it is?"

Jane chuckled softly. "It's a scientist that studies the heavens. I believe there will be plenty of hotels from here to Denver that will be full. According to what I've read, there's to be an eclipse next summer. I expect we'll have all sorts of astronomers flocking to Colorado."

"How long have you known that?"

"Not long." Jane focused on Evie rather than look directly at Sally when she spoke next. "I've reached out to a woman astronomer I read about at Vassar to see if she'd like to come here. Grumblings in the science world suggest she's heading an all-female team to see the event."

"Really?" For the briefest moment excitement warmed Sally's tone. The girl sank back in her bed and lifted her book to hide her features. The next words were flat, "That's nice."

Jane frowned at Cole, then shrugged.

Cole took a seat beside her. He must have gotten her hint not to press the matter. "You want to rearrange the pit?"

"Yes. I have some ideas in mind. I'm no great shakes at drawing, but perhaps Sally or Charles can help me out."

"Fine. Now, about another manager."

"I don't know."

"It'll give you more time for your teas, the library, and the carpentry, and the mines, not to mention all that money."

She laughed outright, immediately groaning as her stomach protested the boldness of the action. On top of that, Evie startled awake. "You stop. I'll be living no different than

I did before. The money will get put to good use, but we didn't have want for anything before I inherited all of that."

"You've still got a lot more on your plate these days."

"The most important things being you and the children. The Inn is a distant third, everything else is a speck in the distance." She pulled him into a quick kiss as Evie let out a small cry. "Now let me focus on our daughter. Then we'll spend time with Jay and Willow, but tonight I want nothing more than to sleep in your arms until Evie needs me."

"You got these arms as long as you want them."

"Forever, then?"

"Forever, Mrs. Mitchell."

Revenge is a kind of wild justice.
—Sir Francis Bacon

Sally slipped downstairs to the kitchen once everyone fell asleep. She had a thought to get a snack, but quickly realized her mistake. The clinic had been almost bursting for two days. While quite a few people had been allowed to go home today, the already limited coffers remained all but empty.

Remembering that Andrew usually kept candy in his office, she made her way there. He claimed he kept the candy to help with the smell during autopsies. She thought he exaggerated the truth a bit because peppermints were all he needed for that. His stash of candy was more widespread than peppermints alone.

Unfortunately, as she approached she heard hushed voices inside. She peeked around the corner to see who it was. Bonnie and Andrew talked quietly near his desk. She moved to leave, but a floorboard creaked at her first step.

"Sally," Andrew called. "Come on in. We were just enjoying some of this bread Bonnie brought with her from the ranch."

Sally's stomach rumbled despite her intention to leave. Hunger won out over common sense to continue hiding away. She stepped in, offering Bonnie an apologetic smile. For all she knew, she'd interrupted an intimate moment between the fledgling couple. "I didn't mean to interrupt."

"Nonsense." Bonnie waved off her apology. Apparently she hadn't interrupted, there seemed to be no annoyance in her tone at all. "Come in and have a bite. I know we've been rationing food with the influx of patients. Thankfully, most of the rest are going home tomorrow. We can return to our usual daily dose of mining injuries."

"And Lor's tendency toward accidents," added Andrew. "I do believe Miss Lorrain Caster can't go a day without tripping on something."

"I think she merely wants to have you as her doctor." Sally gave up on trying to conjure an excuse to escape. She grabbed a slice of the buttered bread off the plate. The bread was still warm, the butter melted to perfection. "Mmmm. Very delicious, Bonnie. I think Lor fancies you, Andrew. You'd best get yourself off the market before she figures out a way to get into your good graces."

Both Bonnie and Andrew blushed at Sally's analysis. Andrew caught his composure, even as his shoulder twitched with his discomfort, a habit she'd noticed early on in their friendship. "Don't be ridiculous, Sally."

"Don't believe me, then. You'll be sorry." Sally polished off the bread in just two more bites. She'd been hungrier than she'd realized. "Who'll be left after tomorrow?"

"Archie, Wil, and two from the fire with the worst burns. We need to keep an eye on them a little while longer. I think Archie should be able to go home in a week or so. He'll need lots of help at the livery, but every day he's getting more function back." Andrew polished off his bread, then licked the butter from his fingers. "Oh, my mother would have a fit to see me like this."

Bonnie laughed, handing him a napkin. "Then stop acting like a mudsill and use a napkin."

"Is Stephen going home tomorrow?" Sally intentionally avoided asking about Matthew. She hadn't seen him since the incident at the barn. Jane hadn't mentioned him coming by to see her after her surgery, and she assumed she would have if Matthew had made such an appearance. Perhaps she'd managed to scare him off for good. The idea both relieved her and broke her heart a little more.

"He is. I think he's upset about it, though. Here at the clinic he's able to see his friends every day without having to wait for Matthew or I to bring him to town." Bonnie turned a piercing stare on Sally. "Not that Matthew minds the excuse to come to town."

Andrew offered a wicked grin. "I don't think he does."

"You two don't know anything. Stop. I've well and good scared him off, and it's all for the better anyhow. Now, if you'll excuse me." Sally rushed from the room. She didn't make it to the steps before Andrew caught her on the arm. "Andrew, please."

"Sally." He turned her to face him, then pulled her into a hug. "I'm glad you're doing better. You must stop scaring me like that."

"Don't you worry about that. I won't be pursuing the ridiculous notion any longer. My life will be without such opportunities from now on." She extricated herself from the hug.

"Wait." He kept hold of her wrist so she couldn't dart away. "You can't mean that."

"I can, and I do. I should go back upstairs before Ma wakes and worries where I've run off to."

"Sally. You had such excitement for what you were doing. Not to mention your intelligence. It's—"

"Nothing. Please unhand me."

"You have an ear for languages, Sally. Look how fast you picked up French a German. More importantly, you have a brain for science. You do so well in my lab. You learned fast."

"I just told you I'm not pursuing any such notions."

"You don't want to be a detective, fine. I don't agree with that decision, but I'm not daft enough to tell you to change your mind. I'd have a better luck turning a feather into gold."

She glared down at his hand where it held hers captive. If he kept talking she'd end up in tears again. She couldn't bear to discuss this. The pain was still too fresh. Look at all those still suffering. "Please, stop. I can't discuss this any further."

"You should consider college. For science."

"What? That's absurd."

"It isn't. I told you, you have a mind for it."

"Andrew. Stop."

He sighed softly, placing a kiss on her forehead. "Fine. I miss my friend, though. She disappeared on me."

"I'm right here."

"I wish you were." He released her hand at last before taking a step back. "I'm around whenever you need an ear, Sally."

"I know." She gathered her skirts and rushed up the steps before he could come up with an argument. None came, and she made it up the stairs in total silence.

With so many sleeping patients still in the clinic she kept her pace slow and quiet as possible. At her room, she opened the door to a peaceful scene. Jay and Willow had returned home as they were too large for the trundle beds, and there were no beds to spare in the clinic. Even the room next to theirs that now sat empty didn't have a bed, as it had been taken to another room to accommodate family.

On the larger bed Cole and Jane lay close together sound asleep. Sally's heart both swelled and ached at the way that even in sleep they turned to each other. Despite Jane's pains from surgery, she curled into Cole. He held her against him, her head tucked under his chin.

Evie lay in her basket, also sound asleep. Her mouth moved as though suckling. Sally couldn't help but smile at the sight, and lingered to watch her a few minutes.

The prospect of sleep didn't appeal to Sally in the least. She grabbed the blanket from her bed to swing around her shoulders. She edged out into the cold air on the balcony. The town lay still and silent, all except the saloons scattered through town.

The Golden Touch was lit brightly from within. Not even the hastily patched hole in the building had stopped the merriment. If only it could be the same for her.

She exhaled a puff of breath that froze into fog. The fog dissipated on the light breeze. She realized from where she stood she could see the upper half of the jail over top of the butcher's shop across the street.

Light shone from a window on the corner, faint echoes of the light shimmered through other windows on the floor. Tommy had said Eckles was being kept upstairs. Was that his room? She imagined most of the town wanted to get their hands on him by now. The hanging would have quite the turnout.

A shadow moved at the window. For nearly a minute it darkened part of the barred window. Then it seemed to stretch out of it, right through the bars. It shimmied down the outer wall, a darker shadow against the night.

Sally straightened with some fascination at the oddness. The figure was small and nimble, too much of both to be Eckles. The shadow disappeared from sight.

She cursed, wanting nothing more than to run and find out what it had been. "It was probably your overactive imagination, you fool. It's so dark, your mind was making up something to see. You're done with such nonsense, remember?"

Though part of her wanted to go seek out what she'd seen, she stubbornly shoved aside the oddity to take a seat on the rocking chair. Her curiosity was a detriment, she'd seen as much plenty. It would suit her no further. She had to ignore it, keep it shoved down in the chasm that had replaced her heart.

She'd been a fool to think she could be anything but what she'd been. Her birth ma had been right, she wasn't good for much of anything.

A movement to her left startled her back into awareness. A shadow moved at the edge of the balcony, then grew absolutely still. As if it had been her imagination.

Sally rose slowly, moving closer to the stairs that led down to the street. A small figure rose from the shadows, giving her a daring challenge of a glare. Sally couldn't have been more surprised to realize it was Linh staring her down with a strength she'd not seen in the diminutive woman before.

A sliver of metal flashed in the dim light. Linh drew the metal between folds of dark fabric to clean it. A sharp, silvery stick that she then placed in the large bun at the back of her head. The surprisingly steel-like and sharp hair pin matched perfectly with another that held the bun in place.

Sally studied Linh, then glanced toward the jail. She smiled as she turned back to Linh. With a small nod, she turned to head back inside her room without another word. Linh slid into the empty room beside theirs.

Soon the alarm would sound, she imagined. She'd best be in bed for it.

The law hath not been dead,
though it hath slept.
-William Shakespeare

Jane startled awake at a loud pounding on the door. "What?"

"*Sally?*" David shouted unnecessarily loud. The room was dark save for a candle lit near Sally's bed. It had to be the middle of the night.

Sally pulled open the door, hushing David as she did. "You woke the baby, and probably the entire clinic. Was all of that necessary?"

"Where have you been, Sally?" David strode into the dark room without apology. It was so unlike him, it startled Jane.

She glanced at Cole, then back to David. Light flickered through the room as Cole turned up the lamp. At that point it was clear David was covered in blood. Jane sat up straighter. "David? What is going on? Why would you wake the entire clinic in the middle of the night with your shouting?"

"Eckles is dead." David stared at Sally. "Where have you been?"

"Right here." Sally gestured to her bed. "Well, about an hour ago I was downstairs with Andrew and Bonnie, then I came up here. I've been reading, I'm having trouble sleeping."

"Wait. Slow down." Cole picked up the squalling Evie. He bounced her in a soothing way as he approached the two staring each other down. "Back up there, Davie. What do you mean, Eckles is dead?"

"Someone murdered him. Not sure how yet, but there was blood everywhere." David didn't take his gaze from Sally for a second. "Did you have anything to do with it?"

"Not a thing." Sally remained perfectly calm, almost amused. Almost as if she expected this whole mess. "I'm not sorry he's dead, but I didn't do it myself. Why come here first?"

"The man had two guards on him, someone had to sneak in." David still didn't look away from Sally. "You've gotten pretty good at sneaking."

"Oh, not that good. The only way upstairs in that jail is past the front desk. Only way I could have done it is by a long shot, and I'm not that good with a weapon. Besides, someone would have heard the shot if such a thing had happened."

"You've sure got this all figured out."

Jane threw her robe on on her way to her feet She set a hand on David's arm, worried he'd run with this as he had with Michael. "You can't honestly mean you think Sally killed him? If she'd wanted him dead, she would have killed him in that homestead instead of tying him up to bring him back here to jail."

"I swear I didn't do it." Sally held up her hands. There wasn't any hint of guilt on the girl, Jane believed her. "You can ask Andrew and Bonnie, I was down there an hour ago, and I've been up here since."

"Well, someone did." David's shoulders sagged. "Marshal Lewis isn't going to be happy when he arrives tomorrow."

"Alfred will manage. I'm certain he's used to frontier justice." Jane urged David toward the table as heavy footsteps approached their door. She took Evie from Cole so he could let in whomever it was. "Let me make you some coffee, David. You look a fright."

David looked down at himself as if just realizing he was covered in blood. "Guess I do. Tommy, Graham. What do you know about what happened?"

"I only know that you came barging in here shouting to wake the devil." Graham rubbed his hand over his face.

"And wake him he did," Jane muttered. It wasn't the time for joking, but she couldn't help herself.

Graham smirked at her. "Linh and I were sound asleep. You woke Jun with your hollering."

"Sorry." David's head drooped. "We just got Eckles over here from the jail. Someone managed to sneak in and kill him tonight."

"Good riddance," muttered Graham. "Too bad we don't know who did it. We could give them a medal for it."

"Where were you an hour ago, Graham?" David eyed him quietly.

"He was sound asleep, for sure," Sally provided. "I could hear him snoring from here."

"Thanks a lot," Graham said drily.

"I was at the brothel, but you already knew that. Plenty of witnesses, too. I didn't want him dead. I had a few more questions for him." Tom dropped into a chair, thanking Jane when she handed him coffee. "So he's dead, eh? How?"

"Waiting on Dr. Cross to figure that out. There was blood everywhere, but no wound that I could see." David squeezed Jane's hand where it rested on his shoulder. "Sorry, Sally."

"No apologies necessary. I did want him dead without a doubt, but not without further questioning. That's the only reason I didn't kill him myself." Sally sipped her own coffee, a hint of a smile on her features. She definitely knew something, even if she didn't do it. When she caught Jane looking, the expression flittered away like a flurry of snow.

Jane leaned against Cole, staring at the men around her table. "Now that that's done, what are we going to do about it? Will there be an investigation? Must we put everyone through that?"

"Once we find out how it was done, we'll have questions. The Marshal will want to know what happened, and will expect me to try to find out who did it."

"Good luck," Jane said quietly. "Anyone that knows something won't say a word. I doubt there's a soul that didn't want to see his end—although I think most were looking forward to the show of a hanging for it."

"They won't now, that's for sure." David took a big swig of coffee. "I guess that means this is all finally over."

"Not a minute too soon, neither." Cole squeezed Jane's arm gently. "All that's left now is the healing."

"We all need a lot of healing," Jane agreed. She held Sally's gaze as she said it. Sally flushed and looked away pointedly. Jane shook her head, turning her attention to the baby. "And many of us have babies that need growing, and a few more that need birthing."

"Kat and Faith, yes?" David glanced her way. "Am I missing anyone?"

"I don't think so. Unless, of course, you and Lee have news to share." She grinned wickedly. "I've seen how she looks at that baby. She'll be happy for another."

"Don't you start with that now." David chuckled softly. He fell silent again, then sighed deeply. "I should probably go check on that autopsy."

"Sit. Wait. I have no doubt Andrew knows where to find you. You woke the dead with your knocking and hollering." Jane set a hand on his shoulder, holding it there to keep him still. "You all keep talking, I'm going to feed Evie."

Sally followed Jane to the rocking chair. Once settled in, she spoke low under the continuing conversation across the room. "I didn't do it, Ma."

"I know." Jane kept an eye on the conversation to ensure they were properly distracted. To her benefit, Tommy set in on a raucous story that had the men chuckling. "I just wonder how much you know."

"Enough. I didn't do it, plan it, or set it in motion. Tommy didn't either. Whoever did it, did it of their own volition."

Jane studied her quietly. There were plenty of people that came to mind that could have happily done it, but how they could have done so without detection she couldn't imagine. She brushed aside her own curiosity, for it didn't matter. "Are you certain you're finished?"

"I have to be. It costs too much."

"I know you feel that way now, but perhaps with time you won't."

"Somehow I doubt it."

"I know how it feels to want to give up." Jane drew her gaze to Evie as she fed. "I've been there a time or two myself. Please, I only ask one thing of you."

"What?"

"Take some time. Let yourself heal. Until then, don't make a final decision on the matter."

"I don't know."

Jane took Sally's hand in hers. Over the past few days she'd seen glimmers of Sally under the helplessness. Somewhere in there the drive and curiosity still existed. "You are stronger than you think."

"I don't feel that way."

"You will. Perhaps sooner than you think."

Hope is a waking dream.
-Aristotle

Jane kept one hand on Evelyn where she lay in her basket, the other hand held her book open. She'd convinced Cole to let her sit in the restaurant for a while. There was something soothing about the hum of normality returning to the town.

Since he insisted on working against doctor's orders, she'd had a strong argument on her side. She'd promised to do little but sit and read, or chat.

A familiar voice called out to her, "Jane."

She lifted her gaze from her book to find Marshal Lewis approaching her table. With a smile, she let her book fall closed. "Alfred. It's good to see you again."

"Despite the circumstances."

"As always. Please, sit." She smiled as he paused at Evie's basket first. "How are your children, Alfred?"

"Well. Delphie is pregnant with our ninth now. Due in about five months." Lewis took a seat. "You're up to nine now, I see. Are you going to aim for a nice round number?"

"I am not. I'll manage with nine and end it there. This one nearly killed me." She waited as he told the waitress he only wanted coffee. "I'm sorry you didn't get to perform your duties properly this time."

"There's still plenty of work to be done around the situation."

"Such an odd thing. Andrew said it was a small blade through the carotid. It went deep enough to hit the voice box which is why he didn't call for help. I have no idea who could have done it. They certainly knew their stuff."

"Much like Tommy and Sally do, though it seems they weren't the ones that did it."

"Sally's alibi is solid enough, and I believe her when she says she didn't do it." Jane sighed softly. "Beyond them, I can't imagine who would be able to sneak into the jail, and have the knowledge to do that."

"You aren't the only one stumped. Tommy doesn't have any idea, either." Lewis sipped his coffee. "We'll figure it, or we won't. Either way I'll have paperwork to submit."

"How long will you be in town?"

"A few days."

"Then let me offer free meals. You cover the cost of your room."

"The town will cover the cost of my room. I'd be obliged on the meals, though."

"Wonderful." Jane pushed herself to her feet. The reception desk was only a few feet away. She got Lewis entered into the ledger and pulled his key. When she returned, she waved off his concerned look. "I was cut open. I'm moving stiff is all. I feel much better than I did a few days ago. Don't worry about me."

"I'm just wondering if you should be up and moving at all."

"Not particularly, when has that stopped me?"

"Never that I can remember, Mrs. Mitchell."

Jane laughed softly as she handed him his key. "Room four has a nice view of First Street. The rooms on Main sometimes have an issue with noise from the brothel."

"I appreciate the consideration. I'm going to get settled in, then head back to the jail."

"Have a good day, Marshal."

"Will do."

Jane had barely picked her book back up when someone else sat at the table. Before she'd set her book down, Lillian had picked Evie up out of the basket and held her. Jane laughed softly. "You simply can't wait for your own grandchild, can you?"

"This one is as good as. You and my Katherine are close as sisters, after all." Lillian smiled down at the infant. "How are you feeling, Jane?"

"Sore, stiff, but overall much better than I was. How about you? Your hands were the worse for wear, from what I'm told." Jane gestured to Lillian's gloved hands. "Are they healing well?"

"Well as can be expected." Lillian turned her attention to Jane. "I've been trying to find people to care for those children from Glorious Valley. It's been rather difficult, even with only four of them."

"Four?"

"Kyle Ross ran off. I thought he'd stay, he seemed protective enough of the younger children. He didn't care for the rules, I suspect."

"What a shame. I hope he has family he's running to." Jane frowned as she thought of the four younger children. "I imagine the little ones will be easier to find homes for. They're young enough that they likely weren't influenced too much. I expect that, and a transfer of bitterness is what's holding up their care."

"Along with the fact that there are still dozens without a proper home in the Settlement. I'd rather they get to remain here in Dominion Falls, but it may be an orphanage in Denver."

"That would be dreadful. Has there been no success contacting outside family?"

"We found family for the oldest and youngest, but they're either rather poor and unable to care, or too old. It's been quite a challenge." Lillian tapped Evelyn's nose gently. "Yes it has, young lady."

"Hopefully we find something for them. Heaven knows I have no more room for any further children. We're rather settled and content now."

"I should hope so." Lillian set Evie back in her basket. "We've decided to push the sweetheart dance until March, perhaps April. While a dance might do wonders for spirits, there's still some physical wounds that need healing. Plus, where would we have it with cold as this winter has been?"

"By April Katherine should have her baby, and be up and about. Any sooner and she could go into labor during it. I've done that, it isn't fun."

"My daughter doesn't have the tendency to disaster you do, my dear."

"Fair point."

"I'll leave you to enjoy the rest of your afternoon. Your mother and I are going to have tea together. Seeing as your husband and governess are both back at work, she actually has some spare time."

"She will enjoy that, I'm certain." Jane nodded to Lillian's departure. She set her hand back on Evie, rocking her gently as her eyes drifted closed again.

Cole approached the table next. He kissed her temple. "Making sure you haven't been up and about. Just saw Lillian go by."

"I got up once to check-in Marshal Lewis, but otherwise I've been sitting here. Chatted with Lillian, Alfred, and read my book. No more, no less. I can behave when the situation calls for it."

"No ya can't."

"I can, if I want to."

"There you go." He chuckled low, squeezing her shoulder. "Think things can get back to normal now?"

"No. I don't think they can."

"How's that?"

"When is anything in life ever normal for us?"

"I don't know that it ever has been."

"Precisely."

Hope smiles on the threshold of the year
to come, whispering that it will be happier.
-Alfred Lord Tennyson

Sally dallied at the edge of the dance floor. A chill still lingered in the late March air, but that hadn't dampened the spirits of those enthusiastically rounding the floor. Jane and Cole were at the center of it. Now back to full form, Jane was all smiles as she and Cole spun about the floor together.

Kat and Norman sat on a bench on the outer edge of the floor, watching their newborn Grayson, and Evelyn as well. Seeing as Kat had so recently given birth, she wasn't up to dancing so she'd happily agreed to watching them both.

Jane spun giddily past where Sally stood with her drink, calling out to Graham to join the fray. The large man did, spinning her in a polka while Linh watched with a smile on her features. Sally wondered at times how Linh had managed to nullify Eckles so completely, but hadn't bothered to question. The woman's secrets were her own.

Linh glanced her way. With only the acknowledgment of a small nod, she turned back to the floor only to be pulled into the dance by Nick.

Sally backed away from the floor before someone found her to pull her into the dance. She'd only come because Jane had made her swear to. For the past couple of months she'd kept her to their apartment and the library primarily.

Tommy had taken to avoiding her, not that she blamed him. For that matter, she'd hardly seen hide nor tail of Matthew. As she'd suspected, she'd likely scared him well off with her antics. It was for the best. The man deserved a good woman. Sally wasn't so certain she was one.

As if the mere thought of him had conjured him, Matthew appeared in the crowd, his gaze on the dance floor. His toe tapped as he leaned against a hitching post, but he made no move to join the revelry.

Sally turned to avoid interrupting him, but not soon enough.

"Sally," he called.

She begrudgingly moved closer. "Yes, Mr. Coleman?"

"Is it Mr. Coleman again?"

"It would appear that way."

His smile softened, his eyes deepening in sadness. "Then I ain't been imagining things. You're avoiding me."

"You're avoiding me."

"I gave ya some space after that kiss made ya skittish. I've been looking for ya 'round town when I come in to get Stephen, at the restaurant at lunch, I ain't seen ya in weeks."

"I've been busy." Sally played with the hem of her bodice. "Taking care of the library for ma so she has more time for the hotel and the baby."

"Hiding?"

A pang hit her heart at his suggestion. He wasn't off the mark. She shook her head, glancing toward the ground.

"Thought we were friends."

"Maybe it's best we aren't." Sally lifted her chin, attempting to appear stronger than she felt. "I'm not a good friend."

"Think that's up to me to decide." He nodded toward the floor. "Look at that. Andrew finally got up the gumption to ask her to dance."

She turned toward the floor, spotting the pair dance by. Bonnie looked every bit as giddy as Jane did. "She looks so happy."

"She does. It's good to see. Would be nice to see ya that happy, too."

"I don't think that sort of happiness is meant for me."

"Ya never know unless ya try."

Sally thought over the past year. "I have tried. I failed."

"Don't think ya failed. Maybe ya got a little lost, but all it takes is a little courage to try again. It's gotta be better than what you're feeling now."

"My courage disappeared months ago."

"Nah. I think it's still there."

"How can you be so sure?"

"Just am."

She actually laughed. "That isn't an answer."

"Sure it is. Sometimes ya just know."

"I thought I did once."

His warm, calloused hand closed around hers. "You gotta be willing to try. Risk it all."

"What if the price is too great?"

"Ya never know until ya try."

To Be

Continued...

In the rest of

The

Dominion

Falls Series

About the Author

Sarah Cass, author of over twenty novels in 4 series, is devoted to giving her readers well-crafted, emotional stories, with depth to even her secondary characters—to give readers a full world to explore. Stories that explore not only the labyrinths of the heart, but the nightmares of the soul. A RONE finalist, she is also owner and creator of Redefining Perfect. By day, she's a nurse, a mother, wife and cat-mom to 4 mischievous beasts. By night she crafts stories that take her across centuries. From the old west of Dominion Falls, to the small town of Lake Point for the holidays, and even into the paranormal land of Shifters and Magic in The Tribe. She loves hearing from her readers. Visit her at www.authorsarahcass.com

Other Books in
The Dominion Falls Series

Independent Brake
Changing Tracks
Derailed
Dark Territory
Green Eye
Runaway Train
Home Signal
Red Zone

Coming Soon in
The Dominion Falls Series

Chasing the Red
Blizzard Lights
Dead Man's Switch
Bird Cage
A Highball Arrangement
Douse the Glim
Blood
Grave Digger
Bad Order

Books by Sarah Cass
The Tribe Series
The Tribe
The Wolf
The Chief
The Raven
The Lake Point Series
Santa, Maybe
Deep-Fried Sweethearts
Stalled Independence
Witch Way
A Thorough Thanksgiving
Eve's New Year
Heartstrings & Hockey Pucks
Luck of the Cowgirl
Stars, Stripes & Motorbikes
Free Falling
Love for Hire
Haunted Hearts
Stand Alone Novels
Masked Hearts
Leap

www.ingramcontent.com/pod-product-compliance
Lightning Source LLC
Chambersburg PA
CBHW070229200726
48293CB00005B/1533